GONE TO TEXAS

VOLUME ONE
JERICHO D. MCCAIN
TEXAS RANGER

R.C. MORRIS

HELLGATE PRESS   ASHLAND, OREGON

GONE TO TEXAS
©2023 R.C. Morris

Published by Hellgate Press
(An imprint of L&R Publishing, LLC)

All rights reserved. No part of this publication may be reproduced or used in any form or by any means, graphic, electronic or mechanical, including photocopying, recording, taping, or information and retrieval systems without written permission of the publisher. This is a work of fiction. Names, characters, and incidents either are the product of the author's imagination or are used fictitiously. Any resemblance to real persons, living or dead, is purely coincidental.

Hellgate Press
72 Dewey St.
Ashland, OR 97520
email: sales@hellgatepress.com

Cover and Interior Design: L. Redding

ISBN: 978-1-954163-61-4

Printed and bound in the United States of America
First edition 10 9 8 7 6 5 4 3 2 1

Other Books Written by R.C. Morris:

The Ether Zone: U.S. Army Special Forces Detachment B-52, Project Delta

Don't Make the Blackbirds Cry: A Novel

Tender Prey: A Novel

*When Legends Lived:
Vol. Two: Jericho D. McCain, Texas Ranger*

What Others Are Saying About *Gone to Texas*

"*Gone to Texas* by Raymond Morris is a remarkable work of fiction that harkens back to the 'lawless west,' in early Texas, a period that marks the first stage of what will be known in coming decades as the 'Wild West.' The hero's journey begins when Jericho McCain, who has lost his parents and sisters, sets out to find his brother Taylor, a member of the Ranger unit in Texas, but the coming-of-age tale of a young Jericho is more than that. It's a history of men called to use violence to remedy the acts of violent men. Jericho's journey to manhood takes place as Texas and Zachary Taylor's army are fighting the forces of Santa Ana. At the same time gangs of lawless men and Indian tribes ravage the countryside. Because the army of the Union is engaged in war and local law officials are inept, only an elite group of Rangers offer hope of interceding in the violence wrought by evil men.

Morris, a retired Army officer familiar with combat, captures the varied conflicting elements through often spare and stark scenes of violent battles that depict both courage and cowardice. Ultimately, as is the tradition in classic Westerns, Jericho's story is a tale of honor. His is also a story that celebrates our deeper humanity as depicted in the honorable actions men perform in battle, as well as in the humor they express and the heartfelt emotions they mask in tragic moments. In the end, Jericho is a stronger and more poised man, and a humble hero as well who echoes the noble virtues embraced in traditional Western fiction, values that seem to have taken a hiatus in 21st Century America."

—H. Lee Barnes, author of *The Lucky*,
a Spur Award Finalist

"If you liked the *Lonesome Dove* trilogy, you will love *GTT!*"

—Aaron Gritzmaker, U.S. Army Special Forces,
Texan and an avid Western reader

R.C. Morris

"In reading *Gone to Texas* it became quickly apparent that the author was writing about times, places, and people he identified with and wanted to portray well! I read the entire book, word by word, story by story, in less than two days. Each time I placed a bookmark between pages to take a break, I found myself being pulled back, almost needing to see where Ray was taking me next! His rich descriptions and well woven events are magic to those of us that love westerns! This book is already a hit for me and reminded me too why I have admired and had deep affection for its author for almost forty years!"

—Major Jerry R. Bailey, U.S. Army Special Forces (Ret)

"Powerful, gripping, suspenseful! This heart-warming and inspiring tale of a young man's survival and success through hardships on the pre-Civil War frontier is a fast-paced, satisfying read. I've been a fan of the late Ray Morris's writing for many years, be it crime novels or military non-fiction. *Gone To Texas* is perhaps his best yet, and will garner him many more fans!"

—Hank Cramer, retired soldier and singing cowboy, Winthrop, WA

Gone to Texas

Prologue

THE YEAR WAS 1845. It was Indian summer and deep in the Blue Ridge Mountains the entire McCain family was being buried – except for a lone survivor. One by one, Jericho McCain dug the holes and carried his baby sister, his mother, and finally his father to the shallow graves he had dug in the rocky soil and carefully covered them over. Jericho McCain was barely sixteen years old.

At this elevation, morning fog tended to hang in the hollows until almost noon. Warm left-over summer days and early cool fall nights intensely collided, with condensation in the low-lying areas and thick vapors cascading skyward as though the world had suddenly caught fire. Rangers who had never seen the phenomenon reacted in uniquely different ways. Some marveled at its beauty, while others shivered with foreboding and anxiety. The region's superstitious hill-folk, especially, tended not to stray far from their homes when conditions were such.

Millions of years of persistent glacial activity had gradually carved deep, ragged ravines through the granite rock. Subsequent volcanic eruptions formed curiously sharp peaks, towering majestically, forever standing sentinel over the eerie terrain. Near the top of one such peak, hidden by tall pines and thick vegetation, a twenty-acre plot of relatively level landscape had been created by some such natural force. It had once been encased within the thick brush and towering trees, but more recently someone had taken great effort to hack away the natural growth leaving a bald spot on the naturally green mountain slope. Several large stone piles dotted the clearing perimeter, removed when the rocky soil had been plowed to make room for the stand of potatoes and corn. Although the patch appeared to have been once well-tended, weeds sprouted between its long straight rows, burnt brown by hot sun-rays and lack of water.

At one corner of the field a narrow road wound up the mountain for nearly a mile, ending at another, smaller clearing. If standing in the exact center, one could see in any direction for a hundred miles. That is, if not for the dense fog — and the fact that a five-room cabin occupied the space. The dwelling, larger than most homes in the mountainous terrain, had been constructed of the same huge timbers from the steep slopes surrounding the site. An observer might speculate about the backbreaking effort that must have been involved in retrieving the logs and meticulously fitting them together. A master craftsman, proud of his work, had obviously built the sturdy cabin, for there were no jagged edges around the windows or doors, nor uneven chinks between the logs. Inside, with the same meticulous care, a large masonry rock fireplace centered along one wall while finely crafted shelves lined the log walls and handmade, intricately carved furniture was scattered throughout.

Several outbuildings dotted the landscape, erected at various intervals with the same precision and skill found within the cabin. Even the split rail fences were finished by someone who took extreme pride in their work. A small barn could be seen two hundred feet to the left of the main house, near a cleared tree line, its rail fence enclosing a graying mule and two large horses of fine bloodlines. Further to the rear, a chicken coop and hog pen in place, and a small fenced vegetable garden was evident, overtaken by weeds burnt brown from the sun.

Between the garden and the tall pine trees, two mounds of dark fresh dirt contrasted with the parched vegetation. A motionless figure sat on one mound. A boy, no more than sixteen, rested with his bowed head, staring vacantly into the deep hole. He had the appearance of someone who had been there for hours. Beyond the livestock, the only other living thing in sight was a lean blue-tick hound, languishing in the meager shade by the chicken coop. The dog's head rested on paws that seemed much too large for such a lean animal, a sorrowful, unwavering gaze fixed on the motionless boy as though sensing his anguish.

At last, the boy raised his head and stared toward the silent house. Noting the movement, the blue-tick also raised his head yet remained in the shade. The boy's face was lean, burned dark from countless hours of toiling in the hot sun. A film of dust and dirt coated his clothing, face and thick shoulder length hair; undoubtedly from the difficult chore of digging the rocky soil. Sweat and dried tears left muddy tracks down his cheeks. Though familiar with hard work, the laborious task of digging had worn blisters on his toughened hands and they'd broken and bled at some point. The boy appeared not to notice.

To the right of the two larger holes, a smaller mound was marked by a wooden cross, etched,

SARA McCAIN
Beautiful Child & Beloved Sister
Taken in her tender years
1840 - 1845

Gone to Texas

He'd dug that grave three days previously when he'd buried his baby sister. His mother had passed the following night, but he'd had to leave her in her bed while he urgently labored for two more days to save his stricken father. Unsure of exactly what to do, he'd placed sheets and blankets over his father's fevered body then doused him with buckets of cold spring water to try to break the fever's hold. Exhausted, unable to function any longer, he'd finally collapsed on the cabin floor and slept for nearly five hours. He'd awakened to the crowing of roosters, only to discover his father had expired while he slept.

Jericho McCain could never understand why the fever claimed both of his parents and sister, but failed to take him. Grieving and exhausted, he didn't much care if the fever did consume him, but direly prayed to first finish the chore of burying his family.

The McCain family had come to these mountains seven years earlier after Thomas McCain heard about the federal government's new homesteading policy. Jericho had been only eight; Taylor, his older brother, fifteen. Their sister Sara was born three years later. Ruth McCain, a schoolteacher in Ireland before marrying Thomas, saw to it her family's education never suffered, although no school was within fifty miles of their new homestead. The nearest neighbor lived ten miles away; a strange bearded old man with a dozen dogs that shared his austere shack. He'd quickly let people know he wasn't friendly and didn't want company. Thomas McCain respected his privacy and went out of his way not to bother him. Their reclusive neighbor Hobbs was also dead of the fever.

* * *

Ruth McCain had proudly and repeatedly told her children

that their father had been a minister before the family's long journey to the United States of America, and if they didn't desert God after coming to this new world, God wouldn't desert them either. Jericho had believed her then. He didn't now.

* * *

Though not overly strict with his children, Thomas had insisted they study the Bible and participate in the family's prayer sessions. He'd also taught his sons to shoot - and shoot well. Thomas McCain didn't hold with the taking of human life, but he'd been a soldier in his youth and had seen awful injustices done toward those who couldn't defend themselves.

He'd told his children, "Never back down from what you believe is right, even if you're outnumbered. It's true you may die, but if branded a coward, the many small deaths you'll suffer from not standing up for your beliefs will be your own personal Hell on earth."

Thomas had felt it was a parent's responsibility to teach their children right from wrong, but if they failed to abide by his teachings after leaving home, it'd be on their own shoulders. Taylor, who had always been a little rebellious and a lot more adventurous than Jericho, mostly just heard the part about "leaving home." He did just that on his nineteenth birthday, two years ago. His only letter mentioned he'd settled in a place far to the west. Someplace called Texas.

Although Jericho had desperately longed to go with him, he considered himself more levelheaded than his impulsive older brother, and also knew how much the others depended upon him to help keep meat on the family table.

Thomas McCain, as a soldier before becoming a man of the

cloth, had been noted for his marksmanship in the Royal British Army, serving with distinction during his country's many conflicts. His skill was such that Regimental Commanders had vied vigorously for his assignment to their units. The casual, disinterested manner, in which he fired both pistol and rifle with unerring accuracy was well known.

Fed up with the death and destruction he'd witnessed, Thomas had finally packed up his family and their meager belongings and sailed for the new world in search of a better life. Thereafter, he'd hated the thought of killing any animal, but knew well the necessity of hunting game for the table. It was for that reason alone that he began to teach his sons to shoot at a very tender age.

Taylor had quickly become a crack shot, seldom needing more than one round to bring home their evening meals. Thomas readily admitted his eldest son was nearly as good as he, but young Jericho McCain showed prowess of an entirely different caliber. When it came to shooting contests between the three, there was never a doubt as to the outcome. Jericho was simply the best. The best Thomas McCain had ever seen. While as fast and accurate as his father with a pistol, with a rifle no one could out-do him. He'd proudly boast, "If Jericho can see it, he can hit it."

Occasionally, they'd travel long distance to engage in turkey shoots. Jericho never failed to bring home the prize, and had won both of the fine-blooded horses in the McCain's corral. With his skill with a firearm, and Thomas's distaste for taking life, it made Jericho the primary family member responsible for keeping meat on the table.

* * *

It'd been a rare event a week earlier, while Jericho had finished up weeding the potato patch, his father had taken the old flintlock rifle he called his squirrel gun and slipped silently down to the creek where he'd noticed deer tracks in the spring. After a few hours of no luck, he'd followed the creek downstream to another clearing he'd remembered from an earlier hunt.

That's where he'd found old man Hobbs lying on the creek bank, ashen, drenched with sweat, gasping for breath. Thomas had carried him nearly a mile to the old man's one room shack and placed him on the bed. At that instant, the old man had opened his eyes and said the only words he'd ever spoken to a member of the McCain family.

"Fever…in the well water…git away…quick."

He closed his eyes and never regained consciousness.

McCain had seen the fever during his European campaigns. The stacks of bodies, their blackened faces twisted and grotesque, would forever remain fresh in his memory. He backed away in horror, brushing at his clothing as if to dislodge any of the clinging invisible death. Outside, he'd paused only long enough to torch the old man's cabin, then stumbled to the stream and jumped in, fully clothed.

He'd frantically washed his face and hands, peeling away his clothing, scrubbing them until threadbare. Without lingering to allow his clothes to dry, McCain had hurried home. He'd ordered his family to stay away from him until he'd scrubbed down more with lye soap. Then he'd burned his clothing.

It was not enough. Within a week, baby Sara was dead and Ruth McCain mortally stricken. Jericho and his father had worked in vain to break the fever's hold on his mother and sister, and it looked miraculously as though the family's two males might be spared. But on the third day, while carrying water from the wellspring, Thomas McCain fell stricken to the ground, unconscious. Shortly afterward Jericho began digging the last two graves.

Jericho stood stiffly, ignoring his complaining joints and muscles, staring stoically at his raw, blistered hands as though noticing them for the first time. With dread, he walked slowly toward the house he'd called home. The blue-tick's eyes followed him as he entered briefly, then reemerged with a heavy, sheet wrapped bundle. Carrying his burden to the graves, he gently lowered it beside a hole and slowly rolled it in. His shoulders sagging, he paused briefly, returned to the cabin once more, reappeared with another bundle and repeated the process. When finished, he sagged to the ground, exhausted.

Thirty minutes passed before the youngster stirred again. Removing a red handkerchief from his pocket, he ripped it in half, wrapped each of his blistered hands, picked up his shovel and slowly began to fill the holes. His task finished, Jericho hammered wooden crosses into each of the fresh mounds. He'd constructed the crosses in the same precise manner as the dwellings had been, and as the one on his sister's grave, impeccably lettered:

BELOVED BELOVED
Thomas McCain Ruth McCain
1801 - 1845 1810 - 1845
Husband and Father Wife and Mother

He lingered, his head bowed, then looked toward the smallest mound of fresh dirt and spoke, his voice soft, raspy.

"Sis, I'll always remember your bubbly little laugh. Every time I see a firefly in the evening or a bright butterfly in the afternoon, I'll see you chasing them through the grass. I'll always love you, Sis."

He stared at the middle grave for just a moment, then spoke again. "You were the best Mom any boy ever had. You taught me how to read and write, sang songs with Sis and me and even when things was scarce, managed to cook the best food any family ever had. For whatever good I process, I have you to thank. I promise each day to try and remember your bible teachings, never hurt another person, and always stride for what's good inside me. Ma...I love you."

His soft voice was beginning to crack noticeably as he finally addressed the last grave. "Pa...you probably never knew you were a teacher, too...but I watched everything you ever did, and from that I learned how to be a man. I don't remember you ever raising your voice, you never broke your word, and never walked away from what you knew was the right thing to do. I'll always try to be the man you'd want me to be. I know this is probably the...the...last time...we'll ever be together as a family. If Taylor had known, I know he'd be here too. I promise you that I will find Taylor and let...him know...about this. I will. You have my word. I love you, Pa."

He stood, sniffed a couple of times, and wiped his eyes with a dirty sleeve.

"Goodbye."

Removing the family bible from a canvas knapsack on the ground, Jericho McCain softly recited the Lord's Prayer and read a familiar passage of the Psalms, then replaced it and solemnly walked toward the barn. The two horses watched unmoving as he opened the gate, saddled the stallion and tossed a rope over the mare's head. He effortlessly tossed another rope over the head of the mule. Tugging it outside, he heaved several canvas-wrapped bundles and canteens onto its back, securing them with hemp ties, then leading the animals to the front of the cabin, he entered for one last time.

Emerging quickly, his father's long-barreled squirrel gun was tied over his shoulder with a leather strap, his cap-and-ball pistol stuffed into the waistband of his trousers. Jericho led the animals toward the three mounds and paused silently. Then mounting, he stared down at the panting dog.

"Well, bonehead - you going or not?"

The blue-tick eagerly bounded to his feet, barked once and followed the boy down the narrow trail. Jericho never looked back as the flames began to flicker through the cabin's open doorway, nor did he notice the smoke lifting lazily into the afternoon sky. He knew where he was headed. He'd been thinking about it ever since Taylor left. He'd have gone to find his brother, even if he hadn't promised his father.

Texas – that's where Taylor said he was going.

* * *

Texas! The name had a good ring to it. A clean "starting over" kind of sound and that's what Jericho wanted - a clean start.

There was no other family he knew of because Thomas McCain had been the first of his kin to migrate to this new world. Jericho swore he'd be damned if he ever considered returning across the water. No, he'd go to Texas, wherever that was, and try to find his brother, Taylor. Between them they could make a new life.

On his mother's old map, he'd often studied the small country people had been referring to as the Republic of Texas. Before leaving his cabin for the last time, he'd wrapped the old map in oilskin and stuffed it inside his shirt. It didn't look too far. Might take him a spell to find Taylor once he got there, but he'd find him! He was sure of that.

How big could Texas be, anyway?

Gone to Texas

One

STARTLED, THE BIG RED stallion shied to the left, the mule and mare kicked up their heels and Blue went into one of his infrequent barking fits as a wild turkey suddenly took flight from beside the narrow trail to their left. Impatiently Jericho had jerked the reins hard, instantly sorry as he leaned forward to rub his mount's neck and speak softly. He was tired and hungry and his butt hurt from several weeks in the saddle. He wasn't in any mood to put up with pesky shenanigans from his animals, but to tell the truth, the turkey had startled him too. They were all jumpy and needed a rest. It was still early but he decided it best to find a camping spot for the night.

Mississippi sure is big, he thought, astonished at how long it'd taken him to reach just this point in his journey. According to the map, Texas looked to be even larger. It might prove harder to find Taylor than he'd first thought.

Mississippi.

That was what the man at the last farm had called this place. Indian for Watery Land. Jericho remembered seeing it briefly on his mother's oilskin map but couldn't recall much more about it. He'd been riding through for the past three days and if the farmer was to be believed, he wasn't even halfway across. Last night, after preparing for camp, he'd retrieved the old map from his canvas bag and studied it by the campfire's fading light. A big place on paper from the looks of it, you could still fit two of its size into the Texas space. For the first time, Jericho had serious misgivings about his venture.

The farmer and his skinny, pale wife had fed Jericho and his animals, letting him sleep in their dilapidated barn for two nights. During the first, a sudden thunderstorm hit in the middle of the night, soaking Jericho and all his belonging through a poorly patched roof. The second night, he'd waited until his benefactors had gone to sleep, then rigged a lean-to behind the barn. He'd arisen early the following morning to take it down so he wouldn't insult the couple's kindness. That had been the last night either he or his animals had a good night's rest. Also the last time they'd had a decent meal.

Ahead, the narrow trail suddenly opened into a wide arch of cleared areas overlooking a swift muddy river. Was this the mighty Mississippi River he'd heard about at the farm? This country was quite different from what he'd been riding through, until now mostly swamp and marshlands. Here was rich, lush land where supple crops and carefully sculptured timbered areas intermittently dotted the countryside. His interest peaked, he decided to ride a while longer before stopping. Within the hour, he topped a rise, and observed two groups of people working in a large cotton field. The nearest, only a quarter of a mile away; the other, a good mile in the distance. Guiding his mount closer, he saw they were colored folks and correctly assumed they were slaves, like the ones he'd seen at the Grouse Point auction block.

Bent low with their sacks over the cotton plants, they didn't glance up as the small column of rider, pack animal, riderless horse and skinny hound quietly passed. The women wore head-rags or tattered bonnets to shield them from the relentless afternoon sun. Only some of the men, bare from the waist up, their backs shiny from the sweat of their toil, wore hats. Intent upon their task, none appeared to notice the lone white boy and his three animals, yet Jericho was sure they couldn't have missed him. He studied them as he passed, eager to question them about the countryside ahead. If nothing else, the sound of a human voice would've been welcome to his ears. Yet, not one of the workers acknowledged him in any way, much less made eye contact as he rode past. He recalled the strange language he'd heard at the auction block years before and wondered if they even spoke English.

This was only the second time he'd ever seen a black slave. His first experience had been at the age of eleven when his father took him to a shooting contest at Grouse Point. It was only his first match but his father had later told him he'd done well - high praise indeed, coming from Thomas McCain. The truth was he'd actually placed second, winning a pair of Dominick hens instead of the fat turkey awarded for first prize. He'd out-shot twenty-three men and boys and one woman. But the last contestant, a man named Wilson Pike, had cleanly out-matched him. Pike could eat an apple with his right hand while driving nails in a fence-post twenty feet away with the pistol in his left. He could toss small rocks in the air and pluck them out with single shots from the boxy stub-nosed pistol he carried in his waistband.

* * *

The Grouse Point shooting match was the biggest county event of the year, and it was there that just last year he'd won the stallion and mare. Folks came from as far away as Memphis to sell their wares and dance to the music. Jericho had listened

Gone to Texas

to juice harps, fiddles, banjos, mandolins, French harps, washboards, spoons, and pot and pans played as drums, and other instruments he couldn't identify. All combined, the event had a carnival atmosphere. It was also where a few slave traders took the opportunity to display their products, hoping to turn a handsome profit. On that particular day, there had been four of them; a strong young man with blue-black skin, an older man who coughed incessantly, a fat woman and a beautiful young chocolate hued girl, about his own age. The only two sold had been the young man and girl. Jericho hadn't fully understood the implications, but remembered afterward how the fat woman wailed when the new owner led the sobbing girl away. The woman had called after them, pleading in a language he hadn't understood. She'd suddenly turned toward him, her eyes empty hysterical sockets. The scene had left him shaken for hours afterward. He also recollected how he'd searched his father's face for comfort, saw his clenched jaw and recoiled at his angry glare as they strode away through the crowd.

If what he'd seen had affected his aim that day he never knew, but it had truly bothered him for days afterward. During the months following the match, young Jericho's memory of the slaves being auctioned off slowly dimmed, until eventually he only recalled that he'd lost the shooting match to a tall, lanky Southerner who, between shooting matches, quietly sipped corn liquor in the shade of an apple tree. The image that hadn't diminished was his mental picture of Wilson Pike leaning lazily against a fence post, plunking rocks out of the air with his ugly little pistol. He'd been so impressed with Pike's accomplishment that he'd practiced hour-after-hour for the next six months, shooting at tossed rocks until he'd mastered the enviable feat.

R.C. Morris

It was only upon his arrival at Grouse Point the second time that he'd thought again about the wailing fat woman and the pretty slave girl. When he and his father returned the following year, Jericho was determined to beat the man named Pike, who many considered the best pistol shot in Tennessee - and this time to come home with first prize. But Wilson Pike hadn't shown up that year. According to the regulars, he was a man who couldn't hit a barn while sober, and required at least four straight sour mashes before becoming the calm, steady-handed shootist he'd proven to be the previous year. With glee, some of the old shooters told Jericho and his father of how, while he'd been preparing for a match in River Town the previous month, he'd consumed some bad sour mash whisky and died from convulsions, drowning in his own vomit.

Jericho had won his turkey prize and the horses that year, and it was only as they were leaving town that they'd passed by the auction block where the slaves had been sold. It was empty, but the scene from the previous year suddenly rushed over him, leaving him with the vision of the old woman's wild eyes. Winning the turkey hadn't seemed so important after that.

Jericho's attention was swiftly brought back to the present by movement in the next field. He was closer and could tell that this second group of workers was much larger than the first. From his height advantage on the stallion, he could count nearly a hundred backs a bobbing between the cotton rows. Disappointed with his initial encounter with the black field hands, he ventured even closer, cutting across the cotton field and riding right through their center. It had little effect, for this group also failed to respond. Only one, an old man with white scars crisscrossing the glistening skin on his dark back, met his eyes, then quickly averted them. In a split-instant, Jericho saw a hundred years of suffering and misery staring back at him. It was as if he were gazing again into the fat woman's frantic eyes at the auction block in Grouse Point. Shaken, he gazed at the horizon to compose himself.

Jericho's eyes shifted to a large man in a flat-top hat, sitting under a lone shade tree in the exact center of the cotton field. A horse was nearby, its reins dangling free, grazing on the small ring of close-cropped green grass under the huge oak. As Jericho angled toward him, the pot-bellied man stood, reaching for and picking up a ten-foot black snake whip from a nearby stool.

From a distance, the man had appeared well dressed and neat in his all-white attire. But upon closer inspection Jericho could tell he'd been mistaken. He was, in fact, disgustingly filthy. The hat that'd loomed so pure in the distant sunshine, was greasy up close, with large unsightly sweat stains around the band. Dirt and grass stains camouflaged his baggy pants, while tobacco stains dotted the front of his once white shirt-ruffle. Never intended to be white were his scuffed knee-high boots, and the black whip he held loosely as though an extension of his hands. The man grinned, his teeth crooked and stained. He cleared his throat and spit out a brownish-gob at the trunk of the large oak, already dotted from many such contacts.

"Hi pilgrim. Got some cool spring-water in the bucket yonder. Hep yoreself."

Jericho lowered himself gingerly to the ground and nodding his thanks, drank long and deeply from the metal dipper. The water was cool and sweet. He nodded approval and dropped the dipper back into the wooden bucket.

"Thank you, sir. I been hankering for that. Been a long dry ride."

"Where you bound, youngster?"

"Texas. My brother's there. Know how far it is?"

The sloppy man placed his chubby hands on his hips, threw his head back and literally bellowed with laughter.

"Texas? Hell boy, Texas is a lifetime away. A good couple o' months anyway. That is if'n Injuns or the greasers don't getcha first. Then there's the heat and lack o'water, rattlesnakes, bandits and deserters. If you do git lucky and actually make it to Texas, the carpetbaggers will skin ya outta them fine-looking animals the first hour. Take it from me son, stay in God's country. Stay right here in Miss'sippi."

Jericho decided right off that he didn't much care for this coarse, unkempt individual, but his pa had raised him right and when the fat man stuck out his grimy hand, courtesy required he grasp it.

"Jasper Gates. Overseer for Pleasant Manor Plantation. Thomas Leonard and Betty Lou Harrington, proprietors. They live in that big place you'll see in a couple 'a miles if ya stay on this road. Have two bright kids, Courtney and Susan. Court ain't much punkin', but that Susan is a mouth-watering little cookie, for sure.

Gates laughed again, winking lewdly this time.

Jericho was sure he didn't like the man. Respect for women folks was something that had been drilled into him since the day he'd learned to walk and talk. "Treat every woman like she was your mother or sister," he could still hear his father saying. It was with some amount of effort that Jericho held his tongue while climbing painfully into the saddle. Trying to hide his disgust, he said, "Is Mr. Harrington hiring? I need a few days work for food."

Gone to Texas

Gates spit out another gob of tobacco on the ground.

"Doubt it. They got more niggers than any white folks in the valley. Anything that needs doing...them niggers usually take care of it for them uppity Harringtons."

Blue barked impatiently and bounded away, stopping fifty feet away to look back. Gates stared after the skinny blue tick hound for an instant, then said, "That's a fine looking animal ya got there, youngster."

Just as Jericho was about to respond politely, Gates went on. "What breed exactly is it anyhow?"

The fat man suddenly burst into loud wheezing laughter as Jericho angrily rode away without answering. Jericho wondered if Jasper Gates had ever shared his water with the suffering field hands; if any of those glistening backs in the hot sun had ever experienced the taste of cool delicious water from his wooden bucket.

The Harrington plantation was exactly where Overseer Gates had said it'd be. Mounting a rise, Jericho suddenly pulled on his reins, stunned motionless by the vastness of the wealth he saw before him. Like a massive compound, the huge white mansion with several large columnar pillars created the centerpiece, surrounded by stables, barns, gazebos, gardens, summer cottages, storage and tool sheds, all immaculately kept. In a small depression near a shallow creek, a quarter of a mile from the main house, it's setting not nearly-so-fine, stood a half-dozen, unpainted, tin-roofed structures, wash drying on clotheslines. A goat and occasional chickens searching for food wandered between the shacks. Several dark-skinned women, each obviously pregnant, toiled over a steaming kettle. Even from a distance an acidic odor stung his nose - the pungent smell of lye soap fermenting in the afternoon air; the sounds of a baby loudly wailing while a woman sang a soft lullaby in another language. This was the slave quarters.

Jericho's gaze returned to the Harrington plantation and he sat quietly, pensive, drinking in the richness surrounding him. Never in his wildest dreams could he have imagined such wealth and luxury - or the vast poverty and suffering that could exist in close proximity. As he tried to reconcile his conflicted feelings, he suddenly yanked on his reins and headed back toward the river. He concluded he'd spend the evening there, rest, and settle his mind before deciding whether to seek employment at the Pleasant Manor. This place made him very uneasy.

Two

JERICHO HAD NEVER ENVIED people with immense wealth as those at Pleasant Manor. He supposed he'd inherited that particular trait from his father who'd been quick to paraphrase from a famous Bible verse, "A rich man has as much a chance of entering the gates of Heaven as a camel has of passing through the eye of a needle." After witnessing the opulence of the Harrington's wealth, he was struck by an acute sense of obsceneness about it. It made the plight of the Negroes even more disturbing.

Closer now, the river didn't appear nearly as muddy as it had from a distance in the afternoon sunlight. Here, it was much slower, moving lazily through the thick trees lining this particular stretch. At first, he'd mistaken it for the muddy Mississippi River, but after studying his map, realized it was a tributary that ran into the main river a few miles to the east. He sincerely hoped he'd find a suitable crossing when he reached it. He'd never been much of a swimmer.

The croaking frogs and the evening glow reflecting off the small river, made it seem almost pleasant as he prepared his camp site. The activity momentarily took his mind off the unsettling scene of the black workers toiling in the hot fields. He tied the mare, mule and stallion to a rope he'd stretched between a couple of saplings, then recalling the swiftness in which the thunderstorm had come in the night at the old barn, he decided to fashion a lean-to from his canvas poncho, then spread his sleeping blanket beneath it. By the time he'd finished, the evening had grown downright chilly. The coals from the dying embers felt good as he reclined against his saddle where he could study the old map and reflect upon his recent encounter with Jasper Gates. He also contemplated the Harrington's ostentatious lifestyle and whether he should just bypass it, keep right on going.

Half-dozing, it was the big stallion's snorting and a twig breaking nearby that forced Jericho instantly to the present. Lying stone still, he listened intently before sliding his ancient pistol from its saddle holster, then silently rolled into the brush beside the lean-to. As his eyes slowly grew accustomed to the darkness, he pushed the flintlock before him and slipped silently through the thick underbrush. His stallion snorted again and begin to prance, this time joined by the mare and mule. Blue also awoke, but was reluctant to leave the warmth of the coals to check out any disturbance. His throat growled deeply, mouth ajar, baring surprisingly long fangs. Jericho felt sure something was out there; something Blue and the big horse didn't care much for. But what? Bobcat? Bear? Maybe an animal, but if so, the animals sure weren't acting as if it was. Nope, they'd be cutting more a rug and sounding an alarm if it was an animal. It had to be a human moving around in the darkness.

That someone was there, Jericho had little doubt. Someone who hadn't just walked up to the campfire and introduced himself - who maybe had something to hide - or worse. The handle of the big flintlock felt slippery in his slender hand, and despite the coolness of the evening, sweat trickled down his back.

There! Just to the right of the mare!

Moving slow and silently - the dark shape of a man. He waited until the shadow got close to the mare so the intruder's true intentions would not be an issue. As the unknown entity reached for the rope tying the mare, Jericho stood and cocked the pistol's hammer. In the quiet evening, the sound was loud - deadly.

The shadow froze instantly.

"Obliged if you'd just stop what you're doing and move out into the open near the fire. If you do anything else, anything else at all, I will blow your head clean off, mister. Last time I heard, it was a killing offense to steal a man's horse."

The shadow hesitated as though deciding whether to take a chance and make a break for it, then Jericho sensed an audible sigh as it moved toward the indicated area. Moving backward into the small clearing near the fire, he carefully followed the visitor's movement with the pistol's muzzle. Stooping, he tossed a handful of twigs into the dying embers and they immediately burst into flame, flaring to illuminate their surroundings. The thief was a black youth about Jericho's age, and while it was apparent he was frightened, he sensed just a hint of rebellion in his dark eyes, unlike the defeat he'd seen in the old man's eyes that afternoon. Jericho kept his body turned toward the youth as he squatted and laid the flintlock on the ground within easy reach, never losing eye contact with his defiant visitor. Continuing his gaze from the corner of his eye, Jericho set his battered coffee pot into the glowing coals, tossing on more twigs.

"A body could get his head ventilated fooling in the dark around a man's stock."

The thief didn't answer, keeping his eyes focused on Jericho's discarded pistol.

"Don't even think about it. I can hit running squirrels with this thing. Gotta name?"

After a long moment, when it appeared he didn't either understand English or didn't intend to answer, his guest muttered softly, "Kepi."

Jericho waited until it was apparent there would be no more, then said, "That's it? Just Kepi?"

The other boy nodded.

Now sensing no threat from the defiant boy, Jericho jerked his head toward the fire. "Sit. There's some hardtack and salt belly still left in the skillet there. Help yourself."

Again, the dark boy waited until the smell of food finally overcame his fear, then squatted across the fire and reached into the heavy iron skillet. Jericho watched from the corner of his eye as the boy fed handfuls of hardtack and bacon into the seemingly endless pit that was his mouth. Without saying more, Jericho poured a tin cup half-full of thick brew and pushed it toward him. At first, the boy just shook his head vigorously, trying his best to swallow the dry fare. When able to speak, he simply muttered, "No."

"Why not? Don't you like coffee?"

"Your cup, Mister."

"What? Sure it's my cup."

Then he understood. The black boy wasn't allowed to drink from the same cup as a white person. Jericho felt his face burn in embarrassment, and then pushed it out again, nodding. "Drink. It's okay."

Glancing around as though to ensure he wasn't being observed, the boy reluctantly took the cup and drank the scalding coffee. Looking up in surprise, he drank deeply again.

"This is coffee? It's good."

Jericho realized his visitor most likely had never tasted coffee before. In a country where coffee was fast becoming the preferred drink of its population, he had somehow been denied this fundamentally simple pleasure. Jericho's ears flamed hot again.

"Where you from, Kepi?" he said softly.

Fear replaced pleasure, as Kepi glanced toward the Pleasant Manor Plantation just over the hill. It was answer enough.

"Why were you trying to steal my horse, Kepi? That's a hanging offense."

His head down, Kepi shook it back and forth, laughing softly. "Hanging? That would be better than what they'll do to me if they catch me."

He looked up, staring Jericho in the eyes.

"Ever seen a man boiled? They do it in a big, larding kettle. After 'bout an hour, the meat comes right off the poor man's bones. They feed it to the hogs, then grind the bones and fertilize the cotton fields with it. Nothing is wasted."

He thought for a moment, then laughed shortly. "We're too valuable to waste. A slave costs a lot of money these days."

Jericho sat like a stone, unable to speak, struggling with his feelings. "You're running away." It wasn't a question.

"Yes, suh. Sure was. Looks like I didn't make it though. I'll make good fertilizer, I guess." He stared into Jericho's eyes for a time. "But I won't let them boil me alive like they did O' Moe Moe. I'll make you shoot me and you can take my body back."

"Enough of that. Nobody's going to shoot you. How did you plan to get away?"

Kepi looked shocked, aware for the first time that he may not die. "There's a German family down river that helps folks like me get away. They call it the 'Underground Railroad.' It's a trail of families that pass us along, hiding us from the trackers until we can get to a place up north. Some have even returned to their birthplace."

"Would you?"

Kepi shook his head. "Nope. I'd go to school and study the law. Become smarter than the white masters who own us. Then someday, I'd make them all pay."

"You sound pretty educated already. How did you manage that?"

"My Auntie Josie can read, too. We're the only two on the entire plantation who can read. She learned from an English missionary before the slave traders came and stole her from her village. She taught me to read from all the books in the Harrington's library. She sneaked them out to me, one at a time. They've got a hundred books. Maybe more. I read them all. I overheard Mister Courtney in his studies once. He's not nearly as good a reader as me. It would have done me good to read for Master Harrington so he could see black people are not stupid animals. But of course he would've had to kill me for the insult."

Jericho couldn't believe what he was hearing. "He'd have you killed for that?"

Kepi nodded, solemnly. "I saw Overseer Gates beat a field hand to death once with an old wagon tongue. Just for swiping a drink of water from his bucket. Master Harrington scolded the Overseer for it. Reminded him how costly we were, but said he wouldn't punish him for it that one time because the old man had a sickness anyway. Not a word about taking the life of a good man."

"I see," Jericho said, though he did not.

"I'm a house boy - was a house boy. My life was easy compared to the field blacks. In a few years I'd have become a Black Overseer - carried a whip and made the others work harder. Plenty of food, water, even the woman of my choice. Several if I wanted them."

"But you left it?"

"I can't explain freedom to a man who has never been a slave...what can I call you? Master?"

"First off, I'm not anybody's master. Call me Jericho. Jericho McCain. Or, if you prefer, just J.D. That's what my father used to call me. Whatever you do though, don't ever call me Master."

"Can I leave then?"

"If you want. Just don't try to steal any more horses though. I don't hold with thievery. Can you get away before they catch up?"

"No. But I must try."

"What's your plan? If you don't mind telling me."

Kepi hesitated, then, "The German man told me where a white fisherman keeps his boat down the river a few miles. If I could've gotten away with your horse, I might've made it to the boat before morning. If I made it there, I had a chance. Once on the river the dogs wouldn't be able to track me any more. And that old Miss'sip River goes all the way to Heaven. Yes, suh!"

"How long you figure it'll be until they miss you?"

"Five, six hours at the most. The house servants get up at four, so when I ain't there to lay out Master Harrington's clothes he'll raise holy Hell. Then they'll mount up and set the dogs after me – three big bloodhounds that'll eat me alive, if they catch me. What they don't eat the kettle will finish off. Like I said, good fertilizer."

"Then we'd better get started. I'll saddle up. You grab what's left of that hardtack and come on." Jericho stood and strode to where he'd left the horses, leaving Kepi to stare after him.

Just over two hours later, Jericho watched as Kepi removed branches from a battered wooden rowboat. In the center, folded, was a tarp and pole he'd correctly surmised was a sail. He helped the young black boy drag the small vessel to the water's edge, then together, they set the sail up and pushed it in the water. Kepi stood silently for a moment as though gathering his thoughts.

"I wish I had known there were white men such as you, Jericho McCain. Maybe some day I will meet another like you and we can be friends. I will tell the other Negroes of what you done for me so they will know as well."

In the darkness, Jericho held out his hand. Kepi hesitated briefly then grinning, grasped it, shaking it vigorously. As he was settling into the boat, Jericho handed him a small packet.

"Black pepper. Drop some of it in your tracks. Dogs hate it. Can't seem to smell for a week after sniffing some of it up their noses."

Laughter drifted back from the small boat as it disappeared into a pool of rushing water that quickly became darkness.

Three

JUST BEFORE DAYBREAK, SEVERAL horses thundered into Jericho's small camp, jarring him wide awake. Startled, he realized the muzzles of a dozen weapons, various large bore shotguns to pocket pistols, were leveled straight at him. Three large short-haired reddish hounds with sad eyes and long droopy ears quickly sniffed their way in and out of the thicket around his campsite. None of the men spoke a word, and Jericho was careful not to make the slightest move. Every few minutes one of the bloodhounds would let go with a muffled yodel like howl. At least, the dogs sounded as if they were having a good time. Beside him, Blue growled deep in his throat. Jericho tightly grasped one of his ears, just in case he was foolish enough to try to tackle the three big hounds. The group's apparent leader, the man with the stained white hat who'd brandished a long black snake whip. It was the overseer he'd met the previous day, Jasper Gates.

"Well youngster, I see you didn't make it to Texas after all."

Jericho, being careful to keep his hands in plain sight, carefully let go of Blue's ear, pulled on his boots and stood.

"If you recall, I mentioned that I intended to ask for employment from the Harringtons. I wanted a good night's rest first." He let his eyes roam around the hostile faces. "What's this all about? Someone think I robbed the Citizen's Bank or something?"

"Na. Looking for a runaway nigger, is all. Haven't seen him have you?"

"To tell you the truth, I was bone-tired when I pulled in and went right to sleep. Heard my horses kicking up a fuss in the middle of the night though."

"And you didn't get up to take a look-see?"

"Mister, try to ride that stallion and you'll see why I didn't worry. He's the Devil in disguise when someone he don't know tries to climb on board. He'd eat any man up that came too near."

Another man, who'd dismounted and had been moving around in the bushes outside the small circle of light, spoke up. "That's the God's truth, Gates. I got a little too near the big bastard and he took a nip outta my shoulder. I sure wouldn't try to put a saddle on 'im."

Gates's eyes narrowed suspiciously, he appeared even more ugly in the half-light.

"Well, the dogs say he came this way," Gates told him. "Hung around for a spell, too. Then they can't pick him up at all. Like maybe he mounted up or something."

Gates looked suspiciously back at Jericho again. "You didn't by chance have three horses, did ya?"

"Nope. Just two. Maybe he stole one from somebody else before he got here. Just hung around to steal some food."

Gates's eyes narrowed, finally nodding as though only half convinced. "Okay for now. I hope I don't find out it's any more than that. Just the same, get your stuff. You might as well come with us to the plantation."

As they rode off, Gates yelled over his shoulder, "Keep after 'im boys. I'll join up with you at the mouth of the river. Never lost a nigger yet and I don't intend to start now."

They took a different path back to the plantation than Jericho had relied on earlier. One that seemed somewhat shorter. Up close, Pleasant Manor Plantation was even more imposing than it'd seemed from a distance. Gates carefully skirted the imposing main entrance, taking him to the servant's entrance in the rear. Outside, a large ink-black woman, her head tied with a bright red bandana, shouted as though agitated, shaking her finger at a thin, obviously terrified older man who was just as dark-skinned. When they rode up, the grateful man was able to slip away unnoticed.

"This is Aunt Josie, McCain. She runs the Manor. Get on her wrong side and she'll feed you to the hogs."

Aunt Josie, her hands resting on her huge hips, laughed loudly. "Now Master Gates! How you do talk! Our young visitor will think we're all heathens right out of the jungle! Lordy al'mighty!" Gates finally left him with her, waving as he rode off to join the men searching for Kepi. Jericho prayed that they didn't find him. He still didn't like Gates, but was thankful the Overseer hadn't pressured him to answer more pointed questions; ones to which his answers might have fallen well short. The black woman spoke.

"Well, young Master. What might your name be?"

Jericho gave her his best smile. "Well, it's certainly not 'Master,' Ma'am. I'm Jericho McCain. Pleasure to meet you Aunt Josie."

"Hungry are you? You look hungry."

"I could eat this saddle right now, Ma'am."

Josie laughed her loud trademark laughter, and jerked her head toward the house for him to follow. The kitchen was a large square room, almost the size of the whole cabin he'd lived in back in Tennessee. His eyes grew wide at the sight of all the food displayed. There seemed to be an abundance everywhere. Fresh pies, vegetables being peeled by other slaves, apples, peaches, and three kinds of meat being carved on a huge wooden table. There were fully ten slaves at work at various jobs in the kitchen.

"Some kind of feast taking place tonight, Aunt Josie?"

Another loud laugh. "Lord no! This is every day around here. We serve breakfast, then start lunch right away. End that meal and start dinner. Cook, cook, cook, all the time. When we ain't cookin', we're cleanin'. All day, every day. Lordy how I do love it. Now, come on and I'll have Sharri'a find you some vittles."

Sharri'a was a light-skinned girl of about nineteen. In the bright sunlight, her skin exuded an almost yellow sheen. At the Grouse Point auction block Jericho vaguely recalled one man referring to someone he'd sold in an earlier batch of slaves, as being a, "high yeller." His remark sounded like it was a much sought after commodity. One thing was certain. There was little doubt that she was absolutely beautiful. Her teeth were white and even as she smiled at him, and it lit up her face, making him want to smile back. It was obvious she was of mixed blood, but the affect of that mixing mesmerizing, having captured the best features of both races. High cheekbones, straight nose, thick coal black hair and dark eyes contrasted brilliantly with her unblemished mocha-colored skin. Favoring him with a dazzling smile each time she approached, she brought him food until he finally protested weakly. Then, she instantly disappeared.

Satiated after three thick pieces of roast beef on yeast bread, a huge slice of apple pie and several glasses of cold milk, Jericho leaned back against the tree, closing his eyes. Feeling stuffed to the point of misery and just drifting off, he heard someone clear their throat politely behind him. Nearly jumping out of his skin, Jericho leaped to his feet and turned.

Gone to Texas

Like Sharri'a, this different girl was also about his age, a gorgeous creature by anyone's standards. Thick copper colored hair cascaded almost to her waist. With green eyes, a starched ankle-length dress and yellow bonnet, and the narrowest waist he'd ever seen, she was easily the most beautiful girl Jericho ever laid eyes on.

He bowed awkwardly at the waist. "Jericho McCain at your service, Ma'am."

The lovely vision curtsied daintily, smiled brightly and stuck out her hand. "Susan Harrington. My father owns the Manor. I heard we had company. I must reprimand Overseer Gates for failing to bring you to us immediately."

Her voice was as sweet as the vision she presented. Now standing aside her, he could see she was very petite, her childlike hand nearly lost inside his. Jericho cleared his throat - then embarrassed as he realized he was still holding her tiny hand, dropped it and stammered, "I'm not…exactly a guest, Miz Harrington. Actually, I'm…seeking employment."

"I know. Mister Gates explained that you're on your way to Texas, looking for your brother, I believe? He said your father was a man of property in Tennessee. There were deaths in your family?"

"Yes, Ma'am. My whole family perished from the fever. All except for my brother, who is in Texas. I burned the place and left. I don't intend to ever return."

He could see how his remarks had affected her, for she turned pale and covered her mouth with a gloved hand. "Oh, please forgive me Mister McCain. I didn't know or I might not have mentioned it at all."

"No, no. It's all right. Really. I've gotten over the worst of it by now."

"It must have been simply horrible for you. I can't imagine what I'd do if anything like that ever happened to my parents. Court, he's my big brother, would probably do fine, but as for myself, I'd simply perish."

As they spoke, Jericho felt himself being drawn to this pale, thin girl, of obviously fine breeding. She was like the great ladies he'd often read about in his mother's old books. Each time his eyes met hers, he nearly lost his breath. How he'd ever been allowed to gaze upon so lovely a creature as this he'd never understand. She departed after a few minutes, after he'd promised to attend dinner at the Manor that evening, then mentally kicked himself for accepting the invitation. Old man Harrington would probably sic the dogs on him if he showed up at all. Feeling absolutely terrible, he started toward the summer guesthouse Aunt Josie had assigned him as his quarters.

As he rested, the pretty mulatto girl, Sharri'a, washed and pressed his only change of clothing. At one time he'd felt well dressed wearing them, even to church. Now, they simply seemed tawdry and threadbare. At least, he'd bathed and shaved the fuzz around his mouth, and Sharri'a had washed and trimmed his long unruly hair. Still dissatisfied with his appearance, he conceded it was the best he could do to look presentable. When the tall immaculate butler greeted him at the Manor's front entrance, he felt instantly turned to stone by the finery he glimpsed inside.

"Evening, Master Jericho. I'm Jonas. Welcome to Pleasant Manor, Suh."

Jericho started to correct him on his title, then simply nodded. Escorted through the immense Harrington home, he was in awe of the crystal chandeliers, polished oak, huge ornate mirrors, marble-tiled floors, and rooms the size of entire schools he'd encountered, with grand fireplaces in each one. Everywhere servants scurried, placing vases of freshly cut flowers about and generally fussing to make things look even better. He was taken directly to the huge dining room, his seat indicated as a high-backed chair in the center of a table that easily could've entertained forty guests; certainly the quantity of food presented would have accommodated that many. Yet, there were only three people seated at the mahogany table; the beautiful Susan, a handsome young man not much older than himself, and a striking older woman, whom he suspected was the mistress of the Manor, Mrs. Harrington. Jericho acknowledged those present with a bow and a brief word, the ladies first, then Courtney. Then he took his seat as indicated by Jonas, the black houseman, who pulled his chair back from the table and stood politely behind to assist his sitting. Properly seated, he suddenly was troubled with what to do with his hands. Everything was so spotlessly clean and shiny he hated to touch anything. The value of the silver utensils and serving pieces alone could've bought the small mountain farm where he'd once lived.

Susan stared at him, as though telling him silently to take his clues from her. He waited for her to begin.

"Mama, this is the young gentleman from way up north in Tennessee, who I was telling you about - Mr. Jericho McCain. He suffered a terrible tragedy and was forced to depart at once. The dear boy lost all his family fortune in the process."

Mrs. Harrington, a beautiful slender woman with fine features and sculptured gray hair, didn't move or reply, nor did she give any indication she'd even heard the introduction. She smiled softly, an odd, distant look in her clear blue eyes as Susan went on with Jericho's story. It took several minutes before Jericho realized she was "touched" - that she would never really know him, or anyone else for that matter. Susan had not prepared him for it yet actually seemed unaware of her mother's condition as she finished her story.

Susan then introduced her handsome brother, Courtney, who put him at ease instantly. "Glad to have the company, Jericho. We don't get a lot of company here. Do you fox hunt? We must go sometime. I have just the pony for you."

He liked Courtney immediately. After only a few moments, it was clear the young man was a rebel and marched to his own drummer. Not too much unlike his sister, Susan, he supposed.

No one had touched their food yet and the aroma was maddening, even though he'd eaten well at lunch. It soon became clear why they'd waited, for they were quickly joined by the family patriarch. Thomas Harrington, strode immediately to his lovely, silent wife, pecked her on the cheek as though she was actually aware of his presence, and took his seat at the head of the table. At six-feet-six-inches tall, with a full white beard and an unusual thickness of chest, he was one the most imposing men Jericho had ever seen. Harrington picked up his filled wine glass and raised it.

"To our young guest. Thank you for honoring us with your presence tonight, Mr. McCain."

He had a deep, soft voice, yet it could be heard without difficulty across the large room. They sipped their wine to his toast and Harrington signaled it was time to finally eat, as he picked up knife and fork and cut into the ridiculously thick, rare beef filet on his plate. As he ate, he kept up a running conversation that was both charming and interesting, his deep voice booming in the large dining room. After only a few moments, Jericho was certain he'd be able to pick his host out of a darkened room from among a hundred others by hearing only a single word.

"Jericho, it's the Harrington family's great pleasure to have you as a guest for dinner. I pray you'll be able to stay for a while with us. We don't get many guests here at the Manor."

"Oh, say you will," Susan gushed, immediately covering her mouth politely.

It was plain Thomas Harrington had warmed to his young guest. Whereas Court Harrington seemed flashy and spontaneous, and undoubtedly more than just a bit irresponsible, his father may have detected Jericho to be more serious and practical. It seemed quite evident to the entire Harrington family that he was educated and well mannered. As Jericho ate, he simply concentrated on his food and missed the frequent subtle eye contact passed between Susan and her father. Had he noticed and understood the subtleties, he might well have bolted before his meal was finished. Education and manners were qualities Harrington admired in a young man, and he'd made it clear to Susan that her future husband would possess them. That was how he'd always been and that was his expectation for her. The body language between them simply meant that this young man was a possible candidate.

Courtney observed it all with a detached sense of amusement and did his best to ease Jericho's embarrassment. Susan ate silently, but occasionally giggled ladylike behind her hand during the evening over witty remarks made by Courtney or her father. This behavior alone would've alerted her brother that she had more than just a passing interest in their young guest. The evening seemed to simply fly by for all of them.

The next morning at sunrise, Courtney banged on the door of the summer cottage. Jericho, always an early riser, was already dressed and had eaten the rest of the sandwich he'd saved from his lunch the previous day. He opened the door to find Courtney wearing riding pants and saddle boots.

"Hey, traveler, let's chase some foxes."

Jericho smiled at his new friend's exuberance. "I really think I should start building some of the birdhouses your father wanted completed for your mother's birthday. That was the agreement. I'm one of the hired hands now, Court."

"Nonsense! My mother wouldn't know if it were a birdhouse, or a stone anyway. Come on, we'll go for a couple of hours, then I'll have a nap while you nail some boards together and cut a hole in one of them. What do you say, Jericho? I've just got to show you some of the most fantastic country you've ever seen. It's the place I go when I want to be alone. Please say yes."

Jericho couldn't deny he wanted to go, so he grabbed his hat and they raced to the stables, turning down the offer of a hunting pony, preferring his roan stallion instead. In seconds, they were saddled and leading their mounts toward the kennels. Courtney owned four large foxhounds, housed in the same kennels as the man-hunting bloodhounds that Kepi had feared so much. Unlike the bloodhounds, these were friendly dogs. It was clear Courtney dearly loved them, and they reciprocated. He held a biscuit between his teeth for each of them, letting them leap and gently retrieve it. Then he roughed up their ears as they sat quietly, staring up into his face, waiting.

Finally, he said, "Let's hunt!" The dogs raced toward the distant tree line before the two boys could climb into their saddles. Within seconds the two men were pursuing at a gallop and yelling after them. It seemed they had picked up the scent almost at once.

It was among the most exciting experiences Jericho could remember. He'd never been fox hunting, and even though he never so much as caught a glimpse of the fox they'd chased for hours, the entire morning simply flew by. Riding at a trot, Courtney yelled that the dogs never caught the fox anyway; they really weren't really supposed to. He explained it was the excitement of the chase that was to be enjoyed. Jericho was certain he would've never understood the sport if he hadn't experienced it, but now that he had gone with Courtney, he was determined to go again.

They ate a lunch that Aunt Josie had prepared for them the previous evening, then Courtney passed his silver flask of Kentucky Bourbon to Jericho as they sat on an outcrop of rocks overlooking the valley and the river far below. Jericho noted an eagle soaring above, heard the cry of a wild turkey and immediately understood what Courtney had meant about the place. This was the "favorite spot" Courtney had mentioned to him earlier, and it was, Jericho had to admit, simply fantastic. He tilted the flask and took a cautious swallow. The liquor burned Jericho's throat like fire, but he choked some of it down.

"Ever been in love, Jericho?"

Courtney's words took him completely by surprise. He was instantly embarrassed and struggled with his answer. "Y . . you mean like my family?"

"No. In love with a woman. Really in love - not just feeling randy and wanting to hop on her for a quick romp in the hay. Certainly not like my father and the other old men do when they get drunk and breed the slaves - pretending they're improving the quality of the race."

"They do that?"

"Occasionally. I used to, but not any more. I suddenly imagined how it must be for them, and now I hate the thought of it. What I meant was, to love the woman you want to spend the rest of your life with - to have your children."

Courtney was only a year or two older than Jericho, but suddenly he sounded much older, more mature. "No, can't say that I have, Court. I plan to marry someday though. I'd like a lot of children. I think I'd make a good father. My dad was a good teacher in the way he raised me and Taylor. I hope I can be half as good."

"My father is a selfish old tyrant. If everyone in the family isn't exactly like he thinks they should be, they're complete failures." Court abruptly jumped to his feet and headed toward the mounts. "Let's get back. Dinner will be ready. Want to race?"

* * *

By the time Jericho had been at Pleasant Manor for two weeks, he'd gone fox hunting with Courtney three more times and taken several long walks with Susan in the evenings, with Aunt Josie trailing behind as their chaperone. He'd been content to stay on at the plantation for at least another few weeks, maybe even through the winter. He'd been treated well by the Harringtons and respected them, and Susan was nearly always on his mind. Court treated him like a brother for certain, but Susan - remembering Gates's coarse statement on his first day at the plantation - well, Susan did actually make his mouth water. Lately, he'd had several disturbing dreams about her that had embarrassed him and lingered long after awaking. He couldn't get her out of his mind, and to make it worse, she always seemed to show up when he was alone.

For the moment, he enjoyed the warm morning sun on his shoulders while he constructed an intricate multi-level birdhouse for Mrs. Harrington's upcoming birthday. It was an identical replica of the Manor, and turning out better than he'd anticipated - except for a small rough area at the peak of a gable. He sanded the spot lightly, then inspected it critically against the bright sunlight, nodding his approval. Courtney chose this moment to come by unannounced, plopping onto a nearby wooden bench.

"J.D.! Stop all that menial labor and let's go fox hunting or something. All you ever do is work."

Jericho grinned up at him from his chore. "Do I have to remind you that's what I'm getting paid to do, Court? I make these silly things and your parents let me stay around for a while. I like the arrangement."

Court leaned backward, searched his pockets, then apparently successful, smiled and stuck a short cheroot into his mouth, lighting up. As he blew a cloud of smoke into the still afternoon, he laughed.

"Hell, J.D., you don't have to work to stay around here. My dad likes you better than he does me. Sis stares at you like she wants to eat you up every time you come around, and Mom wouldn't know one way or the other. Your future is sealed, partner. Marry Sis, give Dad the responsible son he's always wanted, and take over this damned place when he dies. Then I can go to France and live a life of decadence like I want. What could be simpler?"

This time Jericho laughed. "Court, you scoundrel. You can't manage people's lives like that. Even to get what you want."

"Why not?"

"'Cause...well, it just ain't done that way."

Courtney's voice became low and conspiring as he leaned forward. "You like Susan don't you? I mean, don't you lie awake and think about her all night long? Wish she were with you, against you all warm and soft? I see the way you stare at her - like she's a heap of whipped cream. She drools over you the same way. That's love, Pard. If it isn't, it's close enough. Especially, since her daddy owns half of the Mississippi Valley."

Stunned, Jericho stared silently at his new friend.

"Well? Do you love my sister, or not?"

Jericho's face turned a bright red. Court laughed loudly. "You do! Damn right! I knew it!"

"I don't know...and it still ain't right."

This time Jericho's voice hadn't carried the same conviction as the first time he'd said it. He studied Courtney Harrington, suddenly aware of something new about him.

"You feel like that about someone too, don't you, Court?"

It was Courtney's turn to glow red in the face. Feeling a little vengeful, Jericho didn't let up a bit. "Okay, tell me. Who is she?"

"Damn it, J.D.!"

"Who?"

Court contemplated the disclosure quietly for a time, as Jericho stared at him. Then he whispered, "Sharri'a. The mulatto girl. We've been lovers for more than two years. I want to take her to France where they don't even care whether you're both the same color." Courtney fixed his eyes on him again. "I do love her, J.D. I can't live without her. If I don't do this, I might as well die."

"What does Mr. Harrington think about it?"

Courtney snorted loudly. "He thinks it's just a case of a young randy buck hauling his monthly ashes. If he knew for certain how it really was, he'd sell her to the first trader who passed by and I'd never find out where she went. If he did, I might just kill him for it. That's why I have to leave. Help me out and marry Sis, J.D. I know you want to. Take this damned place off my hands and let me have the woman I love."

Jericho watched the embittered young man angrily toss his cheroot to the ground and stalk away, obviously embarrassed about his admission. Jericho sat quietly, studying his options. Courtney Harrington was right about somethings. He dreamed of Susan all the time. He didn't know if it was because he was in love with her or if he was experiencing what the older men called being "in season." He did know Susan was the most beautiful girl he'd ever laid eyes on, and she always smelled really nice. His heart raced like crazy every time she drew near.

"Jericho?"

She'd approached silently, and being deep in thought, he hadn't heard her. He nearly jumped out of his skin when she spoke his name.

Leaping to his feet, he stammered, "Miz Harrington! You nearly scared me to death."

She smiled demurely, primly sitting in the spot previously occupied by her older brother, she patted to the seat next to her. His heart pounding, Jericho eased into the indicated spot and scarcely breathing, waited. When Susan dropped her lace shawl, letting it fall back on her shoulders, he noticed the first two buttons of her dress were not fastened, exposing two creamy mounds. He began to mention it, then faltered, embarrassed, and thereafter just stared at her ample bosom in tortured silence.

"How come is it that we never seem to be alone, Jericho? Don't you like being with me?"

He swallowed, trying to speak through a constricted throat, and finally squeaked, "I surely do like being with you, Miz…"

Susan held up her hand and he ceased speaking. "Let's start off today by you calling me Susan. It makes me feel like an old maid when you call me Miz Harrington. That's my Ma's name, not mine."

Jericho nodded. "Okay, Susan. I like you a lot…Susan."

"Well, that's such a pleasant surprise, Jericho. Now see? If we'd never had this talk alone, I'd never have known that. I like you, too, Jericho. An awful lot. Maybe, even more than a lot. Have you ever thought about how it might be, married to someone like me?"

He started to squeak again, halted, swallowed hard and finally spoke around a thick tongue. "I have…I truly have…I just can't imagine how it could happen, though, Miz…Susan. I left the only property I had when I came here. I'm nearly penniless. How could I ask someone like you to marry me? Besides, there's the question of our ages."

"Property is not everything, Jericho McCain! My daddy says ability is much more important. He says you have more ability at your age than anyone he's ever seen. He said you will be a wealthy man someday. As for our age, my father married my mother when he was sixteen and she was only fourteen. They've been married twenty-one years."

"But…how do you suppose your…father would view you actually marrying a pauper? I know I'd have second thoughts about any daughter of mine doing that."

"I think he would encourage it. When I mentioned it to him, he said I should find out how you feel about it."

Years earlier, Jericho had gotten onto his father's wagon when he was only five. The four mules they'd owned had been skittish and wild-eyed due to some large animal prowling about in the nearby thickets. As his father carried logs from a clear-cut he'd been working, Jericho had climbed unnoticed into the wagon seat and pretended to drive, as he'd seen his father do. Growing bored, he'd loosened the brake and the mules suddenly bolted. That wild, terrifying ride down the mountainside was similar to how Jericho was starting to feel now. His heart pounded loudly and he had a great deal of trouble just getting his breath.

"It's considerable food for thought...that's for sure...considerable."

Sensing his predicament, Susan stood and smiled down at him as he jumped to his feet. "I know you'll reach the right decision, Jericho. Daddy also said you were bright. Coming to dinner tonight?"

"Uh...sure. Sure, I will."

Susan suddenly leaned forward, exposing her creamy cleavage even more, and planted a light but lingering kiss on his lips. She stepped back, smiling.

"Until tonight, then," she said sweetly, her voice full of promise.

With that, she swished away toward the big house, leaving Jericho alone with his tormented thoughts. What was he to do about Texas and finding Taylor? Would Susan and her father wait until he'd finished that chore? He doubted it. No, he knew it was all or nothing. These were rich people used to having their way. They'd never forgive him for any indecisiveness or disagreement. On the other hand, there were the slaves of Pleasant Manor to consider. Perhaps if he were to marry Susan and take over the Manor, someday he could set them all free. He honestly hated the manner in which they were treated, and detested the way they existed in cruel captivity while the Harringtons lived in absolute splendor. Or was he just deluding himself into thinking he could help them simply because he actually wanted to stay here with Susan and run the awesome Manor. Jericho's head suddenly ached from too much pondering. He went inside his cabin and lay down on top of the bed covers.

He must have dozed off, as dreams of Susan Harrington enveloped his mind. In his dream they were married and he'd become the boss over the entire Pleasant Manor enterprise. He'd freed the plantation slaves and paying them an honest wage. They'd stayed on to work for the Manor out of loyalty and because they were so happy just being there. In fact, everyone in his dream was happy. They had kids, lots of kids. He couldn't actually see them, and it wasn't exactly clear how many kids, but there seemed to lots of them running around all over the place. A scene overcame all other visions as he and Susan coupled in a passionate embrace. She was urgently moving against his naked flesh, moaning softly in his ear - the pleasure was painfully exquisite.

His dream suddenly interrupted, he jolted awake, disturbed by sounds from outside. He lay quietly for a moment, listening. A loud clamor was coming from the front courtyard, men speaking loudly, angrily, Gate's harsh voice rising above the din.

"Got 'im Mister Harrington! God dammit, we caught the little black bugger just the other side of the river! Chased 'im most of the way to the state line before we got a rope on 'im. He pert'near made it, too. Got farther than all the others. I figure he had help. Give me time and I'll find out who the black-heart was that helped him get that far."

His heart in his mouth, Jericho peeked out the small window

and saw Gates and four other mounted men. At first, he couldn't make out what they were discussing. Then his eyes wide, he saw standing defiantly in the middle, the bruised and battered youth he'd discovered in his camp by the river. Kepi stood, his hands bound tightly behind, glaring up at his captors. Scratches, cuts and what appeared to dog-bites, covered his torso and legs, indicating he'd been tormented and most likely dragged most of the way back. Jericho's anger surged, quickly turning to rage.

Harrington, in his white plantation suit and hat, stood in front of the injured youth, sipping his favorite drink, a tall Mint Julep. He didn't appear angry like the others. In fact, his face seemed almost sympathetic as he spoke in his familiar deep soft voice that carried well. From Jericho's vantage point inside the summerhouse, his tone sounded kindly, and for the first time Jericho felt a glimmer of hope.

"Kepi, why did you run? We treated you like one of our family. You could've had a good life with us until you died. Now I have to punish you. Why, Kepi?"

Harrington's voice seemed anguished, with real pain at what he was about to order. "Why?" he implored again.

His hands manacled in front, leg irons in place, the defiant Kepi squinted at Harrington through battered eyes. "Freedom, Master Harrington. Just freedom, suh."

"Freedom from what? From plenty of food and shelter? A good life here at Pleasant Manor?"

Kepi grinned, showing bloodied teeth, like a caged animal. "Freedom to not have to call any man 'Master,' ever again, Master Harrington."

Harrington sighed deeply and shook his head slightly, as if he still didn't understand what he was being told. Then he turned his back on the boy he'd known since childbirth and walked away. His words floated back to where Jericho watched with growing dread.

"String him up to the pole and give him his twenty. Leave him hang until morning, then we'll carry out the rest of his sentence."

Harrington walked slowly back toward the big house as though the weight of the world was on his shoulders.

Gates and the other two men were almost gleeful in the way they carried out his orders. First they half-carried the struggling, slightly built youth to a log wedged tightly between the limbs of two trees, placed there for one specific purpose. The Manor's slaves called it the whipping post. Gates tossed a rope over the bar; stringing Kepi up by his hands. His toes barely touched the ground as he slowly swung back and forth. Jericho watched as Gates uncoiled his long black snake whip and took a swig from a small flask before he commenced his task. He tossed the flask to the next man, then moved a short distance away, uncoiling his whip as he positioned himself.

"Ready boy? I warned you once, but you're one of them uppity house niggers, ain't cha? Got a warm bed and nice clean clothes to wear all the time. Ya'll think you're white. Now, we'll see who's the uppity one, won't we? Get set, here she comes."

Gates snapped the whip close to Kepi's eyes and even from his distant vantage point, Jericho could see the youth's startled recoil. Gates and the others whooped loudly as they passed the drink around again, seemingly overjoyed by their captive's horror. The next fling, he didn't snap it overhead. Jericho could hear it distinctively crack, as it's nine braided tails struck the boy's naked back like the report of a rifle in the quiet afternoon. Strangely, in a place where it had been hard to look in any direction without seeing a black face, there wasn't one slave in sight. Twenty, Harrington had said. How could the frail Kepi take twenty lashes? Could he live through something like that? Jericho suddenly remembered the rest of the punishment. The boiling kettle. He slowly slumped to his knees, and with tears streaming down his face, tried desperately to close his ears to the sound of the whip's loud crack. That was where Susan found him hours later.

"Jericho? Why didn't you come to dinner as we'd planned? Are you all right?"

Huddled beneath the window, he didn't move. A large lump seemed to be stuck in the back of his throat preventing him from answering. He swallowed several times before he could respond.

"Did you see it?" he finally whispered hoarsely. It hurt to speak.

"It? What?"

"The whipping," he croaked, his words barely audible to either of them. There was a loud ringing in his ears as he fought off his disorientation.

"Oh, you mean that. Kepi's punishment. No, I never watch those things. That's men's business. The sort of things they do for their own amusement. I have more important things to do with my time."

Relying on the window sill for support, he pulled himself up on his shaking legs, pausing for a moment to get strength back into them, then wobbled unsteadily toward his bed. In the gathering dusk, he could barely make out her pale form across the small room.

"More important?" he croaked in astonishment. "What could possibly be more important than a boy being beaten half to death while the mighty Harringtons eat their supper?"

"I don't like the tone of your voice at all, Jericho. It's...insulting."

Jericho suddenly felt his quivering legs go, as he sat down heavily on the edge of his cot. Sweat popped out on his forehead from the exertion, running unnoticed down his face. He began to feel light-headed and queasy.

Susan had moved closer, peering intently into his face. "Are you sick or something?"

When he could finally answer, his low voice was thick, very raspy. "Yeah, I'm sick, Susan. Do you know what made me sick? The sight of a young boy getting the flesh stripped from his back with a black snake whip, the glee with which his tormentors did it, and how your father ordered it done, as if this were no more than killing a chicken for dinner - and then walking away without a backward glance. The way you dismiss it as just something amusing that the men do, because you have more important things. All of it makes me sick. Every damned bit of it!"

The outline of Susan's face in the dark room became even more pale than usual, as she placed a hand against her bosom and gasped loudly. "Oh! I suppose I make you sick, too?"

There was a slight tremble in her voice and it was clear she'd probably never been spoken to in such a manner. Jericho was too tired to care as he lay back on his bed, covering his eyes with a forearm. "Just go away, Susan. Leave me alone."

He heard the gentle swishing of her skirt as she departed and knew he'd closed a door that could never be reopened. Troubled and fitful, he'd slept fitfully, awakening to the dim morning light through his window, and yet another clamor. Dragging himself painfully to his feet, he stepped out into the morning chill and saw Thomas Harrington, Jasper Gates, Susan and Courtney, grouped between him and the main house. There were about half a dozen other white men with them in the courtyard. To a person, they all looked agitated – and in a very mean mood. Breathing deeply, he strode toward them. Courtney spotted him first and walked toward him.

Whatever Jericho expected, it wasn't what happened. As Courtney drew near, he struck Jericho across the face with the back of his hand. It was a glancing blow, but it cut the inside of Jericho's mouth painfully and blood spewed, dotting the front of his denim shirt. Instinctively recoiling, Jericho sidestepped another blow and held up his hands to fend off any following attack. Although younger than Courtney, Jericho was tall for his age and strong. He was a series of taunt, rangy whipcord muscle, gained from many months of hard labor cutting the family's winter wood and plowing the rocky mountainside fields. Courtney, aware he might not fair too well in an all out fisticuffs with his one-time friend, lowered his fists and stepped back. The assault was apparently over for the moment, but Courtney still screamed furiously at him.

"Damn you to Hell, Jericho McCain! You cur! You damned snake-in-the-grass! I befriended you and what did you do but stab us all in the back? I demand immediate satisfaction. I'm calling you out, damn you! We'll settle this on the field of honor, you…you…damn scoundrel!"

"I'm not fighting with you, Court. Certainly not with any weapons. Whatever it is you think I've done, it's not worth someone dying over."

"Are you a coward then, as well as a thief in the night? What does a man have to call you to get satisfaction?"

Thomas Harrington approached, abruptly stepping between Jericho and his angry son. His shoulders slumped, his eyes haggard and bloodshot from alcohol and lack of sleep. "Why did you help one of my slaves try to escape Jericho? That's a serious charge around here. If you were a Nig'ra, we'd put you to death, too. As a white man, you can take satisfaction with my son and possibly walk away."

"Where's Kepi?"

"We boiled him at daylight this morning."

Seeing the sudden horror, disgust and rage building in Jericho's eyes, Harrington backed up a step and hurried on to say, "That's been the law around here for over a hundred years, Jericho. To some, it may make us out to be barbarians, but that's our way. It keeps the other slaves in line."

Jericho felt nauseous. Spinning on his heel, he started to head toward the stables. "I'm leaving Mr. Harrington. Don't try to stop me."

He slowed his step as Harrington softly said, "Are you a coward like my son said, Jericho? If not, why don't you accept his challenge? Clean the slate of your treachery. We can't just let you walk away. It might cause others to ignore plantation law."

Jericho halted, standing completely still for a moment, then turned and walked slowly back to stand in front of the tall man again. He stared silently at the older Harrington, the others waiting impatiently for his answer - Courtney sullen, angry - Susan, ashen and tearful - Gates and the others spoiling for a fight. Most of the other men either smirked with anticipation or softly swore at him. Jericho chose his words carefully.

"You've been kind to me Mr. Harrington. For that I'm grateful and don't want to kill your only son."

Harrington glared back in disbelief, then smiled sardonically. "Kill Court? Hell boy, everyone in the county knows my son is one of the best shots around. If that's your reasoning for acting like a coward, accept his challenge like a man. He'll kill you before you can blink."

Without replying, silently Jericho stepped forward and quickly slipped Harrington's small pistol from the front of his belt. Startled, the others froze, unsure of his intent. Jericho stuck the pistol into his own belt, bent and retrieved a small round rock. In one fluid motion, he tossed it into the air, pulled the pistol and fired, exploding the rock in mid-flight. Jericho stuck the pistol back into the older man's waistband and turned his back on their stunned faces. This time when he walked away, the stunned plantation owner didn't try to stop him, and none of the others cursed him.

Within the hour, Jericho rode his big stallion back across the cotton fields he'd passed through on his first day at Pleasant Manor. The field hands were already at work in the warm morning sun. The sun and heat would soon be bearing down with a vengeance, but for the moment it felt pleasant on his back. He startled to see a black leathery face watching him among the thirty-odd bent over backs, the same old man he'd noticed on the day of his arrival. While the suffering remained present in his dark eyes, this time he sensed something different. Jericho struggled with it momentarily, then settled on what it was; friendliness – warmth - appreciation. The old man half-smiled and nodded slightly, then dropped his head before Jericho could react.

Pausing briefly on the next ridge, he took a long look back upon the place he'd spent such a short time, yet, where so much had happened that would change him forever. As his father used to say, "Things happen a certain way for a reason. Don't question God's motives." Ahead was one more field, this one with a smaller group of toiling field hands. Beyond lay the foothills and his destination. Somewhere on the other side of those foothills was Texas. He knew he'd made the right choice. Texas was his destiny. He felt it in his bones.

As he rode across the endless fields where the thin, bare backs were bent low in their personal eternities, toiling in the increasing morning heat, his soul ached for their suffering, his heart felt heavy. But the aching wasn't for Susan Harrington.

* * *

It'd been two weeks later when Jericho reached the Natchez Trace, an area well known for treacherous rogues, shysters and violent highwaymen. Twice before his arriving, he'd stopped in some small towns for new supplies and to mend his saddleware, and twice, someone had tried to steal his horses. Had it not been for Blue's vigilance they might well have done so, too. The second time he'd had to fire a few well-placed shots close over their heads to chase them off. Thereafter, he'd decided he'd avoid populated areas and would stop at some of the few outlying farms, and then only when necessary.

He figured he must be near the Louisiana and Texas border when he came upon cleared farmland, and noticed a large house set in a neatly trimmed growth of weeping willows. As tired as he was, he knew his animals had to be even more worn out. If he didn't rest them soon and ensure they had grain to eat, they'd surely become ill and go lame on him. In this lawless territory, that would be the kiss of death for a lone traveler.

Jericho spied a man standing near an old barn, patiently watching his approach. The man balanced a long-barrel goose gun in the crook of his arm. Jericho made sure to keep his hands in plain sight and well away from his saddle holster as he rode up.

"Hello, stranger," the dark-skinned man said as he drew near. "Traveling through?"

Jericho smiled, but made no attempt to dismount. Out here, he knew that if someone wanted you to get down, they'd invite you to do it.

"Sure am, mister. All the way from Tennessee. I think I've grown into this saddle."

The man laughed loudly. "Then light and have a bite of food with us. The missus is just putting supper on the table."

"Sounds mighty inviting to me, sir. I haven't had a meal in a week." Jericho climbed down stiffly from his saddle, feeling his big stallion heave a huge sigh of relief.

The man was smallish, but powerfully built. His grip was firm, his palm rough from years of hard work. "I'm Jean Paul LaPonce," the man said. "A coon-ass Cajun – that's Louisianan for a Frenchman. Everybody calls me Frenchie. My wife Anna comes from the old country, too. She came over nearly twenty years ago for our wedding. My folks arrived in 1811, just before the second war for our independence, with Britain."

"Howdy. Jericho McCain, sir. Pleased to meet you."

They shook hands and his guest suddenly yelled out, "Alexander!"

A tall youth about his own age strode from the barn and was introduced as his eldest son. "Me and Anna have ten children, six boys and four girls. Maria's the oldest. She's seventeen. Katie is the youngest, at two."

Suddenly, Jericho realized he'd only known Jean Paul briefly and already knew more about him than he of his own family's history.

"Alex," Jean Paul said. "Fetch this gent's animals and rub 'em down. Give 'em half a shovel of grain – no more until tomorrow. After having nothing but wild grass to eat for a few weeks, they'd get sick if you grain 'em out too much."

He looked at Jericho and smiled. "Come on, son. I'll have Maria show you where you can wash up, then we'll have some vittles."

A tall, dark-haired girl of roughly Jericho's age exited the house without speaking, and led him to a covered well-spring in back of the main house. She pumped clear cool water into a wash pan and handed Jericho a bar of soap, watching silently as he scrubbed his face and ears. When finished, she handed him a towel and smiled, her teeth even and white. She was completely different than Susan Harrington, with dark creamy skin and large brown eyes, her ample frame soft and rounded, brown from hours spent in the sun. Susan had been beautiful, but almost too thin and pale. Maria also wore her bodice low in the front with the top button undone, but unlike Susan, it didn't seem contrived. It was clear to him that was just the way she dressed. Suddenly, Jericho realized she was very pretty. In her own but different way, just as beautiful as Susan had been. Without a word, she led him inside where the entire family awaited them for dinner. Jericho and Maria took their places at the long table with the other eleven family members, and Jean Paul spoke.

"Join hands and bow your heads to give thanks for this great bounty," he said.

After their amens and signs of the cross, the food was attacked with frenzy. Jericho noticed right away that these were hard-working people who enjoyed good food and weren't afraid to show their appreciation for it. Twice during the meal, he looked up from his plate to catch Maria staring at him. She immediately smiled and dropped her eyes each time.

Unwilling to accept their hospitality without renumeration, Jericho offered to fix Frenchie's barn roof in exchange for his food and a place to sleep until his animals had rested up a bit. By the third day, he had completed the barn and had begun mending the fence and main gate. Somehow, Maria always seemed to show up when least expected, bringing him a cool drink, a sandwich, or just a quiet smile and soft hello. Each time, after she'd departed, Jericho could catch the pleasant lingering smell of her faint lilac scent. Remembering his near disaster with Susan Harrington, it was unnerving to say the least.

After dinner, it was common for he and Jean Paul to sit on the front porch and talk, while Jean Paul smoked his pipe and Jericho whittled. His six hard-working sons usually went to bed soon after the evening meal, eager to get a good night's sleep. He learned quickly that they all put in a long day, and were usually in the fields by the time Jericho arose around daylight. After the evening meal, the LaPonce' females cleaned up the dinner dishes and prepared as much of the following breakfast meal as possible before they also turned in, leaving Jericho and Jean Paul alone to talk.

It was well after dark when Jericho finally stood and stretched, saying, "Think I'll turn in Frenchie. I want to finish up the fence tomorrow, by the time you come in from the fields."

"Good night then, lad. You're a good hand to have around."

Jericho, still basking in Frenchie's praise when he stepped into the dark barn, felt a sudden push against the wall, restrained by something warm and soft. Although she never spoke, he knew instantly it was Maria. The faint scent of lilac water instantly filled his nostrils. Her soft body moved urgently against him, her moist mouth pressed against his, hungrily nibbling and sucking. The sweetness of her breath filling his mouth was intoxicating. His hands slipped around her waist, almost of their own accord, and he felt her tongue dart into his mouth. It took his breath away. Just as he felt as if he would lose his mind, her mother stepped from the back door and shouted loudly, "Maria? Maria! I need you. Come into the house, now!"

Maria tore her mouth from his, lingering, she answered breathlessly, "Coming, Mama."

Her tongue returned immediately and Jericho felt himself slipping into something uncontrollable. Then, in a flash, she was gone, leaving him weak and shaky.

For a long time, he leaned against the wall, his legs wobbly, still feeling her mouth on his, smelling her faint lilac scent. It didn't take long to recover. After a while, he went inside, packed his saddlebags, and secured his equipment for the long trip. After tonight, he knew he couldn't stay any longer. His life was already too confusing without having Maria show up after dark each night, and...well, who knew where it might end? Early the next morning, he said his goodbye to the family, amid joyful well wishes and their urgings for him to return soon. Maria remained back, aloof from the main group, silent, as though she would break into tears at any moment. He paused and glanced back as he reached the main gate, waved, but all he could see were Maria's sad eyes. Women. How could anyone understand them? It seemed they were happiest when they were making a man miserable.

Four

THE SMALL, BUDDING TOWN had been built on the site of what had originally been an ancient agricultural village of Waco Indians. About ten years previously, Cherokees had arrived suddenly and drove the Wacos off. The Cherokees were referred to by the white man as one of the "civilized" nations. A company of Texas Rangers showed up and set up the first white outpost in the area. With the protection the Rangers offered, George Barnard established a trading post in 1844 and a white settlement soon sprang up around it. Then Neil McLennan built a two-story house nearby, and a man named Jesse Sutton immediately started the first blacksmith shop; there were twenty-two white people in Waco at that time.

The Mexican Army, embarrassed by their defeat at the hands of Sam Houston after their bloody victory at the Alamo, returned under the command of Santa Anna and had been placing pressure along the border on Zachary Taylor's small, ill-equipped army of misfits. Many suddenly left their homesteads up north, flooding south by the thousands to answer their country's call for help. By the end of 1844, Waco had swelled to more than five hundred men, women and children, most of the men just passing through on their way to join up with Old Rough and Ready and fight the Mexicans.

Squinting from beneath the brim of his large hat, Handsome Jack Clay watched an odd procession enter Waco's town limits. At its head, a scarecrow of a boy sat easily atop the best-blooded roan stallion Jack Clay had ever seen, leading a mule and a mare. Although a thick coat of dust on his clothing and gear made it readily apparent he'd traveled far, the youngster slouched in the worn saddle in a manner that suggested he was comfortable there. The spirited filly he led behind on a hackamore was equally as fine-blooded as the big stallion. The lightly loaded gray mule appeared to be "rather long in the tooth." A skinny, blue-spotted hound loped awkwardly behind, letting out a surprisingly deep-throated yodel every few minutes.

* * *

Handsome Jack had been sitting on a flour barrel, whittling a knife-grip while observing new arrivals for most of the morning. Up until now he'd seen nothing worth his time. He'd been watching this particular procession with increasing interest ever since they'd first entered the flat area north of town almost an hour ago. The group wasn't particularly interesting as travelers go, nor that much different from any of the others he'd seen ride in lately. What caught his eye and set them apart from all the others was the fineness of the thoroughbred stallion and mare. Upon closer observation, the boy appeared almost as gaunt as the pitiful dog running behind, or for that matter, the plodding gray mule. In fact, only the magnificent red horse with the lightening bolt across its face and the frisky filly seemed like they had any right to be alive.

Handsome Jack studied the boy with growing interest as he dismounted in the dusty street in front of the Sheriff's office. He loosely looped the stallion's reins over a hitching post, but tied the ropes of the mule and mare securely to his saddle horn. The boy wore the attire of a sodbuster – bib overalls, long johns,

Gone to Texas

rough knit shirt, and high-top shoes instead of the standard boots or moccasins of the area. He appeared ill at ease with the activity of the town, startling easily and glancing around nervously at each sudden noise. His gaze lingering on the battered sign for a few more moments, he sighed deeply and entered.

Handsome Jack remained in the shade of the store, his chair tilted back against the wall to escape the hot afternoon sun. A team of horses couldn't have dragged him off that flour barrel at the moment; that intent was he toward the drama unfolding before him. He watched as the half-starved hound bounded about, barking, licking at the stallion's nostrils. The big stallion snorted, playfully pushing the dog away with its nose. The blue tick hound barked once more, then panting heavily, crawled beneath the stallion's legs, plopped down in the small shaded area that the larger animal provided, instantly going to sleep. The large, wild-eyed stallion never so much as moved a muscle.

Well I'll be damned, Handsome Jack thought, staring in disbelief. *I will be damned.*

* * *

Movement caught his eye as two men he'd seen arrive earlier in the week moved toward the boy's animals, appreciably looking them over. From their outfits, he concluded they were either buffalo hunters or trappers. He'd already observed their rudeness toward the town's women folk and their bullying of the local merchants, determining their loutish behavior marked them as some of the low lifes that had been showing up in Waco lately.

Plenty of their ilk around nowadays, he mused. Not to mention mule skinners, ex-soldiers, gamblers, thieves, back country folks, big city folks, hell…even farmers. Hell, only yesterday, he'd met a lawyer. A lawyer! Lowest of the low-lifes! After him, none who showed up in Waco surprised him.

Lately, the town seemed to practically burst at its seams with all the traffic coming and going. Handsome Jack had heard that most of the poor souls had been in such a rush to get here, they'd simply written in bold chalk on their homes, "Gone to Texas." Those in a real hurry had just scrawled, "GTT" on their doors and left everything behind.

Every man of 'em had come to join up with General Zachary Taylor's 4000 regular army troops that had been holding a defensive position just above the mouth of the Rio Grande. In April, Mexican forces had crossed the river and attacked Taylor's army, then once again the following month. Soon after, Congress declared war on Mexico and all these folks were here to answer their nation's call to arms. Or, boiled down to their simple common language, they'd all come to "help ol' Rough 'n Ready kick some Mexican ass."

The problem, Handsome Jack mused, is that Mexican regulars can sometimes be some pretty tough asses to kick – but no one seemed to have heard about that yet.

This was exactly why Handsome Jack Clay had come to Waco, too. He'd been dispatched by Captain John Coffee Hays, and specifically instructed to "skim the cream," selecting only the best of the best of this motley crew for integration into a new elite militia unit Hays had formed, called Texas Rangers. Captain Hays wasn't particularly interested in spit and polish, although he never failed to reiterate, "Cleanliness speaks well for a man." Primarily, he was interested in their character – and skill with a horse and a gun. Even better if they owned some fine horseflesh and guns.

Gone to Texas

The two rascals eyeing the boy's animals looked shy not only in the character department, but as though neither had been on speaking terms with soap and water for several months. Interested in what might develop, Handsome Jack settled back again, carefully looking them over. The larger of the two, dressed entirely in buckskins, sported a wide-brimmed, fringed hat with dark sweat spots around the band. It was of the same type Jack had seen during his only trek to the large plains west of the Mississippi River. A large pistol stuck out, butt forward, plains style, in the big man's beaded waistband. On his left hip hanging from a strap, a wide-blade Bowie knife swung freely with his every step. In one hand, he carried a .50 caliber buffalo gun with a beaded rawhide shoulder strap. The legs and seat of his pants were black with grease and soot, obviously where he'd been wiping them since the first time he'd slipped into them.

The smaller of the duo was attired in a similar manner, although even filthier than his companion, if that were possible. A constant slack smile displayed broken, black teeth protruding from a receding gum line, and a large wad of "chaw" poked his cheek pockets out like a squirrel with a mouthful of acorns.

As the larger of the two men moved closer to the stallion, the blue hound raised its sad eyes, silently following his movements. Paying the skinny dog no attention, the man abruptly reached out to grasp the bridle. At that instant, the stallion lunged forward and clicked its teeth at the outstretched hand. The hound stood and growled deep in its throat, showing its surprisingly long white fangs.

"You son-of-a-bitch!" the man yelled, jumping away from the horse's vicious jaws.

The hound stood now and continued rumbling a caution low

in his throat, this time showing more teeth and crouching as though to pounce. The smaller man literally leaped onto the boardwalk as if to seek the protection of higher ground at a substantially safer distance.

Just as the man's hand went for the knife at his belt and he tentatively stepped forward, the door to Sheriff's office banged open and the boy reemerged, followed closely by Hank Potts. Potts was Sheriff Smith's low-paid, whisky-swilling deputy. The lad immediately sized up the situation and pointed his finger at the buffalo hunter.

"You! Git away from my animals!" he shouted. Like the hound, his voice was strong and surprisingly deep for a youngster.

The burley man glared at the youngster and spit a brown stream at the snarling dog, which moved quickly out of range, but continued to show his fangs.

"This ain't yore animals, snot-nose," the man retorted as his partner snickered from a safe distance away on the boardwalk.

"These two horses was stole from me up on the Arkansas – near Fort Smith. I paid two hun'rt dollars apiece fer 'em, and I aim to kill the man that stole 'em."

"You're a liar, mister," the boy stated evenly through clinched teeth.

The buffalo hunter's hand inched toward his pistol. The boy slightly raised the tip of his long rifle in the man's direction.

Unexpectedly a mountain of a man in a dark vest, white shirt and black string tie, rushed toward the pair, shouting as he drew even. "That'll be 'nuff from both of you!" he yelled, stepping between them. "The first one that starts shooting in my town will hang. That is, if I don't kill 'em first."

The mountainous newcomer gestured toward the buffalo

hunter and rumbled, "Move over there by your little friend, Sikes, so I can watch you both. Don't say a word until I tell you to."

He turned to the boy and in a surprisingly gentle voice, said, "What's your name, son?"

The boy's expression never changed, but it was clear that he was angry. "Jericho McCain. I come from Tennessee. Who're you?"

The huge man gazed down at the slender dust-coated youngster for a moment as though trying to make up his mind if the boy was being cheeky or sincere. Apparently satisfied, he said, "I'm Sheriff Monahan Smith. I run things around here. You got a bill of sale for these animals, Jericho McCain – from Tennessee?"

"No sir. They belonged to my pa who died of the fever. He was a man of property but never held much with signing papers and the like. He always worked on a handshake and a man's word."

"Well, that's right commendable son and it may work back in Tennessee, but out here it won't take you far," the Sheriff responded. Pointing toward the stallion, he continued, "You got any way of proving that horse belongs to you?"

Young Jericho studied his dusty shoes for a moment, then cocked his head and looked directly into Sike's mean eyes. A faint smile played at the corner of his mouth as he said, "I reckon. Let whoever can ride 'em claim 'em, Sheriff."

Surprised by the lad's comment, Sheriff Smith hesitated then grinned and nodded. "Done! You there! Sikes! You say that's your animal? Then climb aboard."

Clem Deeks, his short, dirty partner, knew Alfred Sikes could ride anything with four legs. He winked slyly as the two ruffians grinned confidently at each other. Sikes, recalling his narrow escape from the stallion's sharp teeth moments before, approached the horse cautiously. The big stallion quivered, nostrils flaring – otherwise, he stood unmoving.

Sikes swiftly grabbed the saddle horn and prepared to heave himself into the saddle. Just as his foot hit the stirrup the stallion whirled suddenly and sank his sharp teeth deeply into Sikes's shoulder. Sikes screamed in pain and jumped backwards, backpedaling to get away from the stallion's vicious teeth. Hoofs flying, the animal pursued him relentlessly as he reeled backward, falling into the dusty street. Screaming profanely, Sikes quickly swept the dust and debris from his eyes just in time to see pure hell descending down on him. He rolled, cursed and kicked as he scrambled about in the billowing dust, attempting to squeeze his large frame into a tiny space under the watering trough. Teeth bared, eyes rolled back into its head, the screaming devil horse lunged at him over and over again, knocking huge chunks out of the wooden trough with his shod hoofs, as Sikes cowered between the trough and the high boardwalk.

"Shoot him, Deeks!" Sikes screamed as he scurried on his back towards the other end of the trough. "Shoot the son-of-a-bitch!"

The boy whistled softly and the attack was suddenly over. Sikes jumped to his feet, scampering under the hitching post onto the protection of the boardwalk. His chest heaved as sweat and tears streamed freely down his dirty face. The raging beast that had viciously attacked him only a moment before now appeared to be no more than a pet seeking attention, as it pushed its nose against the boy's breast as though searching for something. It gently nuzzled the slender boy's shirt pocket. He retrieved a treat and fed it to the horse all the while continuing to smile softly at Sikes.

"Maybe you were mistaken about this horse being the one stolen from you – up on the Arkansas, did you say?" Sheriff Smith raised his eyebrows at Sikes.

The shaking man grunted, muttering profanely to himself, angrily dusting off his hat by slapping it against his leg. As he started to leave he turned, glaring directly at the boy.

"You stay out of my way snot-nose. You hear? The next time I see you, I'll slit yore bag and run yore leg through it."

He and Deeks walked away without looking back, the smaller man trying to console his large partner.

Sheriff Smith and Jericho stared after the two hunters as they retreated. When they'd disappeared into the doorway of a cantina, the Sheriff said, "You better give those two fellows lots of elbow room, Jericho McCain. Sikes won't be forgetting this for a while. You got business in town or just passing through? Maybe intending to join up with Zach Taylor?"

The boy seemed confused by the question and remained silent, weighing his options before responding.

"Zach who?"

For a colt, this is one cool customer, thought Sheriff Smith.

Jericho continued. "I'm looking for my brother, Sheriff. He's supposed to be somewhere in Texas, but I don't know exactly where."

McCain briefly explained how he'd buried his family and had spent the past few months on the trail. As he talked, Sheriff Smith could tell the boy was exhausted and more than likely, half-starved.

"...so I figured I'd spend a few days asking questions around Waco while I'm here, then move on. If that's all right with you, Sheriff," he concluded.

"You got a place to stay while you're in town?"

Jericho stared back blankly.

"Lad, I know a widder woman that could use a little handy work around her place. I could talk to her and maybe arrange a cot and 'found' for a few days. She might even be inclined to pay you a little in wages if you're any kind of handy. At least, until you've had a chance to find out about your brother. In the meantime, I'll ask around to see if anyone has seen him. Whad'ya say?"

The thought of a hot meal started Jericho's mouth to watering and he suddenly felt light-headed. "I'd be obliged, Sheriff."

Jericho wasn't too keen about hanging around the smelly little town of Waco for any longer than it took to find out about Taylor, but he also knew that his horses needed rest and he needed time to put together another grub stake for his next leg of the hunt. He figured he could put up with toiling for some cranky old widow woman long enough to get a few square meals under his belt and ask some questions about Taylor. Then he'd be on his way again. Despite his growing hunger, the next two hours were spent hanging around town and becoming familiar with the town's hustle and bustle. Waco was a town of only a dozen wood structures but perhaps four times that number of adobe dwellings. Most of the wooden buildings were businesses, however a few were homes for the more well off citizens of Waco. The size of these homes, although modest when compared to some he'd seen in Memphis when he'd gone with his dad for shooting contests, dwarfed the small five-room cabin he'd once called home.

Gone to Texas

Everywhere he went people were talking about Texas statehood and the recent declaration of war with Mexico.

"Winfield Scott is arriving with nearly 50,000 regulars to fight beside General Zach Taylor – Santa Anna has been recalled from exile and given command of the entire Mexican Army – Zachary Taylor is giving every volunteer a horse, a pistol and sixty dollars a month…"

And so, on it went.

Jericho surmised he'd never seen a bunch so fired up to get themselves killed as the folks of Waco. He certainly wasn't mad at the Mexicans and didn't want to kill anybody. All he wanted was to find his brother.

Reluctantly, Jericho approached the widow's house a mile outside the town limits, leading his horses and mule. He stopped at a framed house with whitewashed fence, as the Sheriff had described it earlier. Even the rocks surrounding the flowerbeds had been whitewashed at one time.

This old gal must dearly love white, he mused, his mouth suddenly dry with nervousness. Well, might as well get this over with.

He knocked on the door and it was opened by one of the most beautiful creatures Jericho had ever seen. He was instantly struck dumb. If this was the "Widder" Matthews, she was definitely not the cranky old woman he'd envisioned! She smiled brightly, a vision of pure loveliness, and spoke in a deep, husky voice.

"Yes? May I help you?"

Despite all his father's Bible teachings, Jericho must've heard the devil laughing with glee for the lurid thoughts that suddenly raced through his young mind. He stood frozen in time, tongue-tied, swallowed hard, and stared at her small waist and heaving bosom.

She spoke again, having the same affect as before.

"You must be the gentleman Sheriff Smith told me about. Jericho, isn't it?" She stuck out her hand, palm down.

"Y...yes Ma'am," he finally stammered, taking her offered hand and pumping it vigorously. "J...Jericho McCain. At your service, Ma'am."

"My, you are a gentlemen. Well, please do come in and we'll discuss the arrangement. I've just made some cookies and you might as well be the first to try them." She smiled sweetly.

Nibbling hot cookies and drinking cold milk during the next two hours, he soon discovered how easy it was to talk to the woman – and to look at her. He told her of the fever killing his parents and sister; of having to bury them; his long trek to Texas; and how he was looking for his brother Taylor. He could've talked on much longer.

The Widow Matthews seemed to know all the right things to say and exactly when to say them. When the last of the cookies were gone, she unaccountably reached out and patted his hand and Jericho felt the hot sting of tears in his eyes. Her cozy kitchen felt almost like the home he'd known just a few months before.

A small room had been added at the rear of the main house and the widow told Jericho to put his things there, and to call her, Jean. Jean Matthews.

Jean. Jean. The sound of it almost sang. He went to sleep that night with the name on his lips.

* * *

During the next month Jericho worked tirelessly, happily whitewashing the fence and rocks around the bungalow, repairing the tool shed, cutting firewood and fixing Jean Matthew's roof. His father had trained him well in the skill of carpentry, and his efforts did not go unnoticed by the young woman. After the first few nights, Jean invited Jericho to eat his meals with her.

They'd usually spend the evening playing checkers and dominos – or simply talking about his home in Tennessee – then her background in Boston where she'd been raised. Although a strong friendship bond formed almost at once, Jericho never quite got over the hammering deep inside his chest every time she lay her hand on his arm or spoke in her deep, breathless voice. It made for some sleepless, unsettling nights for the youngster to be sure.

Jericho learned that her husband, George Matthews, had also been a carpenter and that was, alas, what had led to his demise. It had been the previous year that he'd been helping a neighbor put a roof on a barn when he'd slipped and plunged over the edge. The fall had broken his neck and he'd lingered for two agonizing weeks before passing away.

Although they'd been married for only five years, George had left her comfortable. The house and fifty acres were paid for and they'd been able to put away a small "sock" despite difficult times. No, she didn't want for anything, but after a few glasses of homemade wine, did confess that her family still lived far away in Boston and since her husband's death she'd been terribly lonely. The time went by so rapidly that he rarely thought about his task of finding Taylor.

One frosty morning nearing his second month, Jericho hitched the buggy in preparation for their weekly trip into Waco for supplies. They'd made the short trip every Saturday to buy feed for the few head of livestock and chickens, and a meal at the new hotel. There was a slight nip in the air, signaling a message that winter would not be long in coming. Jericho was glad he wasn't living on the trail now, with cold weather on the way.

Jean Matthews exited the house in a long wool coat with a fur-rimmed hood that framed her beautiful face. The sight caused Jericho to catch his breath.

"Ready to go, Jericho?" she said breathlessly, in the tone that always sent him straight to Hell.

He forced himself to think pure thoughts and busied himself with the harness while he waited for the giant hand gripping his heart to release him. His ears a bright red, he finally replied, "Yes Ma'am. Glad you're wearing your coat today. It's right nippy this morning."

"Jean."

"Pardon?"

"Jean. I thought we'd decided you'd call me Jean when we're alone," she said sweetly.

Jericho felt his face glowing warm again, despite the chilled morning air. The intimacy of calling this wonderful woman by her given name felt almost too sensuous for him. His heart continued to pound wildly.

"Yes…Jean. Begging your pardon."

"Apology accepted," she said, as she settled onto the wagon seat covering her legs with a wool blanket. "Now, sir, let's get into town and have lunch at the hotel cafe. What do you say?"

She knew how much Jericho enjoyed the hotel's hot apple pie and hid her smile at his haste to get started. As Jericho climbed into the driver's seat, he felt at least ten feet tall. He expertly popped the whip over the horses' head, and felt them lurch against the harness. As usual, his blue-tick hound jumped onto the wagon bed just as they left the yard. Riding beside Jean Matthews made Jericho feel so proud that he actually poked out his chest, casting furtive glances at her all the way into Waco.

They headed directly to the hotel for lunch first thing, because Jean knew Jericho would have that apple pie on his mind until it'd been put out of the way. She ordered a small meal, smiling in enjoyment and amusement at the vast quantities of food Jericho could put away. In many respects he reminded her of her late husband, who'd been tall and slightly built, but with whipcord leather-like muscles, and boundless nervous energy. She watched as he pushed back his plate, sighing contently in what she'd lately come to recognize was the signal that he was finished – at least for the moment.

"Ready to go to work, now?" she said in amusement.

Jericho's ears turned red and he nodded, making her smile once again. *Such a dear boy*, she thought as they exited the eatery and crossed toward the Winkler General Store. He hadn't spoken of the search for his brother for a while now, and Jean fervently hoped he would remain with her, at least through the winter months. She did so enjoy his company.

Mr. Winkler's hired hand, Buster Farbis, created a billowing cloud as he swept a pile of dirt out of the store's open doorway. It was well known that Buster Farbis was a bit "touched in the head" ever since his father's mule had kicked him there at the age of nine. No one knew his exact age, but speculation was that he was nearing fifty. Many of the town folks, especially the children and roughnecks, considered Buster odd, looked down on him and sometimes poked fun at him. Jericho McCain was one of the few who never did.

"Morning, Mr. Farbis!"

Farbis didn't look up from his sweeping, but sounded jolly when he said, "Morn'n Jer' cho. Gotta sweep now. Gotta sweep. Bye."

Jericho nodded, smiling to himself as he entered and greeted the store's proprietor. "Morning Mr. Winkler."

"Morning, Jericho. The feed you asked for is stacked out front. Buster's out there if you need help with 'em."

"No thanks, sir. I can manage just fine."

Thirty minutes later, Jericho grunted as he tossed the final heavy bag of grain onto the wagon bed. Just finished, he was startled by the loud howl of an injured dog. Hastily scanning the area for Blue, he ran in the direction of the snarling and yelping sounds.

Jean stepped from the door and saw his retreating back. "Jericho McCain! Where are you going? You come right back here, this instant!"

Jericho sped around the corner of the barber shop where he saw a small crowd around the two men he'd clashed with earlier over the true ownership of his stallion. His blue tick lay on its back before them, teeth bared, snarling viciously. Blood gushed from deep cuts across the dog's back and hip. Sikes maneuvered closer to finish him off with the large Bowie knife, as Deeks watched from the safety of a wood staircase. Attracted by the commotion, a larger crowd had now gathered, most watching with disgust. However, the reputation of these two hard cases was such that they hesitated to interfere in what was happening.

Jericho never slowed a step as he lowered his head and charged headfirst into the large man's spine. Sikes pin-wheeled into a wooden railing, bounced off, and fell heavily into the dust. He barely had time to clamor to his feet when a windmill of flying fists peppered his face and chest. More surprised than hurt, he quickly regained his composure, lunged, and slugged at his attacker, knocking Jericho to the ground. Slowly dawning on him who his attacker was, Sikes grinned nastily through bloodied lips.

Since arriving in Waco, Alfred Sikes had boasted many times of being a brawler; how he loved to fight almost better than anything else. He'd demonstrated to the citizens who'd had the misfortune of crossing him how he loved to feel the crunch of bone and see his opponent's blood flowing freely, laughing loudly as he beat them senseless. He laughed now.

His humor was short-lived, for instantly a barrage of fists pummeled his face and neck again. An erratic but well-landed blow slammed the boy to the ground, but he rolled with it nimbly, instantly back on his feet, his fists hammering away at Sike's face once more. Time-after-time the crowd watched, horrified and amazed at the boy's unrelenting battering, as he was knocked to the ground, instantly recovered and attacked again. While there were some who might've interfered on the boy's behalf, the code of the frontier was clear on that point; a man must fight his own battles. It was evident to those watching that this battered young David had no chance whatsoever against such an overwhelming adversary as the hulking Goliath – Alfred Sikes.

"Stop them," Jean Matthews screamed at the crowd. "Somebody stop it. That awful brute will kill him!"

Jean Matthews continued screaming and berating the men watching, trying to get them to intervene and stop the fight – yet none moved to do so. Discouraged, she ran at the large bearded man and swung her handbag at him, missed and sprawled onto her backside into the dusty street. A handsome stranger assisted her to her feet, tipped his hat and turned back to the fight. Disheartened, her shoulders suddenly slumped and she sobbed, also watching – in horror.

Jericho, bloody and raw from the giant's relentless pounding, took the blows silently, but each time immediately rebounded as though made of rubber, the deafening blows interrupted only by the heavy breathing of the combatants. Gradually Sike's contemptuous smile began to give way to strain, then concern, as his arms became heavy, his breathing ragged. His face was beginning to show the affects of Jericho's rapid fists, his puffy eyes closed, his breathing labored through swollen lips and bloodied nose. Yet the boy's attack never faltered, relentlessly, striking Sikes in the face – then the body. Red welts rose on the big man's face and neck and each body blow now elicited a grunt of pain as he gasped to find more air.

Panicky Sikes sought out Deeks through his swollen half-closed eyes and Deek's hand dropped to the butt of his knife as he stepped toward the combatants. In the crowd, the handsome young man with crossed pistol belts who had assisted Jean to her feet a moment earlier, silently shook his head. Deeks didn't like what he saw in the stranger's eyes and immediately retreated back to the safety of the stairs.

Sikes was retreating steadily now, and finally abandoned the fight altogether as he suddenly turned and attempted to run. It did no good. The demon he hoped to flee leaped upon his back and continued plummeting him with unrelenting blows that had become unbearably painful. Sikes screeched, fell to his knees and tried to scamper away. Still the blows rained down upon him.

"God dammit, help me…somebody…please! Help me!"

Making no pretense of fighting back now, Sikes drew into a

fetal position, covering his head with useless, heavy-laden arms, his once arrogant bravado turning into faint whimpering. It was evident the crowd felt little sympathy for the bully. Most were enjoying it immensely, and not a single man moved to help him.

Jean Matthews screamed again, "Stop it, Jericho! Stop it; you're killing him. Please!"

She grabbed at the boy's flailing arms, backing hastily away in horror as he looked through her with sightless eyes, and slowly drew back his fist as if to strike at her, too. Then reality seemed to gradually set in as his gray eyes began to focus, and he suddenly appeared to recognize her for the first time. Without a word, Jericho lowered his raised fist, rose painfully, and wheeled to kneel beside his injured hound. The dog licked at his hand, whimpering softly, but otherwise lay unmoving as his deep wound was examined with the gentlest of hands. The crowd parted silently as the boy tenderly picked up his dog and walked through them toward the doctor's office.

After his silent warning to Deeks to stay clear of the altercation, Handsome Jack Clay had remained in the crowd and watched the fight.

My God, he thought. *How'd I ever think this boy was just another clodhopper? This beats anything I've ever seen! No one will believe me unless they'd seen it, sure as hell! I got a feeling I'll be hearing more about that young man.*

Five

DOC ROACH WORKED FOR more than an hour on Jericho's dog, as he tried frantically to stem the flow of blood from severed major arteries. At the last, Blue looked up mournfully at the boy as if trying to convey some message, licked his master's hand, then sighed deeply and closed his eyes for the last time. Jericho had seen enough death in the last year to know the dog was dead even before Doc Roach ended his futile efforts and sadly gazed up at him.

"I'm sorry, boy. He's gone."

Jericho's heart ached worse than the physical battering he'd received in the fight. He was devastated by his loss. What had been the last link to his previous life and family now lay unmoving on the table in front of him. Silently he gathered up the limp form in his arms, gently carrying him toward Jean Matthew's house.

Jean had returned home right after the fight and now paced the kitchen floor, angrily awaiting Jericho's return.

He was like a wild man...attempting to strike me...and after all I've done for him, she fumed. *I've never seen him like that.*

Jean was sure that it'd just been the anger of someone hurting that ugly old dog of his that had made him react like that.

But that is no excuse! I simply will not tolerate any such conduct under my roof!

Of course, he hadn't known it was her when he'd reacted that way, still...She suddenly recalled the cold empty stare he'd shown her as she'd attempted to pull him off Sikes. Suddenly, she shivered uncontrollably. She'd seen death there.

Well, I do believe if I hadn't intervened when I did, Jericho would've likely killed that awful man, right then and there!

Granted, he'd ample reason to defend his property, but it was no excuse to behave badly toward her such as he had. She vowed to straighten him out as soon as he returned, and then everything would be just fine again.

Deep inside, she felt terrible, like something precious had suddenly been lost to her. She pushed away those feelings, put on water for a cup of tea, and sat down to await Jericho's return.

The sounds of digging outside abruptly brought Jean back to the present and she moved to the window facing the garden behind the house. Jericho was there, shoveling a hole in one corner of the garden. Nearby lay a bundle, wrapped in his old wool blanket. Tears sprung suddenly to her eyes, her previous anger now completely forgotten. With heavy heart she watched from the window as Jericho labored without looking up. His long hair hid his face, but she had the impression he was crying. It was one of the saddest sights she'd ever witnessed.

Jericho didn't rest until the job was finished, then he gently lifted the blanket-wrapped bundle and lowered it into the shallow hole, carefully covering it with dirt. He stood silently beside the mound when Jean approached behind him. As he finally looked up, she could see there'd been no tears; only an intense pain reflected deeply in his gray eyes. So intensely did it show that she could feel a sharp stab within her own soul.

"Seems like all I do lately is bury things I care about," he said quietly.

With that, he proceeded to clean the shovel and replace it in the tool shed. Jean met him halfway to the kitchen door, placed her arm around his shoulders and walked silently beside him back to the house.

* * *

For three days after the beating he'd taken from Alfred Sikes, Jericho had been too sore to get out of his bed. It'd taken two more days before he'd been able to hobble about. One night he'd awakened to find that Jean nearby. She'd startled him awake by placing a cold wet cloth on his forehead.

"You were moaning," she said, softly. "It's the fever that does it."

"I'm sorry. I'll try to be quiet."

She placed her fingers over his lips to silence him and touched her warm mouth to his forehead, her breath scorching his skin.

He stared at her as she gently wiped his face with the wet cloth. He had never seen her in her nightgown before. The fabric, some flimsy white stuff that floated as she moved, made her appear even more like an angel. He placed his hand over hers, holding it against his forehead, staring into the reflection of her pale face in the darkness. Neither spoke as she abruptly stood, hesitated for a moment as she stared down at him, then she let her white nightgown drop to the floor. Without a word, she quickly slipped beneath the covers next to him. As Jericho lay stiffly beside her, scared to even breath, her soft cool hands instantly brought life into his aching body, tenderly leading him into a secret world he'd only dared to imagine until now. It was an endless, wonder-filled and magical night, like nothing he'd ever experienced before. Near dawn, exhausted—he'd finally slept.

Six

AWAKENING WITH A START, he found the sun in his eyes and that Jean was no longer beside him. For a long time Jericho lay without moving, convincing himself it'd all been a dream. But no, there were just too many details so fresh in his mind – and he could still smell her scent on his pillow.

It really did happen. *Damn! Maybe we'll get married. She's only eight or nine years older than me, and men tend to marry women at least that much younger than themselves. What's the difference?*

He couldn't think of any, but figured there had to be at least one because he couldn't ever remember hearing before about a grown woman marrying a man as young as himself.

But it could happen, couldn't it?

Probably not. Damn!

Suddenly, he felt awful.

Confused by his recent beating and the wonderful night following it, Jericho dragged himself painfully from the bed and slowly dressed. He heard Jean Matthews placing wood in the cooking stove in the front of the house. She was humming. He felt his ears burning as he resolutely headed in that direction. As he entered the tidy kitchen, she greeted him with her wonderful, radiant smile – and his knees turned to mush, just as always.

"Good morning, Jericho! What in the world are you doing out of bed? I was just getting ready to bring you some breakfast."

Not waiting for his answer, she quickly went on. "However,

seeing that you're here now, if you can manage, pull up a chair and I'll put it on the table."

There was not the slightest hint of embarrassment in her voice – nothing to indicate anything had happened the previous night.

Fine, he thought resentfully. *Pretend like it never happened. That's just dandy!*

Stoically, he pushed a chair closer to the large wooden table and painfully lowered himself into it. The kitchen smells were reminiscent of a life far away left in the distant Tennessee Mountains. For a brief instant, heavy loneliness washed over him. Jean placed a large steaming platter of eggs, smoked ham; biscuits and gravy in front of him and the aroma immediately assaulted his senses. Everything else was soon forgotten.

"Sheriff Smith says those two awful men left town as soon as the big one was able to move," she told him.

"The big one…Sikes, I believe that's his name…was hurt real bad. The whole town is still abuzz about how you bested him, and after he'd beaten up a half-dozen others in town, too. All of them grown men."

Jericho didn't look up from his food.

"I don't suppose beating up another man should be something to be overly proud of," he retorted.

Jean paused and just sat staring at him. "Is something the matter, Jericho? You seem…angry."

"Everything's fine!"

He still didn't look up, shoveling in another mouthful of gravy laden biscuit so he wouldn't have to talk.

"Well, that's good! Wonderful," she said, displaying her wonderful smile. "Because today, I have big plans for us! I want to take you some place special!"

Jean refilled his coffee cup from the large iron pot, then set it back on the stove and took a chair directly across from him.

"Today, I'm going to take you to my favorite spot. We're going on a picnic!"

Her excitement was so infectious Jericho couldn't help but smile back.

"That's better," she said. "Now, finish your breakfast and leave me in peace so I can pack a lunch to take along."

Jean reached out her hand and laid it on his and Jericho felt his heart start to race again. "I'm so glad you're up and about again, Jericho. I truly am."

Her special place was ten miles outside of Waco in a small cottonwood grove on the Brazos River. The towering trees were just far enough apart to allow sufficient sun for the short grass to grow among them. Butterflies hovered amid the abundant wild flowers, while singing birds filled the treetops. Every few minutes, a large fish would break the water with a splash.

Jericho leaned back against a tree and watched with rapt attention as Jean spread a blanket on the ground and set out enough food for a family of five. Although it'd been barely four hours since breakfast, she watched as he devoured vast quantities of chicken, coleslaw and apple pie. Satisfied at last, he lay back as Jean loaded the leftovers into her basket. She sat still for a time, gazing at his closed eyes, finally speaking in a soft whisper.

"I came here often with my husband. It was our favorite place."

Surprised that she'd taken him to a place that had been special to her late husband, Jericho's eyes remained closed as he gathered his thoughts.

"What do you suppose he'd think about us?" he finally muttered.

She waited a long time before answering. Just when Jericho thought she wasn't going to respond, Jean said softly, "I think he'd understand."

Jericho still didn't open his eyes, choosing, and then rejecting the words he wanted to say.

She continued. "Jericho, we need to talk about last night."

Jericho finally opened his eyes and he raised himself up on his elbows, but he didn't speak, so Jean went on.

"I think the world of you, Jericho McCain. I don't know how I'd have managed for the past few months without your help. I believe you were hurting inside, too and we both needed someone."

"But…?" he said.

Jean looked blankly at Jericho's question.

"It just sounded like there's a 'but' in there somewhere," he explained.

Tears formed at the corner of her eyes and she took a deep breath. "Oh Jericho, we just can't go on like this. Don't you see? There's no future in it for you, and if folks found out about it… well, I'd have to leave here. There are names for women who take young boys to their beds and I don't want to hear those names from my friends."

She took a lace-trimmed handkerchief from her sleeve and softly blew her nose on it. "This is my home, darling. I don't want to have to leave it," she concluded.

Jericho sat upright and covered her hand with his own.

"Jean, I'm seventeen. That's a man out here…well, I'll be seventeen in a couple more months. You can only be a few years older than me. What's so wrong about it?" he implored.

"I'm thirty-one," she told him, smiling softly.

Her words stunned him. Jericho sat even more upright, staring. He'd have never guessed. Jean sniffed quietly beside him and after a few moments he pulled her gently into his arms. He kissed her eyes, then her lips. Jean sighed sweetly and muttered, "I'm so weak, darling. You have to help me do the right thing."

Then moaning softly, she wrapped her arms around his neck, hungrily pulling him down.

* * *

As the days quickly turned into weeks and the weeks into months, Jean Matthews and her young lover took great pains to ensure their secret was secure. During that time, thousands more ambitious men passed through the small town of Waco, each headed south in search of their individual ideas of fame, fortune or adventure. Many had left families, some were like Sikes while others were simply running away from something.

Handsome Jack Clay had left and returned twice in his search for capable ranger reinforcements, once asking young McCain if he'd be interested in joining Captain Hays's militia battalion. McCain had looked at him dumbfounded as though he'd surely lost his mind, and the young Ranger did not ask again, but patiently bided his time.

Although Jericho continued to share Jean Matthew's bed nightly since their picnic on the river, they were confident their secret had remained safe. That was until just two days previously, when Mrs. Winkler had dropped by unannounced on a Sunday afternoon, just as things were heating up in the widow's bedroom. At the insistent knock, Jean Matthews had quickly disengaged herself, hastily dressed and rushed to answer the door. Jericho quietly remained behind in the bedroom. After the suspicious old woman left, Jean had spiraled into a deep depression; certain her flushed face and disheveled appearance had given away their secret. Indeed, peering through the curtains of the bedroom, Jericho had seen Mrs. Winkler repeatedly glance over her shoulder toward the house as she hurriedly retreated into town. Jean had cried bitterly for more than an hour.

After retiring that evening, they'd talked well past midnight, weighing their options and delaying the decision they both knew was inevitable. Holding each other tightly, and crying, they'd finally agreed Jericho needed to get on about the business of finding his brother and that a separation would give them both time to decide what they should do about things. For the rest of the night they simply held each other, listening to their collective hearts beating, each dreading a bleak future without the other.

At dawn, tired and confused, Jericho McCain went about his morning chores, at last returning to the kitchen for breakfast. Stoically, he watched as Jean placed her typical large platter in front of him and his appetite took over. Jean laughed softly and placed her hand on his arm.

"If I live to be a hundred I'll never forget you, Jericho McCain. Or your appetite. I swear, you should be seven feet tall and weigh three hundred pounds for all you eat."

Jericho forced himself to pick up on the light mood, smiling back. "It's your cooking, Jean. I used to eat like a bird before I got a taste of your cooking."

Jean patted his arm. "I know that's not true, but thank you anyway, Darling."

Jericho wiped out his plate with a biscuit, and popped it into his mouth. He looked up and found her staring at him.

"Do you know what I'd like to do today?" she said suddenly.

When he looked at her blankly, she went on. "I'd like to go back to our place on the river one more time. Take a picnic lunch like before, and spend the entire day." Then more quietly. "So we can make love one last time before you go."

"If it were my last day on earth, I couldn't think of a way I'd rather spend it," he said softly. "I'll go hitch up the wagon."

As he got up to leave, he paused. "Think we could take along some of that apple pie you made?"

Jean laughed loudly and pushed him out of the kitchen.

* * *

While the warm summer sun beat down on their backs, the pace to their secret place was slow and leisurely. Neither felt much like talking, but they didn't need to. The intimateness of their thoughts and the anticipation of the afternoon to come was all they needed for the moment. Jean sat close so she could rest her hand on his arm as they shared the closeness of their silence. Within sight of the river, Jericho saw a familiar figure suddenly step into the road fifty feet ahead. Without warning, something immensely heavy struck the side of his head and catapulted him from the wagon onto the dusty road. He lay stunned, unable to move or see. Through loud ringing in his ears, he could hear some muffled screaming from far away. It came from someone he felt he should know. He knew he should get up and help whoever it was that kept screaming, but he was very tired. So very tired. Then a huge black void ended all conjecture.

John Henry Sommers and Rosa had attended church at the Waco parish every Sunday since it'd been built nearly five years before. That had been right after they'd left Missouri after the

"Old Master," Major Todd Sommers of the Sommers Hill Plantation, had given them their freedom papers and a hundred dollars in gold. As Major Sommers had lain on his death bed and signed the papers, he'd told relatives and staff it'd been for the old couple's "two score and nine years of devoted service" to Sommers Hill and its people. John Henry and his wife had departed hastily, before the old man died – before his stingy son could revoke their freedom papers.

They knew the Major's son, Otis, would presume they'd headed north toward "Yankee land" and immediately give pursuit following the old man's death. That was why they'd struck off toward the south instead, eventually ending up in Texas. Almost by accident, they'd discovered a small partial of land twenty-five miles north of Waco that had enough water to raise food for the two of them, with maybe enough food left over so they might sell it in town.

The Mexican goat farmer who'd owned the property, took their fifty dollars for it and made his Marks on a bill of sale, happy to be rid of the place. He even threw in four goats and a dozen chickens, thus making John Henry and Rosa "persons of property" in the soon to be State of Texas.

Their Sunday trips to Waco usually took just over five hours one way, including rest stops. Therefore, the old couple would rise before dawn to begin their journey, eat along the way, and return following the sermon and the church's basket-dinner. Most of the time it was well after dark when they returned. Cramped in the driver's box of their small wagon for such a long time always aggravated John Henry's "rheumatic" knee, but as he'd just remarked to Rosa, "It's the Lord's way of testing me."

So it'd been on this particular morning that John Henry and

Gone to Texas

Rosa arrived at the small grove of cottonwood trees on the river, which marked the halfway point of their journey, and noticed a wagon blocking the trail ahead. As they neared, they could make out someone laying beside it. John Henry pulled on the reins.

"Whoa!"

Tying the leather straps to the brake-handle, he glanced around apprehensively, telling Rosa, "You wait here. That feller looks hurt. I'll call if I need ya."

The old man picked up his canteen, carefully climbed down and went to the fallen man, kneeling down beside him.

Oh, lordy, lordy! There's blood everywhere!

Flies crawled on the man's face, sucking at the matted blood. John Henry shooed them away and leaned forward, placing his ear close to the man's nose.

Still alive!

Pouring water on his Sunday handkerchief, he dabbed at the bloody face until it was clean.

Why, he's not much more than a boy. Who in heaven's name would hurt a young, handsome lad like this?

He'd barely finished his thought when a low, painful moan emanated from the thick roadside bushes. Temporarily leaving the wounded man, he limped into the bushes and saw a naked white woman, partially covered with leaves and dirt. She was badly battered.

Freezing in place, he shouted over his shoulder, "Rosa! Come quick! Bring the blanket."

Then he removed his "Sunday coat" and spread it over the woman. It was the only coat he owned and he dearly hoped the Lord would appreciate all this kindness. First, his never-before-used Sunday handkerchief, then his like-new-second-hand Sunday coat.

Better not let Rosa catch you thinking like that John Henry, or she'll cut you on that sharp tongue of her's.

He heard her as she slowly made her way through the bushes behind him, then her sharp intake of breath as she sighted the naked white woman.

"Lordy, Lordy."

She quickly spread the blanket over the injured woman, handing John Henry's Sunday coat back to him. With her scarf and canteen, Rosa cleaned the woman as best she could, then the two of them struggled to load the injured couple onto the back of their wagon. After a last look around, the old man tied their horses and buggy behind his wagon, slowly heading toward Waco once again. As they passed by the small church two miles from town, they could hear singing voices from within. It was the first time in nearly five years they'd missed the sermon.

At first, all Jericho could hear had been faint noises around him. Then gradually, the noise turned into words. His sight slowly followed and at last he determined he was in a room with several people.

"Well, you decided to rejoin the ranks of the living, I see," said a deep familiar voice.

Slowly, and with less pain than he would've imagined, Jericho turned his head toward the voice. It was Doc Roach, the man who attempted to patch up Blue, in the failed effort to save his dog's life.

"Where am I?"

"Now, I wish to Jesus I would've bet someone you'd ask that question first. Of all the people I have ever brought back from the dead, ninety-nine out of a hundred will ask it."

Doc Roach removed a small flask from his pocket. "This is for medicinal purposes."

He took a deep appreciative swallow, but didn't ask Jericho if he wanted one. Pulling up a chair, he sat beside the bed where he took another deep pull from the flask, shook it regrettably and placed the nearly empty container of "medicine" into an inside pocket of his worsted jacket. He told Jericho how the old couple had brought him and the Widow Matthews into Waco; him shot in the head, and the missus all beat up.

Shot in the head? Jericho instantly reached up and discovered thick bandages surrounding his head. Doc Roach laughed and took the silver flask from his pocket once more, holding it lovingly against his chest.

"Well, not exactly shot through the head, but close. Damned close."

He continued to tell Jericho how the bullet had glanced off the top of his head and cracked the bone "some." Roach belly laughed again.

"That's probably the only reason you're still alive. You see there is so much blood with any head wound that whoever shot you probably thought you was dead for certain. An inch lower young man, and ya would've been, sure as hell. Just thank the Lord you got a thick head."

He laughed again, and took another swig from his bottle, emptying it. Both actions were beginning to irritate Jericho no small amount. At that moment, the door banged open and Sheriff Smith was suddenly peering down at him.

"Who shot ya boy?" he said so loudly that it hurt Jericho's head. "Who was it? I'll hang the sons a bitches from the first tree I find. Was it that Sikes fellow? Was it?"

Jericho blinked his eyes to clear them, trying hard to concentrate. "How is the Widow Matthews, Sheriff?" he croaked softly. "She all right?"

"Everybody clear out!" the Sheriff yelled, and Jericho grimaced again. After the others departed, Sheriff Smith stood over him again.

"The bastards violated that little woman, boy. It's bad enough to try and kill a man, but to rape and otherwise violate the innocent and pure? I catch 'em, I'll personally torture them into madness! Then I'll hang 'em!"

He leaned closer, squinting meanly.

"Who was it? Just give me a name."

Jericho closed his eyes and once more saw Sikes standing in the middle of the trail just before things went black. Then he opened his eyes.

"Couldn't rightly tell, Sheriff. I was out like a light. Maybe something will come to me after a while. What did Widow Matthews say?"

"She didn't! Claims she kept her eyes closed through it all, and I don't want to pressure her after what she's been through. I was hoping you'd remember something."

"If I do, you'll be the first to know, Sheriff."

Jericho left the doctor's office late that evening despite Doc Roach's protests, and went directly to Jean's house. She was sitting in near darkness, staring out her bedroom window. Jericho came up behind her and gently placed his hands on her shoulders. She shuddered slightly, then relaxed.

"I'm so sorry, Jean."

"It's not your fault, Jericho. It's not either of our faults. It's the fault of those two animals. They should be made to pay for what they've done."

She started sobbing bitterly, and Jericho walked around to kneel in front of her. He took her face in his hands and stared into her watery eyes. In a soft whisper, he said "They will, Jean. You have my word on that. They will pay dearly."

"Promise me?" she said softly.

"I promise. They'll pay."

Jean lay her head against his chest and Jericho gently wrapped his arms around her. After a while he carried her to the bed and lay her on it. Fully clothed, he lay down beside her and held her for the rest of the night while she slept fitfully. Twice she awoke screaming hysterically, and Jericho soothed her back to sleep. Lying beside her in the dark, he vowed to take bitter vengeance upon two men named Sikes and Deeks.

* * *

Three days later, Jean Matthews boarded a stage and departed for the east coast. She'd made arrangements for Mr. Abbott, the only banker in town, to sell her property and send the profits to a bank in Boston. Then, she said her goodbye to Jericho.

They sat and talked for hours on the day she was to leave, each trying and failing to let the other know the extent of their feelings. At last, Jericho walked her to the stage and stood in the dusty street as she waved from its window. The last thing Jean Matthews told him was, "I love you Jericho McCain. I'll never forget you. You'll always have a special place in my heart."

Then like everything else he'd ever loved, she was gone.

Jericho remained in the street, staring at the empty horizon until long after the coach's dust had blown away. Turning finally, he walked into the stage office where he sold the mare and the mule for a decent price. Then he crossed the street to the general store and went inside.

Mr. Winkler was busy stacking items on a shelf behind the counter. When he saw Jericho, he spoke in his heavy accent.

"Jericho McCain. It's good to see you up and about, Lad. You are very lucky to be alive." He smiled broadly. "Now, what can I do for you today?"

"I need a couple hand-guns, Mr. Winkler. Some of those new kinds, like the repeating Colts. Above all, I need something that's reliable and accurate, that shoots more than just once before reloading. Do you have anything like that?"

"As a matter of fact, I do. I just got two of those new Walker Colts in. The ones the Texas Rangers like so much. They don't come cheap, but they're the best handgun ever made, bar none."

Winkler reached down and unlocked a heavy wood cabinet and removed a leather box.

"Got five in yesterday on the stage. Been trying to get some for almost a year now, ever since they started making 'em. The Rangers grab 'em up soon as they come out, so I can't keep them in stock."

He flipped open the box and held them out for Jericho's inspection. If looks meant anything, these were certainly the finest guns he'd ever seen. He reached out and lifted one from the box, balancing it in his right hand, then switching to his left. Perfect. He rolled the cylinders, listening to the distinctive click of each as they rolled over the sear. Balance, grip, weight, all seemed perfect.

"I'll take 'em both," he said, "and fifty loads for 'em."

"Yes, sir!" Winkler jumped to retrieve the nipple and ball-like ammo.

"I want one of those new breech-loaders, too, with a hundred rounds for it." Jericho was still staring at the Colts.

He walked to a table displaying several heavy, hand-stitched leather holsters, and selected a left-handed holster and belt, then a right-handed holster and belt. On his way back to the front of the store, he picked up a small can of goose grease, a bedroll, coffee pot, skillet, several food items, and another canteen. He dumped it all on the counter in front of Winkler.

"Total it up."

Picking up one of the Walker Colts, the right-handed holster, a handful of caps and balls, and the can of goose grease, he headed for the door.

"I'll be back in a couple of hours to pick up the rest of it."

He left the store without looking back.

Five miles outside the town limits of Waco, Jericho sat under a tree and rubbed the thick goose grease into the leather holster until it was soft and pliable. Disassembling the pistol completely, he wiped each piece down with a soft oiled cloth, then carefully reassembled it and loaded it with the caps and balls. Satisfied, he hitched the belt around his slim waist and eased the Colt into it gently, letting the weight of the fine weapon find its own resting place.

"Never jam your pistol into its holster," he could hear his father saying. "Ease it in slowly. You don't want it hanging up if it's needed quickly."

Jericho walked toward a cactus plant with small flowers, until he was the desired distance away. Then in a smooth fluid-like motion, he drew and fired...and one of the flowers disappeared. He fired rapidly three times...and three more flowers disappeared.

"Never empty your gun before you reload," he heard his father say again as he slipped in a fresh load. Jericho walked farther away, spun as he drew effortlessly, firing in a single motion. The target disappeared.

With bent head, he reloaded the round he had just expended. It appeared he was totally involved in his task, but he'd been listening. As quiet as the rider had been in his approach, Jericho had heard him coming even before he spoke.

"Bravo. Excellent shooting Mr. McCain."

Without appearing to, Jericho watched Handsome Jack Clay ease his mount down the steep gully to his rear, then up the other side, where he dismounted.

"I'm not usually easy to impress, but you, young man are one hell of a pistol shot!"

"You followed me." Jericho's voice was chilly, like he didn't want company.

"No, no. I saw you ride out of town, and I headed out here to talk to you privately," Handsome Jack said. "I might know something you would like to know."

"Like what?"

"Like where to find them."

"Find who?"

"Look Mr. McCain, don't you play me for a fool and I won't waste your time," Handsome Jack said without malice. "Do we have a bargain?"

"Talk."

"Let's just start over. I know where Sikes and Deeks are now. Does that bit of information interest you?

"It might. But it sounds to me like you want something in return. I don't like deals with strangers. I always seem to come out on the short end of 'em. I am especially leery of deals made with anyone who goes by some catchy name, like 'Slick, 'Diamond,' Gentleman,' or for that matter, 'Handsome.' Besides, what makes you think I can't find these two on my own? That is, if I was actually looking for them?" Jericho was busy inspecting his new Colt.

"You might well be able to find them, but it might also take you some time to do it, too. Why don't you hear me out first, then if you're not interested, say so and I'll ride away. No hard feelings." Handsome Jack smiled engagingly. "What do ya have to lose?"

"Talk," Jericho said again.

"Captain Hays needs good fighting men for his Rangers. If he doesn't get 'em, there's a good chance the Mexicans will kick us out of Texas, and everything we've gained down here will be lost. I've watched you since coming here and you're about as good as any I've ever seen. You're tough, you talk straight, and shoot fast. I was watching you as I rode up today. You heard me way before I even got near. That's something you can't teach a person. There's another thing about you that I like, too. You just keep coming – you never give up."

Handsome Jack removed the makings from his shirt pocket, hooked one leg over his saddle horn and started to roll a cigarette. He stuck it between his lips, then hesitated.

"I'll give you Sikes and Deeks and won't interfere with it, no matter what the outcome. They kill you? End of deal. You kill them? Well, after it's over, you go with me to meet Captain Hays. You talk to him and if you decide not to join up after that, *adios*."

He struck a match on the leg of his pants and stuck it to the tip of his cigarette, taking a few puffs as he gave Jericho time to mull over his proposition. Then he continued.

"The Sheriff said you were looking for your brother. Over ninety percent of the men that come down here either end up in the army or somehow working for it; hunters, herders, ammo carriers, lots of other things. What better way to look for him than to go where he probably ended up? With the Rangers, you can move around freely. We don't operate like the regular army — don't have to have the same accountability as they do. We cover a lot of territory and see a lot of people, and we pretty much work on our own. In other words, we don't have to answer to the military brass."

Jericho pondered what he had just heard.

"Let's just say that I listen to what this Hays feller has to say and I don't like what I hear. What then?"

"Like I said. *Adios*. Plain and simple."

"I'll get my things."

Seven

HANDSOME JACK CLAY AND Jericho McCain rode south to Austin for supplies before turning southwest toward Uvalde. Austin seemed to be bursting at the seams with inductees and volunteers for Zachary Taylor's new army, even more than Waco had been. In all his young life, Jericho had never seen such a hodge-podge of dress, nor heard so many different manners of speech as he encountered during his short stay in Austin. He had a feeling this was history in the making and despite himself, was beginning to experience a surge of excitement. Additionally, what set Austin apart from Waco, was the extreme level of violence he witnessed, almost from the first moment he arrived in the town. That is not to say Waco was without its share of bloodletting, but by comparison Austin was a nightmare.

Jack watched his young companion as he twisted his head from side to side and stared in amazement at the many open conflicts taking place on the street. Everywhere, men seemed to be cussing one another, plummeting someone with their fists, or with anything else that proved handy.

"It's not nearly this bad in San Antonio, son," he assured Jericho. "Ya see up here, there ain't no proper authority and every man is a law unto himself. Once they arrive in San Antonio, the militia will insure they follow a strict set of rules and regulations."

Jericho watched as another fight broke out between a buffalo hunter and a man who looked like a farmer. The hunter gouged and bit, but the farmer was built like a bull and the outcome was never in doubt. In less than two minutes the buffalo hunter lay unconscious and bleeding in the muddy street, as the farmer repeatedly kicked and stomped his lifeless body.

"Most will oblige, some won't. Those that don't do as they're told will end up getting themselves hung, or else they'll run off and become outlaws. Eventually, we'll catch up with 'em and hang 'em anyway," Clay said, matter-of-factly.

Jericho watched two men drag the buffalo hunter's limp form away, and wondered if he was still alive. A shot rang out and distracted his attention, and when he looked back, the buffalo hunter and the two men assisting him, had disappeared. From his point of view, he could see that Austin wasn't much more than a couple dozen permanent structures, a few scattered adobe huts, several corrals and some large tents set up as eating and drinking establishments. The town seemed to be divided into an orderly functioning community on one side and a hastily constructed tent town inhabited by drunks and riff-raff, on the other. On a hill at the end of the main street they named Congress Avenue, stood an imposing two-story building. Jack saw him looking at it.

"That's President Mirabeau Lamar's house. The President of the Republic of Texas. The long building with the stockade, across from the president's house, is the capitol building."

Concentrating closer, Jericho could see a row of trees and vegetation separating the citizens of permanent Austin, from the rowdy activities going on within the limits of Austin's Tent City. A single strand of rope had been strung between the two communities, running irregularly and tied to the trees at intervals. On the permanent side, a squad of uniformed soldiers with rifles was dispersed along the rope, facing Tent City. In the exact center, the rope had been cut and tied to two posts forming a gate at which two more armed soldiers stood guard.

Clay saw him looking and explained. "I was through here a few months ago, just before Zach Taylor arrived, and this was a nice little town. It changed almost overnight. The new arrivals nearly destroyed the place in the first week. Then at President Lamar's order, the Army sent in some troops and they divided it up into what you see now."

Jack waved his hand in the general direction of the rope.

"Someone tries to cross the rope without going through the gate, those soldiers have orders to kill 'em on the spot. They killed five the first week they put the rope up. Now Tent City folks take 'em serious."

"What happens if you want to go through the gate?" Jericho said.

"Well it all depends on who you are, how you act, and what you want on the other side," Clay explained. "Those two on the gate have absolute authority to turn anyone back...or to shoot intruders – which ever one strikes their fancy."

"I think I'll just stay over here. There don't look like much going on over there anyway," Jericho conceded.

Clay grinned at him. "That's pretty much the way I see it, too."

The tents set up as eating and drinking establishments seemed to be doing the most business even though it was only ten o'clock in the morning. Jack was speaking to him again.

". . . hungry?"

"I reckon I could eat a bite," Jericho answered truthfully. "If I don't get shot or knifed first."

Handsome Jake laughed and Jericho wondered what he had said that was so funny.

As they left one of the tents an hour later, after putting away an enormous amount of food and strong black coffee, they heard a loud bellow come from one of the drinking tents nearby. Looking up, they observed a large hairy man dressed as a backwoodsman charge from the tent flap and stand in the street cussing, shaking his fist at someone still inside.

"Come on out, Jim, ya yeller dog. Yer gonna git what ya got com'n this time!"

The hairy man rapidly paced up and down the muddy street and continued to shout at an unseen adversary.

"That's Henry Strickland. He's well known around these parts for the bully and no-a-count that he is. He's also one tough hombre," Handsome Jack explained.

The front tent flap parted once again and another man that could well have been the twin of the first, stepped into the bright sunlight.

"Uh oh, Jim Forsyth. Looks like this is gonna be a bad one," stated Clay. "Jim's a pretty decent old boy, but he never backed down in his life."

Strickland had shed his rifle and now held a large, broadblade knife in his right hand.

"Bowie knifes?" Forsyth said, drawing his own from a scabbard at the back of his belt.

He slowly moved into the street as observers closed in to form a circle around the two men. Standing on the high plank walk, Clay and Jericho had a clear line of sight as the two backwoodsmen charged each other, swinging their knives as they met. Forsyth's blade struck Strickland's knife hand just above the knuckles, cleaned the flesh from four fingers clear to the bone, and lodged in one of his knuckles. Strickland's knife fell to the ground and he stood at the mercy of Forsyth who hacked at Strickland's arms, cleaving the flesh to the elbow on both arms. Strickland turned to run, but Jim Forsyth followed and with a single swipe, cut his shoulder blade in two. He stood watching as Henry Strickland, bleeding profusely, stumbled away.

"Henry should be in good condition to behave himself now and repent of his evil ways," Forsyth stated as he wiped his blade on the leg of his buckskin pants. "Better to let him live. I jist wanted to make a pious man out of a rogue, a sponger, a horse thief and a peace disturber."

Most of those present, aware of Strickland's past deeds and unsavory reputation, agreed he deserved what he got and that letting him live was a generous act on Forsyth's part.

"Jesus," breathed Jericho.

It was one thing to kill a man outright, but to hack him into little pieces seemed just a bit excessive to the young mountain boy.

"I don't suppose it occurred to anybody to try and stop that?"

"Out here a man pretty much settles his own troubles. After that, if he was wrong, we hang him," Handsome Jack confided.

"That's real civilized of you," Jericho said sourly.

They rode out of Austin in the early afternoon, having spent a total of four hours in the bloated outskirts of the town. That was enough time for Jericho to see he didn't much care for the place. More than enough. The two men rode steadily for several days, skirted west of San Antonio then inclined even more to the west. Ever since leaving Waco, Handsome Jack had been schooling young Jericho in the ways of the trail.

"Every time you come to a rise in the ground, you stop just before you reach the top. That's so you won't be skylined. Then you scan the entire area to your front to see if there is anything that's been disturbed…smoke from campfires…even dust, or buzzards flying. Only when you are satisfied that you can neither hear, nor see anything out of place, do you ride over the rise." Jack chuckled. "Then you'll probably still be in trouble."

He pointed out the edible plants, how to find water, determine how old the piles of animal droppings were, and to constantly identify likely avenues of escape as they rode along. Jericho figured Jack was only a few years his senior and marveled at the depth of knowledge the relatively young man had stored inside his head. He vowed to learn all he could from the young Ranger during the time they were together.

"We're going to a place called Uvalde," Jack told him. "It's a bad place."

"As bad as Austin?" Jericho said.

"Worse. Uvalde is as bad as any place I've ever seen – full of the criminal element, and some of those folks will know I'm a Ranger. I won't interfere while you take care of your business, except to make sure no one else butts in. Once it's over, stay close. We may have to shoot our way back out."

"Why are you doing this for me?" Jericho inquired. "I might just leave once it's over, and ride away."

Jack gazed at him for a minute.

"Yes, you could. But you gave your word and I believe you'll keep it. If you can't keep your word, the Texas Rangers don't want you no how. Besides, I'm just protecting my investment."

He favored Jericho with his brilliant grin, and spurred ahead.

After several more hours of dust and trail education for Jericho, Handsome Jack spoke again. "From here on in, we have to be especially watchful. This is Comanche country. Beyond that, we are just close enough to the border that we might run into a Mexican patrol. Either way, if we do we're gonna be badly outnumbered and out-gunned. Our only chance will be to run for it. If my horse goes down, don't stop. I won't stop for you."

He grinned at Jericho again.

"No reason for both of us cashing in, right?"

When he grinned, Jericho could readily see why folks called Clay, "Handsome Jack." He had the most infectious grin Jericho McCain had ever seen. In spite of himself, Jericho was beginning to find that he liked and admired the young Texas Ranger. He also realized that although Jack was far more confident and worldly than himself, the Ranger couldn't be more than four… five years older than himself. He had never seen Handsome Jack Clay so much as touch either of the two pistols he wore, but Jericho sensed when he talked about potential trouble that he was unafraid and confident in his ability to handle whatever came up.

"Just what makes you so keen on the Texas Rangers anyhow, Jack?" Jericho said. "I never even heard of 'em before I got to Texas. Now that's all I hear from people."

Clay seemed to dwell on that for a while.

"Well, to begin with, there ain't many of us. And to even get in, you have to be a special kind of man. Bigfoot Wallace likes to say that to be a Texas Ranger a man has to ride like a Mexican, track like a Comanche, shoot like a Kentuckian and fight like the devil."

"Who's Bigfoot Wallace?"

Handsome Jack laughed.

"Wallace is six-foot-six-inches, and two-hundred-sixty pounds of pure Southern Texas hell, J.D."

Lately, Jack had commenced to calling him, "J.D." instead of Jericho. Jericho didn't dislike it, but it sounded strange to him. No one but his father had ever called him J.D. before.

Jack spoke up again.

"You'll get a chance to meet him if you decide to hang around for a while. Samuel Walker, too – the man who that Colt you're wearing is named for. Mordecai Jones, Ben McColloch, and Captain John Coffee Hays, too. Captain Hays is our commander and a finer man you'll never meet."

Jack talked for the next hour about the Rangers, people he knew in the organization and their many exploits. Despite himself, Jack Clay's contagious enthusiasm concerning the Texas Rangers began to grow on Jericho and he found himself asking frequent questions to obtain more information.

"Captain Hays developed a new kind of mounted warfare and employed it against the Mex. He sent Sam Walker back east to meet with Samuel Colt about building a new fangled handgun especially for the Texas Rangers. He figured that since there were so few of us and so damned many Comanche and Mexicans every time we had to fight, that we could even up the odds by just out-shooting them. The results are those Colts you're wearing. Durable, easy to load and you can hit a rat in the hind-side at fifty yards."

Time passed quickly for them as mile after mile, Handsome Jack Clay spun stories of the men in the unit Jericho McCain had promised to meet with after he had completed his promise to Jean. Topping one rise, Jack suddenly pulled up and pointed at a small group of shacks and wood facade buildings in the distance.

"Uvalde."

As they neared, Jericho could see that Uvalde was just as Jack

Gone to Texas

Clay had described it; a filthy pest-hole. He was surprised to find that even in this dry country it had apparently rained a vast amount recently, and the dark slushy mud reached nearly to his stirrups in some areas of the main street. Some hard faced women leaned out of windows or shouted from doorways, telling them they had only to enter to find the answer to all their prayers. Even harder edged men leaned against buildings and coldly stared at them as they rode past. A few slept in the deep mud between the buildings. A real pest-hole.

"If those two are here they're most likely in the saloon. They can't have too many friends, even in a place like this," Jack told him. "I suggest you find a place you like and I'll go inside and see if they're here. If they are, I'll try to get them outside. Then it'll be in God's hands."

Not having a better plan, in fact, having no plan at all, Jericho agreed.

"I have to warn you though, if they manage to do you in, I mean to kill them myself." Jack tossed the words over his shoulder as he rode off.

* * *

Bigfoot Wallace stared out over the huge dry stretch before him, watching for the return of his two scouts. They'd been gone since early morning and by now, had plenty of time to have completed their mission and get back. He had a foreboding feeling in the pit of his stomach that he didn't like. Sensing, more than hearing anything, he felt Mordecai Jones ease into position beside him.

"What think?" Jones said, in his abbreviated style of speaking.

Jones had recommended to Wallace earlier that he be allowed

to go along with the two younger men, although he conceded they were worthy scouts and could probably handle the job just fine without him. Still, you could count on every time something went haywire, especially if Mordecai had suggested another way to do it, that he would jaw about it for the next week. Bigfoot Wallace braced himself for Jones's subtle comments to begin.

"Well, they're both damn fine scouts and probably won't have any trouble..." Mordecai waited for a long time, as though he wouldn't continue, then did. "...but sometimes a more experienced man can see things these youngsters can't."

Bigfoot didn't answer, staring sourly at the horizon.

"Still, they're probably all right. Trained 'em myself, ya know?"

Bigfoot grunted and tried to ignore the old man. Mordecai Jones had scouted for the army in every Indian campaign and war for the past forty years. He'd been around long enough that he didn't care if he stepped on someone's toes, or made the army brass mad at him. He knew they had little choice except to put up with his contrariness, because they simply couldn't get along without him. Which was precisely the reason Bigfoot hadn't sent the chief scout on this particular mission. He'd figured it was "iffy" at the least, preferring to risk other less experienced men instead of his best scout. Now, he suddenly wished he'd sent the cranky old man so he wouldn't have to now listen to his jawing – or put up with his drinking either, for that matter.

Bigfoot heard the old man spit loudly again, like he always did when he wanted you to know that he was waiting patiently for an answer to his last remarks. Bigfoot continued his best effort to ignore the old scout, hoping he'd eventually get bored and just leave. He conceded that Mordecai Jones as the best tracker and scout in the military, even when he was drinking, but it was his sharp tongue that Bigfoot didn't care for. That and all those cracker-barrel wisdoms he was always coming up with at the drop of a hat. Like that one last night, when Bigfoot had attempted to quietly chastise the old coot for taking a nip from his rawhide bladder in front of the younger men. He'd simply shot back one of his sharp retorts, then taken another long drink.

"Sometimes, too much drink, ain't enough!"

Now just what in hell is that supposed to mean?

Apparently tired of waiting for Bigfoot's response to his last comment, Mordecai Jones parted his long beard with two fingers and let fly with a glob of brown juice that splattered against a nearby rock.

"Yup. It called for a genuine military decision to be made right on the spot, and aye God, you can sure make 'em, Bigfoot. Yes sir'ee. Course, I like to be just a tad more select in my decision making, having found out that being indecisive is the key to being selective."

There! That was what he meant! Another one of those half-wit comments that made not a lick of sense. Up came the two fingers again to part his facial hair, and the rock was splattered once again.

"Ya want me to go fetch 'em back, Bigfoot?"

"If I wanted you to go fetch them back, I'd have told you to go fetch 'em back, Mordecai. Quit spitting that stuff around me, too. It draws flies."

Mordecai stared at him in disbelief, shook his head and silently withdrew to join the seven men squatted near the horses, a short distance away.

Where the hell are you boys, anyway?

Dread quickly replaced the uneasiness he'd felt earlier, as he thought about the two young Rangers he'd sent out alone. Foley, the youngest, was barley nineteen, and Farmer was a veteran of just a year. Both were competent and could shoot your ears off at a hundred paces; and both could ride like the wind, which was another reason he'd sent them.

Giving up, Bigfoot Wallace sighed and turned to withdraw when a movement suddenly caught his eye. Settling back into his position, he placed the telescope lens against his right eye and watched intently for another five minutes.

Something. There!

He whistled sharply and Mordecai was instantly at his side, all business. He waited as the old man scanned the dry area to their front, respecting the old eyes even over his own, and the long glass he held in his hands.

"It's Foley alright and he's hurt. If you want my advice, don't charge down there like the Huns. Instead, I say we slip down there like someone might be wanting us to come get him."

Bigfoot nodded his agreement to an empty space, because Mordecai Jones was already gone. Five minutes later, he saw the old man several hundred yards to his front. He raised his hand and waved from side to side, which was a signal that meant all clear. With foreboding, Bigfoot led his men down the sandy slope toward the area he had last seen Foley.

* * *

Jericho watched as Handsome Jack Clay trudged through the deep mud of the main street, toward him. When he was close enough, Jack finally spoke.

Gone to Texas

"Your two boys pulled out last night. Headed into Mexico, if you believe the local pack of vermin. Seems they figured there'd be plenty of upset people around that don't care much for the way they treated that lady in Waco, and who'd have strung 'em up if they surfaced anywhere in free Texas again."

Jericho pondered that for a moment.

"Where in Mexico?"

Jack stared back at him in disbelief.

"Surely you can't be thinking about going across the Rio looking for 'em! Why boy, there are already about ten thousand Mexican regulars setting over there and twice that many more on the way. That don't include all the murdering Comanche and Kiowa between here and there either. You wouldn't make it ten miles inside Mexico."

"They hurt somebody I care a great deal about, Jack. I intend to make 'em pay for that. I promised I'd do that, and I keep my word. Where in Mexico?"

Jack appeared as though he intended to protest some more, then staring intently at the youngster, replied, "Just across the border. A place called Piedras Negras. Easy to get into, hard to get out of."

"I'll get out. After I do what needs doing."

"Peidras Negras has a camp of about a hundred Irishmen who have broken ranks and joined the Mexican Army to fight against us Texans. The greasers call 'em *Gringos*."

Jericho looked up surprised.

"Why do they call them that? Is that Mexican for something?"

"Nope. Wasn't even a word until just recently. The Irish tend to sit around the fires at night and drink. And when the Irish drink, they sing. One of their favorite songs is one about how green grows the lilacs. From 'green grows', it seems the Mex's came up with '*Gringos.*' Close enough, huh?"

"*Gringos.* Guess that's me. I'm Irish."

"You don't particularly sound Irish."

Jericho looked serious.

"I can. My father was directly from the old country. I can mimic him if I have to. That's the way I intend to get in…and out, of that camp of *Gringos.*"

"You got sand, J.D. What do ya say about doing me a big favor first? Then maybe I'll ride along with you for a spell."

"What kind of favor?"

Jericho was curious as why the ranger would want to go with him.

"When I was inside looking for your men, I spotted a few bad ones that deserted from the Army and killed three men while they were stealing the payroll. They're to be hung by the Rangers when they're caught. I intend to wait here until they come out and take them into custody."

"How many are 'a few'?"

"Six…though one of them is drunk."

Handsome Jack smiled slightly as he said it.

"Well, that's just fine! Not six, only five sober ones to fill you full of holes."

Jericho wanted more than anything to get on the big roan and head south on his business, but he knew he couldn't leave the young ranger alone to get killed.

"What do you figure to do with them once you have 'em in custody?"

"Those that aren't killed in the shoot-out, I'll hang. Then, I'll ride south with you and help you find the two low-lifes you're chasing."

He spoke matter-of-factly, with no trace of malice or fear.

Just another bit of Ranger business to settle, Jericho thought irritably.

In spite of believing the Ranger to be completely out of his mind, he was beginning to admire Handsome Jack as none since his father. He sighed deeply as though he would regret his decision later.

"All right. What do you want me to do?"

Jack smiled his thanks.

"Take your rifle and position yourself up the street where you can cover me from any of the other's interference. If someone tries to take me out, shoot 'em fast."

Jericho stared at him, confused.

"That's it? You don't want me to side with you? Help you out?"

"Nope. This is Ranger business and you're a civilian. If they do me, you hit the leather and ride toward San Antonio for a spell until these guys forget about you. Tell Captain Hays what happened. That's it."

Jericho watched as the Ranger checked both Colts before easing them back into the leather.

"I think they saw me when I went inside so they won't wait long. Grab your rifle and find a high spot."

"What about you?"

"I intend to go right at them. Not many men are brave enough to stand in the face of two Colts, and still return accurate fire. If they do? Then they win. I think they'll falter."

He flashed his broad grin and walked toward the saloon, leaving Jericho with the awful feeling this handsome young ranger was surely going to meet his death.

Deciding to leave the less familiar breach-loading rifle behind, he slung the long muzzle-loader around his shoulder with the leather strap and slipped the extra Colt into his waistband. Soundlessly, he ran to an outside stairway, rushed up it, climbed onto the railing and hoisted himself onto the roof of the building. Darting across the roof until he could see the street plainly beneath him, he knelt and watched Jack slowly stride down the middle of the street. Movement caught his eye and he swung his head to observe a group of men exiting the saloon.

While he'd never seen them before, somehow he just knew these were the men Jack had told him about. Jericho forced himself not to look at them, instead focusing on the apparently empty alleyways and building top ridges, as Jack had instructed.

"Texas Red! I'm Jack Clay, Texas Ranger. I've come to take you back to San Antonio to stand trial and hang for the murder of the army payroll agent there."

At the sound of his voice, the group halted and stood without movement.

"That's pretty big talk for one skinny Ranger."

It came from the big man in the middle of the group, his hat pushed back to display the bright red hair that had given him his outlaw name, his chin strap hanging loose. Texas Red didn't appear too apprehensive with his thumbs hooked in his gun belt, relaxed and confident. An unlit cigarette dangled from his bottom lip.

The ranger's strong voice never wavered.

"Either drop your gun belt and surrender…or pull your iron, Red. Makes little difference to me. The rest of you? You don't have to die today. I'm only interested in Texas Red and the one calling himself 'Rio Phillips.' That has to be the runt with the black teeth."

Gone to Texas

Still no one moved, and in an instant it was too late. Seamlessly, Handsome Jack held both guns, running straight at the group of men, firing as he ran. Two of the men dropped at once as the others drew and dodged for cover. Jack never wavered, charging straight into the jaws of death; mud and dirt kicked up around him, gun smoke clouding the air.

He was courage itself, as he dropped his empty right-hand pistol into his holster and flipped the other from his left hand, easily catching it with his right, never missing a beat. Another of the outlaws was on the ground while two broke for the horses tied at a nearby hitching post. Texas Red was out of ammo, staring into the muzzle hole of Jack's pistol.

"Yore out of bullets too, *hombre*." Red said as he reached to the back of his belt for a round.

Jack smiled slightly and cocked his pistol, aiming it at the outlaw's shaggy head. Texas Red hesitated, then slowly lowered his pistol until it pointed at the ground beside him. Finally, he just dropped it on the boardwalk near his feet. A clambering of hoofs came around the corner as the two men who'd mounted and fled the scene, came charging back toward Jack, firing from horseback. Without thinking, Jericho shot the lead man through the head. As the second attempted to twist his mount's head around to flee, he took Jericho's next shot, this one from the Walker Colt, through the left thigh. It knocked him out of the saddle, sprawling in the soupy mush of the main street.

When Jericho arrived at Jack's location, the Ranger had just finished tying Texas Red's hands behind his back. Pushing the outlaw to the ground, he went to retrieve the wounded man from the muddy street, binding him in the same manner. The others hadn't moved and Jericho suspected they were dead.

Gone was the swagger, the dangerous cockiness of outlaw, Texas Red. It'd been replaced by only a frightened mud-covered young man who'd been caught at his mischief. With the two outlaws bound, side-by-side on the boardwalk, Jack finally addressed his young companion.

"Jericho, if you'd be so kind to round up two horses, we'll hang these two and be off to Mexico."

Red bellowed in rage, cussing Jake and all his ancestors. Jericho paused.

"You said you were going to take me back for trial," the outlaw bellowed again.

Jack calmly went about his business. "That was before you made me fight it out with you. That changed things a mite. Now, I'm gonna hang you."

Which he did, not more than thirty minutes later. Next to him, Clay hung the outlaw Jericho had wounded, explaining to his bewildered companion, "He's probably wanted someplace."

Later, riding beside the good-natured Ranger, listening to his stories about the people he knew, Jericho McCain was still amazed this polite young man had just killed five men.

* * *

Bigfoot Wallace stood over the fresh mound of dirt with Mordecai Jones beside him, and listened to young "Rosie" Poe as he stumbled through a modified rendition of the Lord's Prayer. He grimaced at one of Poe's butchered phrases, vowing that when he returned to San Antonio, he'd decree that all new enlistees memorize the Lord's Prayer as a requirement to get into the rangers. There just was no way of knowing how many times he had been in the kind of situation that required burying

Gone to Texas

someone and he'd had to listen to a patchwork version such as this. Although this one might just be the worst yet. In any event, this was not the proper way to put a poor fellow soldier into his grave. It just wasn't right! Mordecai seemed to feel the same way. He spit contemptuously and walked off before it was even finished.

Ranger Foley, just three weeks short of his twentieth birthday, lay at the bottom of the dusty hole, having died from eleven separate gunshot wounds and knife stabs. As he was dying, Foley told them he and his partner had gotten into the enemy's camp, the 126th Dragoon Regiment of the regular Mexican Army. They'd gone in several times after dark and drew detailed maps, which he carried back in his shirt pocket. It had been as they were headed back to join the others that they'd stumbled onto a small mounted patrol of Mexican cavalry, who gave chase. That would have been all right because there had never been a Mexican yet that could catch a Texan on horseback, but they had ridden smack dab into a large band of Kiowa that subsequently butchered the Mexican patrol, killed Joey Farmer and wounded him unto death.

The maps Foley brought back were remarkable! Every detail clear and as defined as a picture. Bigfoot couldn't wait to get back and present them to General Taylor and his staff. Old Rough 'n Ready would probably promote him on the spot, or least give him a medal. Bigfoot Wallace was one of the best-known and most feared men in Texas, and one of the most competent among all the Texas Rangers. Although, like most famous men, he had an ego about the size of the state of Texas. He simply liked notoriety and was known to often 'blow his own horn' about his claimed achievements. This time he wouldn't have to. The maps would do that for him. Enemy intelligence had been scarce lately and Old Zach might even make him a Major for this one.

He suddenly looked up and caught old Mordecai eyeing him as though he knew exactly what Wallace was thinking.

Damn you, old man, he thought. *You've been a thorn in my side for fifteen years and if I didn't need you so much, I swear I'd slip up behind you and slit your grizzled old throat.*

Aware of Mordecai's reputation though, that might be pretty hard, if not damned near impossible to accomplish. Determined to make an attempt at a truce, Bigfoot strode to where Mordecai squatted, Indian fashion, and knelt beside him.

"Foley and Farmer were good men," he started. "Good Texas Rangers."

Mordecai said nothing, so he went on.

"I knew if they could get in close enough, we'd get the truth."

Mordecai Jones finally snorted at that. "I've seen the truth and it makes no sense."

More cracker-barrel lore, thought Wallace, attempting to hide his disgust. He made several more attempts to get Jones to talk, but after a while, moved on to manipulate some of the other men. He wanted the others on his side when they returned to Fort San Antonio.

Mordecai stared at the big man's retreating back, dislike clearly written on his dark craggy features. He'd been around a long time and he hadn't found one single shred of evidence to support the notion that life was serious. At least, that was the best way of him looking at it, because it damn sure wasn't permanent. He had seen Bigfoot Wallace kill men just for the way they cocked their hat, and knew him to be a very cold and dangerous man. Jones also knew him to be ambitious, the combination, equally dangerous. It hadn't made one iota of sense for him to send those two young men out alone to get the "truth" he so desperately wanted. The truth, as far as Jones was concerned, was that Bigfoot Wallace just wanted to be the top dog and he'd do whatever was necessary to achieve that end. Even if it meant sending some of his own young men to their deaths.

Yet, he'd seen Bigfoot Wallace commit unbelievable acts of heroism during the time he had known him. He'd seen him face the deadly fire of a dozen outlaws and renegades, unflinchingly returning their fire, and although wounded numerous times, he always came out the victor. He was, for all intents and purposes, a legend in the southwest United States – especially in Texas. Mordecai also aware Wallace viewed the lives of the men who worked for him, in the same expendable manner in which he viewed his own life. Maybe, even more so. And that bothered Mordecai Jones. A lot. He watched as the other men in Wallace's small patrol flocked to be around him, basking in his attention.

Bigfoot Wallace was a giant of a man, even by Texas standards. The heavy caliber rifle he sometimes carried, seemed to be little more than a toy in his enormous hands. He always carried a large Bowie knife in the beaded scabbard at his left side, and those who knew him said he'd used it on more than one occasion to end another man's life. With his formidable size and boundless energy, he left the impression that even if shot, he'd continue to come after you until he'd ended your existence. Nothing could possibly stop a man like him. Herein, that helped give birth to the legendary Bigfoot Wallace.

To Mordecai, Captain John "Jack" Coffee Hays was twice the man as this big idiot who now led them. He'd known and worked for Captain Hays, off-and-on for the past ten years, and found him to be brave, honorable, and a dependable leader. Mordecai worshiped the man and would follow him to the gates of Hell. All he had to do was ask. Captain Hays never took anybody out to fight unless he did everything in his power to bring them back alive; and he never left a wounded man or a body behind. He had watched the Captain build the Rangers into the best fighting force in the world, outfitting them with the finest horses available and the new breach-loading rifles. He'd even sent Samuel Walker back east to see Samuel Colt, and together, they had developed the rapid-fire Walker Colt revolver. Every Ranger now carried at least three of the new handguns. With that piece of equipment, Hays had redefined horseback warfare, and although Zachary Taylor despised the individualistic manner in which the Rangers operated, the old general knew he couldn't win the war without them.

The others were now saddling up and Mordecai, grimacing at their noise, climbed painfully to his feet, careful not to let the others see his discomfort. Old age was going to kill him yet.

Eight

THEY WERE AT THE border in two days. It took another day to find a way through the Mexican pickets and cross a small river that Handsome Jack called the "Bravo." After all he'd heard about it before coming to this retched place, Jericho was unimpressed with the muddy little stream most Texans referred to as the Rio Grande. As soon as they stepped from the water on the far side, Jack leaned closer to whisper, "You are now in Mexico, partner."

Jericho felt a chill carouse through him at the words. He was a long ways from his home in Tennessee, and for the first time, felt like a pilgrim for sure. Tying handkerchiefs around the noses of their mounts and burlap sacks on their feet to keep them quiet, they walked along with their animals for several hours. At last, Jack mounted and declared it safe to ride on. Still, they moved slowly, observing the surrounding countryside carefully as they made their way deeper into the rough landscape before them. Worried, Jericho constantly searched the desolate landscape, wondering if anything were to happen to his knowledgeable companion, would he ever find his way back out again?

During a cold camp that night, Jack told him they would likely be near Piedras Negras by noon the following day. He said the best way to enter the enemy camp was boldly. Just ride right in and declare that they wanted to join the Gringos. The other alternative had been to sneak in, but that would present a problem of finding the men he was looking for. Jericho decided riding straight in was his choice as well, and Jack agreed that was the best solution. Throughout the next day they made no effort to hide, riding out in the open, aware that many eyes were on them, with the strong possibility of receiving a rifle bullet between the shoulders. Just as Jack had reported, they spotted the camp around noon and slowly made their way toward it. A well-armed guard stopped them before they could get near.

"Halt! State your business!"

"McCain and Laughlin looking for the Green Grows," Handsome Jack shouted back. "We've come to join up!"

They waited for what seemed like a long time, then a different voice yelled back. "Come on in. Slowly, and keep your hands where I can see them if you don't mind, laddie."

As they got closer they could observe an older man with flowing silver hair and mutton-chop side-burns, leaning against a knobby wooden stick. They could tell by the manner in which those around deferred to him, that this was their leader.

"Who be McCain and who be Laughlin?" the man said with a heavy Irish accent.

Since they were likely to have heard of Jack Clay, Texas Ranger, Jack introduced himself as Jack Laughlin, and Jericho McCain by his real name.

"What part of Ireland you lads be from?" the old man said.

Handsome Jack told him the truth, giving him the actual places their families had come originally hailed from. "I was born in New York. My family left Ireland years ago, but this lad is direct from the old country," he said pointing at Jericho.

The old man introduced himself as Shamus O'Malley, leader of the "Green Grows." He was anxious to hear from McCain about his travels from Ireland. They were taken into camp and although temporarily relieved of their guns, did not feel as though they were prisoners. Later that evening, as he and Jack Clay were laying on blankets side by side, Jericho whispered, "These folks seem like decent people. I hate to deceive them."

Jack agreed, but pointed out that war was often uncertain, and not necessarily were all the good guys on one side, and all the bad guys on the other.

"You have to keep reminding yourself that you are fighting for a cause, not against certain people."

Jericho fell asleep still uneasy about their mission. It was during breakfast the following morning that he saw one of the men he was chasing. He recognized the weasel-eyed little man he knew as Deeks, as he snatched an extra biscuit from the rack when passing through the chow line. At that instant their eyes locked, then he was gone. Jericho searched for more than an hour for the two men, but with all the others in camp it was unlikely he would find either of them – especially now they knew he was here. He told Handsome Jack what he had discovered, and Jack laid out a plan. Since neither men really knew him, Jack would traverse the camp and seek them out. Once they were discovered, another plan would be hatched to get at them.

Talk was abundant about the "Green Grows" leaving and heading north toward Nuevo Laredo to join up with Santa Anna and take San Antonio back from the Americanos. After days of laying around with nothing to do, suddenly there was a noticeable stir of excitement as men scrambled, seeking friends and misplaced equipment. No resemblance of order or military discipline was evident.

"These fools will be slaughtered like cattle if they go up against Zach Taylor and the Rangers at Fort San Antonio," Jack said in a low voice. "The Mexican officers will place the Irish right up front as cannon fodder, and they won't last two minutes once the Texans unlimber some of them new breach-loading rifles."

Jericho had to agree. It all seemed such a waste. Men killing men over a vast hellhole of wasteland that no one could live in, let alone raise food on. He had found Hell, and it was called Texas. All he wanted to do was settle up with the men that had done terrible things to Jean, find his brother and start over someplace else. Maybe they'd head for California or the Colorados. He had heard a lot of good things about the west. The Devil take it, here he was right in the middle of an all-out war, between Americans, too. If it didn't just beat all. Probably get his skinny backside shot off before this was over, if he wasn't careful.

Deep in thought, he didn't hear Shamus O'Malley's approach. Without ceremony, O'Malley handed back their firearms.

"We'll be moving soon lads, and you'll be needing these. Fine pieces they are, too."

"Where are we going, sir?"

Jericho received a hard stare from the old man.

"Now, ye can't be a'asking all those questions, lad. Aye, just saddle up and follow along. Soon, someone will tell you what to do."

O'Malley turned and walked away, his crocked, knotted stick over his shoulder like a rifle.

That poor old fool will likely end up dead, Jericho thought. Him, and all these other happy fools. They'd probably be singing some senseless Irish jig as they went down, too. The thought left Jericho saddened for the rest of the morning.

After the first day of marching, all singing had mostly ceased and stragglers could be seen for a mile behind. Each time, word

Gone to Texas

would be sent up and the main column halted to allow them to catch up. It was the most pitiful army Jericho could ever imagine being fielded. "Lambs to the slaughter," kept running through his mind.

What a damned waste!

Suddenly, Handsome Jack was at his side.

"I just spied Sikes and Deeks cutting out toward the north. They left the column about a mile back. Drop to the rear slowly until we start to mix with the stragglers, then follow my lead."

Handsome Jack gently pulled on his reins forcing his mount to slow, then dismounted and started picking at it's front hoof as though he'd found a rock to be dislodged. Jericho dismounted and appeared to be helping him by holding the horse steady. Frequently, groups of armed men, some appearing more military than the rest, stopped and spoke with them briefly, moving on only after they were assured the two would catch up. At last, there were only a few stragglers left and Handsome Jack mounted.

"Ready?"

Jericho nodded. Handsome Jack kicked his horse in the side and Jericho raced behind him for the nearby rocks. Not a shot was fired, as no one appeared to notice their retreat. After fifteen minutes at a fast pace, Handsome Jack slowed his mount to a walk and Jericho pulled up beside him, glancing back the way they'd just come.

"I feel sorry for all them fellers back there," Jericho said, looking back. "They seemed like decent folks and they probably won't even be mentioned in the history books. Still, they believe in what they're doing as much as we believe in what we're doing."

"The difference is, we're right…and they're wrong."

Jericho was unconvinced.

"Maybe. But how can we be so sure?"

They found the tracks of Deeks and Sikes early the following morning.

* * *

Taylor McCain checked his equipment for a third time as he watched the American cavalry prepare to charge a long line of men wearing the colorful uniforms of the Mexican infantry. They were standing, unmoving, across the flat area to his front. The line of enemy troops was too far away for him to see any of their features, but Taylor was certain about the unspoken fear in their eyes and faces all along the broken line to his left and right. Only the mounted bunch of men on the right flank of the regular army cavalry, seemed immune to any thoughts of fear. In fact, he could hear shouts…no, that wasn't quite the right word,…more like screams, from the motley crew in mixed clothing of buckskins and broad-brimmed hats. The only thing they seemed to have in common was the three or four pistols each carried, and big knives stuck into their belts. That, and the fact they were all mounted on some of the finest horseflesh Taylor had ever seen in one place.

Listening to their screams, Taylor felt a chill shoot through him. He mused if it had that effect on him, what would the Mexicans feel when they heard it? Everyone in the regular army called this new bunch, "Rangers." Taylor had no idea why. He knew the regular army officers under old Zach sneered with disdain whenever they mentioned them, but he had never heard a disparaging word about the group's fighting abilities. Mexican regulars called that rough bunch a term that when translated, meant the Texas Devils. Having never observed them until just this instant, he had not known why. Now, it was becoming clear. They were, without a doubt, the wildest group of soldiers Taylor had ever seen. Not that he'd seen that many, but he had immediately joined up with Zachary Taylor upon his arrival from Tennessee and been in several battles already.

Though Taylor McCain could probably out-ride any of the regular cavalry, he did not own a fit horse when he'd arrived, so he had been assigned directly into the infantry. He didn't mind that right now. He tried to imagine being in either of the two groups about to charge their horses into that long line of enemy rifles across the bare valley.

Another cannon ball landed in the ranks of the Mexican soldiers; several flew through the air while others simply slumped to the ground. The Mexicans retaliated with a barrage of their own, mostly falling to the rear of the Americans, but one landing on the right flank of the infantry. Taylor could hear men screaming and others shouting for medical personnel. *Fat chance*, he thought, recalling hearing that the Texas Army had only two doctors for all the forces. The bright side of it—a shortage of ammo kept both sides from an unbridled exchange of artillery fire.

Watching the bugle-boy touch the brass horn to his lips, the Rangers gripped their mount's reins in their teeth then pulled a pistol with each hand, as though anxious to have the business over with. At the first blast of the bugle, a collective yell arose from the Ranger's position, starting low then building to an awful crescendo. Then spurs were put to mounts, and as one, they charged down the hill straight toward the Mexican lines. The American regulars followed behind at a somewhat slower, and quieter pace. By the time they'd reached halfway across the flat area between the forces, the Rangers were substantially ahead of the cavalry, and scattered puffs of smoke began to drift skyward from the colorful line of men. As they drew closer, more and more of the Mexican troops hurriedly fired and rushed to reload.

To the observers, their firing seemed to be sporadic. After excitedly jerking their triggers, they'd place the stocks of their weapons on the rocky ground, then frantically ram another ball into the long barrel before slamming the rifle back to their shoulders to fire again. Only about half a dozen of the Ranger's horses went down before they reached the colorful line of Mexican infantry. What followed next could only be described as a slaughter. The Rangers calmly emptied their colts into the disordered ranks, then replaced their emptied pistols into the holsters. Pulling two more loaded ones from their waistbands, they started over. For every Texan that fell, a dozen of the Mexican infantry died. Clearly a hundred Mexican soldiers lay on the ground as the Rangers wheeled and weaved their way through the faltering lines, until at last, the lines sagged, then broke altogether. When the American's regular cavalry finally arrived to complete the slaughter, the enemy infantry was in full flight, many throwing their rifles down, raising hands over their heads.

Taylor detected sudden movement on the hills to the rear of the fleeing Mexicans, as fresh reserves surged down the hill toward the Rangers and regular cavalry, enraged and firing their rifles. Taylor estimated the mass to be close to a thousand, with even more breaking the crest on an adjoining hill. General Taylor's regulars put spurs to their horses and rushed directly back toward Taylor's position, whereas the several hundred

Rangers would continue to race away, then wheel and then charge the Mexicans, then wheel and rush away again. They repeated the maneuver until fresh Mexican troops occupied the original position their infantry had just abandoned. Tremendously out-numbered now, the Rangers returned to their original positions in the American lines. As they closed with the friendly ranks, dusty and reloading their many pistols, Taylor could hear laughing and shouting friendly insults to their comrades. One man, missing an ear and the bloody spot it had once occupied, seemed to cause great mirth among the his peers. Taylor and his infantry companions could only look on in amazement.

The mounted officers urged his line forward, and the infantry moved slowly down the rocky slope toward the thick reinforced lines of the Mexican regulars. An officer with gold epaulets and flowing white beard, rode out front of Taylor's rank, waving a silver sword and shouting encouragement. He heard a voice to his rear say it was General Zachary Taylor himself. A loud cheer arose all along the lines.

God, I hope he doesn't go and get himself killed, Taylor thought. Without old Zach, they'd be lost, sure as hell!

Apparently, the General's staff thought along the same lines, as immediately, he was joined by other officers who escorted him quickly to the rear of the infantry's lines. Taylor McCain was surprised and pleased to hear an almost continuous firing of the American artillery's big guns, far to their rear. Apparently a resupply of ammo had arrived, or old Zach was investing everything he had into this one particular battle.

The pace remained painfully slow as the American line moved down the sloping hill toward the enemy troops. Even from a distance, rounds from Mexican snipers were beginning to find their targets. Several Americans grunted, stumbled and fell to the rocky ground. Taylor stepped over a tow-headed youth he had spoken with the previous night. He remembered the boy mentioning he was from a farm near the Arkansas River. Taylor could tell from the wound in the side of the boy's head that he wouldn't be going home. He forced his mind back to the danger ahead and struggled resolutely up the rocky slope – into an increasingly deadly hail of enemy fire.

The Texan's accurate artillery fire was now taking its toll as well, as large holes began to appear in the Mexican ranks. The enemy officers could be heard above the din, screaming at their faltering troops, encouraging them to hold their ground. Gradually, this encouragement turned to direct orders, then threats, as some in the ranks turned in panic to flee toward the rear. The Mexican officers, now banishing pistols and swords in their hands, shook them threateningly at their own troops. Caught between the two dangers, most stayed and continued to fire their flintlocks.

Before, they had been just a distant colorful line of unknown danger. But now, the enemy finally had a face. Taylor suddenly found himself close enough to make out the sweaty features of the opposing force – see the same fear in their eyes as those he saw around him. He and his fellow infantrymen had yet to fire their weapons, awaiting their officer's command. As if in a slow motion dream, their commander dismounted, raised his sword arm and screamed at them to charge. Without checking to see if he was being followed, the young captain broke into a full run toward enemy ranks. He need not have worried, for the entire line of Texas infantry, tired of being sitting ducks as they crossed the exposed valley, shouted as one, and charged the Mexican forces. Almost at once, Taylor was among the enemy, parrying a blow from a dark youth with his rifle and slashing him across the face with the long attached bayonet. Then onto a rotund private who dropping his rifle, fled in terror. A handsome young officer on a beautiful white horse, a plumage decoration in his hat, rode among them, shouting orders in an attempt to rally the faltering Mexican troops. Taylor brought his rifle to his shoulder and just as the officer looked him in the eyes, he shot the man through the head. Bile rose in his throat and he struggled to force it back as he frantically loaded his ancient rifle.

Shooting had now broken out on the right flank of the Mexican forces and Taylor heard a shout that the mounted Ranger force had taken it upon themselves to attack that point of the enemy's lines. Suddenly large groups of the enemy force began to toss down their rifles and turned to run up the hill to their rear. It was then that Taylor knew why. The first of several mounted men in the recognizable broad-brimmed hats of the Rangers broke into his view. The big, bearded men spewing death from each hand, fired into the backs of the fleeing Mexican troops, seeming to drop one with every shot. Suddenly, there were even more of the mounted Texans, pouring deadly accurate fire into the retreating terrorized men, screaming in fear as they scampered up the steep slope to find safety from the Ranger's lightening attack. The sight of the carnage made Taylor feel sick. Shaken and soaked with sweat, he slowly lowered his hot-barreled rifle, staring in horror and fascination at the spectacle before him.

Almost none of the Mexicans made it to the top and over, so deadly was the fire of the mounted Rangers. The air was heavy with the metallic smell of blood, and acrid with gunpowder, causing bile again to rise in Taylor's throat. This time he lost his battle and suddenly bent double, repeatedly retching. Food had been scarce, and this time nothing came forth. The painful retching eventually passed and the hot air now felt cool against his sweaty face. Exhausted, he slumped to the ground as the battle activity eventually wound down. For a long time, he sat stoically on a large rock and silently observed the Texas Devils as they rode aimlessly through the littered hillside, searching for signs of life from the vanquished enemy. An occasional moan from a fallen Mexican soldier would drift to him, followed by a mighty boom from one of the big pistols carried by the Rangers. That was the only sound that sporadically broke the eerie quiet of the battlefield. Around him, Taylor saw the grimy-faced infantrymen of his company wandering aimlessly among the dead, searching for friends, or their eyes staring hollow-eyed at the awful scene. Taylor's head dropped between his knees and he began to sob softly.

Bigfoot Wallace glanced over his broad shoulder at the five remaining men of the initial eight-man force he'd ridden out with. His chest almost seemed to swell with pride as his gaze touched each smooth un-whiskered face.

By God, there rides Texas's best! Not a nerve among them.

With five hundred like this he could ride to the capital of Mexico City and drag the president of Mexico back by his heels. Damned if he couldn't!

Will Sonnet was the eldest, at the tender age of twenty-two. He packed those two Walkers like he was born with them strapped to his legs. Wallace had often observed the effortless manner in which he drew and fired the big Colts and had determined early on that he was damned glad young Sonnet was on his side.

Gone to Texas

Riding just behind the Sonnet boy, came Raf Palomino, an enigma for sure. Looked to be Mexican...at least partly...yet filled with a seething hatred for all others of his race. Wallace suspected he might be part Indian, too. Maybe one of those South American breeds of Indian. He was as quick with the frog-sticker he carried down the back of his shirt as he was with a pistol. Like all the others, Raf carried two of the new Walker Colts, with a second pair stuffed into his saddlebags. With his fast hands and fiery temper, the others steered clear of him.

Most did anyway. The exception being that new hellion, Roosevelt Poe. The others called him Rosie Poe. Now, that was a silly name, Wallace contended. Whoever heard of a man named Rosie? And the palaver that young man could spit out in a single minute was enough to fertilize an acre of bottomland. He was the only one Wallace had not seen in action and it had been his experience that the ones that talked the most was the most worthless when it came to an actual fight. Cal Tancred and "Black" Bart Stoudimire brought up the rear. Both, Wallace knew, were as deadly as snakes. Yep, a bunch of first-class fighting men – the average age – twenty years.

Bigfoot hadn't seen Mordecai Jones since early yesterday and then, he'd only caught his back as he faded into the dusty dawn just as the others were arising from their bedrolls. He was convinced that the old man didn't much care for him. It didn't bother him none, but he did often take to wondering at the reason for Mordecai's dislike. So far, he had skirted around a confrontation with his most experienced scout, but it might come down to that yet.

He knew Mordecai Jones and Captain Hays shared some kind of special bond, having served together in numerous conflicts in the past, and he didn't want to jeopardize his own position in the Rangers by rubbing out one of Hays's old friends just because he was an irritant. The Ranger Militia was an organization he desperately wanted to command some day, because he was convinced they would play an important part in the building of Texas – after all the Mexicans and Indians had been killed off. Bigfoot prided himself on being a visionary. As a visionary, he was certain that once the war was over, there would be an important place in Texas for a band of fighters as the Texas Rangers. He wasn't yet certain just what that calling would be, but in his bones, he felt sure there would be one. And when it came to pass, he intended to be the leader of such a movement.

He also didn't particularly relish a face-to-face confrontation with the old man, in that Mordecai Jones had a reputation for violence that was built on fact. While Bigfoot Wallace wasn't particularly scared of any man alive, he still didn't want to wake up some morning with an unnatural grin from ear to ear, like he knew some men did after having a run-in with Jones. Besides, no one he'd ever met could trail a man like the famous Mordecai Jones, and the simple truth was, Bigfoot needed the old tracker if he was to succeed in his future aspirations. Still, just the thought of that old man being out there, where he couldn't see him, caused chills to run up his spine.

Suddenly he glanced up and nearly jumped out of his skin. Sitting on his mount scarcely five feet away, was Mordecai Jones, a sardonic smile played at his lips. In a manner he'd perfected long ago that seemed to absolutely drip with contempt, Jones spit at the feet of his unmoving horse and waited for Bigfoot's jumpy nerves to settle down.

"Found the bunch that did in our two boys. Interested?"

Bigfoot Wallace certainly wasn't interested. The trouble was, how did he say so with the others looking on with such great anticipation. His gaze slid over the young faces in the group, as they waited expectantly for his confirmation that they would finally get a shot at the ones who had butchered their friends. Bigfoot's face displayed none of the anger or turmoil he felt inside.

Dammit, you meddling old man! Damn your eyes!

He knew there just wasn't any percentage in going after the Indians who had killed Foley and Farmer. All he wanted was to get the map back to General Taylor and reap his rewards, not chase after a bunch of mangy Indians. Still, he needed the other's backing to attest to the fact he hadn't blundered in sending out the two young Rangers alone. He paused, observing the eager faces of his young band.

You stupid old meddler! he thought again, his fingers aching to close around the old man's skinny, wrinkled neck. He suspected Jones knew exactly what he was feeling, that he actually wanted to rant and rave at the smiling old coot smugly awaiting his reply. At last, Bigfoot sighed deeply, resigned to the task ahead.

"You lead, Mordecai. We'll follow."

Jones spit in his contemptible manner, and led off toward the rocky terrain to the southeast.

* * *

Fifteen miles north of the Rio Grande, Handsome Jack suddenly pulled on his reins, halting his mount in the middle of the old buffalo trail they'd been following for the past hour. Jericho stared at him in question, then lowered his hands toward his pistol grips. Jack's expression alone had caused the hair to raise on the back of his neck.

"Got'cha! You young Texas jackass!"

It'd come from the rocks just ahead, but Jack suddenly relaxed, grinning.

"Is that you, Smith? No one but you would test a man's reflex like that. I might've shot your eyes out before I figured out it was you horsing around out there."

"Eh?"

"I said…oh, the hell with it. Come out where I can see you."

"Eh?"

A bent, buckskin clad figure seemed to materialize from the ground to their front, then, three more men stood, but remained in the shadows of the rocks. As the one in buckskin approached, Jericho saw an elderly white man, a rawhide string around his neck with a long horn-shaped contraption attached to it. The others, remaining motionless behind him, were undoubtedly Indians.

Still grinning, Jack dismounted and shook hands with the newcomer, who appeared to be ancient. He stopped and raised the horn to his right ear.

"J.D., meet 'Deaf' Smith. Mister Smith – Jericho McCain."

Smith squinted up at him, then favored him with a grin that looked more like a wolf's snarl than an expression of mirth. "Howdy, McCain. Been watching you two for a couple 'a hours as you stumbled and bumbled your way across half of Texas. Can't figure out how you could've kept from getting your hair lifted by some drunk Indian, 'fore now."

Smith's tone irked him, so Jericho retorted, "Our hair's on pretty tight. It might take somewhat more than one drunk Indian to do that."

Smith slapped his leg and guffawed loudly.

"God damned, Jack. You got yourself a young hellion here, for sure. Yes, sir!"

Jericho had heard of Deaf Smith, the man who had been with Sam Houston when he'd defeated Santa Anna after the fall of the Alamo. Smith had been the most famous scout of the whole war, and rumors had it, he was also Houston's advisor and confidant.

"Well, hop down here McCain, and let's palaver a bit," Smith declared gruffly.

When all were squatting in the middle of the trail, Smith went on. "What the hell you boys doing out here all alone? I have trouble even getting my God damned Kiowa scouts to venture out this far without the promise of great rewards. I tell them it's safer here than it is in the city, because if they don't come with me, I'll kill 'em. Har, har."

Jack glanced nervously toward the spot where he'd last seen the three Indians. The place was empty now, causing a chill to run up Jericho's back.

"Are they tame?" he asked worriedly.

"As tame as any Kiowa can ever be. I just sleep with one eye open and don't turn my back on 'em. The only thing that keeps those heathens in line, is the fact that they hate the Mexicans worse than they hate me. The Mex's wiped out their entire village just south of the Rio while they was out hunting. I figure once they've killed off all the Mexicans they want, they'll turn their attention back to me. There's a lot of Mex's, so I may be dead of old age by then, Har, har."

"What's happening with the war effort, Mister Smith? Where's General Taylor and his army?"

"Zach is over by the Alcon Reservoir, trying to hold his four thousand man army together. He's got even more of a problem than that, though. The Mexican Army has been lost. We knowed exactly where they was, about a month ago. Then, quick as a wink, they was gone. He can't commit his main force until he finds 'em. So he's done the next best thing. He's dispatched Colonel Roberts with about fifteen hundred troops and four cannon to Laredo, because Johnson and his scouts have discovered a large force heading north to Nuevo Laredo. Whether that's Santa Anna's main force or not, is the question."

Smith finished speaking and dropped his listening horn to dangle around his neck.

"I'd say it is, and Zach ought to get down there before Robert's brigade gets wiped out."

"Eh?"

Handsome Jack motioned for Smith to put the horn back to his ear, then repeated his statement again.

"Oh. Yep, that's what most of his staff is telling him, too. Zach's stubborn though. He thinks the attack will come at San Antonio. Claims he knows how Santa Anna thinks. The Alamo was Santa Anna's biggest victory. Zach says that all the Mex's are superstitious, so he'll want to repeat his victory by hitting there next."

"I hope he knows what he's doing."

"Well, he's got me watching here, Mordecai over near San Antonio, and Memory Johnson down at the Nuevo Laredo crossing. If he comes, we'll see him. I just hope Zach can move his force quick enough to stop him when he does."

Smith dropped his hearing horn again and dug around in a greasy shirt pocket for his chewing tobacco. He drug out a gnawed upon, spongy mess and bit of a hunk, replacing the rest without offering it to any others. That was just as well with both Jericho and Jack.

Handsome Jack seemed to get even more serious, now.

"We're chasing someone who…"

"Eh?"

"Mister Smith, please use your horn, dammit!"

Smith may not have heard his words, but he clearly understood Jack Clay's tone and expression. He stuck the horn back into his ear once more, and waited.

Jack sighed, then started over. "We're chasing two men who done one of J.D.'s own, a great harm. He means to kill 'em."

"Whyn't ya say so? Shucks, the only others through here in a week have been a company of Mex Lancers, a Comanche hunting party, and two fellers of questionable morals. They stopped in San Lupe yesterday to visit the Blue Mule – the only whorehouse within fifty miles. The last I heard, they were trying to drink up the town's supply of hard liquor."

"Big guy and a smaller one? Look like buffalo hunters?"

Deaf Smith spit, then nodded. "That's them. Want me to kill 'em for you, youngster?"

Jericho shook his head. "No. That's my job. I promised someone."

Smith lowered his horn and spit a gob into the rocks beside the trail. "That must've been some powerful wrong they did ya, youngster."

"It was."

"Eh? Eh?"

* * *

Upon their arrival in San Lupe, Sikes and Deeks had gone straight to the "Mulo Azul," the only drinking establishment in the small town. They had been drinking steadily since arriving. San Lupe was nothing more than a dozen dirt dwellings that housed less than fifty local Mexicans and a few tame Indians. Most of these tended to a few head of sheep or raised chickens and small gardens just outside the town in order to subsist. Sikes and his partner had arrived in the small village just after noon the previous day, and already Deeks had stuck his knife into an unsuspecting drunk while Sikes kept him busy arguing. Afterward they had riffled the dead man's pocket as the other patrons looked on, then impervious to their stares of hatred, went back to drinking. Word had spread quickly of the outlaws' presence, and they were given a wide berth by citizens of the poor community.

Deeks laughed loudly as he watched Sikes drag the screaming dark-skinned bar girl up the narrow stairs by her hair. The big man paused for an instant at the landing, grinning down at the men at the bar as though daring them to interfere. When they failed to meet the challenge in his eyes, he roughly pushed the girl into one of the rooms and slammed the door behind them. If it had been his intention to provoke interference from the clientele present, he was disappointed, for none of the peaceful townspeople could fathom trying to stop the well-armed men who had terrorized their small village since yesterday morning. Especially in a village where only two or three rusty rifles could be found, none of which probably worked properly anyway. They were not warriors. They could not fight professionals such as these *Americano Pistoleros*. All the able-bodied fighters had already left to find their fortunes with either the American Army or the general, Santa Anna. They would make no move to stop him – but a smothering hatred could be detected behind their averted eyes.

The woman screamed the entire time Sikes was gone, and then suddenly the screaming ceased abruptly. A moment later, the big bearded man walked slowly down the steps buckling on his pistol belt while grinning slyly.

"Whoopee!" Deeks jumped to his feet and danced a jig among the tables. "Ya sure gave her one hell of a ride partner! The question is did you break her or did she throw you?"

The two men laughed uproariously as the others watched silently, avoiding the newcomers' eyes whenever either looked their way.

"You want one?"

The remaining two females, a short plump Mexican woman of about fifty, and a younger girl with smallpox scars, eased to their feet and moved slowly toward the back entrance.

"Hell no!" Deeks shrill voice split the air. "Them two are ugly as a mud road. You had the purty one. I think I'll jist mosey on up there and pay my respects to her, too."

"Jist don't expect her to be too lively."

More vulgar laughter as Deeks headed for the stairs. Sikes looked up and caught the eye of the Mexican bartender.

"Ya got something on yore mind, greaser?"

"No, *señor. Por favor.* My apology, *señor.*"

"Well bring me some more whisky and I want the good stuff this time, you fool."

"*Si, señor.*"

Deeks was back in a short time and settled into a chair beside the big man.

"She shore didn't have much life. You was right about that. I think you broke her neck."

"You git yore ashes hauled, or not?"

"Well...sure. I ain't complaining or nothing. Hell, I like a quiet woman."

Deeks took a deep drink directly from the bottle and wiped his mouth with the back of his hand.

"Fact is, I'm thinking of maybe going back up there directly and paying her another little visit. Take my time, this time 'round."

He started to rise, then froze halfway out of his chair. Standing just inside the saloon doorway was a young man he was sure he knew from before. Sikes saw his friend's reactions and followed his eyes to find Jericho McCain quietly staring back at him. He didn't speak for what seemed like a very long time. Then, his voice low but clear, he cut through the quiet chatter of the room.

"You two low-lifes drag your mangy hides from behind that table. I'm fixing to kill you both."

His soft tone reverberated through the large room like a bell and suddenly the place became deathly quiet.

Sikes laughter floated through the room. "Why Deeks, if it ain't the snotnose brat from Waco. You remember him. He's the one that had the mean cur and that pretty widder for a boss."

Deeks swallowed hard and glanced nervously at his partner, then slowly lowered himself back into the chair. As his butt hit the chair, Deeks's hand moved slowly toward his holstered sidearm.

"Now you just go right ahead and pull it, low-life," McCain said softly, staring at Deeks. "It's either that, or I take you both outside and hang you. Makes no difference to me. Which ever way it turns out, your passing will only stand to better mankind."

Suddenly made aware that the youth's position was just the right distance away, and that his angle provided sight of their hands under the table, Deeks's hand suddenly jerked away from his pistol as though he had just touched a hot fire. So intent were they on the drama being played out before them, no one in the saloon saw the handsome young man with his crisscrossed gun belts walk through the doorway and move to the corner of the long bar. He seemed completely disinterested in events as they unfolded, but his eyes missed nothing from beneath his low hat brim.

"Stand and pull...or place them on the table. I won't say it again." Jericho still had not raised his voice but his words seemed loud in the quiet room.

"Now what makes a pup like you think he can take two hard men like us, snotnose? Why would you even want to? Hell, we didn't do more than get that little filly broke in for you."

Sikes's voice was smooth and measured as he taunted McCain, but the youngster remained calm and stared back at the seated men.

"Why can't we all just...?"

Suddenly, Sikes jumped to his feet, his chair crashing loudly backwards in the silent room. Deeks was just an instant behind him, as both men's hands streaked for their holstered guns.

What happened next was talked about for years in the small village of San Lupe, and no one present at the time could seem to agree on exactly what transpired next. But in the fraction of the second it took for a slender soft-voiced stranger to end the existence of two "very bad hombres," Jericho McCain became a legend to the Spanish-speaking folks of southwestern Texas.

By one account, probably the most accurate, Deeks's and Sikes's guns were clearing leather before the youth moved. He shot Deeks through the right eye blasting a good portion of his brains out through the back of his head, leaving them to slide slowly down the adobe wall. Then, as Sikes's bullet spun his hat sideways on his head, he coolly placed his next round in the middle of the big man's chest. Sikes backed up several steps until he rested against the wall, his gun hanging from his limp fingers, staring in bewilderment at the large stain quickly spreading across the front of his dirty shirt. Finally, he dropped the useless weapon to the floor and raised his eyes to the boy who had just shot him.

"You killed me, pup. Damn your eyes, I'm done."

With that, he slid slowly down the wall to the floor, where he remained, sucking in loud ragged breaths of air. Then, he slowly toppled over, lay on his side and the loud breaths subsided.

The Mexicans at the bar gave forth a loud cheer and gathered around the boy who still held his smoking gun in his hand, staring as though dazed at the two bodies before him. Jericho slipped the Walker Colt into its holster just as an older man, better dressed than the rest, appeared before him. The old man removed his hat in a sign of respect for the young gunfighter, then spoke politely.

"*Señor*, I am Jorge Gallegos, the village elder. You have done a great thing here today for our small village. The people of San Lupe thank you."

Jericho looked back at him through eyes that still reflected shock over his killing of the two outlaws. "I don't 'spect killing a man is such a great thing," he mumbled softly, turning to walk from the shadowy bar room. He didn't look back.

No one seemed to notice the handsome man quietly following him out. The next day someone penned a song about a slender youth with hard gray eyes and lightening quick hands: *The Savior of San Lupe*.

Nine

POX MARKS WATCHED THE three tall figures and the six small ones as they slowly moved across the lowlands far below. During the past two hours they had covered only half the distance. He was becoming impatient with their laziness, they'd been meandering since the Mexican herders allowed the sheep to pick their way through the edible greens growing in their path before moving on. Pox Marks also knew that Walks Like a Dog was waiting in the nearby rocks with the other two heathens. Unlike him, they wouldn't be impatient. They'd wait as long as necessary for the small band of sheepherders; that was what they lived for –killing the invaders. Unlike him, the Kiowa hated them all – the Whites who came and took the land from them – the Mexicans who were such easy prey. But Walks Like a Dog even hated his own Kiowa for kicking him out of his village and taking away his birthright. Yeah, the Dog had a big hate and Pox Marks could use it to good advantage.

The Mexican sheep farmers, dressed in their light color cotton garments of tradition, were easy to pick out against the dark background of the shadows, growing longer as the afternoon dragged on. The herders tending the small flock periodically rested on rocks or fallen trees, as they slowly made their way toward home for the evening. None appeared to be armed except for an old man with a machete. *Lazy buggers*, Pox Marks thought, tired of waiting for them to reach the rocks on the near side of the clear area. In a land that spawned indescribably cruel treatment of its inhabitants, and possessed more than its share of psychopaths, Pox Marks was unique. He had pride. He was determined to be the worst killer of them all.

The Mexicans, the Whites and the Indians, all hated each other with venom. The new Texicans, it seemed, went further. They even hated their own. Pox Marks really hated no one, except perhaps his old man while he was still just a pup. That made Pox Marks one of the most dangerous. One who simply enjoyed killing – the act of ending life. Any life. He had killed men, women, and children, even animals. He simply loved to kill – mainly by torture. He especially liked to use fire; a very low, slow fire. With that, he was simply feared more than any of the others. The unsuspecting herders were getting ready to experience that fear.

He licked his lips and watched as the three white clad figures slowly egged on the sheep toward the rocks once more.

* * *

Mordecai led Bigfoot Wallace and his Rangers to the location where the ambush had taken place, patiently waiting while they absorbed the bloody scene. He pointed out how Foley and Farmer had accounted themselves well, even though outnumbered and surprised by a much superior force. Somehow they had become separated, Farmer eventually wounded and captured while Foley had miraculously escaped. Between them, Mordecai said, the two young Rangers had killed or wounded five braves, who had been carried off by the others, as was their custom. He informed them that after the Comanche left, Foley returned and carried Farmer's mutilated corpse as far as he could manage before collapsing and dying. Pointing toward the trail of the remaining Indians, he estimated that it had been a party of about twenty warriors. Finished, he led out without a backward glance in the direction the warriors had taken.

Bigfoot stared after him until he was almost out of sight, as though contemplating the effect on the others of letting him go on by himself. Detecting some stirring behind him and a few whispers, he eventually put spurs to his horse and followed the old scout.

They rode south until almost dusk, without even a glimpse of their scout. Suddenly rounding the bend in a deep gully, Mordecai rested against a rock. His eyes lowered eyes until they'd pulled up beside him, he then spit and grinned.

"Just ahead there's a clump of pecan trees and in the middle of 'em is a spring I raked out. Drink yore fill. The savages are still about two hours ahead of us, but I know where. I'll edge in tonight after they're asleep and pinpoint 'em. We can be there by first thing in the morning." He winked. "Join 'em for breakfast."

Once again, he left quickly, slipping into the surrounding rocks at the end of the draw to retrieve his mount that he'd tethered nearby. The others found the spring exactly where he had told them, but Mordecai Jones was nowhere to be seen.

"That damned old man's like a ghost."

Bigfoot looked toward the location the others were unsaddling and deduced that the remark had been made by the new arrival, Rosie Poe. He'd heard undisguised admiration in the youngster's voice and determined right away that he didn't particularly like the cheeky young pup. Anyone who respects that old fool Jones is a poor judge of people, and likely to be a fool.

"Poe, you're on watch first!" he said harshly as he turned away. "Try not to go to sleep or we'll leave you here for the Comanche."

Out of earshot, Poe winked at Raf Palomino. "Now what kind of puddle do you suppose he sat down in?"

"I don't think Captain Wallace likes *Señor* Jones too much… or the man who would speak well of him."

Raf hadn't smiled so it was difficult to tell if he was joking. Poe had only met the Mexican youth a week previously, but was already gaining a healthy respect for his perception and ability to read others.

"Well, aye God! As my old pappy used to say, friends may come and go, but enemies accumulate."

He took an evil brown clump of mass from his front pocket and peeling back the cloth wrapping, took a huge bite.

"You want a chaw?"

He shoved the foul smelling concoction at Raf Palomino, who backed away wrinkling his nose, vigorously shaking his head. Poe winked and stuffed it back into his pocket.

"Grow hair on yer chest. Let me know if you change yer mind."

Poe gathered up his rifle and canteen as Raf watched, and walked to the high point where he would stand his watch. Raf was certain he would never change his mind about that awful stuff Poe chewed. The young man relieved Poe, a scant two hours before Mordecai shook him awake.

"Come on boy. Crawl outta that fart sack. We got work to do."

Peering through his heavy-laden eyes, Poe could tell the others were already rolling sleeping blankets and strapping their gear to their horses. Silently, Jones handed each of them strips of burlap and several rawhide strings. They paid attention as he instructed them how to tie up their horse's feet so they'd make no sound when they neared the encampment.

Gone to Texas

"I'll let you know when I want these put on. I'll give you a sign, like this."….His hands looped around in a tying motion. "Be alert and don't miss it, or I'll just have to cut your throat and leave you on the trail."

Silently, he led them out through the darkness. Two hours later, just as dawn was starting to show, Mordecai turned, made his tying motion, and no one missed it.

Leading their mounts on foot, Mordecai led them up a winding trail that raised several hundred feet before it leveled off. Within another ten minutes, just as it started to drop off once more, Jones remounted again. Determined not to miss any of the old man's signs, those behind also quickly remounted. Slowly, he raised his arm then pointed at a dark spot two hundred yards away to a group of men silently breaking camp. Without a word, the young Rangers lined up beside him, and Mordecai nodded at Bigfoot, who in turn spurred his horse and let out with the most terrible scream the Rangers had adopted as their battle cry. The others followed with thunderous noise, and suddenly, all were charging down the dark rocky slope at break-neck speed.

The Comanche, taken completely by surprise, frantically tried to mount their startled horses as the Rangers commenced rapid firing. Halfway to the Indian's location, the Rangers were met by at least half the Comanche on horseback, screaming their own whooping battle cries. The scrimmage was brief but bloody, the outcome preordained from the start. The Rangers' Colts superior firepower, especially from close range while on horseback was deadly. Within the first few minutes of battle, more than a dozen Comanche lay dead or dying. The horrible cries of dying men and terrified horses, combined with billowing dust and gun smoke, seemed surreal to those occupied in their struggle for survival.

Bigfoot Wallace clubbed a young brave of no more than sixteen years of age and felt his skull crunch under the force of his heavy, steel-capped rifle butt. Ever mindful of what was happening around him, he was aware of the location of his of his men on the battlefield. After the fight he would be able to uncannily ascertain how every one of them had accounted for himself during the fight, and just how many of the Indians had been dropped by which of his rangers.

As suddenly as it started, it was over. Bigfoot began to survey his own loses; one empty saddle was all he could count. Its owner, lying a short distance away, unmoving. He was the quiet one of the group, Cal Tancred. Poe, already at the fallen ranger's side, straightened, shaking his head toward the others. He walked steadfastly through the score of Comanche bodies, putting a bullet through each of the downed Indian's skulls. Nearby, Mordecai watched from horseback with a small approving smile.

He may be an unlikable little cuss, but that boy is one cold-blooded customer, thought Wallace as he watched Poe provide the coup de grace to the last Comanche. He was surprised that it had been Poe who had accounted for most of the dead Comanche; he alone, had been responsible for at least half of them. Bigfoot had caught sight of him, his bridle reins in his teeth and a Colt in each hand, almost nonchalantly knocking the enemy from their horses.

I might have seriously misjudged that boy, he surmised. He concluded that young Poe would bear watching.

The destination they'd picked to make camp was in a small pecan grove on a shallow stream, with what appeared to be the sole water hole from any direction. Since water and shade were both scarce commodities in this barren country, Handsome Jack had recommended that they stop earlier in the day if they located one that hadn't burnt dry by the heat. He normally wouldn't have considered camping on the only water source within fifteen miles, but this particular spot was on level, open ground and should be easily defensible. Notwithstanding, the area they had to cross ahead of them was completely open, dry country, and should they encounter hostiles, would dictate a long hot chase to reach safety. Best to be rested, watered, ready to go. Jericho took care of their mounts while Handsome Jack gathered the dry smokeless wood for a fire. A lack of water had precluded them from cooking anything for the past three days, and coffee would taste good for a change.

Although late in the day, Jericho watched as the layers of heat waffed off the earth's hot surface they'd just traversed. A dust devil cut though the layers in mischief, then disappeared as a gust of hot air dissipated the updraft. He struggled to breath deeper.

"What do ya see?"

Jericho seemed oblivious of his aimlessly staring. He joined Handsome Jack and picked up a handful of firewood.

"Tell me something, Jack. Why would anyone in his right mind want to fight over a place such as this? It's...like Hell! It's worse than Hell! At least in Hell people know they're going to suffer. They come out here to this Godforsaken place, expecting a better life and what do they find instead? Heat, torment and danger – Hell. I say if the Mexicans and Indians want it, give it back to them. It's not worth the life of one more decent person."

Jack came over and sat down near Jericho.

"J.D., what you see here is not all there is to Texas. There are places where the grass grows so high it touches the belly of your horse, and you can't cross it in a week. Clear, pure streams just a busting with trout, rich bottom farming land, deep-water harbors, too. It's so vast that everyone can have as much land as they can work; cattle ranches as large as some states will emerge. Someday Texas will provide the whole world with beef and horses, maybe grain, too. One day, it will be the most powerful state in the Union, J.D. Take my word for it. Texas is worth fighting for."

Jericho stood.

"Maybe. But I can't see it."

He moved toward the edge of a small ravine, bent to pick up several small twigs, then dropped to the ground and froze.

Jack heard a soft whistle and glanced up. He lay motionlessly, staring out onto the sun baked earth and rocks. Dropping the sticks he'd gathered, Jack hurried over and lay down beside the younger man. Scanning the spot Jericho stared at, a lone figure of a woman slowly made her way up a rocky slope toward another grouping of three small pecan trees. They watched silently until she'd disappeared into the bushy area.

"Annie Springs," Clay said quietly.

Jericho looked at him questioningly.

"Annie Springs," he said again, as though in awe. "I've heard stories about her ever since I came out here. Always figured she was a figment of some old lair's day-dream – kind of like the mermaid tales."

Jericho looked stumped, still not comprehending.

"Legend has it that about ten years ago, Annie Springs came out here with her baby girl to join her husband. He'd arrived about a year earlier and built them a small place over on the Brazos. All they wanted was the same as other settlers wanted;

to start a new life, live it in peace. Comanches came upon their camp while she was at a small stream fetching water. She heard their cries and found cover nearby. It must have been horrible for her. She was close enough she could hear everything that went on, and heard them torture her husband and baby to death. They say the Indians stuck a forked stick through the baby and placed it on a bent sapling, then shot it into the air to die. She must have seen the whole thing from where she was hiding."

The sun was sinking rapidly now; still the two men lay, talking without apparent notice.

"She was found days later by another settler group, wandering, calling for her lost child. They backtracked her and found the mutilated bodies, but she never accepted the fact that her husband and daughter were dead. She sneaked off sometime during the night and though they searched, they couldn't find her. Figured she had met up with a bad end out in the wilderness, though nobody ever knew for sure. Since then, there have been reports of her being seen wandering, calling for her lost child."

Jericho looked sadly at the location he had last seen the tattered woman.

"Seems like she'd be discovered and killed by the Kiowa, long ago."

"Indians believe folks like her to be 'touched' by the spirits and therefore protected. Old Comanche who have been left on the trail by their tribes, often end up in one of the settlements. To hear them tell it, she pretty much scares the dung out of them."

"Even from here, she looked about half-starved. What does she live on out here?"

Jericho could feel Clay's eyes on him.

"They say she eats grass, dirt, an occasional snake or horned toad…things like that. Maybe she was after some of them pecans. They're plenty, when they're in season. She'd be better off to just die. Probably blames herself for not trying to do anything to help her family when the Indians had them. Wouldn't have made any difference. They'd have just killed her, too. Still, it'd be a hard thing to have to live with."

Wordlessly, Jericho rose and walked back to where the horses were tied. Retrieving his gear, he commenced to separate his meager food supply into two small piles.

Comprehending his activity, Jack quickly joined him. "Now hold on, J.D.! Giving up your own food won't do a bit of good for her. She's likely to die anyway and the result will be you'll just end up going hungry yourself."

Jericho continued spreading out a red bandana, placing one of the small stacks of food into the center, then tying the corners together.

"I've been hungry," he said, without looking up. "I know what she's feeling right now."

This was certainly a headstrong young man, whom Handsome Jack was convinced wouldn't take quickly to regimentation or discipline by the rangers, or for that matter, any other entity. Still, he liked the young man's independent manner and felt he held rigid principles for himself – probably others, as well. Handsome Jack had known great leaders with similar principles, Captain Hays coming easily to mind. He watched silently for another moment, then sighed deeply and returned to his own bedroll. After a few moments, he was back, dropping several food items of his own near the red bandana.

"I'm a bigger fool than you are," he said, resignation in his tone. "At least, I know better."

Jericho finished knotting the bandana, then picking it up walked nonchalantly down the slope toward the small pecan grove where they had last seen Annie Springs.

He tied the bandana to a low limb where it could be easily seen, sensing eyes on him. Careful not to look in the direction he saw the woman enter the trees, he turned and made his way back up the rocky slope.

They took turns sleeping, turning in at dark then not stirring until just before it was light enough to see. Saddling his horse in the rapidly approaching daylight, Jericho detected the small pecan stand where he'd spotted the woman earlier. The red bandana was gone.

* * *

Taylor received his small portion of the strong aromatic stew without comment, all the while staring into the flames of the big fire. He suspected tonight's meal was one of the horses wounded by Mexican snipers earlier in the week, but his mouth watered at the smell and his stomach rumbled. He hurriedly spooned in the hot food, sucking air around it to cool so he could swallow. If the heavy concoction temporarily eased his stomach's hunger pangs, it did little for his worried mind. The word was circulating among the ranks that tomorrow they would go into the attack again. Now that Old Zach had the Mexicans on the run, he wasn't going to let up on 'em.

He sincerely hoped was not the case, for he'd seen enough death and destruction in the past two days to last him a lifetime.

What a total waste of human life, he brooded for the hundredth time. Feeling a stir beside him, Taylor glanced up to see a rather bookish young man as he stepped from the shadows to stand beside him.

"Mind if I take a seat?"

The polite voice was surprisingly deep for one of such slight stature. Caught off guard by the intrusion, Taylor simply nodded, and the newcomer dropped, sitting cross-legged across the fire from him.

"The name's Johnson. I'm from Ohio. Where you hail from?"

Taylor had found since being in Texas, that it wasn't considered good form to ask too many questions of strangers. But the youth's remarks came in such an off-handed and sincere manner that he quickly discarded any inhibitions and answered immediately.

"Tennessee. The Appalachian region. Came to Texas to obtain property and make my fortune. Found the Mexicans had some ideas about that, too."

The slender man laughed a deep rich laugh.

"That's a fact. Don't suppose I'll stay around after my hitch is up, though. I was recruited for a special contract. Once it's up, I'll be leaving fast'ern a cat with his ass full'a buckshot. 'Bout a year ago, some feller came all the way to Columbus to find me. Offered my daddy a fair settlement for me to come south with him and spend a year in Old Zach's army. 'Course, daddy left it up to me to decide, but seeing as how they offered enough to pay off the family farm, I allowed it was all right. So here I am."

Taylor found himself liking this new man. He whistled softly. "You must have a very special talent for them to come all the way to Ohio to find you. Just what is it you do?"

"I shoot."

It was Taylor's turn to laugh now. "Hell, I shoot. If it hadn't been for my younger brother Jericho, I'd have been the best shot in Tennessee."

"I know. I've been told about it. That's why I'm here. I heard about your shooting skills from some boys in the other battalion. Seems like they were real impressed with you."

Seeing Taylor's confusion, he quickly went on. "I train snipers for the special squads. You interested?"

Now, Taylor knew whom he was talking to. Memory Johnson, the boy from Ohio who had killed nearly five hundred Mexican troops with his large caliber, muzzle-loading rifle. Memory Johnson, the famous Marksman, was well known throughout the ranks of the American Army, the Mexican Army, too, if the truth were known. Until now, Taylor had been convinced he was just another of the rumors always circulating through the units.

"I appreciate your offer, Mr. Johnson. But I don't like to shoot folks all that much. I reckon I'll just do my job as a regular until my hitch is up, then I'll mosey on back toward Tennessee and help my pa get in the winter feed. Thanks anyway."

They talked of Ohio summers and Tennessee hunting until nearly midnight, and then Johnson stood.

"If you should change your mind, just let your officer know and he'll know how to contact me. Maybe I'll drop by from time to time if you don't mind. I kind of enjoyed our chat."

"Anytime, Mr. Johnson. It'd be my pleasure."

Taylor watched as the slender form of the most deadly man in the American Army quickly disappeared into the evening darkness.

R.C. Morris

* * *

Pox Marks stared into the horrified eyes of the dead sheepherder with mild disappointment. The small fire he built on the man's stomach should not have killed him so quickly. He had seen other men, women too, who had lived for days with it.

These Mexicans had no heart. They all died much too easily. That is why they would lose this vast territory to the Gringos. *Gringos.* That was a good word. He had learned it from the Mexican deserter who had just joined his bunch. They initially called them the Irish, but soon that changed to include all *Norte Americanos. Gringos*, yes, they would win, but it would make little difference to him.

From his appearance, it was hard to tell exactly Pox Marks's ethnic background. His squatty muscular build, dark completion and straight black hair foretold at least some Spanish, or perhaps Indian blood; slate-gray eyes spoke of a European influence. To further complicate analysis, he spoke with an undefinable accent. No one in the region knew his real name, for he had been called Pox Marks since childhood after he'd been nearly killed by an outbreak of the dreaded small pox disease. He had barely survived, but the deep facial scars attested to just how close he had come. Pox Marks also came by other names. Butcher and the Manburner, as he was referred to by Mexicans and Indians along the Rio Grande, were but two of them. A psychopath, he loved to kill, and he loved the notoriety received from his killings. To make matters worse, as his reputation spread, it tended to draw more of his ilk to his side. Now he had seven men of varying degrees of derangement working for him. That they were chaotic mad didn't seem to bother him. He respected his disorder for the most part. It was one true human condition that couldn't be faked. So, let them cause mayhem, and let the others come to him. He was pleased they were of the same ilk. All except Walks Like a Dog. He wasn't like the others, just plain mean.

Walks Like a Dog hated the white man and Mexican, as only one who has lost his heritage might hate. Dog would have been Chief of the Eagle Lodge Kiowa, had it not been for one slight mistake. He'd led his poorly armed war party of fifty braves against fewer than a dozen Texans near Adobe Wells and they had all been slaughtered, almost to a man. Walks Like a Dog had survived, but the out-cry from his village had been so vicious and damning he had been forced into exile. Gone were his dreams of leading the Kiowa into victory against the hated Whites. Gone were his dreams of uniting the three noble tribes and becoming the greatest leader in the history of his people. All that remained, his intense hatred, which Pox cleverly used to his own ends.

Of his diverse group of seven, Dog had always been the most difficult for Pox to control. Beyond Walks Like a Dog, he had two other white men, the Mexican deserter, a half-breed Cherokee, and a young Mexican gunfighter, a demented ex-buffalo hunter. Although not much to look at, they were just the type of men Pox Marks liked to work with. They didn't ask for much, and weren't smart enough to ask questions. With the exception of the half-breed and the Mex gun-slick, all could be bullied, manipulated. He'd have to watch those two. They were several cuts above the others in intelligence, and he didn't want any challenges to his authority. Mostly, he hadn't liked the way they always sat off to themselves, not participating in the fun the rest of them had with the three Mexican sheep herders. While he'd observed them kill without reservation, they didn't seem to be interested in the prolonged torture of the victims like the others. They didn't appear to enjoy it, as the others. Pox Marks was suspicious of them.

The killing alone wasn't what kept Pox Marks interested. It was the sensations he received having his victims tied up and helpless, begging, then to slowly witness the life ease from them. As life left his victims, he sensed becoming noticeably stronger, as though absorbing the strength of their helpless souls. The more helpless the victim, the stronger the feeling. He particularly relished women and children. However, often when he could find no human victims, he resorted to the torture and killing of animals. Unsuspecting travelers coming across the scene of one of his gruesome atrocities, knew instantly what had transpired. His parting hallmark, he always left his victims in the same manner, bloody, tied upside-down, gutted like a wild animal. That was how he got his other name. The Butcher.

Pox Marks looked over the three-gutted corpses and smiled. Yes, life was good. He put his spurs to his mount and rode off, the others following behind.

Ten

TWO DAYS PASSED BEFORE Taylor saw Memory Johnson, the deadly sniper again. His unit had just received orders from the commander to pack up and prepare to move to a new secret location, and the camp was abuzz with rumors. The secret had been known for several days, so Taylor already knew it was to be somewhere near Nuevo Laredo, wherever the hell that was. All he knew, it was on the Rio, to the west of his current location. The prevalent rumor was that the ranger scouts had reported Mexican troop movements there, as though they were trying to flank them and hit San Antonio, cutting the main force's supply lines – possibly ending the war before it ever got started. Tying up his bedroll he heard someone ride up behind him and halt. Quickly turning, he saw Johnson, and he was leading a riderless horse.

"You tired of walking all over this God-forsaken country?"

"Reckon I can handle it okay."

Still, Taylor couldn't help but look with longing upon the offered horse. Suspiciously, he ventured, "What are you offering?"

"I cleared it with Major Wheeler for you to ride with me for a few days. Then, if you don't like being a scout, you can go back to walking."

"I ain't killing no folks from ambush," Taylor said.

"You don't have to. Just see how you like being a scout. If you don't care for it, then it's back to pounding the ground again. What'd ya say?"

Taylor finally grinned. "You got a deal, Mr. Johnson. My feet are so sore they cry every morning when I pull my boots on."

He accepted the reins from his benefactor and tied his roll behind the saddle. Swinging easily into the saddle, he hesitated. "Just where the hell is Nuevo Laredo?"

Memory Johnson's scout group was four men, the eldest around twenty-four years old, and the youngest barely seventeen. By the look of their coonskin headgear, Taylor made them out to be Green Mountain boys. The other two young cowboys more likely Nebraska Territory. They didn't talk much and Taylor had the impression they might be hiding from something. He didn't dwell on it, for that pretty much summed up most of the men he'd met since his arrival in this God-awful country. *Texas.* The word sounded so good in Tennessee. *Texas.* Probably means "Hell" in Mexican talk. All he wanted was to finish his hitch with General Zach, then head back up north and help his pa run their mountain farm. *The grass always looks greener on the other side of the fence*, he thought ruefully.

It took them three days to get into the "secret" area, because they'd nearly been caught out in the open by Mexican Calvary on two separate occasions. Young Memory Johnson seemed to know his business, leading them safely into the designated area. By the time they'd arrived, the Mexican Army was fording the shallow Rio Grande, several units already set up on their side. Johnson estimated the force to be about fifteen hundred men and cannons. Considering the fact that Zachary Taylor had sent only five hundred troops to intercept them – granted it was all he could spare – this was going to be dicey, at best. Another thousand was pushing hard to catch up, and the artillery would be with them. Johnson backtracked to the high ground they had passed hours before, and dismounted. He stared over the flat terrain with the small church set serenely in the center, toward the tactically desirable high ground across the valley.

"This is the best we can do. That marshy area next to the river on our right should keep them from trying that route. The high rocky ground to the left will make it too difficult to get their cannons across. Looks like they'll have to climb the back of that ridge, and funnel up this low horseshoe-shaped area to our front."

Johnson sent Taylor and one of the others back to lead the main force into the defensive position, while he settled into a spot behind a boulder and scanned the horizon with his eyeglasses.

"Better tell them to hurry, Mr. McCain. If we don't stop 'em here, they'll be in San Antonio before we get another go at 'em." He seemed to have lost some of his good humor. In fact, he seemed plumb grim.

Colonel Jason Cornell Roberts had pushed his troops fast and when Taylor found them, they were closer than he expected. Passing Johnson's message to the commander, without rest he led Robert's infantry regiment back toward the defensive position above the Rio valley. They arrived on the morning of the third day, nearly exhausted and out of water. It took the colonel only a moment to make an analysis of the terrain, then asked for fifty volunteers to occupy the high ground across the valley. It was clear they would be used only to slow the enemy's advance, buying time for the rest of Robert's main force arriving from the northeast to reinforce them. If the Mexican regulars made it past the small force and pushed them into the open valley, they all knew it could be a deathtrap for the volunteers trapped on the other side. Still, he got his fifty volunteers.

Roberts wanted someone who had been on the terrain to lead them. Memory Johnson immediately volunteered, but denied because he was deemed to be too valuable to risk on something so unpredictable. Taylor also volunteered; he was selected by the Regimental Executive Officer, Major Wheeler, to guide the blocking force into position. Captain Eldred S. Parks, from South Carolina, was placed in command of the force. Without complaint, the exhausted volunteers rose and followed their trusted officer down into the valley below. Taylor could hear the artillery carts arriving in the distance as he departed with the blocking force, and prayed Robert's other two battalions arrived soon.

Several hours later, the small delaying force reached the high ground just north of the Rio Grande, and Captain Parks placed them into positions that provided for the best defense. Ordering a third of his force to remain awake, the others were allowed to sleep until alerted. Just before dusk, the small force was able to make out the beginnings of a growing dust cloud to the south of their position. A faint rumbling could be heard in the distance. Each man knew what that meant; the Mexican Army's artillery carts were coming.

Why did I ever leave Tennessee? Taylor asked himself again. It was a variation of a question each man in the small force asked of themselves.

The sleeping two-thirds of Parks's force awoke to discover long columns of the colorfully attired Mexican Infantry advancing up the narrow trail far below them. Not yet in rifle range, but at the speed they were traveling, they would be soon. All of the Americans had been issued triple supplies of ammo and water for the mission, and scanning the sparsely occupied line of men, Taylor could see the seasoned veterans checking their weapons and laying out extra ammo on the ground beside them for fast reloading. While no one exhibited any outward signs of fear, Taylor's guts were tied in knots, and he knew the others were most likely suffering the same predicament.

The youthful Captain Parks moved up and down the line, cautioning his men not to fire as the long colorful snake moved ever closer. The lead men had been no more than a hundred yards to their front when Parks gave his command to fire. The resulting carnage was devastating. The first thirty-five men in the Mexican column fell at once, and others struggled back, dragging wounded or dead comrades. Suddenly, there was no one left to shoot at. Several of the Americans wet their bandanas and soaked their rifle breeches to preclude a premature cook-off before the round was fully seated. Taylor had once seen a man lose both eyes from such an explosion.

Although they hadn't seen anything move for thirty minutes, they could hear loud commands and cursing from the enemy soldiers out of sight below, behind the rocky bend. The Americans waited patiently, and after a few more moments several squads of infantry burst from the rocks, charging toward them. Following just behind came several more squads, then others. As the infantrymen in the front ranks fell, others instantly took their place. Soon, the entire hillside was littered with men lying in heaps, either dead, or relentlessly moving ever closer to the American position, screaming and firing. Taylor dropped a soldier less than fifty yards away and glanced anxiously over his shoulder at Captain Parks, who showed no indication he was ready to vacate their position. Suddenly, the young captain sat down hard, staring at his chest, astonished to see a bright red spot spreading.

Taylor moved to his side almost at once.

"Take the men to the next ridge-line, Private McCain. Hold as long as you can. If...the Colonel...don't get time to dig in his artillery...all is lost."

The wounded man coughed up a clot of blood.

Taylor turned him to his side and checked his back. Through a hole the size of a cup, blood pumped onto the ground. He carefully eased his commander back to the ground.

"Go now!" Parks gritted out. "Take the water – leave my pistol."

Taylor started to unbutton the dying man's shirt but his hand was grasped firmly, and he observed the fire in his young commander's eyes.

"That's an order mister! Go!"

Taylor moved down the line, giving the men instructions. When he returned to kneel beside Parks, he was gone, his eyes staring though sightless. Taylor removed the pistol from the dead man's waist, strapped it on, secured the dead officer's ammo and water, then gave the word to fall back. A few moments later, the Mexican infantry rolled over their old position, finding the hill occupied only by Captain Parks and six other dead Americans. The Mexican commander scanned the hillside littered with his dead and dying soldiers, then stared at the next ridgeline. He knew it would be a long day.

* * *

Poe had been riding scout detail with Mordecai Jones since the scrimmage with the Comanche. Without making an issue of it, Jones would spend nearly every waking moment teaching the young man the art of scouting and tracking. Poe, who had tracked game for food since he was nine years old, still amazed at the things he didn't know about the skill. On the other hand, Mordecai was quite impressed with Poe's innate ability to grasp what he was told, and pleased to have the eager youngster to teach. During the fight with the Indians, Poe's skill with a handgun had not been lost on either Mordecai or Bigfoot Wallace. Wallace remarked that he seemed to have the same casual offhand manner of shooting used by all the greats, and this young man was sure to be one of those. That is, if he lived that long. A long life didn't seem to be a given in Texas these days. Mordecai nodded his approval as he watched Poe skirt the high ground, pause just long enough at the rim to peer over, before topping it and crossing over.

Yes, sir, he'll do all right!

The old man smiled to himself, remembering the night he had remained in the darkness overhearing an off-handed complement made by Poe to the Spanish boy, Raf. After that, and watching the way Poe used his guns, Jones had immediately made up his mind to take the youngster under his wing and teach him all he could about the art of tracking and scouting. As it now appeared, that wouldn't be too hard. Suddenly, he saw Poe raise his arm and slide behind a boulder. Mordecai came up from behind him and looked toward the spot that had caught his eye. A Comanche warrior had emerged from behind a large rock and staggered toward another, several feet away, falling to his knees once in the process. Soon, he was into the rocks and out of sight.

"What would you do?" Mordecai said.

"Nothing."

"Why?"

"He's likely to die anyway judging from the shape he's in. If we go down and kill him, he might be found before we are out of the area, and his friends would probably just track us down and barbecue us. There is also the possibility that he's playing possum with us, and there's a bunch of his braves hiding out in them rocks, just waiting to lift our hair."

Mordecai laughed low. Without saying a word, he turned his mount and backtracked down the slope. They made camp that night beneath a low over-hang cliff-face where any smoke would dissipate before reaching the top. After a dinner of cold jerky washed down by a cup of strong coffee, Poe broke the silence.

"You and Bigfoot Wallace don't exactly see eye-to-eye, do you?"

Mordecai stared hard at him.

"Don't fiddle with something that's none of your business, boy."

"Figure it is my business."

Jones watched as Poe unwrapped his chaw and bit off a large piece. Seeing the old man lick his lips, Poe passed it over and watched in apprehension as at least half of it disappeared into his whiskered mouth. Grinning his thanks, Mordecai wiped his mouth with the back of his hand and settled back against his bedroll.

"Just how d' ya figure that?"

"I plan to chase pretty women and drink whisky for a lot of years before traveling to the other side. But right now my future is pretty much in the hands of two people that don't agree on much, nor appear to like each other. One might speculate that it could cause a little flawed judgment to develop…just maybe when I could least afford it."

Poe spit at a rock, not looking at the older man. The old man chuckled softly.

"Yep. You'll do all right, boy." he chuckled again. "You needn't worry none. 'Fore I did anything like that, I'd cut his throat while he slept."

"Why do you hate each other so much? He don't exactly light up a room whenever he walks in, but he seems competent enough."

"If you think there's good in everyone, you ain't met everyone."

Poe laughed quietly to himself. "Sounds just like something my pa would say. He had a saying for just about every occasion."

"Yore pa sounds like a right smart feller, young man. What kind of things does he say?"

"Did," Poe said.

Seeing Jones's puzzled look, he explained. "He did say. Pa's been dead for several years. Ma married again and lasted another ten years after Pa passed away."

They sat chewing, neither speaking for a while. Poe finally said, "'There is always one more fool than you counted on.' That was one of his favorites. Another one was, 'you can't tell which way the wagon went by looking at its tracks.'"

He waited until he heard Jones chuckle, then said, "Didn't rightly understand most of his wisdoms, but he always got a big laugh out of 'em."

That was the end of the talk as they settled into their blankets and closed their eyes. They slept almost at once.

* * *

The small group of Comanche had remained in the same location longer than usual, since with the plentiful water there was an unusual supply of grass for the horses. Also, cover and good escape routes, should that become necessary. *Another two days perhaps, then we'll go on to the Kickapoo village*, Gray Wolf thought.

He was a war chief in the Comanche Nation. The youngest to ever become a chief, he took pride in the fact men much older sought him out for guidance and wisdom. With the Mexicans and Texans warring against one another, he had gained great favor among the council by explaining his plan to eliminate both enemies from this land they had stolen. Land that had always belonged to the Comanche Nation. Only a trail of death, burning, and destruction could return this sacred land to its rightful people.

The Whites and the Mexicans had a ridiculous notion that a man could own the land they lived upon. How could you own something that was living? A living ground, far more significant and wiser than the small animals that crawled upon it. Soon, the people who claimed it would all be dead, but the land would still be here, as it had always been. How could it ever be owned by anyone? He snorted, prompting several nearby warriors to look his way. Gray Wolf ignored them.

Tomorrow or the next day he would meet with the Kickapoos. Then, he'd meet with his old enemies, the Kiowa. He would convince them his way was best. Complete destruction of the White's putrid-smelling towns, the killing of their families, the only way. Once they had no place to live, they would leave. Soon others would hear of the Comanche people's determination and stay away, too. It was a good plan. The Kickapoos were important to his plan, for without them he'd never be able to convince the Kiowa, and he desperately needed the Kiowa.

Gone to Texas

While the Kickapoos lacked the determination and the fighting skills to drive off the Whites alone, on the other hand, the Kiowa were a cruel, savage tribe whom Gray Wolf felt to be inferior to his great main band of Comanche. But the Kiowa had tremendous fighting abilities and determination when with others; he needed them. Yes, it was a good plan.

"Where is my baby?"

The cry caught him completely by surprise, startling him from his concentration. He could see by their expressions that others had been caught off guard. Gray Wolf, startled, saw one of his braves, the closest to the strange figure, tip over backwards, then scamper crab-like to put distance between himself and the new entity. It was the old woman again. The touched one, like a spirit, in her ragged clothing and stringy black hair.

Clearly enraged, her dirty face taunt, she screeched and hissed – bared her teeth and nails, threw rocks and dirt – the warriors scampered as they attempted to mount their skittish horses. It was the worst kind of omen possible before making war, and to make physical contact with someone who had been touched by the spirits meant years of bad luck. Angry that she would cause them to leave this fertile place where he wanted to stay for a few days, Gray Wolf reached for his bow, then stayed his hand as the words of the medicine man, Stepping Bear, entered his thoughts.

"If you harm one who has been touched, you will be vanquished from earth to wander, lost among the stars, forever."

"What have you done with my baby?" she screamed shrilly.

She came straight at him now, her face distorted, ugly. Blackened claw-like fingers reached out to him in small gouging motions. Horrified, he backed his horse away from her touch.

"Where…is…my…baby?"

He momentarily stared into the wild empty eyes of the disturbed woman, then wheeled his mount and raced up the side of the steep wall, followed quickly by the other Comanche warriors. Her voice finally fading into silence as she raced up behind them on the rocky slope.

"Where is my baby? Where is my baby? Where is…?"

Eleven

POLLY FARMER RODE BESIDE her father on the wagon seat where she had spent most of her time since leaving Missouri, four months earlier. She could hear her mother, Mary Lou, cooing to her baby brother who had been sick for most of the treacherous journey. They'd left Sedalia in March with ten other families in as many wagons, as soon as the winter snow started to melt. John Farmer Jr. had been born scarcely two weeks later on the trail, which most folks took to be a good omen. They were soon proven wrong when two of the families were suddenly swept away in the Osage River crossing, swollen with melting winter snow and clumps of leftover ice.

Then, Albert Perkins took ill and soon afterward, his wife and son followed. Mable Carter, the recognized local mid-wife, who was believed to have all sorts of potions and remedies for treating ailments and maladies, proclaimed the culprit to be "the croup." The croup was a fever that had claimed several lives in their old community years earlier. After Alfred's lingering illness worsened, the Perkins family was forced to follow the main party at a safe distance, picking up their much needed supplies from those ahead who left them on the side of the trail. Albert buried his son first – no one knew exactly where. Then, two days before the party reached Fort Smith, the Perkins wagon failed to hitch-up and follow the main body. Polly's pa and Mable Carter were the only ones brave enough to venture back to investigate. They found the old lady already dead and Albert with his brains freshly blown out. John Farmer dug two shallow graves beside the trail, under a large drooping elm, and Mable said the appropriate words. Then Polly's father burned the wagon, and they'd carried the news back to the wagon train, unaware they transmitted something else back. Two days later, John Jr. took ill.

By rights the child should have died weeks ago, he'd been on the verge of death several times, but the youngster fought back and clung precariously to life as the Farmers followed behind the others the required "safe" distance. John Farmer never held much faith with doctors and their ilk, preferring to rely upon the home remedies his family and friends used for centuries. But fearful for his son's life, he took the baby to a doctor in Fort Smith and was given a small bottle of red medicine that seemed to instantly ease the child's suffering. John Farmer credited that concoction as being the savior of his dying infant. That, and the power of his prayers. For the past few days Junior had been growing stronger, and Polly now heard his laugh behind her as his mother played with him.

Thank you dear God, she thought. *Thank you.*

* * *

John Farmer had papers on a section of land south, called Austin, but he had decided to travel on to San Antonio where the family would be safe until the dispute with the Mexican government was cleared up. He'd had no idea the dispute was as serious as it now appeared, driving his wagon through numerous camps, each of several hundred armed rough men, each with numerous pistols and rifles. Some carried hatchets on their belts. Upon arrival at San Antonio, it seemed as if this was an armed camp, bloated with every manner of ruffian the young country

Gone to Texas

could muster. Quickly aware of the undisguised, hungry look some of the watching men were giving his young daughter, he ordered her into the back of the wagon and continued toward the center of the adobe village.

After being unceremoniously turned away from the only hotel and two boarding houses in the town, despair quickly set in. At the general store, Farmer inquired about lodging accommodations from the store proprietor. At first, the man laughed aloud, but then appeared sympathetic to their needs. Finally, he offered a small plot behind his store where they could park their wagon until they found a place to stay, in exchange for a small amount of help around the store. John Farmer readily agreed and the family settled in.

The store's owner was Hugo Partic, a fat jolly man with a fat jolly wife, from a place called Nova Scotia. They had arrived six months previously and brought their store with them. Hugo had become a rich man by local standards, and an important one in town decision-making. Farmer considered himself lucky to have made the man's acquaintance. Helga Partic, who was childless, couldn't hold the baby enough, which was fine with Mary Lou who needed the rest. All in all, John Farmer was satisfied with the way things had turned out. That is, he was satisfied with things until two weeks after their arrival. That was when young Roosevelt Poe came into the store to buy powder for his muzzle-loader.

As Poe laid the small bag of black powder on the counter, he glanced up, staring into the bluest eyes he had ever beheld. It was, as he later related to Mordecai, as if a bolt of lightning had pierced him through the heart. Polly Farmer, this most beautiful creature, caught Poe's eyes, and Poe, usually glib, with a remark about almost any subject, was for the first time in his life at a complete loss for words.

"I said would that be all, sir?"

"Uh, hummm, well, um yes, I suppose so. No. I mean, I'll jist look around for…um…a little while."

He swallowed hard several times and averted the girl's eyes as he hurriedly glanced around the small room for something else he could buy. Nothing seemed to register as anything he had the remotest need for. At a loss for words, he pointed toward a glass jar, half-full of brightly colored objects.

"Horehound candies?" she inquired in a sweet voice.

He mutely nodded. The lovely creature broke into a bright smile and Rosie's body seemed to liquefy and melt right into his boots.

"Somehow, I never figured you for the hard candy type."

Continuing to smile, she scooped several of the pieces into a paper and wrapped them, tying it securely with a piece of twine.

"That'll be a penny extra."

Roosevelt dug into his pants pocket until he retrieved the proper amount of money for the black powder, and the extra penny for the Horehound candy. Looking up, his eyes again riveted on her lovely blue eyes.

"I'm Polly Farmer. My father owns a piece of property north of here, and I'm helping Mr. Partic at the store until General Taylor beats the Mexicans and things settle down a bit."

She waited expectantly.

"Uh, oh, I'm Rosie."

The young woman's face screwed up in obvious effort at self-control. She snorted twice, then burst into uncontrollable laughter. Embarrassed, Polly finally tried to stop, then just gave up and continued laughing, holding her sides. At last, her face bright red, she gained some semblance of control and sobered.

"Forgive me, sir. Please. Is..." She was having trouble maintaining a straight face, once again. "Is Ro...Rosie a first name or a last name?"

"It's Roosevelt Wilson Poe, for your information, Ma'am. My friends call me Rosie. Rosie Poe."

He hurriedly gathered his small package and stomped from the store, his ears burning.

Polly watched as he crossed the street, pausing to hand off the package of candy to a small boy sitting on the steps of the local saloon. Suddenly, Polly ceased smiling and felt immediately saddened.

What a nice young man, she thought. *And you were so rude to him, Polly Farmer.*

That he hadn't purchased the candy for himself, told her he probably had just wanted to talk, but her rude behavior had forced him away. She had to admit though, Rosie Poe was a silly name for a man.

* * *

Private Taylor McCain made it to the deserted church with less than a third of the fifty men Captain Parks had initially led in the small blocking force. They'd laid down two more defenses before being pushed off the high ground to seek safety in the church. At each position, they'd killed more than a hundred of the enemy. Still, they came on as though they were an endless stream. What kind of commander would continue sending his men into the face of certain death, repeatedly? What kind of man would just step over the bloody remains of his friends, only to get to the next destination where more of them would die?

R.C. Morris

He didn't relish his new role as leader, but Parks had thrust him into it, put him in charge of the operation just prior to his death. Taylor McCain was not one to shirk his responsibilities, but he didn't want it either. He closely supervised the defenses, as ten of his remaining fourteen able-bodied men used only their hands to shovel dirt against the side of the small wooden building. Several others carried dried sticks, rocks and small tree limbs to place around the walls.

Inside, he tried to ensure anything that might be used for cover had been placed against the interior walls for protection. Surveying the large expanse of level terrain between him and the American forces nearly a mile away, he knew this is where they must stay. They'd never make it to the safety of friendly lines before the Mexican cavalry overtook them. If any of his foot soldiers were caught out on open ground, they would cut them to pieces with sabers and lances. Especially now, since they were carrying the two seriously wounded men that Taylor had steadfastly refused to leave behind for the advancing forces.

"Sir?"

It was the youngest of the bunch that had come up beside him.

"I found some rocks I believe two strong men could carry from the dry creek yonder. What do you think, sir?"

"Take Holloway with you, but keep an eye on the hill. If you see any horsemen coming, you better drop what you're doing and hightail it back here, pronto. Understand?"

"Yes, Sir."

Taylor smiled so to take any sting out of his words.

"Oh, and Thomas?"

The young man turned back to face him.

"I'm not an officer. You don't have to call me 'sir.' Tay, Taylor, or just plain McCain will do nicely. Okay?"

The boys face lit-up as he smiled. "Okay, Tay."

Taylor watched him move away to join up with the big man from Arkansas, Joseph Holloway. As he realized that both Holloway and that young boy might die today, he suddenly felt the heavy weight of responsibility on his shoulders. Within thirty minutes, the Mexican cavalry topped the ridge behind them; Taylor's lookout shouted a warning, all the while scampering down the roof of the old adobe church.

Earlier, Taylor had assigned positions and divided up the remaining ammo between the surviving men. He'd also collected all the water and placed it in the center of the room where he could control the men's intake. It might be a long time before they saw more. Taylor realized he was likely the eldest one in the small room, and smiled ironically at the thought. He knew it could be very unlikely any of them might ever taste of the hoarded water again.

The men, seasoned warriors in spite of their tender ages, and without comment, settled into their new position, checking their guns and ammo. Taylor watched as they sighted along their rifle barrels at the mounted men, unmoving, still just out of range. One of the wounded men moaned softly behind him.

"Hold your fire," Taylor cautioned his men in a soft voice. "The cavalry are not likely to make a frontal charge against a fortified position. They were just hoping to catch us out in the open where they could finish us off quickly. They'll likely wait for the infantry to catch up and do their dirty work."

The artillery, too, he thought. The damned artillery, too.

Hearing the wounded man moan softly once more, Taylor

took one of the half empty canteens and moved to his side to give the dying man a drink of the precious water.

* * *

Handsome Jack Clay and Jericho rode into San Antonio just after siesta, as the local folks were once again beginning to stir in the hot afternoon sun.

"How 'bout a drink in one of those cool, dark, nasty-smelling saloons?" Jack said to his companion hopefully.

"You go ahead. I'll take care of the horses and join you later."

Jack stared at the youngster for a moment, then shook his head in wonderment, dismounted and handed Jericho his reins. Either this young man was the most disciplined person he'd ever met, or he didn't have a brain in his head. Handsome Jack suspected both.

Jericho led the horses up the bustling street as Handsome Jack licked his lips in anticipation and hurried toward the noisy saloon. Neither looked back.

San Antonio was Waco times ten, Jericho realized as he emerged from the makeshift livery stables. Observing his surroundings, he was suddenly reminded of the bloated body of a dead horse he had once seen in his travels. Like maggots feeding off a dead carcass, they'd be gone instantly if word came that the Mexicans had broken through General Taylor's thin defense lines and were headed their way. Card-sharks, medicine men, gunfighters, all were here; only in greater numbers than had been evident in Waco. The only difference, there were no soldiers here to help keep them in line. He heard two distant gunshots from a row of tents behind the so-called permanent structures. A man yelled out in pain, followed by a third shot, then silence as another fortune seeker gave up his dream. Was this just Texas, or really Hell? The prospects washed over him frequently.

Looks like I made the wrong choice, he thought dishearteningly, as he walked toward the plank facade of the saloon Jack had entered earlier. I should have chosen Hell instead.

Even this early in the day, the place was jammed with people. Jericho searched out Handsome Jack leaning against a far wall, facing the rowdy crowd. Jack caught Jericho's eye as the young man walked toward him, just as a large man in a soiled suit backed into him. The man angrily jerked about to face him, exclaiming loudly, "Why the hell don't you look where you're going, sprout?"

Jericho gazed into the drunken man's eyes, smiled softly, and then said mildly, "You're right mister. I was clumsy and I apologize."

He nodded slightly to the uncouth stranger, stepped around him then headed toward Handsome Jack's position on the wall. The large man simply stared at his retreating back, cursed then went back to his game.

The encounter was not lost on Handsome Jack. Far from having the effect of making Jack question the bravery of his young protégée, he considered it an attribute that the boy had not simply blown the trouble-maker out of his boots, as most men in town would have undoubtedly done. He had seen the way Jericho handled his over-sized Colts when he gunned down the two rogues in San Lupe. He knew the lad didn't need to back down from anyone. That he hadn't resorted to use them to settle the disagreement impressed the ranger, who pushed it to the back of his mind for the future.

A pretty girl, obviously with some Spanish and maybe Indian blood, about sixteen years of age, approached Jericho as he neared Jack's location. She carried a wooden tray and wore a loose, belted cotton shirt over little else, and a large lovely smile.

"Can I provide the handsome young cowboy a drink?"

Jericho stammered for a moment and Handsome Jack ordered for him, as the girl hurried away, smiling over her shoulder.

"Now that's what I call an invitation." Handsome Jack smiled at him, which only added to the boy's discomfort.

"Don't know about that," was all he muttered.

In a short time the girl returned with the drinks, the "invitation" still glowing on her pretty face. Finally, disappointed, she made her way back toward the bar, nimbly dodging several of the drunk's groping hands as she went. Jericho took a tentative sip of the foul smelling liquid and winced. Holding it up to peer at it through the light, he wrinkled his nose.

"What do you call this stuff?" he said.

"Tequila."

"Tastes like mule water," the boy said with distaste.

Handsome Jack laughed loudly. "You'll get used to it if you stay here. The Mex's make it. They put a grub worm in the jug and it sinks to the bottom. It's a custom that the one who gets the last drink also gets the worm. It's just something they do to show who has the biggest *cajones*."

"I'll be careful, then."

Jack laughed again. He was beginning to really like this young man. Jack downed his shot and Jericho did the same. Shuddering, he declined a second. As they left, he caught the dark-skinned girl again favoring him with a pretty smile. She reminded him of Maria, as he still vividly recalled that last night in her father's barn. He felt his face burn as he hurried out.

Handsome Jack took Jericho to the headquarters of General

Zachary Taylor, commander of the combined U.S. forces in Texas. It seemed as though everyone knew him, as they walked unchallenged into the office of the commanding general's adjutant.

Jack shook hands with the major as though he had known him for a long time, and then introduced Jericho.

"Tom, meet Jericho McCain...J.D., Major Tom Kettle."

The two men shook hands and Kettle motioned toward several straight-back wooden chairs. Seated, Handsome Jack started in, wasting no time.

"Tom...J.D. is looking for a brother that he thinks might be around here some place. Their folks died of the fever back in Tennessee, and he's carrying the bad news to his brother."

The major nodded. "Sorry to hear that, Mr. McCain. What's your brother's name?"

Jericho had been studying the army man while he was talking, and answered. "Taylor McCain. He's twenty-three by now, I suppose."

"Alright, I'll get word out to the units and we'll see what turns up. We're pretty spread out so it might take some time to accomplish."

They continued to talk another ten minutes, Jericho agreeing to return the following morning. After shaking hands and departing, he said, "Nice enough man. Not at all what I would have expected from a military man."

Jack laughed his deep laugh. "Oh, you'll find your share of pompous asses in the ranks of the American Army, J.D. But you'll also find those like Tom Kettle. They say old Zach thinks of him like a son."

"I just hope he can help me."

"If anyone can, it'll be Tom."

Jericho was up early the next morning. He bathed, shaved a sparse beard, then rinsed out his second pair of socks. By that time, he was starved, and as soon as he was joined by Handsome Jack, they hungrily sought out the nearest eating establishment for a breakfast of eggs, steak, biscuits and gravy, washed down with a gallon of black coffee.

Jericho eyed the two remaining biscuits, sighed and pushed his plate toward the middle of the table, leaving it within arms reach.

"I thought I had an appetite, J.D., but feeding you is like pounding sand down a rat hole. There ain't no bottom."

"That's what someone else used to say. She said I'll never be fat though, cause it all goes to energy."

"You got enuff of that, I reckon. I was there when you beat the whey outta that Sikes feller. I didn't see an ounce of quit in ya. I pity anyone if you get the notion in your head that you owe him one. This…person ever say you got a bit of stubbornness in you…and maybe just a streak of mean, too?"

"Nope. Taylor, maybe…not her, though."

When they arrived at Regimental Headquarters they found Major Tom Kettle standing outside the small building speaking among a rough group of well-armed men, none of whom appeared to have shaved nor washed for at least a month. They were all mounted on well-fed horseflesh, sporting saddles decorated with Mexican silver, from which one or more of the fast-firing Walker Colts and rifles hung. Some of the rigs had two rifles attached, a breechloader and a muzzleloader, one under each stirrup. The leader, in tight riding pants, buckskin coat, and an over-sized rawhide hat, was at least six-feet six-inches tall and broad at the shoulders. He was also the loudest. In fact, none of the others seemed to have anything to say, except for Kettle and the giant.

"…killed a dozen of 'em, Tom. You should've seen my boys shoot! Not a round wasted. It'd have made ya proud. Damned if it wouldn't."

"Mordecai come back with you? Captain Hays asked about him."

"That old heathen don't feel comfortable in towns, Tom. You know that. He must've come in yesterday though and left right away, because he dropped Poe off."

As he said the name, the big man gestured toward the only one in the mounted group who appeared to have had a bath and shaved lately. The young man he'd nodded toward whittled away at a small piece of wood, one leg wrapped around his saddle horn, seeming as comfortable as most folks might be in their own living rooms. Poe nodded silently, spit a brown stream into the dust, and went back to his whittling.

Handsome Jack took his time reaching the group, allowing Jericho sufficient time to scrutinize them and reach his own conclusions. Although Jericho suspected from the condition of their clothing and gear that the men had been in the saddle for weeks, none seemed inclined to dismount, appearing relaxed and content to stay atop their mounts. Of one thing he was sure. He'd never seen a tougher bunch in his life – not even Sikes and his skinny sidekick Deeks came close.

Kettle saw them approaching and shouted out a greeting. "Morning, Gentlemen! J.D., this is Captain Wallace of the Ranger Militia."

He went on to make the necessary introductions, then got right down to the business at hand. "Captain Wallace and his company have just returned from three weeks in the field and he tells me there's a small contingent of Zach's troops, commanded by Colonel Roberts, near Nuevo Laredo. They're facing about thirty-five hundred Mexican regulars who are probably trying to cut off our main force and isolate San Antonio. If they succeed, we might well be finished in Texas. I've sent runners out to our other local units and the word is, your brother is with Colonel Roberts."

"How do I find this place, Major?"

"I wouldn't suggest you even try, McCain. That's going to be just about the most dangerous place on God's green earth in a few hours."

He studied Jericho's face for a moment, then sighed.

"I guess you'll be going anyway, huh?"

From the corner of his eye, Kettle saw Handsome Jack smile smugly. Resigned, Kettle went on. "It's about two day's ride on a good horse. But you're likely to run right up the business end of a Mex cavalryman's pike, stumbling around out there alone." He turned to Jack Clay. "Have you been that far south lately, Jack?"

"Once, several months ago. Back then, lots of Kiowa between here and there."

Bigfoot Wallace broke in. "It's the same now, but Mex patrols are thicker than fleas on a hound's arse in the hills around the place. If the Kiowa don't get you, the Mex patrols will, boy. You'll need someone who's been there recently and can weasel their way around them." He turned toward the mounted men and bellowed. "Poe! Front and center!"

The clean-shaven youth stuffed his whittle block into a shirt pocket, slipped from his mount and stood next to Wallace. He was about an inch taller than Jericho and a few pounds heavier. Other than that, nothing remarkable about him. In turn, he sized Jericho up, then offered his hand to him.

"Roosevelt Poe at yore service. Most folks call me Rosie."

"Jericho McCain...J.D., if you like."

Wallace placed his ham-sized hand on Poe's shoulder, who shook it off, appearing uncomfortable by the gesture. It was clear he didn't like to be touched. His action didn't seem to faze the big man.

"Poe here is the best pistol shot in the company, and that says a lot. Fact is, he might be the best natural shot with a handgun I've ever seen. He's also spent the better part of the past month being tutored by Mordecai Jones in the finer points of reading 'sign.' He's your best bet for getting through the Mex lines and finding Colonel Robert's command. When do you plan to leave, McCain?"

"As soon as I can saddle my horse, sir."

Jericho's answer didn't please Poe very much; he still had plans to once more visit the pretty girl he'd met earlier. As he grabbed his horse's reins, he was already figuring how he might finagle a quick stop at Partic's general store before they left.

"Well good luck. You're sure as hell gonna need it."

With Jericho and Poe a half block away, Wallace turned to Handsome Jack. "Your young farmer will likely get my man killed, Handsome Jack. Can he use a gun?"

"Dot your eyes at five hundred paces with that squirrel gun he carries, Bigfoot. Better than average with a sidearm, too. Don't you worry none. He can handle himself just fine. 'Sides, I'm gonna be there to make sure he does."

Handsome Jack smiled and turned on his heel.

As Jericho and Poe passed Hugo Partic's general store, a pretty red-haired girl swept the boardwalk in front. She glanced up, then broke into a broad smile.

"Why, it's Mr. Rosie Poe! And how are you today, kind sir?"

The change that came over young Poe was instant and complete. Gone was the brash youngster Jericho watched as he brushed Bigfoot Wallace's hand from his shoulder with disdain. He'd been replaced by a red-faced, stammering fool of a boy, as unsteady as if he might just trip over his own feet...or his tongue.

"M...morning...Miss P...Polly Farmer. I...I'm just f...fine."

"And who is this you have with you, Rosie Poe? You might at least introduce me to your handsome friend."

This remark brought a sour look to Poe's face, who scowled deeply and buttoned his lip.

Jericho touched the tip of his hat and nodded. "Jericho McCain, Miss Farmer. Pleased t'meet you, Ma'am."

Polly Farmer eyed Jericho coolly. "Well, I didn't know Rosie knew any gentlemen. I can see I was wrong. Won't the two of you come inside and have some Horehound candy?"

Jericho, taken aback, clearly puzzled by her remark. Polly quickly covered her mouth and giggled. From behind her hand, she explained, "Rosie Poe likes Horehound candy. He buys it here all the time. Right Rosie Poe?" Another giggle.

Suddenly, Jericho felt Poe's strong grip on his arm and a sharp tug.

"C'mon, J. D. Let's be on our way. We ain't got time to stand here a jabbering over some old Horehound candy."

Jericho glanced over his shoulder as Poe pulled him along, just in time to see Polly Farmer flash another smile and wave as she entered the store. Poe kept him in tow for nearly a block before Jericho was able to finally jerk his arm free.

Gone to Texas

"Now just what was that all about?"

"What was what all about?"

"All that stuttering and stammering, talking about Horehound candy and such...and jerking my arm pert' near out of joint?"

"Nothing."

"Well, it shore seemed like something to me. Anytime a pretty girl like that comes on all a'smiling and a'flirting like she done... it ain't nothing. No siree. It's something all right. Sure as shooting, it's something! And that's likely to spell misery for some man."

Entering the stables, Poe grabbed his chinch strap and jerked it so hard the mare grunted. He picked up his canteen, stomped outside and filled it from the watering trough. By the time he returned Jericho had saddled his own horse and was tying his bedroll behind it. Looking up, Poe stared at him, a strange look on his face.

"Something eating you?"

Poe attempted to put his foot in the stirrup, missed, then succeeded and swung aboard. "Just stay away from my girl, that's all."

"Your girl? Is that who she is? Your girl? Well, you could've pretty well fooled me about that."

"Well she is! So just stay away from her or I'm liable to thrash you. Hear?"

Jericho visually checked his gear a final time and mounted. Peering from beneath the brim of his hat at Poe, he muttered. "I wouldn't be running right out and buying a wedding suit if I were you."

Poe's face flamed red once more. "I damned well mean it, you...you clod-hopper! Don't make me have to whup you."

With that he spurred his mount and rode out of the stables in a cloud of dust. Jericho sat and stared after him for a full minute, shaking his head in puzzlement and followed.

*   *   *

Poe and Jericho both covered their mount's noses with their hands and watched silently as the platoon of Mexican Cavalry passed below them, finally disappearing from sight. Jericho could see right away that Bigfoot Wallace had been right about Poe's abilities, as far as scouting and tracking was concerned. He surely knew his onions about reading sign, too. A pity he wasn't much of a hand with the ladies.

Poe seemed to have gotten over his mad spell once on the trail. That was just fine with Jericho, who figured they had enough trouble without having a hot young wench like Polly Farmer cause more angst between them. Besides, she seemed like such a child, after…Jean. He hadn't thought about her for almost a month, but suddenly there she was again, just like it was yesterday. He could almost feel her warm hand on his arm as she leaned out of the stagecoach window and smiled her goodbye. At the thought he was instantly sad, then pushed Jean from his mind and concentrated on the business at hand.

"They're gone," Poe said as he swung into the saddle. "Nuevo Laredo is just over that next ridge line. I suppose both sides are trying to save their cannon shot, or you'd heard them by now."

"Have you been in a battle, Roosevelt?"

Poe let the "Roosevelt" slide. He didn't particularly like having someone call him by his first name, but reasoned that there was enough friction between them so he avoided a direct confrontation. However, some retaliation was called for so he replied in kind.

"Bet your boots, Jericho. All of us Rangers have been in it

from the first. Most soldiers don't have the grit it takes to be a ranger though, so they joined up with the regular army where all they have to do is what they're told. Me? I like my freedom, so I became a Ranger."

"What's it like when the cannon balls start falling on you?"

Poe's face grew instantly serious.

"Like Hell, J.D. Just like Lucifer's Hell."

Within the hour, they topped one final ridge and found Colonel Roberts's rag-tag regiment spread sparsely along a lower ridgeline a hundred feet below. Poe instinctively headed toward a clump of standing men, periodically staring through a spyglass at the terrain across the valley. A big man in a mixed uniform with colonel's insignia, ceased talking, and stared at them as they approached. The others, taking a cue from their leader, did likewise. Poe gave what probably passed as a salute among the rangers, but caused the other officers nearby to grow red in the face. Roberts appearing not to notice, returned the cocky salute.

Before any could speak, a galloping horse drew their attention. They looked back to see Handsome Jack Clay rein up beside them. Like Jericho and Poe, he was covered with trail dust and parched from hard riding.

"Where did...?" Jericho started.

"Covering your backs, is all," he answered. "Just followed along behind in case you young fellows ran into trouble. Figured I could give you some covering fire to get away, if you did."

Colonel Roberts's face beamed brightly and he bellowed, "Handsome Jack Clay! You scoundrel! What are you doing hanging around with us regular army types?"

Handsome Jack swung down and the two men grasped hands warmly. Then he said, "These two fellows are traveling with me, Colonel. This is Ranger Poe, and the other is Jericho McCain. It's a long story, but young McCain came all the way from Tennessee to tell his brother about the death of their parents and baby sister. We think his brother, Taylor McCain is with you."

At the mention of Taylor's name, a slender young man holding a long-barrel rifle stepped from the group of officers.

"My name's Johnson. I know your brother, Mr. McCain." Johnson looked at Colonel Roberts and said, "He's with Captain Park's company, sir."

Jericho didn't particularly like the look on Robert's face. "Where's my brother, Colonel?"

Colonel Roberts's face clouded for an instant, then he motioned for Jericho to follow him. They walked alone to a large boulder on the lip of the ridge. He stared at a small battered church on the valley floor, where several hundred men in bright uniforms were charging at the building from three sides. They watched as the attackers fell back, bodies littering the battlefield, then they'd tenaciously regroup and rushed the small church again. He slowly raised his arm, pointing.

"Your brother's down there, lad."

Jericho watched the carnage for a full minute and when he faced Colonel Roberts again, his voice was hoarse.

"Why don't you get him out of there?"

"Can't. We're outnumbered four to one. Our mission is to delay them until General Taylor can get into a blocking position. We go charging down there in full force, the Mex Cavalry flanks us and gets us in a crossfire. If I send a smaller group, they end up like your brother's bunch – cut off and hacked to pieces as soon as their ammo is gone. Your brother's group needs ammo real bad right about now. The problem is, I can't order any of these men to go down there with a resupply, cause I'd be sending them to their deaths as certain as we're standing here."

He saw the horrified look on Jericho's face, and hurriedly went on.

"It's a bitter pill to swallow, lad...to stand by and watch family killed. But you've no choice in the matter...and neither do I. If General Lupa's force gets by us here, there's nothing between here and San Antonio to stop them until General Taylor gets in position. There's women and children in San Antonio. After what Santa Anna did to the defenders of the Alamo, I hate to think what would happen to them if we can't hold them here. Zack Taylor needs one, maybe two days to reach the Duck Bill and set up defensive positions. I intend to give him that time...even if nobody walks away from here."

"What can be done for my brother then, Colonel?"

"Nothing."

"What if they get the ammo they need?"

"That can only prolong it for a while. Maybe let them kill a few more of Lupa's men before they're overrun. But in the end, it'll all be the same."

"Get that ammo ready, Colonel. I'll take it with me when I go."

Roberts stared at the slender youth before him, saw the steady determination in his eyes and knew further discussion would be fruitless. He sighed, his eyes sad.

"Aye, lad. I'll get it packed."

* * *

A thunderous percussion jarred them just as they reached the others. The Mexican Army had finally figured out a way to get their cannon up the steep slope across the valley and began to fire on the small church. Their first shot had been wide by fifty yards, but the gun crew was making rapid adjustments.

Roberts bellowed in Jericho's ear.

"Johnson! Memory Johnson! Front and center!"

The young man who had spoken earlier ran to stand beside them. He held a long-barrel rifle with peculiar hand-made sights. The rifle was old, but appeared clean and well oiled.

Roberts pointed at the enemy gunners.

"Can you hit them from here, Johnson?"

Johnson was already pouring extra powder into his rifle as he replied. "If I do, sir, it'll be the best shot I ever made."

He flopped behind a flat rock and breathed deeply, letting it out. Then he breathed deeply again and let half of it out, paused and squeezed his trigger. After what seemed like an especially long time, the major spotting with his telescope shouted, "Short by fifty feet, and to the right by ten."

Another attempt showed little improvement and the cannon boomed again, this time caving in a portion of the chapel's roof and blowing a large gap in one wall.

Roberts shook his big head sadly.

"Too late, lad. Too damned late."

Jericho didn't answer. Instead, he rapidly walked back to the horses, pulled his long-rifle from its scabbard, checked its prime, and added extra powder. Squatting briefly, he scooped up a handful of fine dust and clutching it tightly, returned to the large rock. Opening his hand, he let the dust drift in the slight breeze, then stuck a finger in his mouth and held it in the air for an instant. Apparently satisfied, he dropped into the spot vacated by Johnson earlier and slowly took aim.

Gone to Texas

"Foolishness," Roberts swore, stomping halfway up the incline, then pausing, looked back. Fascinated, he watched Jericho elevate his rifle's barrel well over the point of aim for the target, as if he were shooting at a hawk...then almost nonchalantly, squeezing the trigger. The roar of the old rifle was followed by silence along the line of men. They waited as the heavy round traveled the remarkably long distance across the valley...then the man swabbing the cannon's barrel clutched his chest and crumpled to the ground.

A cheer arose from the ranks of the Texans, then another as Jericho quickly reloaded and fired again. This time he missed hitting anyone, but the round careened off the cannon's barrel. That appeared to be too much for the gun's commander, who led the gun crew's retreat back up the rocky slope – leaving the cannon deserted.

Memory Johnson was suddenly thumping Jericho on the back and pumping his arm up and down as he shouted, "My God! I've never seen such a shot! That's got to be half a mile! My God! That must be that Kentucky windage I've heard you mountain folks use."

Roberts began screaming at his staff to get ammo packed for Taylor's group in the church, as Jericho rejoined Jack Clay and Poe.

Poe spit and cocked an eye.

"Fair shot."

"Best I ever made."

"Missed your second, though."

"Missed my first, too."

Poe looked puzzled, so Jericho grinned sheepishly and explained. "I was aiming for the gun's commander...further up the hill."

Poe broke into a broad grin, then a chuckle as he slapped his leg with his dusty hat.

A ragged private ran up leading a skinny mule loaded with powder and a wooden ammo box. The scared soldier, his eyes darting as if he'd be much happier if someplace else, preferably far away. The ornery critter loaded down with ammunition and water didn't look too pleased either, kicking at him and anyone else coming into range.

Jericho calmed his stallion by rubbing his nose, then mounted and checked his pistols. He twisted about in the saddle as he heard a stir behind him. It was Poe who had also mounted.

"Where you going?"

Poe grinned and spit.

"These regular army soldiers walk around so stiff they make my arse itch. Thought I'd keep you company, if you don't mind."

"Know anything about mules?"

"Rode one all the way from Missouri. If you want him to run, I'll get him to run."

"Good enough. Ready?"

Poe spit a wad into the dust, yanking his hat down tighter.

"Let's dance."

Handsome Jack Clay joined them in a cloud of dust and debris before they were halfway down the steep slope, riding full speed.

"Thought I'd come along and watch your backs," he yelled over the rushing wind.

Jericho was scared, his heart pounding in his throat, his mouth like cotton. It was worse than having to face Sikes and Deeks alone. At least, he had known then what he was up against. There might be thousands of Mexican soldiers out of sight in the hills just beyond him.

Gone to Texas

Well, what the hell! Tay's in there...if he's still alive...and he's my brother.

The Mexican Cavalry spotted them before they were halfway to the small church, but taken completely by surprise, they had difficulty getting everyone mounted. Only twenty-five of the regiment's better horsemen were able to intercept them, less than three hundred yards from church. With their sabers and flintlock pistols, the Mexicans were totally unprepared for the firepower unleashed upon them. Jericho, Handsome Jack and Poe rode fast, bridle reins held tightly in their teeth. Slamming into the saber-wielding front line of the advancing cavalry, they spewed death into their ranks with both hands. In less than a minute the ground was littered with the colorful uniforms of fallen dead and wounded, and as a path miraculously opened for the three men, the remaining horse soldiers beat a wild and undisciplined retreat.

Dust clouds billowing, Jericho slid his horse to a halt near the gap in the wall blown out by an earlier cannonball. There was only room for one animal inside the small church, so he and Poe dismounted and pushed against the mule's flanks, which stubbornly refused to budge. Poe finally stuck the hot barrel of his Colt against the mule's flank. It brayed loudly and jumped inside.

Poe grinned at Jericho, his teeth white against his dusty face. "Told ya I know how to handle mules."

Jack Clay, who had been providing cover fire, bolted from his saddle and swatted their mounts back toward the American lines as the few capable men left inside fired into the backs of the retreating cavalry. It was over in less than a minute. Suddenly the battlefield was clear, except for dead and dying Mexican soldiers.

Jericho ran inside and pulled a knot loose from the mule's pack, allowing one of the ammo boxes to drop. It split open, spilling smaller boxes onto the stone floor.

"We brought powder, lead, water and some medicine! The rest is in the other bundle! Get it quick before that blasted mule bolts on us!"

A mad scamper ensued to subdue the braying, kicking mule, and to unload its contents, and it took nearly all of the able bodied men to accomplish the task. Only one man stood frozen in place, staring at Jericho as he fired off orders to the other men. In mid-sentence Jericho paused, ceased shouting, and stared back. The face blackened from firing rounds of black powder and he'd gain a full thirty-five pounds of muscle, but Jericho's eyes met those of his older brother, Taylor McCain. He had failed to recognize his own brother under all the dust and grime. In two giant steps, they had their arms around the other, hands pounding against backs.

"You young fool! Why the hell did you come here?"

There were tears in Taylor's eyes as he scolded his younger brother.

"Came to get your butt out of this mess, big brother. Pa always told us to look out for each other."

"I wish you hadn't come, Jericho. But, God, you're a sight for sore eyes! How are Ma and Pa – and Sis?"

Taylor knew instantly something was amiss, for Jericho's smile froze and he stepped back.

"What happened?" he asked again. The pain he saw in Jericho's face told him all he really needed to know, but he waited for his brother's answer.

"It was the fever, Tay. Pa caught it from old man Hobbs,

brought it back to the farm, and they were all dead in two days. I thought at first it would skip Pa and me but in the end, he just kind of gave up, too. I buried them all under the big Maple near the cabin and came looking for you. It's been more than a year now, and I've been looking for you ever since. You didn't write so I didn't even know where to start…except for Texas."

Taylor looked ill at ease.

"Well I've been sort 'a busy."

"I can see that. Never figured you for an army man. Pa said you'd never have the discipline for that."

"He was probably right. I just kind 'a got caught up in all this Texas spirit and was swept along. I wish I had been with them when…."

A shot rang out and a skinny tow-headed youth with corporal stripes shouted, "Here they come again!"

Twelve

BY MIDDAY, POLLY AND her dad arrived at the property he'd purchased sight unseen prior to leaving their home in Ohio for Texas. It was clear he was proud of his decision, once he'd actually seen it. Her mother had arose early and packed a lunch for them, which Polly spread out on a table cloth under a small willow tree. Her father walked about, poking into the soil with a silly grin. Repeatedly, he'd point out the spots he intended to build their house, a barn, and dig a well. Nestled in a small valley beside a running creek, aligned with pecan and willow trees along its banks, surrounded by rolling hills, Polly had to admit it was a beautiful place.

As John Farmer paced off plots on the land, periodically pausing, kneeling to sift a handful of dirt through his fingers, Polly's thoughts returned to the two young men she'd met earlier at the store.

Rosie Poe. Quite good-looking, but what a silly name for a man.

He did seem awfully nice though, and she sensed under all the bashfulness that he was brash and confident – perhaps even daring. He'd have to be as a member of the Ranger Militia. Talk all around town was rampant about their exploits and heroics against the Mexicans, Indians and outlaws. He might even be...romantic.

Jericho McCain, however, why he was something else altogether. He actually disturbed her. Handsome as sin, but not

Gone to Texas

open and honest like Rosie Poe. Something hidden deep inside, maybe missing altogether – or perhaps just a great sadness she detected.

Her father had once taken her to see a play with the renowned English actor, Sir Charles Blighton, when she was eleven. Sir Charles played the role of a secretive and exceedingly dangerous man. She mostly recalled each time he came on stage, the music struck a certain tone to make the audience aware of his potential danger. When she'd looked into the calm eyes of Jericho McCain, she could sense that same tone of music…danger ahead.

Nonetheless, dangerous or not, Jericho McCain was definitely the most interesting of the two. Polly smiled.

* * *

They'd beaten back two more all-out attacks by the Mexican infantry before the enemy commander had finally managed to hoist three of his artillery pieces up the steep slope to the top of the ridge. They finally had the deadly fire needed to breech the small church's defenses. The outcome a foregone conclusion. The small but deadly guns rained death and destruction upon the fortified church for forty minutes, while the Texans on the far ridgeline watched and fret.

At last, the cannon fire lifted and a few disheveled figures could miraculously be seen crawling from the rubble. The major with his telescope pronounced their identities.

"Looks like the two McCain brothers, though one appears to be badly wounded. Handsome Jack Clay is there, and Ranger Poe…young Thomas too, and that big guy from Arkansas… Holloway, I believe his name is."

The major lowered his eyeglass but continued staring at the

valley. "That's all of 'em. Out of the original fifty men who went up that ridge, six are all that's left."

The Texans saw the small group of prisoners herded over the bloody ridge – back into Mexico.

* * *

The days had been unbearably hot and their captors provided them almost no water until the evening stop. Even then, they were not fed. The nights in Mexico proved to be bitterly cold, causing the six captives to huddle together for body warmth. Jericho spooned his body against his wounded brother's back and thought about the warm woolen blanket he'd left among the other articles on his horse. In a way, he was glad they had sent the horses with their gear trotting back toward the American lines. Otherwise, their captors would now be the beneficiaries of its warmth, and in possession of his new Walker Colts and rifle.

He'd been allowed to doctor the youngster Thomas's wound after the evening camp had been established, and what he saw worried him greatly. The shrapnel had passed through his right shoulder and exited under his right shoulder blade. While it had bled little, it was purple and ugly. Jericho had seen enough such wounds to know if it didn't get proper medical attention soon, Thomas would die. He'd attempted to seek help from his captors and received a beating for his efforts. One of the guards struck his face with his rifle butt, and if Jericho had been just a fraction of an instant slower, he'd likely have lost an eye. As it was, the left side of his face was swollen and discolored.

Taylor was his main concern, however. Taylor was blind. One of the cannonballs had collapsed a portion of the wall onto him and when Jericho and Poe had finally dug him out, his chest was severely bruised. Only later as they prepared to move out, did they discover he couldn't see. Jericho assured him it was temporary, but now...well, he just didn't know. He was certain Taylor had several cracked or broken ribs, and he had bandaged them tightly with his long john tops. He didn't know if anything else had been crushed or damaged inside, – or if the blindness was permanent.

What the hell were he and Taylor doing in a place like this? Killing people they didn't even know, probably just end up getting killed by them in return. What was the sense of it all?

He had to find a way to get himself and his brother out of this mess. Taylor, sleeping restfully beside him, grunted, stopped breathing for just an instant then breathed regularly once more.

Jericho didn't like the way Taylor's breaths rattled each time he exhaled either. The breaths like bubbles deep inside him. Carefully, not to alarm the guards whom had convinced them early on that they would shoot their prisoners at the slightest provocation, Jericho unbuttoned his denim shirt and pulled it partially over his sleeping brother. He laid his head against Taylor's broad back, closing his eyes. Although totally exhausted, sleep was a long time in coming.

Young Thomas, who had been wounded even more severely than Taylor, groaned loudly in his unconscious slumber. One of the Mexican guards grunted a derisive comment from a nearby shadowed area. The other guard laughed sharply. In the early morning hours, he finally slept.

At daybreak, they were kicked awake; each received two flour tortillas and a cup of water, which they eagerly consumed, convinced it would be their last until the evening stop. As Jericho fed his brother, Taylor spoke from behind the dirty bandages covering his eyes.

"One hell of a fix I've gotten us into. Hey, little brother?"

"Shut up before I eat your tortillas, too."

Jericho tore off another chunk of the sticky pancake and fed it to Taylor, then holding the canteen cup to his brother's lips, allowed him to sip.

"First chance you get little brother, you skedaddle, ya hear? Don't worry about me. They're probably taking me and Thomas back to a field hospital."

"Uh huh."

He stuck another bite of the tortilla under Taylor's nose; he turned his head stubbornly.

"Dammit, Jericho, I mean it. Pa's gone now so that makes me the boss. You get out and that's the end of it."

"Quit jumping around before you damage something inside. I've got to think and I can't do it with you cussing up a storm."

"Jericho....!"

"*Vamoose, vamoose*! *No hablar*! Hurry!"

Their two guards suddenly appeared and began to poke at them with their rifle barrels, prodding them to their feet. Jericho had secretly named the guards Ratface and The Pig. Ratface, like his namesake, had a sharp, angular face with half-dozen stringy hairs growing to each side of his long, humped nose. His button bright eyes constantly shifted side-to-side as if searching for a way to flee…or to attack. The Pig was forty pounds overweight and absolutely filthy. With small mean eyes, he tended to grunt a lot, too. Jericho sensed the only reason their two guards didn't kill them outright, was because they'd been ordered not to by their superiors. Maybe the officers had other plans for them, still convinced that anyone slowing the column down would be instantly dispatched in the most expedient manner, left on the trail for the coyotes.

Thomas couldn't stand by himself and when Poe and Handsome Jack saw the guards discussing his condition, they'd quickly pull him to his feet and half carry, half drag him with them. Concerned for his brother's safety, Jericho grasped Taylor's elbow to help steady him, leading him up the rocky trail. Holloway paused long enough to grab the uneaten portion of Taylor's tortilla from the dust, stuffed it into his own mouth, then helped with the injured brother.

The sun was at its hottest just after the mid-day rest stop, when their attempts to get Thomas on his feet finally failed. Despite repeated attempts to hoist his limp body to a standing position, he remained on his back, eyes glazed, breathing shallowly through his half-open mouth. The young southern boy had clearly gone as far as he could. The others watched in fixed horror as the Mexican captain spoke briefly to their guards, saw them salute with the customary "*Si, Capitan.*" They chased the other prisoners away with their bayonets then dragged Thomas to the side of the trail. He made only a small whooshing sound as they both punctured him repeatedly with their long bayonets. Finished, they continued to stand over his bloody body, seemingly disappointed that he hadn't been more aware of the act. Nonetheless, they'd appeared to take great pleasure in the sport. After that, Jericho never left Taylor's side.

His brother had grown more drawn and weakened, each step requiring great effort just to maintain his balance. Jericho stumbled through ankle deep sand dust, over rocky stretches, supporting more than half his brother's weight at any one time.

However, the difficult journey had taken its toll on him and severely weakened by the ordeal, he was also near collapse. Suddenly, Poe and Handsome Jack, their burden lifted now that Thomas had been killed, were at his side. They carefully removed Taylor's arms from around his shoulder, and carried the blind man between them. Tears of gratitude flooded Jericho's eyes as he stumbled along behind them.

By the fourth day, after the prisoners had gone as far as they could possibly go, the column halted at a small Mission near a shallow river called Rio El Perro, River of the Dog. There, the commander ordered his soldiers to set up camp. He appeared to be waiting for something or someone. Jericho didn't know what his motive might be, but he was grateful they'd be able to rest for a while, thus allowing Taylor time to regain his strength.

He'd counted forty-six foot soldiers in the column; only the Captain was mounted. Earlier, he'd overheard one of the sergeants refer to him as Capitan Cruz. Cruz was one of the privileged class found in abundance in the Mexican officer corps. Jericho speculated he was wealthy, educated, and one who held his rank as a political appointee rather than from experience or military training. He possessed the refined good looks of Mexico's early settlers – pure Spanish bloodlines – a legacy of their Castellan conquerors. His uniform immaculate. Four beautiful women accompanied him.

With his apparent education, Jericho had hoped he might show compassion toward the captives, providing them with medical attention and comfort items once the long march was over. Any expectations quickly dashed. Upon their arrival at the new camp by the river, they'd been thrown into an old meat-curing house, reeking of carcasses long ago devoured by the mission workers. A one-gallon bucket in the corner the only concession to their comfort. Soon even that would be denied, as it was already nearly half-full. It was clear Cruz hated the "Gringos" with a fierce passion, never failing to humiliate or torment them at any opportunity. At their first meeting, he'd ordered Holloway to wipe his boots clean of the thick trail dust. Holloway refused and was beaten with the captain's riding-crop until he couldn't stand.

While grateful for the halt, Jericho was nonetheless concerned about the extra time Cruz could now devote toward his bedevilment of them. The prisoners knew their time was quickly running out; Jericho spent his every waking moment searching for a weakness in the guard's security. So far he'd been disappointed.

Poe watched Jericho wipe the trail grime from around his brother's milky eyes with his ragged bandana, then gently replace the dirty cloth that covered them from future dirt. He'd correctly assumed that it was best to hide Taylor's embarrassing blindness. The tenderness the youngster administered to his older brother caused a sharp ping deep inside Poe's physic. Perhaps a forgotten memory from when he was just a baby, of a father, brother or uncle who had taken a moment to show an act of kindness. He quickly brushed it away. It'd been so long ago that he couldn't really remember it. He passed off other memories, how it'd been as he got older; a gentle mother who'd married a mean-spirited man, brought him home, and informed him he was now his stepfather.

Poe endured eight hard years under the rule of his stepfather's iron hand. The day after his mother was buried he'd dared his stepfather to just try and stop him, then left Ohio and struck out for a wild untamed land he'd only heard rumors of, south, near

Mexico. Gone to Texas, he'd joined the exodus along with thousands of others seeking a better life. He'd been fifteen.

He'd lived by his wits for the next three years, mostly laboring for food when he could find work; stealing it when he couldn't. Somewhere along the line he'd stumbled across an old pistol and the moment he picked it up, he'd been changed forever. Remembering it, he almost always smiled. The damned thing had seemed like a natural protrusion of his hand. Hitting a target as simple as pointing at it. He was what James Butler Hickcock would call him after meeting him years later; a born natural shootist.

Shooting came as natural to him as breathing. Either hand. Conscience wasn't a big hindrance with him either. He figured any man who took after another with a loaded weapon usually got what he deserved…and he wasn't about to lose any sleep if it just happened to be him that dished it out. Oh, that didn't mean that his first couple of shootouts hadn't unnerved him to a certain extent, to the point of causing him a few bad dreams. But he'd quickly overcome that sensation, an innate feeling that he'd eventually die by something other than a bullet, anyway. Now, he wasn't so sure.

That young McCain was another man who could shoot! His shot with the rifle was the best he'd ever seen. Not two…three men in the world could have made that shot, and he'd seen others by McCain at the church that had convinced him that his first shot was more than just a lucky hit. The youngster wasn't bad with a Colt either. Maybe not as good as himself, but better than nine out of ten men who considered themselves gunhands. His sense about McCain, Poe figured, was no matter how skilled others might be with a gun, if that young man ever got it into his head to kill you, Poe felt he wouldn't be stopped until he'd done just that!

Gone to Texas

Mordecai Jones had told him about a man named Sam Buffer who'd been shot more than a dozen times by the three McKenzie brothers. Jones claimed he'd witnessed the whole thing and swore that Buffer was dead on his feet, but still managed to kill all three of the brothers with an axe before laying down to make it legitimate. He picked up the same determination and resilience in Jericho McCain. He wondered if they'd have a chance to become friends.

The following morning another column of Mexican infantry, accompanied by a troop of cavalry, arrived with a somber swarthy officer riding in front. Six pretty *señoritas* trailed along behind him in a fancy carriage. The prisoners speculated that with his magnificent uniform and arrogance in his saddle, he had to be at least a general. He was. It was his Excellency, General Santa Anna. General of the Mexican Republic's armies. Jericho heard his name whispered by one of the guards and shuddered. Many in Texas had heard of the extreme cruelty dealt by the general to the few survivors of the Alamo. There wasn't a Texan who didn't hate him with a vengeance – now, they were his prisoners. May God help them.

The arrival of Santa Anna was cause for great celebration among the troops. They confiscated all the livestock owned by the small mission, and the commander broke out rum and tequila for his soldiers. By mid-afternoon, they were all drunk, including Captain Cruz and his Excellency, General Santa Anna. The prisoners sat quietly in the confines of the smelly locked room and whispered among themselves, convinced the festivities didn't bode well for them.

Just before dusk, startled by the sound of the heavy door being unlatched from outside, their two scruffy guards entered, followed by Captain Cruz. Although the commander's eyes were bloodshot and red, his uniform was still immaculate. The group stood silently for a few moments, then Cruz pointed at Holloway.

"That one. Take him."

Rat Face and the Pig stepped forward and quickly bound the big man's hands behind him. Cruz paused in front of Jericho and his brother, a half-smile lingering at his lips.

"So, *dos hermanos* — two brothers. Which of you would willingly give up his life for the other? I wonder how deeply brotherly love goes. I shall leave that question up to you. In five minutes I will return. You must decide which of you will go with me for the General's pleasure. If you have not decided by the time I return, I will take both of you. *Cinco minutos, Gringos!*"

He spun on his heel and marched smartly out the door, followed by the guards pushing the bound Holloway before them.

Holloway yelled over his shoulder as he was being dragged away by the guards.

"I won't be coming back, boys. They mean to do me sure as hell! God bless Texas!"

As Holloway's echoes drifted away, they sat silently, afraid to meet the others' eyes. Taylor pulled himself to his feet first and stood with his head toward the door.

"I'll go."

"No!"

Jericho jumped to his feet to stand beside his brother.

"I'll die fighting them right here in this cell before I'll let them take you, Tay!"

Taylor smiled in the direction of his brother's voice. "Listen, J.D."

Lately, Taylor had picked up Handsome Jack's habit of using

his initials instead of his given name. "There's more at stake here than just the four of us. Tell him, Jack."

Jericho turned to Handsome Jack, seeking his friend's help; clearly puzzled by Taylor's words.

"He's right, J.D. Didn't tell you before 'cause I figured you might act differently around me if you knew – perhaps give me away. I speak Mex 'bout as well as old Santa Anna himself. Kept it a secret so's I could find out what they had in store for us. I only let Taylor know this after we moved in last night, 'cause I saw something like this coming. I wanted someone else to know what I'd heard, in case we got separated...or something like this happened."

Poe moved closer to stand beside Jericho and his brother, listening intently.

Handsome Jack lowered his voice.

"I heard some of the new bunch telling our guards that Santa Anna's main force is setting about twenty-five miles from here, just south of the Rio. All that ruckus at the church was a lead dollar, a diversion to throw a scare into Zach Taylor and have him cut out of San Antonio to try and help Colonel Roberts. When he's far enough away that he can't get back in time to help, Santa Anna plans to ride into San Antonio unopposed, kill every man, woman and child, burn the place down, then swoop a wide circle and do the same to the countryside. Then get back before Zach can turn around. Most of Zach's ammo and supplies are stored at San Antonio so he'll be in a bad situation if he loses it. When he finally returns to confront Santa Anna's bunch, they'll be in the positions they've already dug along the valley wall on this side of the Rio Grande. When he attacks, the rest of Santa Anna's army near the old church...the six regiments that didn't show themselves to Robert's force... will catch Zach's forces in a pincher movement – and that'll be the end of the Texas dream."

To a man, the others looked stricken.

"They still ain't taking my brother." Jericho was adamant.

Jack laid his hand on Jericho's shoulder.

"J.D., think about it clearly. Without you, Taylor can't survive. Without him, you might. It's a matter of basic survival. One of us has to get back and let Old Rough 'n Ready know about Santa Anna's plans. If we don't, four hundred civilians will die, as well as most of the Texas Republic's army."

Jack laughed shortly and turned away.

"Hell, we may all die right here, anyway."

Taylor touched Jericho's arm lightly.

"He's right, little brother. It has to be me. I can't run with you and I won't hold you back. This is the only way."

For the first time since he'd buried his family, Jericho felt hot tears rolling down his dirty face. "Aw heck, Tay. Aw, heck!"

He felt Taylor's arm wrap around his shoulders and they stood clinched together until the heavy door clanged open once more; Captain Cruz walked in, the tight cruel smile still on his lips. Rat Face, rattling a chain with two iron bracelets followed him. Additional guards stood just outside the door, pointing their rifles at the four prisoners.

"Well, which brave brother will it be?"

Taylor stepped forward, ripping the dirty rag from his eyes. The milky stare, though empty, seemed to radiate hatred.

"Me, you smelly bastard. When this war is over the Texans will hang you and your fat general, side-by-side."

Cruz's face flamed. He nodded to Rat Face who jumped forward, roughly forcing Taylor's hands behind his back. The sound of the snapping of the wrist clamps loud and final. As Rat Face pushed Taylor before him, Cruz smiled once more and said, "Rest well. Tomorrow the General may require more entertainment."

He started out, then paused and turned.

"If you care to look out the slot in the door, you can see what will be in store for you tomorrow."

Jericho lunged at him but was instantly restrained by Jack and Poe. Held fast he screamed, "I'll kill you...you greasy bastard! I will personally cut off your head with a rusty knife!"

The door slammed in his face, loud and final. He sank to his knees, silent tears streaming down his face.

* * *

It'd been over an hour and still the three men stood with their eyes glued to the small slot in the smoke-house door, watching Holloway and Taylor labor in the mid-day sun as they each dug a deep narrow hole in the loose sandy soil. Neither had headgear and their backs had burned a deep lobster red in just that short period of time. A tent shelter opposite from the smokehouse, seated General Santa Anna, Captain Cruz and their women, protected from the scorching sun. Two enlisted men fanned them. Other officers seated behind the guests of honor, sipped drinks in the shade and laughed as they waited for the festivities to begin. The rest of the regiment's soldiers, most of them already drunk, and numerous local villagers, lined a makeshift parade ground. All appeared to be enjoying themselves immensely. The holes Taylor and Holloway were digging, placed in the exact center of the long, narrow courtyard.

Suddenly, Cruz shouted a command and several armed soldiers approached Taylor. Two of them grabbed his arms, bound them, and lowered him into one of the holes. After a short heated exchange, Holloway spit at the boots of a guard and jumped into the other hole, his cuss words drifting back to them in the stifling heat.

"Santa Anna, you son of a *puta*! The Texans are on their way and you can't stop 'em. They're going to cut yore *cajones* off and feed 'em to that sweet smelling Captain sitting beside you. I'll be waiting in Hell for you when you arrive, you greasy *bastardos*!"

The holes were so deep that with the dirt mounded up around them, the three observers could not see their friend's heads. Using their boots, two of the guards kicked dirt into the holes until they were filled, then smoothed the dusty soil level so that only the heads of the two men showed above the ground. From that distance, they looked like two of the pumpkins Jericho and his pa used to raise in the cool sweet mountain air of the Appalachians. Sick, he closed his eyes, trembling in horror as he realized what was about to happen.

A loud cheer from the crowd caused him to snap his eyes open again, despite himself. A squad of Mexican Lancers in colorful dress uniforms, had lined up at the far end of the courtyard, gallant in their flashy attire. Each of them held one of the ten-foot lances the Texans called "pig stickers" and even from that distance, they appeared wickedly sharp and evil. A cavalry sergeant and a portly well-dressed villager stood just to the left of the tent where the General's entourage relaxed. The sergeant held a metal pot and a sturdy wooden spoon; the villager, a pocket watch. The crowd grew silent in anticipation…then the silence was shattered by a loud clang as the sergeant struck the pot with his club.

Gone to Texas

At the signal, one of the Lancers spurred his horse savagely and charged toward the two buried men. At the halfway point, he lowered his lance and his intentions became vividly clear to everyone watching. A collective cheer arose from the crowd, as Jericho closed his eyes again and slumped to the floor. Another, much louder cheer went up from the crowd.

"Did he...?"

"Nope. Missed."

Unable to restrain himself, Jericho scampered to his feet and stared out through the slot. A broken lance protruded a scant foot from Holloway's head. The villager with the watch shouted out the time, then waddled over and measured the distance, which he also shouted to the audience. His chore finished, he hurried back to join the sergeant, who clanged the pot again as another Lancer charged toward the doomed men, this time toward Taylor. He also missed by inches. Not until the last man in the squad charged, did any of them draw blood when he cleanly severed Holloway's left ear from his head. Blood spurted from a deep gash on the side of his head that had almost taken out his right eye, a bright red gusher spewed onto the thirsty ground. Flies quickly converged on the wound in the hot afternoon sun as the squad galloped to the reviewing stand where the General rewarded the lancer who had cut off Holloway's ear. As a bugle sounded, the mounted men exited the field as another squad of Lancers lined up to take their turn.

The three watching men slumped to the dirty floor and sat with their backs to the cool wall. They knew the squads would keep coming until their comrades were dead...then, they would be coming for the rest of them. After listening to the sound of repeated charges by the individual Lancers, a loud cheer suddenly went up from the crowd and Poe sprang to his feet to peer out. He stared quietly for a full minute, then returned to his place on the floor.

"Holloway. One of 'em ran his pig sticker right through his eye. He's surely dead. May God bless him."

Jericho slowly looked up from where he sat, hugging his knees. "Taylor?" he whispered.

"He's alive. Saw him move a little...but he's wounded some, I reckon."

They heard the loud clang of the old pot and each lapsed into the silence of their personal horror-ridden thoughts.

* * *

It had been nearly dark by the time the festive crowd dispersed hours earlier. Still the three men remained huddled on the dirty smokehouse floor, where they had been for most of the day. None moved, and in the darkness of the small room, Jericho supposed the others were sleeping. He didn't know for sure because they breathed shallowly, unmoving as he'd been for hours. He felt listless and dazed – sick enough to vomit but not feeling as if he could move to do so. So he sat and waited...like the others.

The sturdy door latch clanked as it opened and Rat Face and the Pig stumbled in, their first slurred words affirming them to be as drunk as they both appeared. Each carried heavy chains with metal clamps attached to the ends, the same as they had used on Holloway and Taylor earlier.

"Hey, *Gringos*! You sleeping?"

None of them moved. Rat Face kicked at Handsome Jack's leg, missed, and stumbled against the wall where he remained, breathing deeply through his mouth. Trying to right himself, he shouted, "Come on, *Gringos*. Get up. El Capitan Cruz wants you to dig up the garbage in the parade field. Then dig more holes so the three of you can start training his Lancers early tomorrow morning."

This time the Pig kicked Poe's leg and he reacted in a flash. Poe grabbed the Pig's extended leg, jerked it viciously upward, and pulled the startled guard to the dirty floor. Quick as a wink, Poe wrapped the chain around the fat man's neck and clamped down. As drunk as he was, Rat Face's befuddled mind told him something was amiss as he struggled to push away from the wall. He staggered again and tripped over Handsome Jack's conveniently outstretched foot. It would be his last mistake. He strained to suck air past his own chain tightly held by Handsome Jack, as it cut deeply into his windpipe. After a few moments of silent struggles, both men abruptly stopped kicking. Poe rose silently, moved to the door which stood partly ajar. He peeked out, then closed it nearly shut.

"Looks like the party's over, and the kids have all turned in."

Handsome Jack tossed him one of the rifles, keeping the other for himself. Jericho pulled the old bayonet from Rat Face's scabbard and stuck it under his belt. Jack motioned them around him in the center of the floor. He whispered as he drew a map in the dirt, pointing.

"I figure we're about here, at least fifty miles inside Mexico. If we follow the North Star until we hit the Rio, then bear off easterly, we'll eventually get to San Antonio. We'll have a better chance if we stay together, so let's get started."

"I'll catch up."

It was Jericho.

Jack stood and glared down at Jericho who'd remained seated.

"No! We stay together!"

Jericho rose and stared calmly back. Jack had seen that look before and he didn't like it.

"Look, Jack. I owe you. But I'm not in your army. I'm a free man and I'll go where I want. I have something important to do…then, maybe I'll join your fight."

"What would that be?"

When Jericho didn't answer right away, a realization slowly spread across Handsome Jack's face.

"Oh no. Tell me it's not true. You're not thinking of going after Cruz? Are you out of your mind? There's two hundred soldiers out there. Hell, we'll be lucky if we even make it out of here, let alone seek vengeance on a scum-sucking pig like Cruz – no matter how much he deserves it."

"Mind's made up, Jack."

"Well that's just dandy! Bull puddles!"

He sounded resigned to the fact he couldn't change his young protégée's mind. After all, he'd seen the stubborn streak in Jericho McCain when he'd steadfastly traveled into the lion's den to track down the men who'd harmed his lady friend. He knew without a doubt there would be no changing the young man's mind in this matter either.

He finally just sighed, and then nodded. "Well then, come on Rosy. Let's put some trail between us and this place before this young fool stirs everything up so bad we can't get out."

Poe stood near the door, looking out. In the dark he heard Poe spit.

"Reckon I'll have to catch up, too."

Handsome Jack turned to face Poe, his hands on his hips, perplexed. Quietly, he said, "You too?"

"Nobody does something like that to two of my friends, then just walks away."

Handsome Jack's shoulders slumped in defeat.

"What do you two plan to do?"

Poe jerked his head toward Jericho.

"It's J.D.'s party. I just came to dance."

They slipped out of the darkness of the door into bright moonlight, but a cloud quickly obscured the half-moon again. Before it darkened, Jericho paused to stare across the deserted parade field at the two dark objects in its center. He felt Poe at his shoulder.

"Come on, Pard," he whispered softly. "You can't help him now."

* * *

The officers slept in tents, off to themselves. The enlisted men usually slept wherever they could find a comfortable place to spread a single blanket. This night, men were scattered around, snoring where they dropped after consuming the strong fiery liquor they always seemed to carry in vast amounts. Jericho had heard the Texans' claim that the Mexican generals had to get their army drunk before the officers could persuade them to charge into battle. Maybe they were right.

Silently, they stepped over a snoring guard and while Jack stood watch outside, Poe and Jericho slipped inside to check its occupants. They were lucky on the first try. They found Captain Cruz laying between two of his camp followers, all were snoring heavily. Poe went back to the door and snapped his fingers. Instantly, Jack joined them inside the tent.

Jericho quickly strapped on Cruz's holster and stood over the bed with the officer's pistol cocked and aimed directly at his head. He saw Handsome Jack's horrified look and smiled, shaking his head slightly. Poe and Jack slapped their hands over the girl's mouths as Jericho stuck the barrel of the pistol into Cruz's snoring mouth. He was awake instantly.

"Ommmph…?"

"Good morning, Capitan," Jericho whispered as he stuffed his dirty bandana around the pistol barrel, filling the frightened officer's mouth. When satisfied Cruz could make no sound, he pulled him up by his hair, sat him in a nearby chair and bound him to it with strips of bedding. Behind him, Poe and Jack stuffed torn sheets into the naked females' mouths and used the rest to tie them to the center tent pole, back-to-back.

Slipping the pistol back into its holster, Jericho watched Cruz's eyes as he pulled Rat Face's rusty bayonet from his belt. The eyes grew wider until it seemed they would pop right out of his head.

"With a rusty blade, I believe I said. Right, Capitan Cruz?"

When General Santa Anna stumbled from his tent the following morning to relieve himself, there were three heads in the middle of the parade field. Upon closer inspection, he discovered one of them, his second in command, Captain Cruz.

Thirteen

"IF WE DON'T FIND water and food pretty soon, we're gonna both be deader 'n dirt."

Jericho hadn't realized Poe was awake until he'd spoken through the tattered hat placed over his face to protect himself from the vicious black flies that continually feasted upon them. Poe lay in the shade of a large boulder with his hat still pulled down over his eyes as he spoke again.

"My insides are drier than a popcorn fart."

He chuckled softly as usual, and that made it difficult to tell just how much he was actually suffering. But Jericho knew that if his own thirst was any indication, Poe's was also substantial.

Jericho didn't answer. That would've taken too much effort, so he just continued to stare at the top of Poe's dusty hat. His newfound friend had a knack for pointing out the obvious. To Jericho's way of thinking, anything that was plain as the nose on your face needn't even be discussed. Besides, Poe's folksy sayings were beginning to get on his nerves more than a little these days – right along with his soft, irritating chuckle – which he usually exercised at the most inappropriate times. Like now. What was all that funny about the situation they'd found themselves in lately? Jericho himself was never one for talking too much anyway; in fact, he didn't trust anyone who sat around shooting off at the mouth all the time. His Pa had always said, "Deeds speak louder than words."

The reason he didn't confront Poe about his irritating little habits was the fact that the young man from Ohio seemed more than able to stand behind his words. For Jericho McCain, that also counted. And he was right about one thing. If they didn't find water pretty soon, they were all going to die out here. Handsome Jack had left an hour earlier, telling them he thought he recognized the area, and if he was right, they might be able to find a water hole in the pocket of rocks to their northeast. The trouble, he'd warned them, if there was still water to be found, the Kiowa also knew about it, and with the scarcity this time of year, they wouldn't be too far away. That didn't make Jericho feel all that happy about the prospects, but as thirsty as he was at the moment, he was willing to fight for it if necessary.

He'd given Poe the pistol in exchange for the breech-loading rifle that Rat Face had retrieved from the body of one of Taylor's men at the old church. There were only five loads for the pistol and all of them so old they probably wouldn't fire. The rifle, on the other hand, had ten rounds, and with Jericho's skill with a long gun they had hopes of killing a wayward antelope or wild pony that could feed them until they made it to San Antonio. Handsome Jack had taken the other rifle, an ancient muzzle-loader with a scant supply of powder and six lead balls, in the hopes he might get a shot at some wild game also. Nothing would count however, if he failed to find water in that clump of boulders.

The report of Handsome Jack's heavy muzzle-loader shattered the afternoon quiet, reverberating through the rocky canyons like thunder. Jericho and Poe scampered to the edge of the large boulder from where they could see for nearly a mile. Half running, half sliding down the opposite slope, they saw Handsome Jack being pursued by about twenty Kiowa braves on horseback. The treacherous, loose rocky slope made riding a horse about as difficult as trying to run full-bore down it afoot, like Handsome

Jack was attempting to do. In all, they stirred up so much dust that at times Jericho actually lost Jack in the great dust cloud enveloping the surroundings. One thing for sure, the Indians were gaining on him. Jericho took off like a jackrabbit, trying to get close enough to help Jack out before the Kiowa got him.

Aware of his plight, Jack paused just long enough to slam another ball home, tamp it in, and drop the leading Kiowa's horse. Two others stumbled over it, tossing their riders like rag dolls down the steep slope, creating enough havoc for him to gain another ten yards on his pursuers. Now in the low area and running hard, the Indians had closed to scarcely a hundred yards. Jack tried to load the clumsy old rifle as he ran, but he must've felt it was only a matter of time before they were upon him. Arriving at a large flat boulder at the base of the ridge where he'd initially left Jericho and Poe, he nimbly leaped upon it, finished loading the rifle, whipped it up, and firing from the hip, skillfully shot a pursuer through the head. He'd shot two more before they reached the large rock.

Winded from their sprint, Jericho and Poe arrived at a different large boulder lying between them and where they'd first observed Jack's predicament. Jericho thought the new location would put them in marginal range, and afford a better field of fire for the breech-loader. He'd have given his place in Heaven to have his dad's old squirrel gun at the moment. Upon arriving, he could see he'd been right. Quickly, he and Poe climbed up on it and flattened out. From there, they could clearly see what was happening to Jack, but the range was still great. Jack was clubbing at the howling warriors with his now broken rifle, as they swarmed over the rock from all sides. Suddenly, Jack was down, but still swinging and jabbing with his useless weapon.

Jericho dropped a big Kiowa attempting to swing his war ax with the first shot. Then he shot another as rapidly as he could load and fire. By the time he had killed two more, they were in full flight back toward the rocky ridge in retreat. Jericho didn't slow his killing rage, firing five more times before they were out of range, concealed from his deadly view – missing only once. Between him and Jack, they'd killed more than half of the hated Kiowa who'd mostly been armed with bows, lances and hatchets. Jericho said a small prayer of thanks that they hadn't had rifles.

Under the bodies of three Kiowa, they found Handsome Jack's body, nearly hacked to pieces. Jericho turned his back and puked over the rim, then took the dead man's feet and helped Poe lower him to the ground below.

"If he'd taken the breech loader, he might've had a chance."

It was clear Jericho was consumed with self-blame for his friend's death.

"Now don't go to beating yourself all about the head and shoulders over this, J.D. He's the one who insisted you keep it in the first place."

Jericho didn't answer. Instead, he pulled Rat Face's old knife from his belt, dropped to his knees and started probing in the hard, rocky soil. Poe stared at him in disbelief.

"There's at least a dozen of them left out there, J.D. We ain't got time for a proper burying. Let's just toss some stones over him and skedaddle 'fore they decide to come back. Jack won't mind now."

Jericho kept digging.

"I'd mind. You go and I'll catch up."

"You got the rifle."

"Take it…only one bullet left anyway."

Gone to Texas

Poe slapped his hat against his leg, the dust billowing around him. "Som'bitch! Dang nab it, if you ain't the most pig-headed, perplexing young fool I ever met. I swear, you're gonna get me done in yet! And before I can even marry. Som'bitch!"

Jericho still didn't look up from his task. "I'm not asking you to stay. Go on. Get!"

Still grumbling, Poe snatched up the rifle and stood staring across the valley where the Kiowa had disappeared, then stomped off. Much later, when Jericho was about ready to place Handsome Jack Clay into the rocky hole, Poe suddenly returned to help lower and cover him. Jericho mentally noted his return, but never commented. When they'd placed rocks over the shallow grave, Poe fidgeted nervously while Jericho said as much of the Lord's Prayer as he could remember. At last, casting anxious glances over their shoulders, they hurried up the dusty slope, heading away from the hostiles that were possibly waiting on the other ridgeline – headed away from water.

Hours later, sitting in the meager shade cast by a small boulder, Poe leaned back against it and watched Jericho roast a large rattlesnake over a low smokeless fire. He'd been at it for barely a minute but the aroma of splattering juices was beginning to drive Poe wild. He smacked his lips and leaned over to better see the simmering meat.

"You can't cook rattler too long, ya know. Dries 'em out. Makes 'em tough."

"Who caught it?"

"Well, you did. Just offering you a little advice, is all…based on experience."

"Well, thank you kindly. Your interest in my cooking ability is sorely appreciated."

Several more moments passed, then Poe said, "You aim to share that, don't you? My stomach thinks my throats been cut."

"Depends on how dry and tough it gets." Jericho squinted up. "Wouldn't want you to choke on a tough old dried-out piece of rattler."

Poe bit back a retort and leaned back again, bidding his time until the meat was done.

"J.D., you ever think how it'd been if we'd took up running a dry goods store like old man Partic? Maybe even married and raised a family?"

"It'd been a damned sight safer…and we wouldn't have to eat rattler."

"Been thinking about marrying that Farmer girl. Polly Farmer, remember her? She runs the store for Mr. Partic."

"The one with the sharp tongue and a hankering for Horehound candies?"

At the mention of that, Poe's face flamed. He started to rile up, then remembering the rattlesnake meat simmering over the fire, calmed down again.

"Oh, that's just her way. I think she likes me more than she lets on. Anyway, I intend to pop the question as soon as I get back to San Antonio."

He cocked an eyebrow, watching the back of Jericho's neck. "Unless of course, you got some objection to that."

Jericho snorted loudly, a mannerism that Poe was beginning to dislike a lot.

"Why should I care who you do or don't, marry? It just seems like you're buying yourself a whole lot of grief marrying that particular filly though."

"None prettier in San Antonio, no siree! A mighty handsome

woman, if you ask me." When Jericho didn't respond, Poe prodded him. "You in disagreement with that, too?"

"Nothing to disagree with. She's striking all right...maybe a mite too narrow between the eyes, though."

This time, Poe did bristle.

"Now see here! I won't have you speaking about a lady like her in that manner. The girl's a saint! A bonafide angel! Any man would be proud to marry someone like Polly Farmer."

"If you say so. My apologies."

Poe eyed the darkened meat again.

"Accepted. That ready yet?"

At least for the moment, the aroma of smoked rattlesnake had won out in the tussle between his ravenous hunger and his desire to defend Polly Farmer's honor. A short time later, his hunger partially satiated, he rested against the rock again and wondered where Polly was at the moment.

* * *

Polly Ann Farmer and her father had made the trip to their new homestead twice, over the objections and stern warnings of the post Adjutant, Major Kettle. He'd told them of a settler family found mutilated just fifteen miles west of the town, only a week earlier. John Farmer replied as he always did, that those who minded their own business needn't live in fear of other men. Having just returned from his property earlier in the day, they'd eaten a hearty meal that Mrs. Farmer had prepared for them before retiring for the night, and now, tired but happy, discussed the family's future.

"Once we get settled in our new quarters, Polly, there is the question of marriage that we must discuss."

"Pa, I don't intend to marry some fat old man with a lot of land just for the sake of prosperity. I told you that!"

"Now, Polly Ann. I know how you feel about that. I believe we can come to an agreement on someone. Just because a man has property doesn't always mean he's unacceptable."

John Farmer realized early on that his daughter was a headstrong young lady if there ever was one, and he'd discovered that if he really wanted her to do something he had to get her to see the value in it and convince her it was the right choice. He wasn't always successful. Like with the idea of marriage. His daughter was a strong-limbed young woman, capable of bearing numerous children for the right man, and as such, had many suitable men to court her. He dearly loved his daughter and just wanted to have a say about who the right man should be; preferably one of property. There had been ample opportunity for her to marry a respected and wealthy landowner back in Missouri, but she had steadfastly rebuked the elderly gentleman's affections. Now, with the state of affairs in this God-awful place called Texas, there were few acceptable, or even likely candidates. Still, he had made a mental list of the eligible men and from his perspective, it wasn't all that bad.

He gazed with affection across the dining table at the stubborn tilt of his daughter's determined chin, and smiled.

"Tell me, Polly, if you were considering marriage tomorrow, which suitors would you favor?"

Polly's manner softened substantially and she giggled quietly. She and her father had always had an open relationship, and had discussed the topic often. Still, it never failed to embarrass her.

"Well…there is one or two young men who have been hanging

around the store lately. The one I favor most is a serious gentleman with, what I believe to be, high potential."

"Not that fool Ranger with a girl's name, I hope."

Polly giggled again, then become somber.

"No, Father. Though I have seen this one with Rosie Poe. The one I favor is named Jericho McCain. He owns a fine-blooded horse and well-tended gear. He appears to be a man of means, or at least one of some potential. He speaks with intelligence and manners. I believe he has had some formal education."

"Jericho McCain, huh?"

Polly knew her pa liked men with biblical names and could see him seriously pondering what she'd just told him. At the thought of the McCain youth, she felt her face redden again. This time, not with embarrassment, but with a warm glow of desire. *Why Polly Farmer! You don't even know him!* Her self-rebuke did little good. She'd been reacting the same every time she'd thought about him since the day they'd met outside Hugh Partic's store. He'd held a strange attraction for her; a lonely, hurt feeling that could invade her soul every time she looked into his eyes. Was it love? Or just…what? Motherly instincts? There was also something else. Like he was just on the verge of striking out. It gave her an unsettled feeling – an excited one.

"Yes, Father. He is also very handsome, in a dangerous sort of way. I would like to explore it further and maybe we can discuss it more when you've had a chance to meet him."

"Jericho, huh? I like the name."

* * *

Pox Marks squatted and ran his fingers over the wagon tracks in the soft soil, then moved to another set and did the same.

The others remained mounted and watched silently. He next moved to a small pecan tree and studied the area where a mashed pocket of grass indicated someone had recently sat down. At last he arose, remounted, and spurred his horse toward a tree-covered knoll half a mile away.

He reined up at the knoll and nodded toward one of the others, the big man called Tao.

"You. Stay and watch. Come get me if someone shows."

He moved further into the trees followed by the others, westward toward the high ground. Not in a hurry, just a steady even pace…like hunters.

Pox Marks was pleased. Someone had been there all right. Two people, a man and a woman. Not just once either. They'd returned several times over the past couple of weeks. That meant whoever it was, they'd probably come back again.

The possibility of catching the woman made his thoughts race.

* * *

Jericho didn't know just what he expected to find when he and Poe topped the small rise they'd been chasing all morning. He simply hoped it wouldn't be more of the deserted desolate landscape they'd been crossing for the past three days, but it was. Endless, scorched, barren land that couldn't sustain a decent life for even the rattlesnakes and horned toads that called it home. Wavering layers of heat floated above the ground, reminding him of the water they so craved. Beaten, bone dry, they'd dropped heavily into the dirt and lay unmoving.

After a time, Jericho dragged himself to a sitting position and observed Poe's closed eyes. With his boot, he nudged Poe's foot.

"You dead?"

"Yeah...leave me alone."

"We got to get up...keep moving. Otherwise...we're buzzard food for sure."

Poe didn't open his eyes.

"You go. Send back help if you make it."

Jericho stared at Poe for a moment, and then with great effort used the breechloader to push himself to his feet. When his partner still made no effort to move, his eyes pinched closer and he said, "I'll do that. But I've been thinking about what you said earlier, and the first thing I'm gonna do is marry that little Farmer gal. What you said has got me all worked up. Made me think. This just ain't no way to live. A man needs a family and Polly Ann looks like she was just made for having babies. We'll probably have a dozen or two. I'll name the first one after you."

He stumbled away without glancing back; he could hear Poe struggling to his feet.

That had been four hours earlier, and Jericho had thought at the time they were finished for sure. But Poe had come across a certain kind of cactus and cut the core out, from which they'd chewed the juice. That'd given them enough moisture to continue a few more miles. But now they were finished, and they both knew it. Jericho had always just assumed they'd make it back to San Antonio, save the folks who lived there from Santa Anna's army, and live out a full rich life. Poe would marry that Polly Farmer gal he was so stuck on, and as for himself, well, he'd light out for Colorado, see the mountains there.

Since Jack's untimely death, however, he realized how foolish he'd been to assume anything in this Hell on earth they called Texas. If lack of water and the oven-hot temperatures didn't kill them during the day, and the frigid Texas nights didn't freeze them to death as they slept, then the Kiowa would likely return and butcher them the first time they let down their guard.

As he observed Poe's blistered, swollen face and licked his own dry lips, he knew they'd reached the end of their endurance. They presently were lying in a deep crevice between two large boulders, formed several million years before when a raging river had once cut through the area. Some of the water likely still flowed freely below the dry arid surface and blistering heat that baked their flesh, but neither of them knew of it, and it wouldn't have done them much good.

Jericho didn't know if Poe was unconscious or merely sleeping. He'd been lying in the same position for nearly an hour, his face against the hot ground. He knew his companion was still alive with an occasional groan, and by measured shallow breaths that stirred powdery dust in front of his nose. He wanted to help Poe sit upright, get his face out of the dust, but he hadn't the strength. He watched the dust stir with each breath his friend took and waited for it to finally stop altogether. At last, he too drifted off.

Someone was with them. His mind in a gray area, between drifting off again and consciousness, and he couldn't seem to pull himself back far enough to see who it was. Probably Kiowa. They were the only ones dumb enough to live in a place like this. Better to not wake up at all, than to face what they had to offer.

Don't matter none. My race is over.

His decision made, he faded off once more.

He became conscious of coolness on his face and moisture drops sliding down his tongue. It was like heaven. Through his swollen eyes he could see nothing. Thinking he was blind, he wiped his eyes and found a wet rag covering them. Poe grinned at him, as he gnawed away on something resembling a rabbit leg.

"You dead?"

He tried to move, then groaned and fell back. Remembering his friend's words earlier, he moaned. "Yes. Leave me alone."

Poe laughed and continued eating. Jericho observed they were in the middle of a cave measuring about forty feet long and ten feet wide. He'd been lying on a pallet made of twigs and a wool saddle blanket. Half of the rabbit Poe was devouring still roasted over a small fire in a circle of rocks a few feet away. It looked as if someone had been living there for quite some time.

"How did we come to this place?"

At that moment, a third person entered the cave, carrying a bundle of twigs. He strained against the bright light of the opening but could only make out that it was a woman. As she moved forward, he noted her tattered dress, but she seemed vaguely familiar. She dropped her load near the fire and stared back at him as recognition slowly flooded his eyes.

Annie Springs!

She nodded at Jericho and he did the best he could to bow his head in respect.

"Thank you for the hospitality of your home, Ma'am."

"Jist repaying a kindness, young man."

Poe looked on astonished.

"You two know each other?"

Up close, the legendary frontier woman wasn't nearly as old as he'd thought she would be. He'd guess no more than thirty... thirty-five years old. Under all that grime, probably not unattractive, neither. Something about her reminded him of his mountain home...and his dead mother. Suddenly he felt saddened by the plight of this strange creature before him.

"Rosie, meet Annie Springs," he finally said softly.

Poe whistled low, then said, "Pleased t'meet cha, Ma'am. No disrespect, but I always thought you was a figment of some old buffalo hunter's imagination, Missus Springs."

"Maybe I am. You want any of this rabbit carcass before I clean it up?"

Simultaneously, both of them reached out for it.

Most of the time during when they were awake, Annie Springs stayed gone, returning only after they'd turned in for the night. Each time she brought food and water, making Jericho believe there had to be a spring close by. Jericho surmised the reason she left was her searching for her long-lost infant daughter. She seemed sane enough when near, still he knew that whatever kept her living out here, all alone, would probably have touched on insanity. The mere thought made him terribly sad.

By the second day, both Jericho and Poe noticed a substantial improvement in their strength. Another day and he figured they'd be back on the trail for San Antonio. That evening after Poe started snoring, he waited until Annie Springs returned. She slipped into the cave and upon noticing he was still awake, turned to leave. Jericho held out his hand to stay her.

"Please. Don't go. I have to leave and I want to speak with you before I do."

She walked out anyway, then a few minutes later, returned to squat across the cave from him. She stared at him but didn't speak.

"Missus Springs, I never got the chance to properly thank you for saving our lives." He waited. Her eyes stared a hole through him, not answering.

"Well anyway, for what it's worth, thank you from the bottom of my heart."

This time she did answer, so softly he had difficulty hearing her.

"You helped me once."

Remembering the handkerchief he'd placed in the scrub oak, he smiled, and she smiled back. Encouraged, he hastily hurried on.

"Maybe some, but nothing like what you've done for us. You saved our life, Ma'am."

As she looked up he saw tears in her eyes.

"Have you seen my baby, sir?"

She positioned her hands about eighteen inches apart. "Just a little bit of a thing, hard to spot if you don't look real close. Have you seen her?"

A huge lump formed in Jericho's throat and he swallowed hard to make it go away.

"No Ma'am. I'm terribly sorry. Do you want…me to look for her?"

"No. I'm the only one who can find her. I have to look for her."

Jericho stared into the fire, embarrassed over what he could not understand. After a while he said, "Me and Rosie have to leave tomorrow. Old Santa Anna is going to burn San Antonio to the ground unless we can warn the folks who live there."

"Santa…Anna? San Antonio…"

Suddenly, he realized that living here all alone she was totally unaware of the events taking place around her. All that existed for her in the world was her lost baby.

Jericho stood and walked to the entrance of the cave. There, he motioned for her to join him. As she stood beside him, he pointed to the northeast and said, "That town. The folks there and their babies are in great danger from the Indians. I must warn them. Will you show me how to get there?"

Without a sound, Annie Springs returned to her spot and squatted against the wall again. In a matter of seconds, she was snoring loudly. Disheartened, Jericho made his way back to his blanket bed and dropped onto it. He pondered the turn in life that brought Annie Springs to this remote area in the first place, and caused her to meander through it, searching for a dead child that she could never find. For that matter, what had brought him here? And Taylor? So much tragedy, so many lost lives. What a waste of life – for a place as Texas. The next morning, he was suddenly awakened by Annie Springs roughly shaking his arm.

"C'mon. Get up. The Kiowa have been hiding out in the rocks all night watching the place. They must've found your tracks and suspect you're in here. That means you and your skinny friend got to get to getting, or they're likely to skin ya both…and eat ya!"

She started cackling loudly, waking Poe who sat up wide-eyed, clutching his pistol. "Glad to see everyone's in fine spirits this morning," he said sourly. "If there's a Kiowa within a thousand yards of the place, I hope he's in as fine as spirits."

"There is."

"Huh?"

"Right outside. Annie just told me."

"Well, if that ain't just Jim Dandy."

Annie rummaged through an old wooden trunk in the back of the cave. Finding what she was seeking, she pulled it over her head and turned around. She'd placed an old yellowed-white wedding dress over her tattered one. Without a warning, she

Gone to Texas

ran out the entrance horrifically screaming as she stumbled down the side of the rocky slope toward the spot where she'd indicated the Kiowa were waiting.

"Where's my baby? What have you done with my baby? Howling!"

Jericho sighted his rifle at the rocks and waited for a target, fully recognizing the fact that he had only one round and wanted to make it count. By the time they were close enough for Poe to use the five rounds remaining for the pistol, it would pretty much be all over.

Annie was more than halfway to her destination, and still there was no movement from the clump of rocks. Then, without warning, a great cry went up from the rocks and seven mounted Kiowa charged from their protective enclave – away from Annie Springs. None looked back until they were out of sight.

Within a few moments she returned and went directly to the old trunk, refolded the wedding dress and placed it inside. Returning to them, she cackled to herself.

"Fools. One old woman hollers at them and they ride away like frightened school children." Then her face sobered and she said, "They think I'm touched – believe touched people can see into the spirit world. That's why they leave me alone."

She walked to the opening of the cave and stared toward the spot Jericho had pointed to the night before.

"If you want to find that San Antonio town, you best get started young man."

Fourteen

MORDECAI JONES PUFFED HIS pipe and watched as regiment after regiment of the colorfully attired troops crossed the river in four columns. Last came the ox-drawn cannons and the supply trains. It was nearly dark before the last of the long columns finally moved away from the river and commenced setting up camp. Through the still evening air he could hear men coughing, farting, strumming guitars and some, officers most likely he thought sourly, bedding with their camp followers.

He grinned and scratched his groin. Hot damn! To be a Mex colonel! What a way to live!

Ensuring his horse was securely tethered, he removed anything from his person that would rattle, shake or make a sound; even leaving his rifle and pistol on the saddle. The wide-blade knife always present at his belt, he slid into the top of his boot; the thin one, he suspended on a rawhide string down his back where it rested between his shoulder blades. If he needed more, it'd likely be too little to help, anyway.

In his moccasin-encased feet, he slipped noiselessly through the scrub oaks until he came to a long string of horses. Silently, he slid under the rope and continued toward the sounds of the encampment. A guard suddenly arose out of the darkness, less than five feet in front of him, pulled up his baggy trousers, tying them with a rope around his waist. Jones wrinkled his nose disgustedly and froze in place.

Must be that mashed bean stuff all these Mex's eat, he thought. *Never find an American smelling like that. No siree!*

As soon as the sentry was gone, Jones drastically altered his route and paralleled the camp before he again edged closer to the night activity. Behind a makeshift shelter he heard someone moving inside; he waited for nearly thirty minutes. Finally, his patience was rewarded when another soldier stepped outside to relieve himself and ran into the thick handle of Mordecai's heavy knife. He crumpled without a sound.

Mordecai removed his hat and his rifle, then moved toward the front of the tent, careful to stay in the deeper shadows. There, he leaned against a tree and smoked one of the unconscious soldier's strong cigarettes.

"*Amigo. Buenos noches.*"

He'd heard the man come up behind him so he wasn't startled. Without speaking, he passed the lit cigarette to the dark blob before him and felt it leave his hand. When the soldier took a deep draw on it Jones could see he was an elderly Indian with a sparse gray beard.

Good! An Indian.

Mordecai Jones had lived in Texas far longer than most white men and at one time had taken an Indian wife from one of the small coastal Mexican towns. She had died nine years before, but he had learned to speak the language from her and her family and still spoke the dialect of the coastal Indian people.

"I'll be glad when this is over and I can get back to my fat wife," he said in that dialect. "I'm too old for this soldiering life."

The old man laughed, had a mild coughing fit, spit, and then answered.

"My wife too is fat. It is good to have a fat woman when the night air turns cold. They are also stronger and more hot-blooded than the skinny ones the *Gringos* like."

He broke into another coughing fit.

"I hope his Excellency, the General, lets us go home to our wives soon," Jones said.

"I believe he will as soon as we burn San Antonio and wipe out the Texans when they come to help. It should not take too long. My sergeant is allowed to attend all the staff meetings because he can write. He said we will be there within the week."

Jones scratched his groin and headed toward the back of the tent.

"This bad food has given me the trots. Don't get too close or you may die."

He heard the old man laughing as he slipped into the woods, back the way he had come.

* * *

From the hidden trails she located, Jericho felt that Annie Springs must know every water hole in Texas and all the game paths, too. She also knew how to catch small critters and cook them without pausing to build a fire. One way, she cut them into thin strips and attached them to her belt, letting the hot sun cook them as she moved. Some things she found for them to eat left something to be desired in the taste department, but it was certainly better than starving like before they met her. Jericho made a map of the trails and the watering holes for future reference, not that he planned on coming back this way once he got back to civilization. Cool mountain air, that's what he wanted from now on.

One night after making camp, Annie Springs told them her

baby was named Emma. Her husband was Garfield Springs, a successful wagon builder in Virginia from where they had come. She seemed to recall that part of her life with little difficulty, describing the home they'd left, names of friends, and family. And she remembered this part of her life, the searching part – but nothing in between. It was the in between part that convinced Jericho that she'd seen her husband and baby tortured and killed by the Kiowa, and had been helpless to do anything about it. In a way, the blotting out of what happened when Cruz had taken Taylor away to die. At least he'd made Cruz pay for it and he supposed that counted for something. With Annie, since she couldn't remember it happening, it simply didn't happen. So she continued her search without end for her baby, Emma.

"After you find your daughter, what do you intend to do then, Ma'am?" Poe asked.

Jericho shot him a hard look, but it was lost on Poe.

Annie looked confused, then brightened. "Why there ain't nothing else. Just looking, that's all there is. Don't you know anything?"

Poe started to follow up, but this time caught Jericho shaking his head and let it drop. After she'd gone to sleep, Jericho sat close to the lingering coals and contemplated Annie Springs. In the sand, he wrote down the names of everyone she'd mentioned back in Virginia. Then he memorized each of them. If he ever got out of this mess, he intended to contact them and tell them about their courageous relative. Someone had to let them know she was still alive, and what had happened to her husband and daughter. It was the least he could do for her. Still saddened for this lonely demented woman and a lost child, Jericho finally slept.

Two days later, Annie brought them to the crest of a hill and simply sat down in the dirt. Since Jericho and Poe had seen her act strangely before, they plopped down beside her and silently waited. After a time, she stood.

"Well, that's that. I gotta go back and look for my Emma."

She started to return the way they had just come and Jericho and Poe leaped to their feet.

"Annie! Wait, please!"

She turned back, clearly agitated.

"Well, what?"

"You said you'd take us to the town. We're not there yet."

"Said I'd take you and I did." She pointed at a saddle in the next ridgeline. "From there you can see the smelly place. Now, I gotta go."

As she turned to leave again, Jericho ran to catch up, causing her to pause once more.

"Annie? I…well, you take care, Annie. I hope you find your Emma real soon."

She placed her hand on his arm and for just a second, he saw a kind, intelligent person in her wet eyes as she said, "God bless you, Jericho McCain. You're a good boy. I hope that Emma grows up to be just as good."

Then Annie Springs struck off back up the trail and in only a few moments lost from their view. It was as though she'd never been there at all.

Poe was waiting for him when he returned to the top of the ridge. He stared at the empty place Annie had left when she'd disappeared.

"Do you think she knows her baby's dead?" he asked.

Jericho thought he caught a glimpse of movement among the rocks, but couldn't be sure.

"I don't think that matters. It's all she's got left, Rosie. All she's got left."

With one final look, they headed toward the saddle in the ridge, their thoughts on a brave, small woman, alone in the wilderness, searching for a baby girl that she'd never find.

Fifteen

JERICHO MCCAIN LEANED BACK in a wooden chair on the boardwalk in front of the town's only hotel, his feet crossed on the rail in front, relaxing as he soaked up the first sun of an early spring morning. To those who'd known him before, he would have looked remarkably different. He'd put on almost twenty pounds of muscle, gaining another inch and a half in height. Although his face still that of a young man, his eyes appeared older; a mature man's eyes that had experienced a lifetime of pain and loss in a few short months. The townsmen referred to him as the "quiet one" whenever the company of Rangers were discussed. His slate-gray eyes held just a hint of the hardness that would come later.

His outward appearance had also changed substantially. Missing were the bib-overalls and high top brogans of his farm days. These days, he blended in with hundreds of others either living in San Antonio, or just passing through; heeled boots and spurs, jeans, a large brimmed hat, bandana and pistol belts a more practicable wardrobe. The object that set him apart from other travelers was his shiny Silver Star pinned to the left pocket of his faded denim shirt.

The winter in eastern Texas had been as severe in its own way, as the summer months had been in the opposite extreme. When winter had come, it had been all at once. Just a chill in the air one morning, then blizzard-like conditions by late afternoon. Those not familiar with the region, or unable to find shelter in time, simply froze to death – them and one hell of a lot of livestock. All in all, it did little to change his opinion of the area. He still missed the deep serenity of his beloved Blue Ridge Mountains. But at melancholy times like this, his thoughts often slipped back to the preceding summer, and his capture by the Mexicans.

At first, he'd suffered terrible nightmares about his ordeal, but managed to compartmentalize the bad aspects of it and mostly remembered only the good. Taylor and the way he died still came to mind every now and then, but Jericho could abruptly push it away, force it back into its small room in his head until he could deal with it better – someday. He simply wasn't ready to face that episode. Maybe never would be. Each time he thought of Taylor, tears would sting his eyes and he'd have to force himself to concentrate on more pleasant things. Taylor had been the last of his family, and the world was now filled with only strangers.

He also missed the young ranger, Handsome Jack Clay, who'd been as much a friend as anyone he'd ever known. He'd learned a lot from Jack that you couldn't get out of a book. He figured he was a better man for having known the fiery Texas Ranger. Several times while playing poker, a pastime he'd recently picked up during the dark winter months, he'd heard a clear, honest laugh and had to turn to assure himself that it wasn't Handsome Jack.

But Jack was dead, just as everyone else that he'd ever cared for; except Jean, and she was as lost to him as if she were dead, too. Still, when he least expected it, her face would suddenly pop into his thoughts and a sharp pain touched his heart. It was then that he missed her the most – the small orderly cottage, the happy smells from her neat kitchen, and yes, the intimate love they'd shared together. Other times, he had trouble simply recalling what she'd looked like at all.

He seldom thought of the beautiful Susan Harrington or the young French-Cajun girl, Maria LaPonce. They'd just been strangers he'd passed on his way to Texas to find Taylor. Polly, the spicy filly Poe was so hung up on these days, seemed to fall into the same category as Susan and Maria. After Jean's mature, loving warmth, none of them seemed to measure up very well. He supposed that just having Jean for the short period he had with her ruined him for all other women he'd meet, forever. He realized that she too was now lost to him. He didn't feel sorry for himself – just terribly alone.

Sometimes the men he'd killed returned in his dreams to haunt him, but Jack had told him that would happen for a while and not to let it bother him too much – they needed killing, Jack had said, and he was just God's instrument in the affair. Still, it was difficult to fathom that until just over a year ago, the largest animal he'd ever killed was an occasional deer or elk for the family dinner table. Now, he was a killer of men.

A lot had happened since he and Poe escaped from Santa Anna down on Dog Creek. The Kiowa had killed handsome Jack and Ol' Zach had sent Santa Anna crawling back to Mexico with his tail between his legs, no thanks to him and Poe. By the time they'd made it back to San Antonio, Mordecai Jones had already spread the alarm and the citizens had prepared for the defense of the city, while riders left to warn General Taylor of Santa Anna's deceit. Armed with the information, Zach Taylor had circled far to the south, coming up behind Santa Anna's army as it positioned its cannon for the siege. Taken completely by surprise, the Mexican army had panicked, threw down their rifles and left their cannon in place as they ran back toward the Rio Grande in terror.

The Texans captured over a hundred cannons that day, a complete supply train, and inflicted heavy casualties as the enemy fled the field. With its new armament, for the first time Taylor's army had now became a formidable force. An army, he surmised, that Santa Anna wouldn't be eager to face anytime in the near future. The word was that the United States government was putting together a large task force to invade Mexico in the south and capture Mexico City.

True to his word to Handsome Jack before his untimely death, Jericho had spoken with Captain Hays about joining the Rangers. He'd had his own reasons. He wouldn't have made it two miles out of town in the frigid winter conditions suddenly thrust upon them; and, he needed food and shelter to get him through until spring. When Captain Hays offered him a trial period of six months, he'd readily accepted. He had two months left of the commitment, then he anticipated he'd bid Texas *adios* and strike out for new parts. He was thinking the Colorados would be a good choice. He wished Taylor was there to go with him.

To his way of thinking, he'd picked a pretty good time to join the rangers. With the Mexican army in full retreat, the Indians occupied full-time trying to find enough food to stay alive through the winter, and most of the riff-raff holed up someplace warm, the Rangers' job had been relatively easy. Jericho really hadn't had much to do all winter. Now that it was finally warming up though, he expected that to change right away. He was planning to be far away soon.

The truth, the inevitable restlessness and violence of the renegade Indians and growing number of outlaw bands, wasn't the only reason he was so eager to be rid of the place. An uneasy sensation rushed over him as it did each and every time he thought of this particular problem. The main reason he needed to be gone from Texas was that red-haired Polly Farmer and the look she got in her eyes every time she came around him; like he was a big piece of apple pie, and she couldn't wait to sink her teeth into him. It seemed as if she'd set her cap for Jericho McCain, for sure, and somehow found a way to be the same place as him at every opportunity.

Poe on the other hand, behaved a lot like old Blue used to act every time he came around a female in season; prancing in his finest duds, not a hair out of place, talking about Dear Polly all the blessed day. He'd even shined his boots, for cat's sake! Also, it seemed that lately Poe had been eyeing Jericho suspiciously every time Polly Farmer was around. Jericho snorted loudly, drawing glances from an elderly couple entering the hotel lobby.

Why in tarnation would he be suspicious of me? I don't want Polly Farmer! I don't want any woman. Can't handle the misery that comes with 'em.

Of course, those long winter nights would get any man to thinking about company, but he was determined not to be weak in this matter. He had a feeling she was bound to cause trouble between him and Poe before it was over, and he wanted to be far away before that happened.

Jericho's mind shifted to the night's festivities ahead of him. The local folks called it the Bluebonnet Spring Cakewalk. Named, he'd been told countless times, after the dainty blue flowers that were soon to blossom. There'd be music, dancing, liquor galore, and more food than Zach Taylor's army could devour in a month. They claimed it was just their way of celebrating that winter was all but over, with fair weather just around the corner. He didn't know much about that, but the sound of all that food had his mouth to watering – if he could just stay out of the sight of Polly Farmer.

A man picked his way across the muddy street as if he was trying not to get his boots soiled. He had an idea who it was, yup, it was Poe. Despite the fact he'd been choosing his path carefully, he still seemed to be in somewhat of a hurry. He started talking as soon as he reached the boardwalk.

"Better put some gitty-up in it, J.D. Bigfoot Wallace wants to see us both at headquarters, five minutes ago."

"What about?"

Poe eyed him like he was from another planet.

"Now, how in the name of Lucifer would I know that? When Bigfoot Wallace beckons, you jist drop whatever you're doing and git to gitting. Enough talk about it."

Poe had been acting uppity ever since he'd been made corporal, and had even began to develop some of Wallace's unattractive airs. Jericho snorted, straightened his hat and reluctantly pushed himself to his feet.

"Well, pardon me, Corporal Poe. I'd plumb forgotten somehow that Bigfoot Wallace sat on the right hand of God. I'll surely take precautions to see that don't ever happen again!"

Poe stormed off without commenting, this time kicking up splatters of mud as he stomped back across the muddy street, unmindful of his shiny boots. Jericho was pleased he had managed to get under his friend's skin. Served him right after the way he'd been acting over that red-haired city gal. As he picked his way across the deserted street and upon reaching the other side, he noticed Poe waiting at the corner, near the gun repair shop.

As he neared, Poe simply stared in the window and spoke as if nothing had happened between them.

"I'm thinking about having some work done on my Colts. Heard of a feller in Missouri who had a gunsmith file off a little gadget in his Colt's trigger. Speeded up his shooting considerable. Less pull, he said. What do ya think?"

"I think it's a lot of horse apples. Probably just end up shooting his toes off."

They moved toward the small Ranger headquarters building, the last one at the end of Main Street. A square corral made use of the far wall of the building as its fourth side, confining half a dozen wild-eyed mounts. These were mustangs the Rangers had been working with to break before spring. If unsuccessful, they'd issue them anyway to new recruits who'd have to finish the job on the trail. Eyeing them cautiously, Jericho was glad for the hundredth time that he'd left his stallion with the army when he'd attempted to rescue Taylor at the church. Colonel Roberts had kept it safe and returned it to him as soon as he learned Jericho made it back alive.

Poe was jawing along side him.

"Why in tarnation is it that every time somebody tries a new-fangled way of doing things, you think it's silly? Ain't you never heard of progress?"

Poe knew it was coming. He could have bet money on it. Jericho McCain's famous snort.

Jericho snorted loudly. "I heard of it. Don't want no part of it neither."

"Well that's just Jim Dandy! Without progress, there would be no Texas."

Another snort. "Now that had to be a tremendous loss, wouldn't it?"

"I just don't understand you, J.D. Here you are smack in the middle of the greatest place on earth, a member of the finest fighting outfit in the world, about to meet one of the most famous men in the world, and you're not satisfied. Beats all I never did see."

"You ask her, yet?"

Poe was so surprised by the question that he gulped, nearly swallowing his plug of chaw. He coughed, spit it into the street, and glared at Jericho.

"No, I ain't asked her yet," he said. "I'm abiding my time for just the right moment. Women like that sort of thing, ya know. They call it romance. Don't you know anything at all about women?"

"Not much, I reckon. But I know they cause a lot of misery, and I also know this much. As anxious as that little filly is to get married, you'd best do it quick or someone'll beat you to it."

"Like who? What have you heard, J.D. McCain? Are you...?"

Before he could ask it, they were there. Jericho opened the door without knocking and entered. Chagrined, Poe followed him inside, mumbling to himself. A corporal cleaned a rifle he had disassembled on the office floor while Bigfoot Wallace sat at a desk in the far corner, drinking from a tin cup. He didn't look pleased.

"Didn't anyone ever teach you to knock?"

Jericho looked puzzled.

"My Pa taught me how to knock."

"Then why didn't you?"

Poe stood back watching. His expression on display that he

was enjoying the possibility of his friend being dressed down by the acting commander.

"He said to knock when you went to someone's house you didn't know, and who weren't expecting you. Far as I know, Poe said you were expecting us."

Bigfoot squinted at the youngster, then said, "Where you been? I've been asking for you since yesterday. You're a day late."

"Came as soon as I heard. If I'd heard yesterday, I'd come yesterday."

Bigfoot, befuddled, as if he couldn't make up his mind if the slender young man before him was being cheeky or just honest. At last, he pressed on.

"A family of five was wiped out near Sandy Point. Butchered – every last one of them."

"Indians?"

"I don't think so. There's a few renegade groups riding around causing grief, among 'em, is Pox Marks's bunch. This is the kind of thing he usually does, so it could be him. Mordecai Jones read the sign and he said it was. Enjoy the cakewalk tonight. Tomorrow at daybreak, I want you two colts, Sonnet and the Mexican boy to get out there and see if you can put pressure on him. You may get lucky and whack a few of that bunch. I expect you'd have to be damned lucky to do even that, but if we can just put a little pressure on them maybe Pox Marks will get tired of all the attention and take off for greener pastures."

"You're in charge, Corporal Poe. Take Mordecai to scout for you. Just chase 'em around a bit and come on back. I don't want to lose any more men to that heathen." Bigfoot waved his hand in dismissal. "Go on. Take off!"

Poe headed for the door as though pleased to be let off the

hook without a Bigfoot Wallace special reprimand. Halfway to the door, he cringed as heard Jericho say, "Maybe we'll get lucky."

"I said to git!"

They hurried back toward the livery stable to check their gear and insure their mounts were given a double feed for the trail. Poe was fuming.

"Now that's a sure fire way to end up having to shovel horse manure for the next nine months, J.D. You're lucky Bigfoot Wallace didn't take that long knife he carries and slice three layers of hide off your butt. You got to watch that quick tongue around folks of respect like Bigfoot Wallace."

"I'll work on it."

* * *

As the sun dropped below the horizon, Poe met Jericho. on the street in front of the church, boots shined, freshly shaven, and not a hair out of place. Jericho, who'd changed shirt and dusted his boots, felt tattered by comparison. That was just the way he'd planned it, too. Maybe Miss-too-eager-to-be-married Polly Farmer would overlook him in favor of the spit-shined, just-as-eager-to-get-married Rosie Poe. In any event, he hoped to avoid possible conflict with either of them this night. From inside the church, the fiddle music was tuning up to the loud cheers of the inhabitants.

At Pastor Lang's insistence the liquor table had been set up in the street, completely off the church's premises. He'd reluctantly approved the dancing, but drinking liquor would have to remain separate from holy ground. Jericho didn't really understand that, since the pastor could usually drink about everyone else under the table without half trying. Poe spotted the liquor table immediately, smacked his lips, grinned at Jericho and made a beeline for it. Mainly because he didn't relish entering the lion's den alone, Jericho followed and grabbed a glass of tepid beer, watching Poe's Adam's apple bob repeatedly as he swilled down the fiery corn liquor straight from a crock jar. Poe lowered the jar long enough to loudly belch, wipe his mouth with the back of his hand, then tilted up the crock once more.

Mordecai Jones sat sprawled in the mud with legs spread, his back resting against a watering trough. He was cradling an identical crock jar in his arms, as tenderly as someone would hold a baby – already passed out from too much of the homemade brew. Each time he breathed, his thick moustache would float up to tickle his nose. Jericho wondered just what shape he would be in to scout for them the following morning – or Poe either, for that matter. He sipped his beer and silently observed Poe who'd already turned glassy-eyed, tilting up the crock jar for another long pull of the fiery liquid. He'd entered into a spitting contest with two other men – both were having trouble remaining upright.

Taking a chance he wouldn't be noticed, Jericho moved to the church door and cautiously peeked inside. Dancers had formed two large circles and were square dancing to the music of two fiddles, a banjo, juice harp and two mandolins. The mandolin player, an old man of about eighty who seemed to be playing a different song then the rest of the musicians, kept falling off the small platform into the dancers. He appeared to be about as drunk as he could get without passing out. Not spotting any trouble in the form of Polly Farmer, he edged toward the long food table, picked up a tin plate, and started filling it.

Feeling eyes on him, Jericho looked up and saw Bigfoot Wallace sitting with a pretty woman and a small boy. Wallace's eyes were cold and didn't waver as they bored into him. Jericho stared back without malice for half a minute, then turned away. He could still feel the man's eyes on his back.

He may be a hero to Poe, he thought, *but as far as I'm concerned, the man's a cold-blooded killer.*

He'd heard stories of how Wallace had killed two men in a knife fight during the past winter. He had no doubt Captain Hay's second-in-command was brave and could fight, but he doubted the honor of the big man and vowed to be vigilant whenever he was around.

A man with eyes like that wouldn't think twice about cutting my throat and rolling me into the river.

As he sopped up the last of his gravy with a hot bun, a soft touch at his arm brought him back to the present. He almost choked on the last bite. It was Polly Farmer. She was wearing a revealing green dress, hair piled high on top of her head, with a matching green ribbon in it. Jerking his eyes up from her exposed bosom, he felt his face flame.

"Why Mr. McCain! What an unexpected pleasure seeing you here."

Yeah, I'll bet. He muttered something unintelligible around a mouthful of biscuit.

"Oh, that's my favorite song. Come. Let's dance. Please?"

Not waiting for any response, she grasped his hand in a vice-like grip and dragged him reluctantly across the floor while he searched for a place to set his half-filled plate. He dropped it into an empty chair as he passed, then jolted to a sudden stop against her soft body. They were standing near the middle of the dance floor. Jericho felt as if everyone in the room was staring at them when she slipped smoothly into his arms and led the dance as he struggled to keep up. He tried several times to move back a respectable distance from her soft rounded front, but she kept pressing her warm breasts into his shirt, making it extremely difficult for him to breath. She smiled up at him, as though unaware of any problem. Embarrassed, he felt his body responding and was sure he could light a match on his face. At the song's end, he rightly anticipated her next move and broke away before the next one began, heading for the food table again. She was only a step behind him and hurriedly followed him to his destination. They arrived almost together, and he could hear her panting softly through moist red lips.

"My, that was the nicest dance ever, Mr. McCain. Maybe we could do it again after a while?"

Jericho stuffed half a slice of gooseberry pie into his mouth and mumbled around it, "'Fraid not, Miss Farmer. Soon as I finish eating this pie, I got to hit the sack. Captain Wallace gave me and Roosevelt orders to ride out first thing in the morning."

Her pretty face registered such genuine disappointment, that for just an instant he was tempted to agree to one more dance. Besides, it was awfully hard to forget the way she'd felt, pushing against him as they danced. Poe suddenly appeared at his side, swaying greatly, his face red, angry.

"Whatcha doing with my…girl, Jericho?"

He belched loudly, stumbled again and nearly fell down.

"I said I was gonna whup ya…and aye God…feller turns his…back…for just one minute, and damned…(*belch*) if you don't stab…him in the…"

Poe's eyes rolled back in his head and Jericho watched as in slow motion, he spewed a stream of vomit that arched in a rainbow of colors, landing on the front of Polly Farmer's new green dress. Then, without another word, he pitched forward into Jericho's arms – out cold.

Jericho struggled to keep Poe on his feet as he finally managed to touch the brim of his hat politely.

"If you'll excuse me, Ma'am, I'll just take old Roosevelt home and put him to bed now."

The last he glimpsed as he carried Poe out the door over his shoulders was Polly Farmer, standing where he'd left her, her pretty features stunned, bewildered and frozen, her once green dress, a collage of muted, dull colors.

Sixteen

THEY'D BEEN ON THE trail since daylight, and the midday sun was starting to bear down with increasing intensity as Poe moaned again, causing Jericho to covertly observe him swilling water from his rawhide canteen. They were still in country where water was easy to find for now, but when they reached the plateau area that might become a problem. Jericho vowed to keep an eye on his friend for a while. Raf Palomino and Will Sonnet rode well to the front where the air was fresher, occasionally casting glances over their shoulders and snickering between themselves. Poe had vomited constantly for the first two hours on the trail, and then suffered the dry heaves for another. Finally dehydrated, nauseous and pale, he just clung desperately to his saddle horn and groaned from time-to-time.

The scene brought to mind a jovial story his pa liked to tell about himself when he was a youth. Jericho remembered how his pa used to belly-laugh as he said, "My ma always told the neighbors, 'I know my boy don't drink any of that potato liquor, 'cause I see him going to the well too often."

Right then, Poe was going to the well again, as he hefted the large canteen and drank deeply. Moaning softly as he lowered it, he replaced the plug and slung it over his saddle horn within easy reach. Hiccupping and belching profusely, he hung over the side of his saddle and waited for another fit of dry heaves to pass. Jericho urged his mount a few steps ahead to get upwind from him.

After a few moments, Poe pulled up beside him again.

"I didn't really puke on Polly Farmer, did I? I mean really?"

"Yep."

Another groan.

"My life is over. Ruined. Not only do I get drunk and make a complete arse out of myself, damned if I don't puke all over the woman I plan to marry. I hope Pox Marks kills me so I don't have to face her again."

Secretly, Jericho was taking no small amount of glee in Poe's misery. He was fed up with the way Poe had been mooning after Polly Farmer all winter.

"Look at it this way, Roosevelt. All this just might be a blessing in disguise."

Poe didn't want to be placated. "And just how did you arrive at that brilliant deduction?"

"Suppose you and Polly had already been hitched and this little shenanigan happened. Why, she'd probably make you swear off hard liquor for the rest of your natural life. Now just how serious would that be?"

Poe looked thoughtful, then horrified. "I can see what you mean, J.D.! A whole lifetime without another little snort of corn. Why…why, no woman is worth that!"

"My sentiments exactly, Roosevelt. Especially since it makes you feel so good the next day, too."

Jericho's sarcasm was completely lost on the ailing Poe, but he appeared a little more cheerful after that, although still quite pale and shaken.

By the second day it appeared that Poe might actually live after all, for he no longer wished for a quick death at the hands of their prey, the outlaw, Pox Marks. He even ate a meager breakfast of beans, several biscuits Jericho smuggled out from the cakewalk, and about a gallon of strong black coffee – while joshing with Will Sonnet about someone slipping poison into his corn liquor when he wasn't looking. By noon, the color had partially returned to his face and he was sitting easier in the saddle.

As they took an early afternoon break near a running brook, Mordecai suddenly rejoined them. He just walked into camp and squatted down beside them like he'd been gone only a couple of minutes, instead of the past two days. He cleared his throat and spit a profuse volume, then leaned back on his heels even further and half-closed his eyes.

"That pack of polecats split up. Four went angling off the west and the other seven continued due south. You recovered enough to make a decision yet?"

He'd addressed his question to Poe, who looked decidedly better than the day before, but was still hollow-eyed and a little shaky.

"'Course I am! I'm re-cov-ered enough to make several decisions if need be!"

Poe appeared agitated as the old man turned his head away, a shadow of a smile playing at the corners of his mouth. Poe's hangover hadn't entirely gone away, and Jones's smirk didn't set well with him.

"Bigfoot put me in charge cause I know my business. He said to chase 'em around some and let 'em know they can't just ride around butchering God-fearing folks without raising the ire of law-abiding citizens. I say we go after the small bunch. That way, if we're lucky enough to catch up with 'em, we'll have 'em outnumbered. Hee hee."

Gone to Texas

Jericho snorted.

Mordecai remained silent except for spitting at a swift lizard running full-tilt for a low-growing bush. Brown juice covered the lizard by the time it reached its destination.

Poe ignored Mordecai, staring hard at Jericho.

"Well, what? Come on, out with it! I'm beginning to recognize that little snort of yours. And that particular one sounded like you're less than pleased about my decision to chase the bunch that split off. Come on, let's have it Mr. Smarty Pants."

Jericho appeared interested in something at the bottom of his empty tin cup. Finally, he looked up, faintly amused.

"As I told our famous leader, Mr. Bigfoot, I intend to get lucky and bring some of these heathen back to answer for their sins. I figure we have a better chance if we trail the main bunch."

Poe's previously pale face was now beet red.

"And just how do you figure that? I've been a Ranger for more'n a year. That's why Bigfoot Wallace put me in charge. Just what makes you think you always know so danged much more than anybody else?"

Jericho's stubborn streak had now risen to the surface as he set his jaw and stared straight ahead. There was no power on God's green earth that was going to make him back down at that point.

"I've hunted most of my life and learned the habits of creatures. Bear, elk, man – makes no difference. They're pretty much all the same. A lone animal or one in a small herd is careful – skittish – constantly ready to flee at the smallest sign of danger. They smell everything, including the air, check a familiar clearing a dozen times before crossing, and will stand in a stream bed, frozen for hours before taking a simple drink of water. You take that same deer or elk among a large group of their kind, and they tend to do things that are likely to get themselves killed. They mistake numbers for safety, much like you or me would. That's why we have a better chance with the large bunch. They feel safe."

Poe's mouth hung open for an instant.

"Well if that ain't the most…what do you think about those buffalo chips, Mordecai?"

The old man was eyeing the bush where the lizard had hidden, his mouth filled, ready to fire at the slightest movement. Finally, he splattered the brown gob in the dust near his boot and wiped his mouth with the back of his hand.

"Lad's right. I had to look hard to even see the trail of the four that split off. They were careful and they knew how to cover their tracks. Split off in a rocky creek bottom. Almost missed it – and I was looking, too. On the other hand, the big bunch just kept merrily on their way like they hadn't a care in the world. So…I gotta agree with the lad, here."

Poe jumped to his feet and slapped his hat against his leg.

"I was testing you Jericho. Just wanted to see if you have the makings to be a real Ranger. Aye God, ya done right smart. Yes, Sir! Let's saddle up! Mordecai, see if you can pick up the trail of the main group again, and this time try to leave us a little sign to follow by."

The place near the rock where Mordecai Jones had rested was empty. He had already disappeared.

* * *

Polly and her father reached the pecan grove just before noon. The shade near the water felt cool, almost luxurious after the warm ride. In another month, they wouldn't be able to make the trip during the hot part of the day, but now, it seemed almost like Paradise to her. She'd heard Mr. Partic say it was sure to be a hot summer, since the spring days had grown so warm all at once. Polly didn't doubt it. She spread the blanket on the grass beneath the largest tree and set out the picnic lunch she'd prepared for herself and her father, fantasizing about the time she would come here with Jericho McCain.

Mrs. Jericho McCain.

She had little doubt it'd happen. She'd seen the way he'd stared at her after she'd pressed against him during the short dance. If she could just get rid of that pesky Rosie Poe long enough to spend some time with Jericho…Well, she had a plan for that as soon as he returned from that silly old chase after some so-called bad men.

The food ready, she leaned back against the tree and watched her father go through the same ritual he did every time they visited their future ranch site. He knelt and dug into the rich soil, let it sift through his fingers, then moved on to another spot and repeated the process. As he reached the third large pecan tree along the bank, a tall figure stepped from behind the tree and smashed a rifle butt into her father's face. Uncomprehending, she watched as he crumpled onto the cool grass without a sound.

Polly screamed and jumped to her feet to run to him, but suddenly a man with a horribly disfigured face blocked her path. His grin was so evil.

Then she faded away.

* * *

It was on their twelfth day out that their chase finally bore fruit. As the shadows grew longer in the aging afternoon, Mordecai met them and led them into a spot where they lay and watched the seven men they were pursuing cook their evening meal. The outlaws didn't seem concerned about the bright fire they'd made attracting attention. They seemed content with their surroundings, overconfident. Poe grinned at Jericho in the fading light.

"Numbers makes 'em brave – that what you said?"

"Something like that."

"Well, they're gonna wish they'd been just a mite more careful before this night's over." Poe looked around, suddenly nervous. "Now where in tarnation did that old heathen run off to?"

Jericho knew he was speaking about Mordecai Jones, but since he didn't have an immediate answer, he remained silent. Suddenly, the old man returned, beside them again.

"They're all there, 'cept for the four that split off earlier. How'd you want to play it, Rosie?"

It was nearly dark but Jericho saw Poe glance toward him, as if seeking advice. When he didn't take the bait, Poe said, "You had a pretty good idea back at the forks, J.D. Got any more?" He sounded sheepish.

Jericho squinted through the thickening darkness at the dying campfire.

"If it was me, I'd get a couple hours sleep then move into position so we have 'em in a three-way cross-fire. I'd place a couple of men on that small peak, one on the large rock across the gorge, and two more at that mound with the four scrub oak on it. Any way they tried to hide, we'd be staring right down their throats."

Poe breathed, "Aye God, son, I hope you never come after me."

He pondered Jericho's suggestion, and then nodded.

"Mordecai, let's do as J.D. says. You tell Will and Raf to move over to that peak. Me and J.D. will take the mound. Since you got that buffalo gun with the longest range, slip around to that rock pile and take up position there. Be ready at daylight cause that's when I'm going to cut a rug."

Mordecai didn't t answer, just slipped silently into the darkness.

* * *

Mesmerized, Pox Marks stood exactly as he'd been for almost a full hour, staring at the blackened grotesque shape twisting gently in the afternoon breeze. He ignored the three mounted men a short distance away, and they knew better than to rush him at times like these. He was in a spell and the others knew to wait until he was completely finished. Finally, he shuddered violently, groaning, his eyes half-closed. For several minutes he stood, shoulders slumped forward, then straightened and turned to them as if nothing had happened.

"What did I tell you? The old man and his sweet little clam returned just like I said they would. That's why I sent the others on – no reason to share her. Besides, that would have made too many of us. You boys'll sure owe me after this."

Walks Like a Dog sat on his spotted mount like a statue, his face and bare chest smeared with blood. His demeanor evil, downright ferocious. Taos appeared smug, dangerous, like large mountain cats after they'd gotten their stomachs full of prey they just killed. Carlos too remained mounted, his arms wrapped around the red-haired girl's waist, nuzzling the hair on the back of her neck with his nose. She didn't stir, just blankly stared at the horizon. Pox Marks knew what they were feeling. The slow torture and eventual killing of the old man had taken hours – then the games with the girl. Instead of draining him, it made him feel stronger – invincible. It always did.

There had been others before and there'd be many more expected in the future. Texas was a big, open land and more and more settlers were showing up every day. Soon there'd be a farm or ranch on every hill. All those newcomers and no law to protect them. Pox Marks grinned at the thought of it.

The red-haired girl had been feisty at first, fighting them fiercely, eventually giving up and pleading with them. Pleading mercy for her father – then for herself. But she'd given up too quickly. Most of the city-bred women he'd known did that. They were too soft, had no will. A Mexican peasant or an Indian girl would fight them every time they came near, then might try to cut their throats at the first opportunity. City girls screamed a lot, but in the end, they crumpled.

He'd always let them keep the girl for a while, then when they'd grown tired of her he'd cut her throat, or sell her to one of the Mexican whorehouses across the river. Maybe he'd build a small fire on her soft stomach to see what she would promise them to put it out.

"Let's ride. I told Mills we'd meet up with them at the Four Corners."

* * *

A prairie dog stuck its head out a borough a few steps from where Jericho and Poe lay motionlessly, watching the enemy camp beginning to stir below them. Men coughing, spitting, breaking wind and speaking in profane terms. It sounded to Jericho much the same as the Texan's camps had during the short time he'd been with them. He kept reminding himself these were men who butchered families – small children and women. These weren't soldiers sharing comradely exchanges before the day's battle, but brutes who'd stepped over the boundaries of human decency and must pay for their transgressions with their lives – or at least their freedom. He didn't relish the task at hand, nor did he shrink from it. It was simply something that needed to be done.

Small twigs could be heard splintering and soon a smokeless fire was going. Something metal struck a rock nearby, a sound clear and sharp in the morning calm, as camp aromas drifted up to them – someone was preparing coffee. Still, it was too dark in the shadowy draw to get a fine bead on a moving target, and the Rangers knew these were experienced and deadly men despite their apparent disregard for possible danger.

Jericho's clothing was damp from the morning dew, causing him to repress an urge to shiver, thus momentarily distorting his point of aim. He felt exposed in the approaching morning light which was rapidly growing brighter on the ridgeline, where they waited. He and Poe forced themselves to remain, frozen in place, despite cramps and other bodily functions urging relief. They knew that any movement would likely be spotted from the men below and the element of surprise lost.

"Any of 'em makes it to the horses, it'll be your job to bring them down with your long gun," Poe whispered hoarsely, the strain showing in his voice.

Jericho nodded silently as an answer and kept his eyes fixed on the camp below, now becoming much easier to see in the expanding light. He watched from the corner of his eye as Poe inched his rifle up to rest against his shoulder, heard him sigh.

"Time to dance."

Poe squeezed off a round, the loud report vibrating through the endless draws and canyons, then suddenly disappeared from ear range. At his shot, several things happened simultaneously. The man he'd aimed at dropped like he'd been struck by a sledge-hammer, and in the smattering of rifle fire from three directions, four others also spun and fell to the ground, one crawling between two rocks, dragging his leg behind him. The rest simply disappeared.

They waited. After what seemed like a long time, a rough voice rose from below.

"Hey out there! Who you be? What you want?"

Poe, careful to keep his head down, shouted back. "Texas Rangers. Come to kill you or take you back. Makes no difference. You decide, but do it quick."

"Wait...wait! You've made a mistake. We're horse traders from Louisiana. We've done no wrong."

"Well, then you won't mind just lying down your guns and coming out so's we can apologize for this little mistake, right?"

A few seconds later a volley of fire raked the grove of trees where they waited. As soon as the dirt stopped falling over them, Poe and Jericho raised their heads and saw two of the men running for where the horses were tied. Amid a hail of bullets, the two outlaws reached the horses, leaped upon their backs and sped away. Almost at once, one of the animals somersaulted head over heels, catapulting its rider headfirst into the hard earth. Both animal and rider lay motionless where they'd come to rest. Will Sonnet and Raf Palomino had appeared from nowhere, dragging the downed man from between the two rocks where he'd tried to seek shelter from their withering fire. His mount lay without moving.

The last rider had apparently made it out of range and viciously spurred his mount to greater efforts, nearly to the crest of the hill. Jericho rose to one knee and brought his rifle to his shoulder, carefully sighting along the slim barrel as Poe fidgeted and looked on with worried eyes.

"Well, dammit – shoot!"

Jericho waited until the rider was outlined against the bright morning sunlight at the very top of the ridge, ready to slip over the other side, before he startled Poe with the gun's thunderous report. Poe watched, agitated as the rider vanished from sight.

"Ya missed."

Jericho didn't answer, climbing down from his perch and heading down the dusty slope toward the place Will Sonnet and Raf guarded prisoners.

"Guess everybody misses once in awhile," Poe said again. "I just didn't know you was that human."

"I didn't miss," Jericho said quietly.

"Huh?"

"I said I didn't miss."

"Looked to me like you did. And I got the best eyes in the Ranger Militia, outside of Bigfoot Wallace."

Jericho snorted.

They'd reached the others and it was clear the man with the wounded leg was in considerable pain. His thighbone prominently poked through his right pants leg, blood spurting like a small red fountain into the air. The outlaw who'd been thrown from his horse was slowly coming around, groaning softly, trying to sit up. Finally aware of where he was, he dropped his hand to an empty holster, and then looked up into Raf Palomino's grinning face.

Disgusted, Poe kicked a stick ten feet into the air.

"Pox Marks ain't here. I sure hope that one you missed wasn't him."

"I didn't miss."

The man with the broken leg attempted to sit up, screamed horribly and fell back unmoving in the dust. Sickened, Jericho looked away to find Poe and the others watching Mordecai Jones pick his way down the rocky hillside. When he arrived, he reached for the canteen Sonnet held out to him, swallowed deeply and wiped his mouth with a greasy buckskin sleeve. He reached inside his shirt and rummaged around for his plug of tobacco.

"What's that?" Poe pointed toward a dripping mass of hair attached to Jones's belt.

"Scalp. Found him just over the ridge there." He jerked his head toward the spot Jericho had fired at the escaping outlaw.

"Breathing his last, so's I just relieved him of his hair. He won't be needing it where he's going."

Poe stared at Jericho, amazement written across his face.

"Well I'll be dammed! Ya didn't miss! Ya hit the son-of-a-bitch at nearly half a mile away! I'll be double-damned."

Mordecai walked over and squinted at the wounded man, who stared back at him through pain-filled eyes. After a moment he nodded and continued to stare until the wounded outlaw grew agitated with him.

"Well? What's your problem old man?"

"Not nearly as serious as your'n young feller. Tomorrow morning I'll have breakfast, take a crap and maybe get drunk. Because I'll still be alive – you, on the other hand, will be deader'n dirt."

"I'm not gonna die you crazy old geezer! I've had worse than this and lived!"

"'Peers to me like you're 'bout finished heathen. Bleed to

death before the night is through – that is, if the wolves and big cats don't get to you first. 'Course if you do manage to make it until morning, we'll hang you anyway. Like I said, I'm doing better'n you." Mordecai winked and stood. "I wouldn't be making any long-range plans if I were you, son."

The man moved as if to stand, then screamed in agony and fell back again as Jones continued to stare at him, grinning wolfishly.

"What do we do now?" Jericho asked uneasily. Suddenly, he didn't like the way this way going.

Mordecai turned toward him, laughing right out loud this time.

"Do? Hang 'em. That's all we can do."

"We can't just hang them without a trial," Jericho replied, beginning to feel even more sorry he'd come along on this excursion.

Jones squinted at him in apparent sympathy.

"What would you have us do, lad? We're five-six days ride from a friendly soul...if we don't run into Mexican deserters, Kiowa, or the rest of his ilk. Now that the weather's turning warmer, the Comanche will be drifting back into the area, too. Maybe already here. Ya better think about that, pilgrim."

"They can't be any worse than the men we're chasing."

"I can see you ain't been here long enough. There are several kinds of Indians around here, lad. The Kickapoo are pretty good fighters, but have no imagination and will run if they think it's going to be a hard fight. If they outnumber you, and if it don't cost them too much, they'll usually just kill you, maybe eat you too, if it's a particularly hard winter. If they do decide to engage in any torture, which is unlikely, they'll most likely just bury you up to your neck and ride off. Like I said, not much imagination."

Jones spit a brown stream at a nearby rock, and then continued.

"Kiowa are a whole different proposition. They like to play with their victims. Sometimes they'll tie a prisoner over an ant hill and dab a little honey on all of the poor soul's body cavities – then throw a party that can last for a week while them busy little critters store up for the winter. Or sometimes, they'll start a little tag of skin – they like to start on the back of the neck – wrap it around a stick and peel a strip off inch by inch. They keep it up until a body's practically skinned."

Jones looked around for a place to spit, but by this time the others had moved in closer, blocking his aim – so he swallowed it, then fiegned momentarily ill. It was all part of the play, because he knew he had his audience hooked and wanted to savor it.

"But when it comes to torture and just plain being nasty, nobody beats the Comanche. They can keep a man alive for days while they work on him. One of their favorite tricks is to build a small fire, hang someone over it and cook a prisoner's feet. Once I seen the remains of a man and they'd burnt his feet clean off halfway to his knees. Kept him alive the whole time too. I know, 'cause Comanche don't torture the dead."

Mordecai turned away from Jericho's sick expression, satisfied he'd made his point. He spit, this time at the wounded man.

"That one won't live out the day, if I have to shoot him myself."

Then he turned and nodded toward the other outlaw.

"That one'll likely weasel outta them ropes first chance he gets and cut our throats while we sleep. You'll learn out here that prisoners are a luxury you just can't afford. I say, hang 'em right now, and save ourselves a passel of trouble."

Poe appeared distressed. As leader, the weight of the decision now rested entirely upon him. He reluctantly turned to Sonnet.

"Will, get some ropes. Raf, bring a couple of horses over – and check out those scrub oaks to see if there's a limb strong enough for us to use. We might as well get this over with and hit it back to headquarters."

Jericho felt as though he were sleepwalking.

"Rosie? Roosevelt?"

Poe wouldn't look at him.

"Mordecai's right, J.D. It's got to be done. Wallace told us over and over exactly what we had to do with these types – not prisoners of war – but heathen like this don't have no right to live anymore. He said we got to be judge, jury and executioner for the Texas Republic until the citizens are able to do it for themselves."

"Everybody has a right to a fair trial," Jericho insisted.

"Not these two. And even if they do, they sure ain't gonna get it this time. Wallace told us what they done to that family. You heard it same as me. We take 'em back, the folks in town will likely just tear them apart piece by piece, anyway."

Jericho, sick to his heart, stumbled over to a rock and sat down heavily. Since coming to Texas he'd killed other men – men he didn't even know. But they were armed and might have killed him or a friend if he hadn't. This was different. Hanging men without a fair chance to defend themselves in court, no matter what they'd done, went against everything he'd ever been told by his pa – against all his mother's Christian teachings. He looked up as Raf approached, leading two horses. Hanging the outlaws didn't appear to have diminished the good humor of the slim Mexican youth in any way.

"That lowest limb looks strong enough to hold them both," Raf said with a winning grin.

The two outlaws now looked terrified. The wounded one lay back, closing his eyes and groaning softly. The other, who'd been thrown from his horse, jerked his head from side to side, eyes darting as though seeking an escape. Seeing none, he grew belligerent.

"You mangy sons of bitches! You can't hang us out here! You're lawmen. The army'll likely shoot ya when you return if you do this."

"Yeah," moaned the other one without opening his eyes. "It ain't no skin off you one way or the other. We done wrong, I admit it. But that don't give you no right to just up and hang us without a trial."

Poe's face looked drawn, pale, but he remained determined.

"You get the same kind of trial that family got when you and your friends butchered them. Bigfoot Wallace said you gutted the little girl and stuck a timber into the woman, raised it up and burnt her. Said he seen the results personal and it made him sick. That don't call for no trial."

The wounded man moaned loudly.

"I'm injured almost to death," he said pitifully. "Ya can't hang an injured man. If you just gotta hang someone, hang Mills. He ain't hurting like me."

The outlaw Mills made as if to lunge at his partner, but Raf's pistol suddenly appeared in his hand as though by magic, so he just settled back, glaring at the other outlaw. Finally, he screamed, "You scum sucking pig! You keep your stinking mouth shut fore I rip your head off!"

Mordecai chuckled.

"Now, now girls. Let's not fight. It'll all be over soon." He and Raf seemed to be the only ones not affected by the approaching execution.

Gone to Texas

A pale Will Sonnet arrived carrying several rawhide strips. Poe pulled his pistol and pointed it at the man leaning against a rock.

"If you move, I'll put a round in each of your legs so your partner won't have nothing to complain about. Will, tie his hands but leave his feet free. Then do the same to the other one. I want to be gone from here in the next half-hour. I don't know who might've heard our ruckus earlier."

With the outlaws securely tied, Will Sonnet and Raf half-carried them to the mounts and placed them into their saddles. The wounded man screamed, nearly fainting with pain, but soon they were both mounted with Mordecai holding their horse's reins. Without a word, the party moved to the old scrub oak and Poe tossed the rope ends over the lowest limb. Jericho remained seated where he'd been all along, staring out across the valley. Behind him, he could clearly hear the proceedings, seemingly deafening in the morning stillness – the creaking of leather, horses snorting, stamping their feet nervously and the ragged breathing of condemned men. Even the sound of flies buzzing in the warm morning sun. Poe's voice carried to him.

"Any last words? Anybody I can notify? Family, friends?"

"My leg's on fire. You can't just hang a wounded man like this! Dammit, it ain't right!"

"Your pain will be over soon, friend. Any last words?"

"Go to Hell you son of a bitch! I'll be waiting for you when you arrive!"

A loud slap and the snort of a startled horse drifted on the still air, followed by galloping horses, then the cracking of the old limb as it took the dead weight of the two outlaws. Finally, there was only the rubbing of ropes as the bodies swayed back and forth in the quietness. Jericho still didn't move when he heard Mordecai say, "Cut 'em down?"

"No. Leave 'em," Poe answered. "In case their friends come looking for 'em. And leave a note on 'em that this is Texas Ranger law."

For three days after the hanging Jericho remained in a foul mood. Having already heard about his flaming temper, the others steered clear of him. For two more days, he kept to himself, brooding. On the sixth day Poe ventured near, bringing him a cup of coffee.

"Should be in San Antonio late tomorrow. The first thing I'm gonna do is buy me a cow. A big cow. Just gonna bash in his head, wipe his butt and singe the hide a little. Then, I'm gonna eat the whole damned thing, bones, horns and all. I don't care if I never see another bean and tortilla again as long as I live. My ribs are poking right through my shirt."

When Jericho didn't answer right away, he persisted. "What about you, J.D.? Got any plans?"

Jericho sighed and raised his head to stare at him.

"I've got less than a week left on my hitch with the Rangers. That's all I'm committed to. I'm going to tell the Captain I ain't cut out to being a Ranger, then I'm going to light out for a place I heard about a while back."

Poe, encouraged he'd finally penetrated Jericho's shell, inched closer.

"Where's that?"

"It's a bunch of mountains running all the way from Canada to the Mex border. They say you could set all of the Blue Ridge Mountains down in them and never see them again. It must be something to behold. I just want to see the place before I die."

"Probably not many people there."

"I 'spect not."

Poe didn't say much for a while, then embarrassed, he ventured, "I'd miss not having ya around, J.D., I reckon."

Jericho looked surprised. *Poe would miss him?* He'd always figured the young Ranger resented him a little, especially when it came to Polly Farmer. Suddenly he felt a little saddened and knew he'd miss Poe, too. Probably Will Sonnet, Raf Palomino, and even that old killer, Mordecai Jones. He tossed a stick into the small fire.

"Hell, Roosevelt. You're just going to end up married to the Farmer gal. After that, we wouldn't see each much other anyway. I mean, with you working in the store, and all."

Poe squinted at the darkening horizon.

"I reckon. Depends on what her long range views are, concerning drinking corn whiskey though."

Neither spoke for several minutes, then Poe blurted, "You ever love a woman, J.D.? I don't mean like we all do in them saloons and whorehouses. All that's fine as far as it goes, but it ain't real love. I mean a woman you'd want to go home to every danged night, lay off the whisky and never stray again?"

Jericho hadn't thought of Jean in weeks. Now, suddenly he could see her face as clearly as that day under the pecan trees by the river. All the pent-up pain and emotion of her departure rushed over him, leaving him shaken. He hesitated, regained his composure and wondered how much to disclose to the talkative Poe. Finally he nodded, and then realizing Poe couldn't see him in the darkness, said, "Once. Felt like I was missing a part of me when I lost her."

"She dead?"

After a long silence, Jericho whispered, "Yeah. She's dead."

"Well I guess you know how I feel about Polly then. I think about her all the blooming time, J.D. If I don't get her, I swear I'll probably just up and die."

"I could think of some better places than this to raise a family if it was me getting married – which it ain't."

"Now just what've you got against Texas, J.D.? Ever time I turn around, there you go again, bad-mouth'n Texas."

Jericho considered dropping the subject, then decided to explain.

"Back where you came from, was there lots of trees – rivers – tall hills?"

"I reckon. My family lived so far back in the hills the damned road finally came to an end running right up a danged tree."

Jericho chuckled.

"I know what you mean. We lived smack-dab at the end of our road, too. Pa made it by dragging a load of logs, back-and-forth, back-and-forth. Took him almost a month."

He swished his coffee around and tossed it into the weeds.

"You ever miss the cool breeze and fresh air of that place, Rosie?"

"Can't say I do. Jim Stafford – not my real Pa, he's dead – well, he used to get us kids up at four o'clock in the morning to start working in the fields. Many nights we didn't get in until hours after it got dark. I was just a pup, but I couldn't remember when I didn't have sores and scabs on my hands from toiling in the fields. It wasn't his fault really. Weren't nobody's fault. If we didn't do it, we didn't eat come winter. Then, when it did turn winter, it got so cold spit cracked. They say it has to be twenty-five below zero for spit to crack. I don't know about that, but I do know that until I left home, I never had a winter coat of my own. Me and my younger brother Tass had to share one. Leaving home was the best thing I could've done for Tass. At least now he has his own coat.

"I cut out as soon as I turned sixteen…damned if I was going to be a danged farmer like Pa was – and mean old Jim Stafford. When I came to Texas to join the new militia, John Coffee-Hays asked me to shoot a rifle. I done passable. Then he tossed me one of them new Walker Colts and it felt like a part of my own hand. I flat couldn't miss. Impressed him so much, he gave me a job on the spot. Been in the militia ever since. Best deal I ever got. Get to sleep in until five every morning. Most Sundays, I don't even have to work. Hell, I thought I'd died and gone to Heaven. Guess I did in a way…and they call it Texas."

Jericho sat silently and drank the rest of his tepid coffee. Then he said, "A lot of people have it tough. I admit, I had a good life with Ma and Pa, but I knew others who suffered like you did. I still say you could just strike out for the Colorados with me. Lots of room out there to get lost in – room to raise a family."

Poe looked like he was concentrating on something serious. A rare feat for him.

"Part of me wouldn't mind that too much, J.D. But something great is going to happen here in Texas, and I want to be part of it. Besides, I'd always wonder how it'd been married to Polly Ann."

"I wish you both the best, Rosie. I truly do. Name one of your boys after me."

"Danged if I won't! Come to the wedding, J.D.? You wouldn't take off until after the wedding, would ya?"

"No. I reckon I'll stay until after the wedding. But then…I gotta see them mountains."

* * *

Walks Like a Dog completed his circle and returned to the three men and a girl waiting under the old scrub oak. A dozen vultures, disturbed at their morning meal by the riders, waited impatiently in one of the nearby oaks. Only an occasional loud squawk indicated their displeasure over the interruption. A small pack of coyotes waited in the shade of a thorny bush halfway up the steep slope, where Poe and McCain had waited the previous morning. Both fowl and beast knew that if they waited long enough, their patience would eventually be rewarded.

Pox Marks leaned back against the trunk of the old tree, his eyes closed, apparently sleeping. He heard Walks Like a Dog approaching in the same manner all those hunted hear such things. He snapped his eyes open, as the big Indian squatted down beside him.

"There was five of them. Army or militia I'd say, because the horses were shod. They shot from there – there – and there."

He pointed at the high points around the camp.

"Waited until daylight. Took Mills and the others by surprise. Bochman was wounded. I don't know how they took Mills alive though. I wouldn't think he'd just give up. He was too damned mean for that."

Pox Marks listened until his man was through, then spit.

"He gave up all right. Acted like such a hard case all the time, too. I'll bet he messed his pants when they put that rope around his fat neck."

He climbed to his feet and stood, staring at the tattered remains of what had once been two of his men, then laughed.

"The birds sure like him though."

Pox Marks mounted and stared at Walks Like a Dog who hadn't moved from his spot by the tree.

"Find out who did this, Dog. Get me some names and where they're at. Then join up with us at the Buffalo Wallow. I needed those boys. Someone's gonna pay for this."

Seventeen

EAGER TO WASH THREE weeks of trail dust off, Jericho headed for the bathhouse first thing. Old Chin Li owned the only bathhouse and laundry in town, and three of the four opium dens. Folks surmised he had more money than the U.S. Government, but you'd never know it by his appearance. His tattered coat and pajamas with large golden buttons, the same as he remembered the first time he saw him, a year earlier. He always provided good service for a dollar spent.

Jericho burst through the door like a cyclone, yelling at the old Chin Li to bring hot water – lots of hot water. He tossed a coin to the old man and watched him as he broke into a gappy-toothed smile, stuffing the dollar into his sash, then shuffling off to do as bid.

That's where Poe found him thirty minutes later, soaking up to his nose in an over-sized tub and smoking a long foul-smelling cigar, a habit he'd recently picked up while gambling. Jericho knew straight away from his friend's expression, that something was terribly wrong. Poe's face was deathly pale, lines burrowing deeply across his usually tan brow. To make matters worse, he'd just walked in and plopped down quietly, staring at the far wall.

"What's eating you? Somebody steal your horse?"

As Poe finally looked over at him, Jericho sensed the true depth of his friend's despair.

"It's…Polly Ann. She's…gone."

"Gone? You mean she just up and left?"

To give himself time to adjust to the news, Jericho held up his cigar and studied it, seeing it was soaked. He grimaced disgustedly and flung it against the far wall.

"She leave by stage? Her family go with her?"

"No, no. Not gone like that. Just a minute, will ya? I gotta get things straightened out in my head!"

Jericho respected Poe's silence until he was finally ready to continue.

"I just came from seeing Bigfoot Wallace. He said Polly and her pa rode out to some property they'd bought'n back when they first arrived. In spite of his warning to them, they'd done it before. When they didn't return, Bigfoot provided the shopkeeper a few militia to ride out and see what'd become of them. They found the old man, hanging in a tree by his feet, gutted and burned to a chitling. They think it was the man-burner; Pox Marks."

"Polly?"

Poe started to speak, but his voice cracked. He lowered his head and waited for a moment, then said, "They took her, Jericho. Took her with them."

Jericho couldn't think of anything to say right away, but when Poe looked up, he comprehended the full impact of the torment in his friend's eyes.

"What am I gonna do, J.D.? Poor Polly, all alone with that mangy bunch. You know what they'll do to her."

Jericho stood up, grabbed a towel, drying his body. As he slipped into his clothing, he covertly watched Poe. Now that he'd said his piece, didn't move. Jericho didn't like the way he looked – like a man who had just given up.

As gently as possible, he said, "Rosie, would it make a difference what they did to her, as long as you could get her back?"

Poe jerked around to gaze at him.

"Good God, no! I just want her back! I'll help her get over it, but I can't go on, not knowing if she's alive or dead."

"Any idea which way they're traveling?"

"After we hung them low-lifes, I sent Mordecai back to the place they split-up, just to see if he could pick up the trail. He showed up late last night. The smaller bunch that took Polly joined up a few more low-lifes along the way. Then a couple of weeks later, they ran into Comanche west of here and four of them didn't make it. The signs said most of the men and a woman must have gotten away and lit out toward Uvalde. Mordecai said it was a large band of the heathen, led by Gray Wolf. The Comanche either killed the other outlaws out-right, or burnt 'em if they found 'em alive. One of the bunch that got away was wounded bad, Mordecai said. He followed a trail of blood almost to Uvalde. There, most of the group swung around Uvalde and the wounded man went in with the woman and another outlaw. Possibly for treatment of the wound. There is no way of knowing if the woman is Polly, but I got to try and find out, Jericho."

"Did Jones go into Uvalde? See who the woman was?" Jericho said.

Poe shook his head.

"Mordecai was fearful of riding in because most of the low-life there know he's been working with the Rangers for years. He hung around for a few days, but when he left, they were still there. Could be they're still in Uvalde. If not, maybe I can pick up their trail."

"Bigfoot Wallace gonna be any help?"

"I doubt it. When I asked him about getting some help to

track 'em down, he said he had trouble along the Mexican border right now and needed to send every available man. Some self-styled bandit-turned-revolutionary has gathered up a few hundred men and fancies himself the next Bolivar. They hit a few outposts and farms along the border and seem to be getting bolder. I refused to go with them until I knew beyond a doubt that Polly is dead, and it was only at the insistence of the shopkeeper that he finally said if I wanted to go after them, he wouldn't try to stop me. The bastard knows a lone man don't have a chance in country like that, but damn his eyes, Jericho, I gotta try."

At the last, his voice broke.

Jericho studied him silently. Poe sat unmoving, his long hair dangling in front of his face. He rubbed his eyes wearily – a man shaken to his core. This wasn't the brash young gunfighter-killer Jericho had first met – courage itself, wilder than the wind, believing himself immortal to every danger he flaunted. This was a beaten young man, uncertain of his course – shaken in his own belief of himself – and that was dangerous. Jericho knew because he'd been there before.

He too had lost every thing that had ever meant anything to him; his family, Jean, Handsome Jack, even old Blue. It'd left him empty, seething with rage, searching for something he couldn't identify. Now a small, rarified, improbable spark of friendship began to grow between them, – a man with whom he shared not one nugget of commonality – a friendship that seemed all the more precious...because of the improbability of it.

"You ain't gonna be alone, Roosevelt. Not this time. In that poke on the chair is my wages. Take it. Lay on the supplies we'll need and I'll meet you at the stables in half an hour."

Poe jerked his head up, stunned. Then he leaped to his feet, exclaiming, "Aye God, Jericho! You'd help me? You'll stay here and help me get Polly Ann back?"

"It's nothing more than you'd do for me if the tables were turned. Now quit jaw-jacking and lay down tracks. We still have a few hours until dark."

* * *

The Comanche arrow had embedded itself in his thighbone and it'd taken the doctor a long time to cut it out. Pox Marks's leg throbbed beneath the bandage that the old horse doctor had dressed it with in Uvalde the previous day. He couldn't take off until he let the "doctor" look at it again in a few days. He'd seen the effects of advanced gangrene infection and he surely didn't want that. No, he and the others would wait. He may have to sweeten the pot a little to get them to stay, by letting them sample the girl some. But whatever it took, he'd hang around until he was sure there was no danger of infection setting in.

He sat apart from the others, like the lead wolf covertly studying his pack as they reclined around the outer edge of the fire, wagering no collectable bets, yet cursing one another over real or imagined slights. Taos, a big sloppy man with bullish neck and chronic bad breath, had absolutely no scruples, pride or honor. Pox Marks had seen him whine, beg and snivel to get what he wanted, then after his benefactor turned his back, he'd simply slipped his thin blade between the man's ribs, and robbed him of his shoes.

Carlos dressed flashy, grinned broadly, and looked like a dandy, but Pox Marks figured him to be the deadliest of the lot. He'd witnessed the blinding speed and accuracy when he used the

Gone to Texas

brace of pistols he shoved into a red sash around his waist. He carried another hidden in the top of his boot. Pox Marks had noticed that one accidentally as they were drying out after crossing a flooded stream. He'd been impressed that the youth kept it hidden from those with whom he rode. Carlos had also been the first to attempt to rape the red-haired girl despite her tortured screams and pleadings. He'd been purposely crude in his approach, relentlessly cruel. It was a side of the youngster Pox Marks had only suspected, and now finally witnessed. He was pleased with the discovery.

Pox Marks reluctantly had warned him off, astutely realizing it was the promise of such things that would keep he and the others in line. Once they'd sampled the heifer, his hold card would be gone. Carlos had not given in to his demand willingly. He's seen just a hint in the young gunfighter's eyes that led him to believe he was nearing the point when he'd be ready to take on his leader soon. Facing Pox Marks's cold smile, he'd stomped away, cursing under his breath. Carlos had taken a nap while the others butchered and burned her father, then when awakened, he'd taken out his rage on the girl by viciously and repeatedly kicking her, spitting on her with contempt after he was through with her.

Pox Marks had no interest in intimate things and it often surprised him that men placed such high value on the fleeting pleasures derived from lying with a woman. Not that he wouldn't partake of the whores along the border now and then, but they had never brought him the pure bliss he experienced when he dealt death in his own special way. He couldn't explain it, but those acts were as near to the physical pleasures of the flesh as he could come. Almost religious, in a sense. Yes, that was the word. The others in his group would never understand. It was mainly why he felt he was better than the others, occupying a higher plain than the riff-raff he commanded. The deaths of others by his own hands made him more…whole.

None knew Pox Marks's real name, and it didn't really matter to them. In fact, no one in the new territories knew who he really was. But earlier, when he'd been called by another name, he'd been a learned man, well read and educated. He'd owned property and traveled extensively; discovering the pleasure another's death could bring – first in London, then in New York City. He'd needed to be careful in those cities. As large as they were, there were really few places to hide – not like here in this huge country of Texas. Every man was a law unto himself – free to take and do what he wanted as long as he had the power. This place was made him.

He glanced up to see Taos shoot him a scorching grimace while Pox Marks sneered back contemptuously. The fat man was still fuming about when Pox Marks had taken Carlos and the two drifters with him to scout for an overnight camp site, and he'd been left to watch the girl because he'd been too drunk on rot-gut whisky to ride any further. They'd returned to find him with his pants around his ankles, pinning the squirming girl to the hard ground, passed out cold, either during, or before consummation of the act. Pox Marks had watched dispassionately for several minutes as the unconscious man's gross weight held the struggling girl's body beneath his own before she was able to slip away cowering under her blanket. Disrobed as she was, he'd almost had a revolt keeping the others from mounting her. He didn't care about her disgrace; he just didn't want her out of her mind when he finally decided to burn her. She had to be fully alert. Otherwise, what was the point?

Gone to Texas

When Taos finally sobered up, believing the others had been with the girl while he'd been passed out, he demanded his turn with her, too. Pox Marks had just laughed and told him he'd already had his chance; reminding him that they'd drawn straws earlier. When he was ready to turn her over to the others, Taos had already lost his turn.

He knew the others, in their drunken stupor, wouldn't care one way or the other, but in Pox Marks's own mean way, he wanted to watch Taos stew in his juices. He knew the pathetic creature wouldn't try anything as long as he was being watched, but he'd have to keep an eye on him and not provide him an easy target, or else he'd end up with the fat man's knife between his shoulder blades. The stress of living like this might have adversely affected most men, turned them into nervous wrecks. But Pox Marks thrived on it. It made him feel alive.

The two new additions to his group would cause him few problems. Of lower than average intelligence, and pre-conditioned toward expectations of reward and punishment, all he needed was to keep them supplied with rotgut and a promise of sharing the girl, and they'd do as they were told. When he'd first picked up the two half-breeds off the trail yesterday, foot-sore, half-starved, glancing nervously over their shoulders every few moments, they'd been belligerent and totally uninterested in joining up with his group. But Pox Marks had quickly recognized them for the cold-blooded killers they were and he needed the extra guns, so he'd let them see the girl and their attitudes changed immediately. They'd initially been after her like a pack of dogs. Once he'd pistol-whipped the youngest one into unconsciousness, then plied them with some of the rotgut whisky he always carried for emergencies, they barely paid her any attention now. Reward and punishment, that's what would keep them in line. He'd gotten two more men in the deal, too.

Of the others, only Walks Like a Dog had no thoughts to use her in that manner. His hatred for Whites so deep, he'd never consider copulating with a vile white woman. Instead he sat, unwavering, sharpening his deadly knife – staring at her like she would soon know of his hatred. He seemed to terrify the girl more than any of the others.

Pox Marks watched through half-closed eyes as Polly Farmer, her fine red hair now filthy with tangles and weeds, dropped an armload of twigs beside the fire, then stumbled tiredly to a dirty blanket a few yards away. She stood as though too exhausted to even fall down, then her knees suddenly buckled and she crumpled heavily into a heap. After a few moments, he observed Taos hit her on the back with a small rock. She didn't move except to hug her knees tighter. Discouraged, the fat man scratched his crotch and lay back. In less than a minute he was snoring loudly.

The girl would be useful for gathering wood and fixing their meals – keeping the others close. He'd dangle her before them for a while, providing them a reason to remain, then maybe he'd give the white *puta* to them for a time. When they tired of her, he'd burn her, too.

Eighteen

UNDER NORMAL CIRCUMSTANCES Jericho would have trusted Poe to put together the essentials they'd need for an extended time on the trail. But Poe wasn't himself these days, so he disregarded the gnawing need to hurry while he carefully accounted for each item he figured they'd require to see them through a long and dangerous ordeal such as the one they contemplated. It was just as well, for Poe had overlooked the winter coats and extra blankets they'd need in the event their chase took them into the higher elevations inside Mexico, or the mountains along the west side of the Texas territory. He made a brave effort to ignore Poe's temper and incessant jawing as he went about his chore.

"A body would think I'd never been on the trail before, the way you're checking everything over and over. We're wasting precious time, J.D. We got to be getting!"

Poe paced rapidly back and forth, stirring up a fine dust from the stable floor with all his stomping around, but it didn't dissuade Jericho from his task. He said, "If I hadn't checked, we'd been short coats and blankets and would've likely froze if we encountered a northern on the trail."

Poe squinted at him, and then spit a brown gob of tobacco toward the rafters, where it hung for an instant before dropping like bird dung into the stall below. Jericho, who'd caught the act from the corner of his eye, thought for the hundredth time that Poe's chewing habit the most disgusting mannerism he'd ever encountered. He resolved to tell him about once on the trail.

"It don't take a genius to spot a cow in a pig pen!" Poe prophesied.

This remark caused Jericho to look up, his face a puzzled mask.

"Now what in tarnation is that supposed to mean?"

It'd been one of Poe's daddy's favorite sayings, and it made little difference that he'd never quite figured it out either. He smirked knowingly and shook his finger at Jericho.

"That's for me to know and you to find out. You always claim to know so much more than anybody else, you figure it out."

With that, he stomped angrily out the stable door, leaving Jericho to shake his head in bewilderment.

Poe appeared in a much better frame of mind an hour later as they passed the town limits, finally in pursuit of the woman he planned to marry – and anxious for a confrontation with her abductors.

"Mordecai said once they'd split off from the others, and they didn't seem too concerned about hiding their tracks. He said after they'd ran into that large bunch of Comanche, the trail had headed straight for the Pecos. There's a pass through the mountains near the Piedras Negras Mountains inside Mexico. He thinks that's where they were headed. If we don't find 'em still in Uvalde, we can circle around and try to pick them up near the Pecos."

"Might need them coats, then."

Poe squinted at him dangerously, spitting into the bushes along side the trail.

"Now don't you start with me on that subject again. I already said I was wrong. So let's just leave it at that."

This time, Jericho's mouth sagged open as he stared at his friend.

"You said you were wrong? That must'a slipped right by me! When did it happen?"

"'Course I did. Back there at the livery stables. Said in my haste to bring that innocent young girl back home, that I might have overlooked some little something...like them blamed coats."

"I noticed you didn't forget your favorite plug of chew, and a bottle of corn whisky when you were putting everything together."

"Medicine. Plain and simple. A man needs such to help him survive the rigors of the trail."

"And the extra blankets?"

"I believe I mentioned at the same time, that I made a mistake by forgetting about them, too."

Poe had a knack for acting as if he were the person being wronged – totally indignant at the smallest possible slight – even when he was clearly at fault.

Jericho snorted. Poe by this time had grown accustomed to the sound, but still could just barely tolerate. He tried to close his ears to it – and to Jericho's cryptic remarks.

"I must have dozed off at some point back there, because for the life of me, I don't recall any such comments."

Without answering, Poe kicked his horse's sides and galloped ahead.

* * *

Five days later, tired but still determined, they sat on their horses and gazed down at the outlaw town of Uvalde. From a distance, it looked like any of the other small towns that dotted the barren west Texas plains. Having been through it earlier, Jericho knew that was where any similarities ended. As far as he was concerned, it was the den of iniquities written about in his family bible; clearly, Sodom and Gomorrah and a few other bad places, the names of which escaped him for the moment. Poe didn't hesitate. Kicking his horse in the ribs, he rode off down the bare hill towards the livery stable on the outskirts of town. Jericho sighed deeply, and then followed.

Other than the fact the sloppy mud had dried to hard deep ruts in the town's main street, Uvalde was unchanged from what Jericho remembered when he'd been there with Handsome Jack Clay, months before. Heavily face-painted women still leaned out of their upstairs windows, calling coarsely to them as they rode in. Men cussed one another in the street, seemingly on the verge of gunplay. They slowly rode by as two men lifted another from a pool of dark blood on the boardwalk, loaded him onto the back of a wagon from which several digging tools protruded. Two loud pistol reports shattered the morning calm from within a two-story building at the end of the street. These were quickly followed by the loud blast of a shotgun. Jericho and Poe dropped their hands to rest closer to their pistol grips, wearily eyeing the alleys and doorways along the cluttered street as they rode along.

Uvalde had only two established saloons, but more than a dozen other destinations where one could buy liquor or women as the urge required. Jericho discovered on his earlier trip to the outlaw town that liquor often costs more than the price to have someone killed. They decided to hit the saloons first, then gradually work themselves through the town until they located Polly Farmer, or were satisfied she was no longer there. Poe hoped to kill the villainous Pox Marks in the process.

They stepped inside the first saloon and immediately moved to the side of the lighted doorway to allow their eyes to get accustomed to the darkness of the damp room. Two men leaned on the bar, a bartender behind it. At one of four tables sat another man, clearly a gambler, and a fat bar girl. They had their heads close together, sharing a bottle of dark cloudy liquor. Neither the woman nor the liquor seemed very appetizing. The man, with a soiled gray suit and a filthy shirt that was once white, appeared so drunk he couldn't sit upright in his chair. Sensing no danger from that quarter of the room, Poe and Jericho turned their attention back to those at the bar.

The bartender was old, with transparent skin and a sickly cough. He had the pallor of death about him and it was evident he suffered from some fatal disease. When he set a bottle on the counter for them, his hand trembled. When he spoke, his voice weak, dry.

"Step up, gentlemen. Name your poison. It don't really matter what you name, everyone gets the same. It's all we got."

Poe and Jericho ignored the bottle and studied the other two at the bar. The youngest, a man in his late twenties, dressed as a Mexican, but clearly he was not. His long stringy blond hair stuck out from beneath the headband of the big sombrero, low over his eyes. He also brandished the ornamental holsters so popular with *pistoleros*, and his handguns sported bone-handle pistol grips. The other man was covered from head to toe with trail dust; except for his one pistol worn low on his left hip. It was oiled and clean. Of the two, Jericho figured he'd be the one that needed the most watching. The two men did not appear to be together.

Poe didn't waste any time.

"We're looking for some people. One is a young woman – pretty with red-hair. The man she is with would have scars from smallpox on his face. I'll pay for information."

Jericho caught recognition in the eyes of the old man. He suddenly looked very frightened. The other two didn't glance up, nor acknowledge the remark.

"Well?"

This time Poe spoke loud, and his tone was sharp.

"This ain't no place to be asking questions like that, hombre. Not if you value your health."

It had come from the dusty man. Poe didn't back down.

"You know something? If you do, spit it out before I lose my patience."

The stringy blond in the Mexican outfit, shoved his hat back so the string around his neck held it on. His eyes were dangerous, eager for trouble.

"You on the prod? If so, you might find it here."

The dusty man stared at Poe and Jericho, his eyes unafraid, but tired, like he'd seen too much of life and didn't like what he'd seen.

"I just got into town a hour ago," he said. "All I want is a drink and maybe a woman for the night before I head out again. The drink tastes like turpentine and women look even worse, and suddenly, I've lost my appetite for both. But no. I haven't seen your man, so I'll be leaving now. There are other drinking places in town."

He spoke with finality, as though he just wanted to leave, but if prevented, he wouldn't hesitate to fight. He clearly was among those fearless travelers who'd seen their share of trouble, and who were not afraid.

Poe nodded slightly and the man gathered up his change and backed to the door, disappearing out into the bright morning sunlight. The youth in the Mexican attire, fidgeted, nervous and uncertain of himself now that he was alone, facing two possible antagonists.

Poe's eyes bored into him.

"Well? How 'bout it? Ya seen 'em?"

The youth's hand trembled slightly as he lifted his drink, but he wasn't backing down.

"I told you. You don't ask questions in Uvalde."

The old bartender broke in with his weak voice.

"Please, Mister. Don't start shooting in here. I just cleaned up the mess from one gunfight last night, and I ain't as strong as I used to be. They was in town. Not in here, but in the Blue Goose whorehouse across the street. Stayed about two days 'cause the pox-marked man had a hole in his leg. Only saw the girl when they rode in. Didn't see them leave, but Cory Wilson, the bartender at the Goose said they left before dawn. That was six days ago. He said the girl was with them. Pretty little thing, too. Seemed scared to death – kind'a in a daze all the time."

Poe looked stricken now that he'd confirmed Polly Farmer was still alive, at least up until a week before. Seeing his friend in some difficulty, Jericho interrupted, "Anybody see which way they headed?"

"Like I said, Mister. Left before daylight. Just sneaked away. Your guess is as good as any."

Keeping his eyes on the young gunman at the end of the bar, Jericho said, "Who else was with Pox Marks?"

At the name, both men stiffened.

"P...Pox Marks? That was the Manburner? Holy Jesus! We had the Manburner right here in Uvalde and we let him go. Imagine that!"

Jericho asked again, "Who was with him?"

Excitement shining in the old man's eyes, his voice sounded stronger.

"Don't know. But Cory would. Beware of him though, Mister. Cory can be a mean son of a bitch if he don't take to you."

Poe laid several gold pieces on the counter.

"Thanks, Old-timer. Get that cough taken care of."

He and Jericho backed to the door, keeping the blond man in view until they were well outside. Poe strode hurriedly across the street, leaving Jericho to catch up.

"Let's see what ol' Cory has to tell us," he said over his shoulder.

This saloon wasn't quite as dark as the other, and held more people. Three men and a bartender stood by a handmade bar, just rough planks lying on up-turned barrels; the bartender with a dirty apron, his darkly stained teeth brown from chewing raw tobacco leaves. From the old man's description, the heavy-set man was Cory Wilson. Four more men sat at a table in the rear, dealing a dirty deck of cards. Another, either sleeping or passed out from too much drink, on the floor in a corner, snoring loudly. He was a heavily bearded man with a large pot-belly, a bloody butcher's apron and greasy clothing. As Poe and Jericho entered no one looked up, but both knew they had not gone unnoticed.

Poe headed straight to the bar. Jericho hung back so he could observe the entire room.

Poe's voice cut through the air like a knife. "You Cory Wilson?"

The bartender glared back with contempt. "I serve drinks. Order, or git out."

Never breaking stride, Poe leaned over the bar and lighting fast, grasped the man's shirt, pulling his face close to his own. In the same movement, Poe's pistol suddenly appeared in his right hand, slamming into Cory's surprised open mouth. The sound was one of teeth breaking.

Poe was aware of the loud scrape of a chair against the rough flooring, as someone attempted to rise. He heard Jericho softly say, "I wouldn't do that if I were you." The retreat of sitting back down quickly followed. Poe didn't turn to look.

"Ya got bad breath and bad teeth, hombre. I'm fix'n to cure your bad teeth problem by blowing 'em out the back of your head. Now, when I remove the barrel of my pistol just answer politely and say 'yes sir or no sir.' Nod if you want to keep your teeth."

Cory's head nodded vigorously.

Poe pulled the wet nozzle from the bartender's slack mouth, but laid it against the side of his head. Holding it still, he began to ask questions, which Cory Wilson answered politely, ending each with a "yes sir or no sir."

Thirty minutes later, they were well outside Uvalde, headed towards the mountainous area to the west.

Once more on the trail, the two friends had quickly developed an uneasy truce, each going about their chores professionally and competently. Still the bickering continued, quickly making them aware that whatever level their relationship might develop, it would forever encompass the eternal constant bickering present since it's inception. Unbeknownst to either, this might well be the key to the very foundation of their enduring and strengthening friendship.

The first two days after leaving Uvalde were spent attempting to pick up the abductors' trail. Poe had learned his tracking lessons from Mordecai Jones well, and Jericho was dully impressed at his ability to explain things, such as the time they'd occurred, the speed they'd be moving, and often their intentions. Poking around in a few horse droppings, he'd patiently explain when the outlaws had last allowed the mounts to graze, accessibility to water, and the approximate time the horses had dropped the piles.

About four days from Uvalde, Poe estimated they were only three-to-four days behind their quarry. Relentlessly, they pushed on each evening until darkness forced them to abandon the trail, believing the outlaws would stop several hours earlier, thus allowing them to gain substantially on their prey each day. There was beginning to be a scarcity of any materials to make a smokeless fire. He and Poe took to breaking twigs off the bushes as they rode by, hanging bundles of them over their saddles for the time they'd be finally forced to halt for the day. By then it would be too dark for them to gather wood for a fire.

Now into the most dry and barren sections of the country, just prior to reaching the mountains where there were no trailside bushes to gather for firewood, they simply ate a cold meal of jerky and hard tack, washed down by tepid canteen water. Neither ever complained. Initially, Poe talked about Polly Farmer and the life he had planned for them, attempting to draw Jericho into his plans, seeking a commitment by his friend to remain in Texas. Jericho did not commit, nor did he link himself with any of Poe's other plans. Despite a growing friendship between them, he seemed resolved to remain a consummate loner.

Their conversations usually occurred just as the fire was dying down, in the few moments before they dropped off into an exhausted state of sleep. Poe lay against his saddle and a rolled up blanket, carved himself a plug of tobacco, and then as always, offered it to Jericho. As usual, Jericho declined his offer and he shoved it back inside his vest pocket.

"You ought to try it just once, J.D. Makes a man ponder things better."

"Makes 'em look better, too." Jericho said deadpanned. "Remember Cory Wilson's teeth?"

Poe squinted in the diminishing firelight, as though attempting to decide if there was any sarcasm intended. Although not completely satisfied, he finally lay back and half-closed his eyes.

"You know how many boys I want, J.D.? Nine. That's a good number. Nine."

"Why nine? To help you make a living?"

"Shoot, no! Gonna send them all to school, get them a good education, right up through the eighth grade. I plan on every one of them being a preeminent instigator in this new state of Texas. Aye God, won't that be something?"

"Preeminent instigator? What's an instigator?"

Poe provided his irritating chuckle as an answer.

"I surmised ya didn't know everything. For your information, an instigator is a man who starts things, important things."

"You mean like wars? Fist fights? Things like that?"

Poe raised himself on his elbows and glared at Jericho across the smoldering fire.

"No, I don't mean like fight'n and such! I mean like governments, schools, and law. That's what I mean!"

"Oh."

"What you don't realize is this state is going to be the greatest addition to the Union since the original colonies. Hell, Texas could be a whole country all by itself. We got seaports; grazing and farming land, ore and things like that ain't even been discovered yet. And my boys are going to be part of all that! Won't it be a wonderment?"

He was answered only by Jericho's soft snores. Poe raised again on his elbows and stared at his sleeping companion, then shook his head.

"Yes, Sir, J.D., a real wonderment," he said softly.

* * *

Gray Wolf held to the high ground and observed the drama unfolding below him. One group, the one with six men and a woman, had caused great excitement among his warriors. He knew it was primarily due to the woman, and the fact they'd been away from their wives for so long. The other smaller group, two well mounted white men, seemed to be tracking the others, unaware they were being hunted. He had long ago ceased to be surprised or amused at some of the antics of the white men.

Gray Wolf had twelve men. More than enough to take either group. But white men were certain to be well armed and he'd pay a heavy price if he didn't have complete advantage over his opponents. He couldn't afford to lose any of his warriors. The larger group was a mixed one; several half-breeds, a Mexican, a white man and the female. He'd even picked out Walks Like a Dog. He spit in disgust at the thought of any Comanche crawling so low as to live in consort with the white man—even the outcast, Walks Like a Dog. Even though that group was larger, his instinct told him it might well be an easier target than the two following.

The heavily armed hunters of those two groups looked dangerous, cautious, always on-guard. The others appeared too full of themselves to be afraid of anything and that might be their downfall. Still, it was too early to make a decision.

Nineteen

"NO MORE THAN A day...maybe, day-and-a-half ahead, Jericho. They'll still be in the foothills, but nearly to the base of the mountains before we can catch up. More, if we travel the way we should in these hills."

Poe glanced around the horizon, letting his demeanor translate his concern.

Jericho had been in the field with Poe long enough to know there wasn't much he was frightened of. Yet, something in these rocky hills had him spooked.

"Dangerous country, Jericho, and I got me a feeling. Could be Kiowa, Mex, or God-forbid, Comanche moving around here with us. If we don't take our time we could end up riding smack into a bunch of 'em."

His concern caused the hair to rise uncomfortably on the back of his neck, and forced him to also anxiously search the high ground around them. He vividly remembered Mordecai Jones's horrific tales about how Comanche captors tortured their enemies for days, sometimes weeks before allowing them to die. His actions told Poe he was also anxious to get out of the unprotected draw and he swung into his saddle, leading off toward a higher point between two ridges to their front.

"If we can reach that high area in the middle before dark, it might give us a good view of the valley below. Maybe we'll get lucky and see something."

Jericho didn't answer. He was busy checking the high ground on their flanks, holding his rifle across his saddle.

They reached their objective well before dark, but disappointingly, saw nothing before them but more peaks and rocky draws. Careful not to highlight themselves against the sky, they passed through the saddle and stopped for camp a short distance down the opposite slope, in a large grouping of large boulders the size of barns. While there appeared to be easily over a dozen ways in, or out of the rocks, Poe said that would help provide them the security they needed to get some rest for the night. They made a cold camp, neither reckless enough to chance even a small fire to cook coffee.

"That stallion of your's is the best watch dog you can have out here. In the daytime watch his ears. As long as they're standing straight up, ya got nothing to worry about. But if you see them lay back or start to flop around, you better figure out the reason mighty quick. At night we'll keep both mounts in close, in case we have to make tracks. That way, he'll let us know if another horse comes within a mile of us. You hear him start to stomp and snort around during the night, we'd best be moving."

"You learn all that from Mordecai?"

Poe chuckled.

"Most of it. The rest comes from stumbling along half-asleep behind my pa's ornery, mean-tempered, cantankerous old plow horses. I learned to sleep with one eye while keeping the other eye on them critter's ears. At the first sight of someone approaching, they'd start waggling their ears to beat the band and I'd straighten right up, just like I was a 'loving my job."

Jericho laughed in spite of himself, realizing the value in the meaning of the message and tip. At times like these it just felt good being with the unpredictable Poe. Almost like when he'd been with Taylor when they were kids in Tennessee. Then immediately, he withdrew inside himself, resolving once again not to grow close to anyone.

They slept completely clothed and armed, so all they had to do in the predawn darkness was roll a single blanket and tie it behind their saddles. By the time it was light enough to see, they'd already finished their breakfast of jerky and hard tack and were five hundred yards from their overnight position. When Gray Wolf's braves stormed over their old camp at dawn, all they found had been imprints where two bodies had lain in the dust, and overnight horse droppings.

* * *

"Look at 'er, boss! She's getting skinnier and for the worse every day. What are ya saving her for anyway? We ain't gonna hurt her none. Just wanna treat her to a little bit of down home loving."

Since getting away from the Indians and rejoining him in Uvalde, Taos was showing more backbone than Pox Marks had given him credit for. Maybe because of the festering hole the Comanche arrow made in Pox Marks's thigh; or perhaps he felt he had the backing of the others. Looking around the group, Pox Marks saw it was true.

"You get her when I say you do. Not before." He didn't raise his voice.

Carlos had slowly drifted around until he was standing well to the side of Pox Marks, his left hand out of sight near his gun grip.

Pox Marks shifted slightly, and then said, "I'm going to allow you about another inch gunfighter, then I'm going to kill you. Now get back where I can see you."

Grinning, Carlos drifted back into his line of sight where Pox Marks was able to focus all of his attention back on the fat man. Carlos wasn't scared of his boss. He knew he was faster, but there was something about the madman that told him to be careful. When he looked into Pox Marks's crazy eyes, he knew if it ever came to that, he'd be up against his most formidable and dangerous opponent to date. He didn't want to push that right at the moment.

Pox Marks was speaking again.

"So you think, Taos. You really think, do you?"

The big man backed up a step, sweating profusely.

"Naw, Boss. I was just making conversation. Hell, I don't care if you cut her throat and leave her right here. Honest I don't."

"Why don't I just cut your throat instead right now, Taos, and save myself a lot of trouble later? You're worth nothing to me anyway, and I'd be able to sleep much better nights. Give me a reason why I don't."

Taos was really getting worried. This hadn't gone as he'd planned at all, and he could see he was getting in deeper by the moment.

"Now, Boss, you know I don't mean nothing. Don't I always do like you tell me?"

They had seen the same look in Pox Marks's eyes when he was ready to butcher one of his captives. They had watched his eyes change to an almost milky white, a cold snowy glare that seemed to border on the fringes of insanity. It was raging in his eyes now. The others backed away, leaving Taos to face the mad man alone.

Taos too, tried to back off, but Pox Marks followed. The big man stumbled, then toppled backward, landed heavily in the dirt, stirring up tiny dust devils. The dust stuck to his face, clearly outlining tear-tracks down his fat cheeks as he crabbed backward on the ground to keep away from his antagonist.

"Aw please, Boss. Don't. I never meant nothing. I swear I didn't."

These were tough, hardened men. Men who wouldn't beg for an inch if their lives depended upon it. Men who'd killed many times, who'd seen death face-to-face so often they no longer feared its coming for them. But to face down the mad man before them, none could fault Taos's pleas for his life. If he lost, they knew it would be at such a great price that none of them could withstand it.

In that instant, a shot rang out from the lookout's position, followed by the sound of a galloping horse.

"Comanches! Comanches coming!"

Poe slid down the rocky hillside in such haste that he created a small landslide behind him. Mindful of the noise, Jericho watched him with disapproving eyes as he dusted off the seat of his pants.

"Find anything?" he said, hoping whatever it had been was worth all the racket. It was.

"Comanche, J.D. They're following right behind Pox Marks's bunch of riff-raff. Probably getting ready to pounce on 'em again. There seems to be an awful lot of unshod ponies in these hills, pard. Like the Comanche are gathering for something big. We got to think of a way to get Polly out of that bunch before the Comanche do decide to hit 'em."

They hurriedly mounted up and struck out at a gallop. It was three days later when they found the remains of Pox Marks's outlaw band.

R.C. Morris

* * *

Poe saw it first. Turkey buzzards making slow lazy circles in the afternoon sky. Dozens of them – something drawing them in from miles away to come and feed – something big. Jericho watched him look at them, as they angled their horses in the direction of their deadly feast. At quarter of a mile the smell was strong. As they moved closer, overwhelming. Finally, he and Poe soaked their neckerchiefs in a little precious water and tied them around their faces. It was of little help.

The killing ground was large, as though the outlaws had put up a tremendous running fight. But the horrific conclusion had been preordained from the outset. The Indians had set up on both sides of a long draw, concealed in the large rocks above. Those, whom the deadly opening fire hadn't killed outright, had later been tied to boulders and burned...then butchered.

Jericho heard Poe whisper, "Polly. Oh God, Polly."

Attempting to identify whether the bodies were male or female would be difficult, because of the condition the Comanches had left them in. They went from body to body, trying to identify the dead and determine if Polly was among the mutilated corpses. Neither Pox Marks nor Polly Farmer was among them. Poe's ability to read the signs confirmed what they already knew. The outlaws had been strung out more than usual when the trap was sprung, probably before they were all inside the killing area. Pox Marks, Polly Farmer and maybe one or two of his henchmen had apparently survived the initial onslaught and gotten away. Poe found their trail immediately, for they couldn't possibly have hidden it in their haste to flee the hellish scene in the draw a short distance away.

Poe pointed toward the setting sun.

"That way. About a dozen unshod ponies in hot pursuit, too."

"Anything out there?"

Poe squinted for a moment as though thinking, and then said, "Pollo Rio. The Chicken River Mission. That's all."

"What's there?"

"Used to be a large Spanish mission, if it's still there. The Spaniards built a high stonewall surround to protect it. Once kept a small contingent of soldiers. After they left, a village sprung up around the mission, and the last time I was through here it'd turned into quite a little town."

"Any possibility of Mexican soldiers being there?"

"Always a possibility, but that's all that's out there, so we've got little choice. Nothing on the other side of the border for several hundred miles either, so usually it ain't worth the bother for most folks to try and get further. Those that go just have to turn around and backtrack. But I suppose if someone had a dozen or so wild Comanche breathing down their necks, they'd hightail it for anyplace that provided them a little safety."

"Let's go. Try not to lead us into that bunch of heathens, will ya?"

* * *

Pox Marks, Polly Farmer, Carlos Reyes and the half-breed kid had successfully out-distanced the tired Comanche ponies long enough to reach the small village of Pollo Rio. The kid had been wounded severely and Pox Marks had left him along side the trail to die, hoping their pursuers would stop and torture him long enough for them to reach their destination.

Compared to other towns they'd been through, Pollo Rio was

larger and substantially cleaner. It had a constabulary of half a dozen officers. That hadn't worried Pox Marks or Carlos Reyes, but it was best for them to stay out of sight as long as possible. When the old Mexican Sheriff came to visit them in their sparse hotel room, Pox Marks had slipped his arm around the half-dead Polly's waist and introduced her as his wife, Mrs. Smith.

Not want to make trouble, especially from the *Norte Americanos*, the old Sheriff had left suspicious, yet not willing to start trouble as long as the uninvited guests caused no problems.

Pox Marks and Carlos laughed uproariously about it later. Then Carlos's eyes narrowed as he said softly, "When do I get the girl?"

Pox Marks realized he'd held the young gunman off as long as possible, so he quickly conceded his loss. Jerking his head toward the exhausted girl, he said as though unconcerned, "Help yourself. She ain't much good to us now, anyway."

Carlos grinned, standing to unbuckle his gun belt. Pox Marks closed the door behind himself, hearing a faint "no" from their captive. Suddenly he was starving, and he'd always enjoyed Mex grub. Even his injured leg felt better.

Polly lay on the sagging bed under a tattered bedspread, listening to the faint street sounds outside. The rough cover irritated her skin but the thought of moving was too painful to contemplate. Unmoving, she let her eyes roam the room as far as she could see, searching for a gun or some other means of ending her miserable existence. What Carlos had done to her was too hard to live with. She'd never have the family she'd always dreamed of. No decent man would ever want her again. Not Jericho McCain, not Rosie Poe. Not anyone.

She couldn't bear to think of facing her mother either, especially after witnessing what Pox Marks and the others had done to her father, and making her watch. She had prayed time and again that she'd be able to get through this ordeal without the inevitable happening. But now that one of them had used her, there'd be no end to it. It was better that she died now than face any more of the same. Shivering, she wondered if she had the courage for what she was contemplating; the courage to place a gun-muzzle against her temple and pull the trigger. She feared she did not, but somehow, she must.

Cowering naked beneath the rough bedspread, for Carlos had taken all her clothing, she knew he'd be returning soon as he'd promised.

God help me! What can I do?

She began to cry.

Twenty

"SO THAT'S POLLO RIO," Jericho said. He was tired, dusty and hungry.

More than anything, he longed to take a bath and find a steak large enough to make a meal for two big men, then he'd eat it all himself. Afterward, he'd sleep for a week. But first, he knew they had pressing business. Polly Farmer, if she was still alive and if she was here, needed them. After this outcome, with a bit of trepidation, if he were still alive, maybe he'd turn back into something human. But first, there were people who needed killing – needed it real bad.

He felt Poe pull up beside him and glanced over to see him staring back.

"What'd you say we get this over with, Roosevelt?"

Poe still hesitated.

"Jericho, there's something you've got to know before we go down there. That bartender, Cory, told me the other man with Pox Marks is a young Mex by the name of Carlos Reyes. He ain't too well known North of the Rio Grande, but down in Mexico people only whisper his name. They say he's killed over twenty men in face-to-face shoot-outs. Even more out of just plain cussedness. He's good, Jericho. Very good."

"We've been up against gun-hands before, Roosevelt. Why the lecture?"

"Not like Reyes we ain't. He's different."

"I thought Pox Marks was the bad one here. I never even heard of this Carlos Reyes fellow."

"Pox Marks is bad enough – bad to the bone. But what makes him that way is that he's mad as a hatter. Reyes ain't crazy. He just don't have a soul and he'd as soon kill as spit. On top of that, he may be the fastest gun in Texas."

"Faster than you?"

Poe didn't answer, just nudged his horse down the winding trail leading toward the sleepy little town resting on the banks of the Chicken River. His silence caused Jericho more concern than his words.

They entered during siesta time when few people were on the streets. Pollo Rio was larger than it appeared from the ridge; about fifty houses and shops. They were both keenly aware that if the men they sought were in town, they'd likely be spotted riding in. They'd already discussed it and agreed they'd just have to take that chance, because they weren't going to wait until after dark and allow Pox Marks to slip away again if he was indeed there.

As they halted in front of the town's Sheriff's office, and dismounted, a short portly man with a bushy, snow-white beard, exited. He paused when he saw them and waited. He was unarmed.

Poe didn't waste any time.

"Where can we find the town Marshal?"

"I am the Marshal," the old man said politely.

Poe tried not to show his disappointment at the revelation, instead said, "Can we talk inside, Marshal?"

The old man politely stepped to the door and held it open, nodding his white head.

Inside, there was simply a plain-boxy-desk and three straight-back chairs. The old man motioned for them to sit and plopped down behind the desk.

"What can I do for you seniors?"

Jericho kept his eyes on the open door, while Poe answered.

"I'm Poe and this is McCain. We're Texas Rangers from San Antonio, chasing two men and a woman. Have you seen anyone like that come through here? Strangers."

"This is not the United States…nor do I think it is Mexico or Texas. No one wants this small place on earth. Even the Comanches leave us alone."

"Well, there may be some folks that would argue that point with you, Marshal. But I don't have the time, nor the inclination. Now please, have you seen them?"

The old man averted his eyes for a moment, then said, "What do these people look like, *Señor* Poe?"

"The girl is an American, like us. Pretty little red-haired gal. One of the men is a good-looking Mexican youth; dresses fancy and wears two pistols. The other man has scars from small pox on his face. They here?"

"What have they done?"

Poe was beginning to get warm under the collar, and he could hear Jericho fidgeting behind him.

"Their names are Pox Marks and Carlos Reyes, old man. Cold-blooded killers, both of 'em. Now for the last time, are they here?"

At the mention of the two names, the old man's dark face turned a sickening pale as he closed his eyes and slowly made the sign of the cross.

"*Dios*. Holy Mother," he whispered.

He wiped his face with a trembling hand, and then slowly nodded his head.

"*Si*. They are here, *Señor*. I spoke with them only yesterday. The pox-marked one said he and the red-haired woman are married. The other was a handsome boy – very polite. I did not know…"

"Got any deputies that can give us a hand?"

The old man still appeared shaken by the information he'd received.

"Regretfully, no, *Señor*. I have six men who help me. They are not *pistoleros* – like I can see you are. They handle mostly disputes between neighbors…over who's goat is eating who's garden… and carry drunken fathers home to their families. Nothing dangerous. There are only three rusty rifles to share between them – maybe these do not even fire anymore."

At Poe's expression, he mumbled. "I am sorry, *Señor*."

"Well, no matter. What we came to do still needs doing. Tell your deputies to stay out of our way and not interfere, no matter which way this goes. These are bad hombres who won't hesitate to kill anyone who gets in their way – or burn your little town down around your ears for that matter."

* * *

In the shadows of an alley, Pox Marks flattened himself against the wall of the old general store, watching the two strangers walk down the far side of the main street. He thought he might have a chance of picking them both off, but the smaller one's eyes never rested, darting from doorway to alley. He was sure those restless eyes would spot him at his first movement. Judging from their two tied-down pistols, they didn't look like anyone he'd want to tangle with in a fair fight. So he waited until they'd passed and entered the saloon, then sprinted for the outside stairway leading to the second floor room where he'd left Carlos to play games with the girl.

Maybe they're just renegades, on the run like me.

His instincts told him they were not. The arrogant way in which they strode the street, unafraid, challenging, almost belligerent, left him with a far different impression. They might as well have had signs on their backs proclaiming them to be – Lawman. Intuition he'd come to depend on informed him these two were Texas Rangers. Maybe they were after him, maybe not. But he didn't want to be in the same town with them if he could help it. Not as easy as he was to spot.

* * *

Walking in silence, Jericho followed Poe to the only drinking establishment in town, one of three, two-story buildings on the main street. Cautiously they entered the room, letting their eyes grow accustomed to the darkness after leaving the brilliance of the summer sun outside. Except for one bartender, no one else was present. They hadn't really expected anyone because it was still the traditional siesta period, observed by most of the locals in the hottest part of the day.

Poe walked to the bar and leaned on it.

"Speak English?"

The skinny Mexican bartender licked his lips nervously before answering.

"*Sí.*"

"I don't have much time, so I'm only going to ask my questions one time. Savvy?"

Again, out came the nervous tongue, wetting thin lips.

"*Si, Señor.*"

"Two men. One a young Mexican, the other with a scared-up face. They have a woman with them. Seen 'em?"

The thin man's eyes involuntarily drifted up at the ceiling, then returned to stare widely at Poe. It was answer enough. Poe took the steps two at a time, Jericho a few steps behind him.

On the second floor landing were four doors. Two stood open, the others closed. Poe's pistol magically appeared in his hand, as did Jericho's. He stepped beside the first door and peered inside. It was empty. As was the second. The next door was closed but not latched, so Poe shoved it open with the muzzle of his Colt. On the sagging bed, lay a fat Mexican man and an even fatter female. They were both nude, snoring loudly.

At the third door, Poe flattened himself to one side and hesitated long enough for Jericho to reach the other side. Then he jumped in front of it and with a mighty kick, sent it flying open. He stared at the large bed where someone had just recently lain, a strained look on his face. The used bed caused vivid images to flash repeatedly through his mind. He forced his attention back to the task at hand. The room was empty. They whirled as one and raced back down the steps to find the thin bartender, still frozen when they'd left him.

"Where'd they go, hombre? Pronto!"

Poe's voice left little doubt he was in a killing mood, and the thin man's Adam's apple bobbed rapidly. As he stuttered, trying to get the right words to come, another voice drifted to them from outside.

"*Gringos!* Inside the saloon. Stay inside and listen. If you come out, you will not find me until I want you to."

Jericho and Poe rushed to the window and peeked out over the windowsill. The street was entirely empty. They waited.

"I am Carlos Reyes. Perhaps you have heard of me. I have always wanted to kill a Texas Ranger and now it looks like God has been good to me."

"If you're so anxious to kill yourself a Ranger, why don't you show yourself, ya mangy cur?" Poe suggested, struggling to keep the fury out of his tone. Jericho searched the deserted street for some indication as to where the voice was coming.

"Even I, Carlos Reyes, am not so foolish as to try two Rangers at a single time, *Gringo*. No, one is enough for me."

"What ya got in mind, Reyes?"

The hidden voice drifted to them.

"Pox told me to hang back and do one of you. He said he'd take care of the other. Sounded like a good plan."

"Where is the Manburner, Reyes? Waiting to bushwhack us when we come out?"

Laughter drifted to them this time.

"No. He is gone…with the girl. He said to tell you he will be waiting for you in the desert."

Jericho caught Poe's horrified expression for an instant, and then it was gone.

Poe hid his feelings well as he said, "Which one of us do you want to try first, Mex?" There was an edge in Poe's voice this time that even the distance between the antagonists could not hide.

More laughter.

"Not so fast, *Gringo*. Pox said to hold you both here until he has a little head start. Then I will oblige you."

Poe slid down until his back rested against the wall. Jericho

Gone to Texas

joined him, waiting. When Poe didn't say anything, he ventured, "How do you want to play this, Roosevelt?"

"We could both just take off out the back, come up behind the Sheriff's office where our horses are tied, and light out after Pox Marks and Polly. Leave Carlos Reyes here to stew in his juices."

"Wouldn't work, though. Would it?"

"No."

"Carlos would probably just perch himself on top of one of these buildings and pick us off with a long-gun before we got out of range. Even if one of us were lucky enough to get away, we'd have to contend with his bird-dogging along behind us as we tracked Pox Marks. I don't relish having to watch both directions at once in that situation, especially up against someone like them two. Throw in the Comanches, too and...well, you see what I mean."

Poe looked defeated.

"Help me out with this, Jericho. You always did have the best head when it came to cooking up a plan."

"One of us has to keep Reyes occupied while the other gets away to pick up Pox Marks's trail. The important thing here is getting Polly back."

From the corner of his eye, Jericho could see Poe nodding in agreement. He stood, careful not to show himself in the window, then walked to the center of the large room. The bartender remained as they had last seen him, rubbing the same glass with his rag, staring at them with his wide unblinking eyes. He was clearly trying not to draw attention to himself. Jericho pulled out one of his Walker Colt's, then the other, checking them for dust and ensuring they were fully loaded. Poe joined him.

"Rosie, go get your girl. That's your place. I'll stay and take care of Reyes."

Poe reached out, grasping Jericho's hand.

"I never had a friend like you before, Jericho. I don't know how I'll ever be able to repay you."

Poe's eyes were wet, embarrassing Jericho, unaccustomed to expressing his own feelings. He quickly averted his eyes, saying simply, "No repayment required. It needs to be done. Now git."

Poe started toward the rear door but stopped halfway, his head bowed. After a moment, he returned.

"Carlos Reyes is good, Jericho. Real good. He may be the best around anywhere."

"You told me that. Go find your gal."

"No. Listen to me, Jericho. Against Reyes, you have no chance at all. None."

"Maybe I'll get lucky."

"No! You came along on this business because I asked you – and because you're my friend, I have to say this. I never had a real friend before, Jericho. I can't let you go out there to certain death. Not if there's some way I can prevent it."

"How you gonna do that?"

"You go after Pox Marks. I'll handle Carlos Reyes."

"Can you?"

"I have a better chance than you do."

Jericho knew how Poe felt about Polly Farmer, and was instantly touched by his friend's offer.

"You'd trust me to get Polly back?"

"Who better? I know you. You won't stop. Not ever. You're just that way. Handsome Jack said it better. He said even if you were killed, you'd keep coming until you got done whatever you had in your head to do. Go get her, Jericho. Bring Polly home. Please."

Jericho still hesitated, searching Poe's eyes, trying to read behind them. Finally he nodded.

"I'll get her, Roosevelt – and I'll send Pox Marks to Hell in the getting."

Somberly the two friends shook hands, and as Jericho rushed for the rear door, he heard Poe mutter, "Okay Reyes, you murdering son of a bitch. Let's dance."

Jericho found his stallion tied exactly where he'd left him. Trusting Poe to keep Carlos Reyes occupied, he led his mount behind the Sheriff's office before he swung into the saddle. Taking advantage of every scrap of cover available, he worked himself to a point where he was convinced he was well out of rifle range, then put spurs to his horse's flanks and headed for the high ground. When well enough away, he paused for a moment, staring at the small village below.

Good luck, old pard. Send him to Hell.

As he nudged his mount down the far side, scanning the dust for fresh hoof-prints, he heard the first smattering of pistol shots far below.

Twenty-One

"GIVE ME SOME INDICATION where you're located, Reyes. Then I'll come out."

Poe caught a dark hat with silver band raise above a stack of boxes at the mouth of a nearby alley. A good choice, it was one of four spots he'd selected as possible hiding places. The alley had an added advantage of giving the outlaw an avenue of escape should it be needed.

"How do I know you won't pop me when I step out into the open, Reyes?"

Quiet laughter. Then, "What, and spoil my sport? Not a chance, *Gringo*. I want to see you lying in the dust at my feet. You've probably heard of me. I'm no back-shooter. I don't have to be."

"I heard of you alright. A murdering scum is what I heard. Old men and women mostly. Made your reputation riding with that butcher, Pox Marks, 'cause you can't think for yourself. Yeah, I heard of you, Reyes – plenty."

"Enough talk! Come out now, *Gringo*. I want to kill you very badly."

Fifty sets of ears listened to the exchange as the town patrons huddled inside their shops and homes, certain that the young ranger was about to die. They didn't know of the Ranger, but they'd all heard of Carlos Reyes – El Lobo – one who had never lost a gunfight, even when outnumbered two, or even three to one. Most of the villagers had heard the songs of his terrible deeds for years. No, the handsome young ranger would be dead in a very short while, and they would make up yet another song about El Lobo.

Gone to Texas

Poe inched around the doorway and spotted Reyes, standing partially hidden behind the stack of heavy wooden boxes. He sighed, loosened his pistols in their holsters, and stepped outside. Standing motionless, he waited, praying Reyes would honor his promise to give him a fair chance. His prayers were answered as Reyes stepped away from the alleyway.

"So, Ranger. We see who is best. Do we not?"

"Did you hurt the girl?"

"The girl? The little red-haired *puta*?" He laughed. " Na, I didn't hurt her. I made her feel good, *Gringo*! She cried and begged me for more, but I told her I didn't have the time right now – that I had to go kill a Ranger today."

He laughed again. A cold nasty little laugh. Poe had heard enough.

"Ready to die, low-life?"

"It is you who will die today. Whenever you are ready, Ranger."

Those who watched from behind their windowsills said the hands of Carlos Reyes were so swift that even those with fine eyesight could not follow them. Like the strike of the rattler, he moved. So certain were they that he would kill the young Ranger, that few eyes watched the Texan's draw, stunned when they saw Reyes hurled backwards into the stack of wooden boxes, to lie unmoving in the dust – stunned to see the Ranger, unscathed, walk toward the still form of the badman, Carlos Reyes, while reloading his empty chamber.

Ay-ya-yi-yi-yi! There would be a new kind of song to sing this night – one of a handsome young Texas Ranger who had finally killed the notorious bloody outlaw, Carlos Reyes.

Ay-ya-yi-yi-yi.

* * *

Jericho had little difficulty finding the trail, even less in following it. Somehow, he had the feeling Pox Marks wanted him to follow, but he had little choice in the matter. It was late afternoon already and he felt he had to catch up before it got dark, or he may lose them and never find their trail again. If only he were half the tracker as Poe. He'd just have to improvise the best he could. Roosevelt was counting on him.

A faint stirring off to his left caught his eye. Dust. Pox Marks, or just a dust devil? Worse yet, a Comanche? He shuddered at the thought, remembering Mordecai Jones's stories of the Comanche horrendous deeds.

God take the heathen devils! Don't let it be Comanche!

The trail entered a rocky draw and in an instant Jericho become more alert. His hair rising on the back of his neck, he carefully scanned the high ground on both sides, expecting at any moment to feel the crushing impact of a heavy rifle slug or feathered arrow. He felt like a sitting duck. Then the draw leveled out once more and the trail angled toward the foothills further west. If they reached the mountains, he knew Polly would be lost forever. Oblivious to the danger, he urged his horse into a trot. With two hours of daylight left, his eyes caught a glimpse of something on the slope leading into a canyon, half a mile away. Something white that shouldn't be there. Something that moved.

* * *

Polly struggled against her binds and felt warm blood as the rawhide dug into her flesh again. She'd been without water since leaving the hotel and her tongue felt parched, swollen. Dark spots occasionally floated before her eyes, and she was beginning to feel light-headed, detached from her body. She wondered how it would be to die of thirst. Did one suffer, or simply go to sleep and drift away? She hoped she wouldn't suffer any more. She really wanted to die now that Carlos had defiled her, but she didn't want to suffer – no matter how much she deserved it.

Pox Marks had informed her when he'd tied and left her here that Rosie and Jericho had come for her. He'd lied of course. No one would come. She'd die in this God-forsaken land, eaten up by the snakes and coyotes – or those big birds floating lazily overhead. Hawks? Eagles? She should know their name, but it escaped her.

"Mommy, oh please help me, Mommy."

The sound of her own voice startled her and she sat upright, scanning around her. She knew the evil Pox Marks was up in those rocks there; at least that's where he said he'd be. He'd also told her what he was going to do. Struggling to remember, yes, he said he'd be waiting for Rosie and Jericho. Yes. That was it. He was going to wait for them to come get her. That was silly of course, for they weren't coming. No one would come.

Something else...something bad. She remembered now. Yes, he said he was going to kill them – burn them up. He'd do it, too. She'd seen him do it to her father.

Please Rosie, don't come. Stay away Jericho. Let me die.

Pox Marks said he'd just leave her here for the Indians to find if she didn't die first. She really hoped she died first, for he'd described in detail what they'd do to her if she was still alive. Oh, how she wished she could die first.

"Mommy...Mom..."

Pox Marks moved to a higher position from where he could

better see the entire slope of the small rugged foothill. That pup following him had probably dismounted in the shallow draw a quarter of a mile away. He'd have to come out some time. Pox Marks would simply wait until he reached the girl, then put a round in each leg. Afterward, he'd go down and cook him – real slow. Then the girl.

The sun was unbearably hot, even though it was less than two hours until sunset. Pox Marks risked a sip from his goatskin, just enough to wet his lips. Unable to resist, he glanced to the spot where the half-dressed girl was lying fully exposed to the burning rays of the evening sun. She'd been without water far longer than he, and had ceased her whining. He doubted she was dead yet, but by tomorrow morning she'd be completely out of her head. He may just give her a drink so she'd be able to comprehend what he had in store for her and that meddling ranger pup. A small fire lit in the center of their bellies always captured their interest. He chuckled softly.

Now where in Hell did that pup get to?

* * *

Gray Wolf sat silently, watching one of the Whites crawl up the shallow drain ditch that captured run-off whenever there were flash floods in the mountains. He moved well for a white-eye. He'd seen the man before. It had taken him a while to discern exactly where, but at last it had come to him. He'd been with the Protected One – the "touched" woman who searched for her spirit baby. He was certain of it. He'd been the one who killed twelve of Gray Wolf's warriors with his long-gun.

Gray Wolf also knew the other man, the one who waited on the canyon bluff. He was the Manburner. Gray Wolf had tried unsuccessfully for the past month to end his existence, but the Manburner was crafty. He'd burned many of Gray Wolf's people through the years, but what made him take a vow of death against the scar-faced one, was the loss of his son Desert Mouse, and wife, Winter Sun. The Manburner had caught them as they swam in the river over one year before, and had allowed his men to disgrace his wife before he burned her and his son. All else must wait for his settlement of that debt, and then he would take to the warpath once again.

He'd sent all but five of his warriors on to Adobe Wells to wait for him. Black Crow and the others waited in a draw below. They'd be there if he needed them. This was his personal business and he'd take care of the Manburner alone, then he'd rejoin the others and drive all Whites from this land. The Manburner had one of the rifles that fired many times, and Gray Wolf had seen his skill with it, so he proceeded with care. The introduction of the long-gun white man and the woman, made him pause to see what would develop. He had time. He could wait. There was no way out these hills alive.

Jericho had detected the lone warrior on the high ground, watched him from a distance, and wondered how many more might be hidden in the rocks, unseen. Mordecai always said where you saw one Indian; there were a dozen more you didn't see. He didn't dwell on it. There wasn't any need to, for he'd also seen Polly Farmer staked out on the bare slope of the small foothill. From her position in relationship to the high rocks, he was pretty sure he could guess where Pox Marks lay in wait. It was exactly where he'd be if the tables were turned. He stared at the clump of small boulders for a long time, seeing no movement. Then he glanced back at the tall unmoving form on horseback, watching them from the high ground. Comanche! God how they made his skin crawl.

That's it heathen. Stay right there and watch. Don't give me a reason to kill you, too.

Jericho flattened out in the draw and began scooting along on his belly. The sun, intense heat, and limited airflow in the small draw was taking its toll on him. When he finally reached the cover of the large rocks, he collapsed against one of them and watched the mounted Indian – watching. It was really beginning to get on his nerves.

Breathing easier now, Jericho sprinted between the boulders, up the slope to higher ground. He disregarded the noise at this point. Unless Pox Marks caught him crawling up the shallow wash, he'd be okay until he drew closer. Praying he was right about the renegade's position, Jericho removed his boots, hung them around his neck with a strap of rawhide, and slipped across the rocks on stocking feet toward the clump of rocks. He had come far enough around that he'd approach anyone waiting from the rear.

God, please let me be right!

Then, he heard a soft chuckle.

Pox Marks, watching the still form below, chuckled softly, started to raise the goatskin to his lips – then froze. He clutched the rifle grip tighter, his eyes darting from left to right. Body taunt, ready to spring – but he was too late.

"Don't even think about it, low-life. You can't see me, but I've got a bead on your back and I couldn't miss from here if I closed my eyes."

Pox Marks relaxed, still not moving.

"You the Ranger pup that's been chasing me?"

"Just push your rifle over the edge in front of you and let it fall – or try your luck if you're so inclined. I'm hot and thirsty, and I've got to get that little girl out of the hot sun."

Pox Marks pushed the rifle forward, listening to it smash against the rocks below.

"That was a fine repeating rifle, pup. Cost me more than the damned Rangers pay you in a year."

"You won't need it anymore."

"What do you want with me?"

"Shut up and toss your pistols over the edge, too."

"There's Comanches up here, pup. Without my pistols, I'll be dead."

"You are dead. Now in less than a second I'm gonna blow your head off if you don't. Now toss 'em."

Pox Marks growled and flung his gun belt over the rock.

"On your feet and turn around."

Pox Marks's eyes reflected a cold burning hate when he saw Jericho had commandeered his horse, now holding the reigns in one hand as he leveled his rifle with the other. Pox Marks spit out a vile curse.

"Down the slope, low-life. Keep your mouth shut. Don't give me even a little excuse to kill you – cause I really want to."

As they approached, it was hard to tell from the way she laid if Polly Farmer was alive or dead. A large turkey buzzard had taken up residence a short distance away, and startled into lazy flight as they neared.

"Pray she's still alive, Manburner. Because if she's dead, so are you."

Jericho pointed to a small rock thirty feet away.

"Sit."

Fire still shot from the outlaw's eyes, but he held his tongue and lowered himself onto the indicated rock. There would be time. He just had to be patient.

Jericho knelt and lifted Polly's head to rest on his arm. Keeping a careful eye on Pox Marks, he lowered his ear against her nostrils, and then smiled. She was alive.

Hurrying to Pox Marks's saddle, he removed the goatskin he'd retrieved on the bluff, and knelt beside her again. Lifting her head gently, he placed the canteen against her parched lips to let her drink. It was only a few drops, but Polly coughed, sputtered and finally opened her eyes. Her voice was weak, her words slurred.

"Jericho? Are you really here? Am I dead?"

"You're alive, Polly. But I've got to get you on that horse before those Comanches I spotted earlier come calling."

His eyes told Pox Marks to move at his own risk, as he lifted Polly into the outlaw's saddle.

"Now hang on tight. We're going to pick up my horse, and then we'll make a run for it back toward Pollo Rio. Rosie's waiting for you there."

As she swooned in the saddle, he first tied one foot, then the other to the stirrups with short strips of rawhide. Then her hands to the saddle horn. It'd be uncomfortable but a lot better than passing out and falling off if they had to run for their lives.

Pox Marks suddenly stood but when Jericho's gun appeared in his left hand, he quickly sat back down.

"What 'bout me," he complained. "I can ride double with the girl and hold her on. With those damned Comanche out there, I won't have a chance on foot and unarmed."

"I don't 'spect Miss Farmer wants you anywhere near her again, low-life. Take a walk out toward those boulders. If you hustle I may not cripple you before I leave."

Pox Marks jumped to his feet once more, shaking his fist at Jericho. "Damn you, pup! Damn you to Hell!"

"You're probably right, Manburner, but you'll likely get there before I will. Now git!"

Pox Marks glowered for an instant but the sound of Jericho cocking the hammer of his Colt started him back toward the canyon. Every few feet he glanced back in hatred.

Pox Marks was tough and he was determined. He'd been in bad spots before, and he was still alive while all the others were probably burning in Hell. If he could just reach the place where he'd dropped his rifle over the edge, and if it was still working, well…that might just be another kettle of fish. He lengthened his stride.

Jericho found his stallion where he'd tied him earlier. He hadn't seen the tall Indian since he'd captured Pox Marks, but his instincts told him the Comanche were still around. He checked Polly again, making sure her feet were secured to the stirrups and her hands maintaining circulation. Then he checked his rifle and both handguns again before he swung into the saddle. The big horse snorted and pranced nervously, like he was just as anxious as Jericho to leave this sorry place behind. In the thick waves of rising heat across the vastness, Pox Marks ran toward the boulders, already nearly halfway across the open area to the foot of the canyon wall.

Jericho scanned the distance between them and the safety of the ridgeline that seemed so far away now. Not even a jackrabbit moved. There was no cover to speak of until they reached that ridgeline nearly three miles away. If the Comanche wanted them they would have to join in an all-out chase. He and Polly broke for it; if they weren't jumped before they reached the ridge, they had a chance.

Well, time to dance, right Roosevelt?

He gripped the other horse's bridle tighter and using his knees, nudged his stallion up the steep bank into the open. As he put spurs to his mount, Jericho glanced back toward the canyon and saw Pox Marks still running toward the canyon wall. He knew he'd try to fetch the guns he'd dropped earlier. Jericho hoped they were smashed to bits from the fall. At that same moment, riding from the mouth of the canyon, Jericho saw the Comanche he'd spotted earlier, and with him, five of his brothers. It was obvious they were not after him and Polly for they were loping their ponies towards Pox Marks.

By now, seeing the Indians in his pursuit, Pox Marks redoubled his efforts to reach the canyon wall. It was clear he would fail. When Jericho reached the far ridgeline, he paused once more and looked back. The Comanche had formed a circle around Pox Marks. Even from his distance, the Manburner could be heard swearing and screaming at them as they sat motionless on their horses – quietly watching him. As he and Polly dropped over the ridge, the Indians started to slowly move closer toward the hated Manburner.

Twenty-Two

"JERICHO? JERICHO!" POE shouted every time his left foot hit the ground.

Jericho straightened from his task of shoeing the big stallion, placed his hands in the small of his back and bent backwards. The ordeal of stooping for so long had been a discomfort, but he was finished, and as soon as he was packed, he was ready to ride.

Poe skidded to a halt, sawdust blinding them both for just an instant.

"Roosevelt Poe – for cat's sake! Don't you know running in cold weather like this will make you catch your death of the croup? Ain't you got a lick of sense?"

Poe had an exasperating way of flinging his arms when excited. Jericho secretly thought the gesture made him seem like a chicken with a busted wing. Poe stopped waving his arms long enough to respond with some degree of indignation.

"Well, 'course I know that. Everybody knows that. But this is important, J.D.! Captain Hays sent me to fetch you. He's gonna hold a formation for you and me on account of us getting Polly back from that skunk Pox Marks. Mordecai and Raf said he was gonna promote you to sergeant, and give me a pay raise of ten whole dollars a month. Hot damn, won't that be something? Ranger Sergeant J.D. McCain! Hot damn!"

Jericho silently stared at Poe's exertions. From his expression, one could assume the news didn't sound quite as grand to him as it did to his excited friend.

Poe calmed down some as he slowly picked up on Jericho's mood.

"Well? What is it? Get it off your chest and you'll sleep better for it."

Jericho led the stallion into a nearby stall and closed the gate. When he returned, his face was troubled.

"I told you when we brought Polly back last summer that I was going to see the Colorados, and that's what I intend to do. I let you talk me into staying for a while longer, and here it is winter again – and I still ain't left yet. Now you say the Captain wants to promote me to sergeant and I suppose then he'll try to talk me into staying too. Why don't he just promote you instead? You like it here! I'm gonna leave."

"J.D., everyone knows I ain't a leader. Hell, tell me what to do and I can do it as well as the next feller can. But leave it up to me to hatch a plan and it'll fall apart before it gets out of the corral. The Rangers need men like you. Captain Hays is ailing, Big Foot Wallace talks about getting married and settling down, and me, Raf and Mordecai won't have no one to tell us the right way of doing things anymore."

Poe turned his face away so Jericho couldn't see his furtive cunning. He had that much respect for Jericho's ability to read people. Furthermore, he felt not an ounce of remorse for conniving to keep his friend in Texas with the rest of them. After all, it was for his own good – and the good of the others, he reminded himself.

"Like as not, we'll end up getting scalped by the Comanches first time we get sent out on our own. You wouldn't leave your friends in a pickle like that, would you?"

Jericho had been expecting something like this ever since he

Gone to Texas

and Poe had returned from bringing Polly Farmer home. Word of their killing the gunman Carlos Reyes and the Manburner, Pox Marks, had miraculously beaten them back to San Antonio. It wasn't any wonder, for with Polly being in such bad condition, it'd taken them twice as long to return as it normally would have. As it was, they'd rode in to a swell of well-wishers generally raising cane for most of the afternoon. He'd never seen such a bunch of shouting, clapping and backslapping as went on that day. He'd just wanted to find a hole and crawl into it.

* * *

Polly had finally recovered somewhat and looked almost the same as she had before her abduction by Pox Marks. That is, she looked the same, but those who knew her well enough, sensed the deep dark changes taking place with her. Poe asked her to marry him at least once a week after their return, but Polly quietly refused to talk about it. That had left Poe withdrawn and moody, so Jericho tried to avoid him as much as possible.

Poe took to drinking nightly and tried to lick every able-bodied man he encountered when in his inebriated state. He walked around all stove up, sporting bumps and bruises most of the time. He eventually developed into a passable bare-knuckled fist-fighter – although he was known to occasionally resort to kicking, gouging and even biting on occasion when his latest opponent began to get the upper hand and things started going badly for him. Most knew enough not to challenge him with their guns. Having Poe put knots on your head was one thing, facing his pair of Walker Colts was quite another.

"Pickle or not, I told you I was leaving and that's what I intend to do. I ain't got nothing to keep me here now that Taylor is gone. Can't say I'll miss this place none. It ain't good for much 'cept raising rattlers – and the likes of Pox Marks and a lot of wild Comanches."

Having failed with flattery, Poe decided to take another approach. He spit, still eyeing Jericho's reaction.

"Be full winter in a week or so."

He glanced slyly from the corner of his eye, so he could judge if he was having any luck with his new tack. "Anyone caught out in the open when one of them Northerners hit will probably freeze into a snowman. If you don't care anything about yourself, at least think about that fine stallion. He don't deserve to die that way – not that you do, either, J.D."

Jericho paused in his task of tying a slicker around his bedroll to keep out moisture, his brow wrinkled in thought. To Poe's surprise, he actually seemed to be considering it. Finally, he stood.

"I ain't saying I will mind ya, but if I was to, what do you think the Captain would say about me staying on with the Company just until spring? Then, just as soon as the snow melted in the foothills, I'd be on my way. Do you reckon he'd consider that?"

"Hot damn, J.D., I'm sure he would!"

There went the arms flying around again. Jericho wanted to toss a rope around him just so he'd stop it. Poe was so excited again he didn't let up.

"He's never promoted anyone in the Company to sergeant before. Well, not since Big Foot Wallace, and he don't count. I'm sure he'd consider it! Let's try it out on him!"

Knowing Poe's high regard for Wallace, Jericho let his last comment pass.

Poe locked a vise-like grip around Jericho's arm and pulled him toward the stable door.

"Come on, J.D. Let's tell everyone the good news!"

Jericho allowed himself to be pulled along, his reluctance showed.

"Now, Roosevelt, I said I'd consider it. Not that I'd actually do it – and only 'til spring, too. After that, I'm off to see the Colorados. Plain and simple."

"Now don't you fret, J.D. We'll talk about that again, in the spring. You might even come to like Texas. It ain't such a bad place to..."

Jericho McCain did get to see the Colorado Mountains eventually – but that's another story.

Afterword

RAY ENDED HIS LAST chapter simply, with Jericho McCain being prompted by his friend Rosie Poe to remain in Texas: "It ain't such a bad place to…"

Then he left the reader hanging with anticipation: Jericho McCain did get to see the Colorado Mountains eventually—but that's another story."

Turning the page to the *About the Author*, some might scratch their heads and ponder, how did a US Army Special Forces officer with these credentials, and an illustrious and legendary military career spanning twenty-six years, ever decide to write a Western?

Good books often become even richer with an understanding of the back story. I'd like you to know this one. Like many other veterans of the Vietnam War era, the enemy followed Ray home in the form of Agent Orange. He passed away in February 2022.

Whenever Ray and I had brief discussions of family items of importance, the topic of his manuscripts always came up. His imagination with writing genres knew no bounds. I always prompted him to save them, which he heeded, and to inform me where they were located. With his creative juices in gear as a storyteller, he left it up to me to manage the business end of his endeavors; it was a team sport. While rummaging through some papers and boxes, I came across a copy of his first manuscript, a Western, only shared with a few friends.

As a young man growing up in Missouri, Ray frequently remarked how his love of books came from reading the Westerns

Gone to Texas

his father shared with him, circa Louis L'Amour. When his father passed, Ray wanted those books. They remain on our bookshelf, yellowed, the spines devoid of glue, his treasures. I began to reread Ray's manuscript. I was familiar with it from many years before.

Prompted by his spirit, and nudged with inspiration, I reached out to his publisher. "Any chance of taking on a Western genre, among your other categories of historical fiction, military memoirs, etc.?" He responded that he personally LOVED Westerns, and to send it to him for a "look." Then, while he was taking a "look," I discovered another in his manuscript files, same characters, different time.

Holy smokes, this was a series! Readers have just been introduced to the first volume of the series, which is his second Western. The craft of storytelling is not always a linear process. He couldn't seem to get those characters out of his head and proceeded to write a prequel to their adventures together. McCain's friendship and adventures with Roosevelt Poe endure through the second volume, *When Legends Lived*, the one I was familiar with.

Ray lived in a generation that if you were an avid fan of Westerns, you might have experienced some of Elmore Leonard's best novels—*Valdez is Coming*, *Hombre* and *Last Stand at Sabre River*—and several of his short stories. These, along with *3:10 to Yuma* were made into revered movies. Taking nothing away from Zane Grey, Larry McMurtry (with the classic mini-series *Lonesome Dove*), et al. You might have been hooked on every episode of *Bonanza*, *Have Gun Will Travel*, *Wild, Wild West*, *Gunsmoke*. Much of this might have come from your childhood when eight out of ten of the top shows on TV were Westerns! All exciting fodder to discuss at the kitchen dinner table, that is, when families still ate together at the kitchen dinner table.

Ray's book is a gritty, period-authentic Western for hardcore Western aficionados. Yes, it's a different time now, but a Western is a Western. It was a different era, a sweaty, tough life; those who made their homes in the West were of sturdy stock. The Wild West was WILD, the dastardly foes quite adept at torture; not for the faint of heart of how folks survived and died! You'll find many villains to loath. The lawmen righted wrongs, justice prevailed.

You were always rooting for the good guys even when a bad apple was among them. Those who read Westerns likely relish the violent moments in the "Name of Justice"! From Ray's point of view, these men smacked of character, integrity, honor. Ray knew what made them tick.

Ray never got around to dedicating this book, as he did with his others.

It's only fitting, then, that it should be dedicated to him:

Lieutenant Colonel Raymond C. Morris (Ret)
24 June 1941 to 6 February 2022
For a life well-lived, loved by many, a good man.
He will never be forgotten.

Moreover, I would be remiss if I didn't acknowledge the friendship, professionalism, support, and assistance of Hellgate Press, Harley Patrick and his remarkable creative team, who have shepherded all his books to the public eye over the years.

A sense of nostalgia permeates the soul when reading a good Western, much like looking back at the patchwork quilt of our lives, frayed around the edges. It seems quite remarkable that I have been able to bring these two Westerns of Ray's to life, and there may be others! It has been a labor of love, and he lives through me.

I invite you to continue the journey with the sequel *When Legends Lived*.

—*Brenda D. Morris*

**The sequel to *Gone to Texas* —
When Legends Lived — is due out in Summer 2023!**

About the Author

RAYMOND C. MORRIS was born in Jefferson City, Missouri and entered the Army at the fuzzy-cheek age of seventeen. Following basic training, he was assigned to the 101st Airborne Division. With a rank of staff sergeant, in 1963-1964 he attended Officer Candidate School at Fort Benning, Georgia.

In May 1964, as a freshly minted 2LT and the OCS Honor Graduate, his new orders led him to the 6th Special Forces Group. On 2 January 1966, he was assigned as team Executive Officer for the 5th Special Forces Group Operational Detachment (SFOD) 106 at Bato, Vietnam, followed by an assignment in May 1966 with SFOD A-103, Gia Vuc, Vietnam.

In October 1966, he was selected as the Long Range Reconnaissance Platoon Leader (LRRP) for Mobile Guerilla

Force A-100, with operations throughout the A Shau Valley. In 1968, an assignment transferred him to the 46th Special Forces Company in Thailand where he trained Thai Black Panther brigades in reconnaissance tactics and inserted them into Vietnam. In 1970, he'd been detailed under the auspices of CIA operations in northern Thailand, to train Laotian commandos and deploy them into Laos.

In 1968, Ray returned to the U.S. for Ranger School, again distinguished as the Honor Graduate, winning the Darby Award. A new assignment led him back into Southeast Asia, where for two years, from April 1971-April 1973, he was a B-detachment commander with the 1st Special Forces Group (A) in Okinawa. During this time, he was sent to Vietnam twice for temporary assignment with the classified Special Forces FANK Program.

Returning Stateside, he continued his military schooling and went on to hold other key assignments, including Deputy Commander, 6th Region Criminal Investigation Division in San Francisco, CA. In 1983, he was selected to be the Deputy Commanding Officer to reactivate the 1st Special Forces Group (A) at Fort Lewis, Washington. Ray retired from active duty in 1985 after an illustrious military career spanning twenty-six years.

His love for the military has never waned. As a civilian he returned to Fort Lewis, in charge of training the Army's new Stryker Brigades prior to Iraq deployment.

His awards include: Legion of Merit, Meritorious Service Medal, Bronze Star, Vietnam Cross of Gallantry w/silver star and Cross of Gallantry w/bronze star, Army Commendation Medal (2) and numerous service awards. He proudly earned his jump wings, U.S., Thai and Vietnamese Master Parachutist badges, Special Forces and Ranger tabs.

Ray, never one to sit on his duff too long, holds a BA in Criminal Justice from the University of Nebraska, an MBA from City University in Seattle, Washington and a Masters in Justice Administration, Wichita State University.

A lifelong history enthusiast and prolific writer, Ray has used his keen observation of the human condition as the catalyst for expansion of his interests into writing and mainstream fiction. R. C. Morris's 2004 suspense thriller, *Don't Make the Blackbirds Cry*, and psychological thriller, the 2006 *Tender Prey*, are now available as ebooks. In October 2005, commissioned by the Project Delta members to write their story, his love of Special Forces forced him to place pending fiction novels on the back burner to write *The Ether Zone*, published by Hellgate Press.

OTHER BOOKS BY R. C. MORRIS

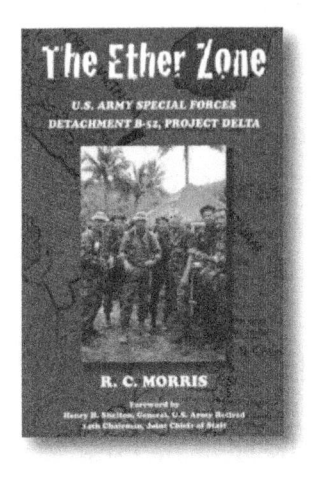

THE ETHER ZONE: Project Delta and its clandestine special reconnaissance operations proved to be one of the most successful Special Operations units of the Vietnam War, yet few Americans have ever heard of them. This small unit, comprised of less than 100 U.S. Army Special Forces men, amassed a record for bravery second to none. Now, for the first time, the Project Delta "Quiet Professionals" finally share their story.

Highly trained as experts in special reconnaissance techniques and procedures, the covert Project Delta missions were accomplished through recon team insertions into enemy territory. The primary sources of intelligence collection for Project Delta, these tough and tenacious men recount hair-raising adventures.

Enter the world of a highly classified project to learn what makes U.S. Army Special Forces soldiers tick—and learn the legacy of these men of honor, their breathtaking heroics, humility, humor, camaraderie and brotherhood.

ISBN: 978-1-55571-662-2
Paperback   392 pages   6x9 $24.95

Available through most major bookstores,
online at Amazon.com and others, or direct from Hellgate Press.

DON'T MAKE THE BLACKBIRDS CRY: Murder, Hatred, Corrupt Politics, the Klan...A Great Thrill Ride! An orphaned and homeless teenager has just broken in and robbed the local store. Hiding in the darkness of an alley, he witness's five young men brutally rape and murder three teenage girls, two black and one white. One perpetrator is the town's star high school quarterback while another is the sheriff's son. When one of the five turns up dead a short time later, he knows he can't come forward!

Morris's debut novel, a gritty mystery of southern culture clash and racial hatred, reminds us that the quest for justice is not always free, and often, when seeking truth or trying to right a wrong, many lives can be affected by dire or unexpected consequences.

What the critics are saying:

"*Don't Make the Blackbirds Cry*, with all of its unexpected twists and turns, makes this first novel by R.C. Morris a difficult book to put down!"
— *Northwest Guardian*

"....truly a page-turner...a fully packed adventure. This author has writing talent and showcases it well in his first debut novel. Terrifying and exciting but most certainly entertaining! ...Well crafted...a must read book."
— *Military Writers Society of America*

Available on Kindle at Amazon.com
or visit Raycmorris.com to read excerpts

TENDER PREY: Fear Grips Seattle! A Deranged Serial Killer is Loose. Have you ever known someone who has been sexually abused? Do you think they'd be conscious of the effects these childhood perversions might have on adult behavior? Do you ever question what could possibly motivate the bizarre acts you learn about your friends and neighbors who appear so normal? Then you'll want to meet Corky!

Detective Frank Murphy and his side-kick, John Henry Drake, get the nod to head up the task force. Who is committing these heinous acts?

What the critics are saying:

"Compelling, tantalizing and filled with complex characters and plot twists...an intelligent treat and great entertainment! It is a terrific read for all mystery lovers. The MWSA gives this book its highest rating of Five Stars." — *Military Writers Society of America*

Available on Kindle at Amazon.com
or visit Raycmorris.com to read excerpts

www.hellgatepress.com

Made in the USA
Monee, IL
19 September 2023